ANNE ZOELLE

The Destiny of REN CROWN

EXCELSINE PRESS

Other Books by Anne Zoelle:

The Awakening of Ren Crown

The Protection of Ren Crown

The Rise of Ren Crown

The Unleashing of Ren Crown

The Destiny of Ren Crown

House of Scepters

Cage of Shadows

Crown of Starlight

Tender of the Garden

Contents

1. Chapter One
AWAKENING ONCE AGAIN   1

2. Chapter Two   27
OF MAGIC, NEW AND OLD

3. Chapter Three   49
OF ANGELS AND DEVILS

4. Chapter Four   80
REMINDERS

5. Chapter Five   110
THE WEIGHT OF THE LOST

6. Chapter Six   144
OTHER HANDS DO BURDENS HOLD

7. Chapter Seven   164
COILS OF THE TEMPEST

8. Chapter Eight   182
REMINDERS OF OTHERS

9. Chapter Nine   208
WHEN IT ALL BREAKS

10. Chapter Ten   231
CRACKED PIECES OF ICE

11. Chapter Eleven   253
COMMENCING in 3...2...1...

12. Chapter Twelve   287
RUNNING

13. Chapter Thirteen   314
ERSTWHILE COMPANIONS

14. Chapter Fourteen   334
BODY OF THE SUN

15. Chapter Fifteen   382
THAT WHICH IS UNBEARABLE

16. Chapter Sixteen   401
PLOTTING

17. Chapter Seventeen   434
THAT WHICH IS FREED

18. Chapter Eighteen   465
THREE MAN SNEAK

19. Chapter Nineteen   494
ASSAULT ON CRELUSSA

20. Chapter Twenty   538
SECRETS OF A CANVAS

21. Chapter Twenty-one   560
GENESIS OMEGA

22. Chapter Twenty-two   608
EMPATHY OF THE LOST

23. Chapter Twenty-three   647
WHAT WAS LOST

24. Chapter Twenty-four   670
WHAT WAS FOUND

25. Chapter Twenty-five   711
     REUNIONS

26. Chapter Twenty-six   745
     SHADOWED PLOTS

27. Chapter Twenty-seven   780
     UNSEALING THE DEVIL

28. Chapter Twenty-eight   789
     REPRISAL

29. Chapter Twenty-nine   806
     ALL IS LOVE; ALL IS LOST

30. Chapter Thirty   840
     ANOTHER PERSPECTIVE

31. Chapter Thirty-one   850
     ENSNARING AND ENSNARED

32. Chapter Thirty-two   874
     GOLDEN CIRCLES

33. Chapter Thirty-three   887
     HOW IT ENDS

34. Chapter Thirty-four   897
    HOME

35. Author Note   903

Chapter One
AWAKENING ONCE AGAIN

THE BOY LOPED down the street with the easy, unconcerned grace of a teenager never expecting to encounter danger in the shadows. Spiky hair was weighed down by giant headphones as he bopped his head to an internal beat and hiked his backpack higher on one shoulder. A violin case was securely strapped across his back, and the sharply bent fingers of his left hand syncopated a line of music against his thigh.

He absently scratched the underside of his left wrist against the side seam of his jeans—a motion that had no doubt been repeated with greater frequency as each minute passed.

He was oblivious to the shapes detaching from the long, spiked shadows of the trees.

Being suddenly half surrounded registered fully on his danger index, though, because he jerked to a stop, ripped his headphones down to circle his throat, then took a defensive step backward.

Lightning streaked the sky, sending jagged lights through the unnatural shadows that surrounded the black-clothed men around him.

A combination of jazz, violin, and synthetic beats grew louder—unnaturally projecting from his headphones and becoming a haunting, cacophonous melody that wrapped around the space.

"Definitely him," one of the men said.

"Definitely me what?" The boy's gaze was quick—intelligence weighing variables and options and trying to make sense of the reality in front of him. "What's going on?"

Where did you come from? The unsaid question was clear in his gaze as he looked toward the lawns on either side of the street.

"Hands where we can see them," the leader ordered in a graveled voice.

The boy's hands shot into the air, open palms face out.

"Listen, I'm on my way home. Rehearsal ran late—"

"Shut up."

The boy did, his wary gaze assessing the way the black-clothed men with scanners in their hands were slowly surrounding him. More than one was looking outward, searching the distance. He shifted his body.

"They said she'd be here," one of the newer recruits complained, a lethal look in his beady eyes. "This was supposed to be—"

"Well, she's not," the leader said, his eyes not leaving the boy. "And we have a job to do, and a feral to drain."

"Feral?" the boy murmured and took another step back.

The music grew in volume, turning harsher and more frantic. The boy was going to run. It was obvious from his gaze, his motion, and the burgeoning magic emanating from him that he couldn't yet control.

He wasn't going to survive a standoff—and if he ran, he wouldn't make it home.

We hadn't.

From my vantage point in the trees, the rage started at my toes and slithered up to join the violent tingle in my fingers.

A haze of crimson glazed over my vision threatening to overtake me, but solar lights stuttering to ignite in a neighbor's yard flashed white through the haze, bringing objects more sharply into focus and reminding me of where I was. First Layer. Civilians. Innocents. Life.

"The abomination is only half of it," the cruel-eyed man said, looking around. "It's not a fully completed job if we don't—"

"Crown didn't take the bait. You'll get your chance to take her down on the next one, Doogin," the leader snarled. "But this half-paycheck isn't going to neutralize himself."

He motioned for the men to surround the boy, and they did so with careful movements.

"Now boy, you just stand there, and this will all go much easier for—"

The boy doubled over, half-compressed notes of magic oozing from him, dripping like sweat down his skin.

His sputtering magic opened the allegro of a symphony, and I gripped the notes as my heels lifted, releasing my body from its careful perch. The soles of my shoes started a slow slide down the thick branch into freefall as each note echoed the tapestry of magic that made up this world. I let my breath release steadily and silently as I fell through the air, ticking off each movement I was about to make with each note harshly and vibrantly drumming from the boy.

Magic worked best when joined.

"He's Awakening fully," the leader said harshly. "Secure—"

I dropped into the circle in front of the boy, and thrust out my palms, letting the boy's musical crescendo flow through the visual patterns I formed in the air. The two figures at either side of us flew backward, impacting with abnormal crunches—one hitting a tree, the other a car. A second set of patterns disabled the men to the front and back, but the remaining ones sprung into motion.

Containers on the belt of the leader clanked together—one filled with defensive spells, another an empty container awaiting the boy's magic.

Never again. Never again would I allow a feral to be drained.

I spun and let my cloak take the brunt of the first hit, and used my momentum to fling sticks to pierce both containers. The containers exploded, the men swore, and magic from the full container abruptly filtered into the First Layer air, even as the grasping magic of the empty container sucked the leader dry.

The boy was hunched over, looking at his fingers, an awed look overtaking his expression. "I feel—"

Additional figures ran toward us, and red descended over my vision like a single shade of old 3D glasses. I pulled the freed magic through the molecules of existence into a riotous whirlwind of colors. Gigantic, autumnal leaves formed in the slowed motion landscape, then shot free of the wind—plastering the approaching figures to the ground and forming hard shells over the top.

Music notes were swirling more wildly around the boy, building to a crescendo. "I feel like I can do anyth—"

I whipped a shield over his body and pulled it tight, tripping him. He crashed to the ground, and I threw out my hand, rolling the pavement over him like a burrito shell and propelling him away from the fight with the last of the free magic in the air.

A jolt of energy hit me from behind, reverberating in my bones, but it was to my benefit—my cloak sucked the magic inside and I pulled it from the coiling conduit in my cloak to rest in my palm.

"You idiot, she can absorb and use our magic. Throw the—"

I threw myself into a tucked roll that opened into a crouched, magically-enabled skid along the concrete as the second man followed the commands of the first. The magic in my hand scraped against the ground and I added just a bit of layer magic to slick a curved path in front of me as Delia's beautifully made, flexible boots attached to the magic I was infusing underneath them.

The same idiot withdrew a device and threw it into the air. I felt the shimmer of the magic as a containment dome mushroomed around me.

Found the new guy.

"No, no, you fool—"

I didn't let the other man finish before I sucked the dome into my center, out through my palms, then shoved it into the ground.

The earth cracked and erupted around them, downing everyone still standing, and forcing them to use the remaining magic in their containers—the only magic they could use—to heal themselves and avoid falling into the fissures.

Power filled me. The sweet, sweet ambrosia of infinite possibility.

I called magic to me like Mike had taught me to call the wind, sifting a little of each crossed thread into the elements whirling along the thin lines of my left palm—letting them cross-ruff into a ferocious storm of elemental parts. A bridge formed, and I let threads trickle out before carefully—carefully— knitting the area back together—closing fissures, righting street lamps, and soothing active heartbeats nearby.

I flexed my right fingers and let other threads envelop the groaning, twitching Department figures around me—pinning them in place. I lifted the leaf shells and lined up the bodies, applying one tracking sticker, two, then a slightly forceful application of the third on the man who'd called the boy an abomination.

Power hovered in my hands. Paint bubbled within me. I could remake them.

The layer trembled.

I could do anything right now. I could force open their minds. Make them tell me what they knew. Make them repent for killing teenagers whose only mistake was being born open to magic.

I knew exactly who could help me do it, too. I nudged the closing cracks into a different kind of opening. A small push, and—

Shadows erupted from the ground, like a freight train of terror, blowing chunks of concrete into the sky before morphing into the most unscrupulous of the Department's henchmen.

I swore as I pushed the remaining stickers onto the Department grunts—hoping they bled into their skin as fast as promised.

I turned to the boy who was staring at me in shock from the cave of his pavement cocoon. I lifted my hand, visualizing what I wanted while pulling the layer magic into a pyramid in my palm, then flipped it and shoved downward, pushing the pavement and the boy through the ground.

The ground vibrated around me like it always did when I used magic between layers in haste. My stomach heaved. The earth split in a deep vee. I grabbed for the edge and drew the vee into a sheer line.

"That's going to cost you, little girl," growled the familiar voice. Kaine smiled ominously and threw down his shadowed hands. Large chunks of pavement ripped upward to hover menacingly in the air. "Destroying another town, tsk. You just made national news."

I ducked the concrete slab he threw but the impact caused a large fault line to split the earth.

Repair, repair, repair, I ordered my magic.

A net flew toward me as I repaired the slice, and at the last moment, I rolled to the side. The net grazed me, and blood streamed down my leg.

"I've been waiting for weeks to play." Kaine laughed as he threw a shadow that I barely dodged.

The static sounds of a First Layer broadcast stuttered forth from a praetorian who looked like a Dali-assembled version of his boss.

"A town that hasn't experienced an earthquake in a hundred years has just been torn apart by—"

"Miraculously, the destruction has mended itself—"

"What were we just talking about, Raymond?"

The suppression spell had taken hold.

"Too bad that the spell doesn't work on mages," Kaine cooed. "They will all know how you rend the world. They will know how you can never be trusted. So much destruction. And all for an unknown. A feral."

A shadow wrapped around me, and I sliced through it.

He smiled darkly. "You can't save them all. Your little pets. Do they remind you of someone—of your brother, of home? Sad little girl."

I pulled magic, letting its power fill me, then released it in three concussive waves, pushing the shadows back, and quickly erecting a barrier. My gaze spun to the house across the street—its sad solar lights reflecting the flames shooting up the side of the house.

Rain. Rain.

A downpour began at my directive, but lightning struck the yard with a too forceful push of power, and Kaine's shadows slipped around my barrier. The neighborhood sizzled and shook dangerously. I grabbed the next lightning bolt with a slipping grip and wrapped it around me.

I had expected Second Layer reinforcements—a second wave of Department hitters, but not the praetorians. As Prestige Stavros's personal guards and enforcers, the praetorians were banned from the non-magical world unless Stavros was physically present or during emergency events. Which meant that Stavros had politically succeeded and been granted emergency powers to capture me.

"You aren't going to last," Kaine sing-songed as he gave chase, shooting shadows at the whirling storm cloud around me.

I stopped before I reached the park at the end of the block, raised my hand and threw concrete toward a shadow shrieking around a stop sign. I tried not to think of where I had conceived the idea. The shadow slipped through with a moment to spare, unlike the Department grunts in Ganymede Circus, who'd fallen to Raphael.

"I've lasted this long."

The First Layer was my battleground advantage, not theirs. Power filled me again, this time with an edge of heady exultation.

Kaine's eyes narrowed, but there was something glinting beneath his expression that I couldn't read. Something akin to pleasure.

"All that magic building up within you. You aren't going to last, Origin Mage."

I blasted away the first praetorian that swept toward me, and caught the second in a tornado of crimson swirls that coiled the metal climbing structure into a rising, misshapen cone.

No.

Kaine laughed, then Stavros's face flipped onto that of the praetorian I held in my grip.

"You look tired. Terrorist," Stavros said in a voice that was both dignified and world-weary—a politician dealing with an unruly populace he was feigning to protect.

"You are the one who deals in terror," I said.

He smiled. It was an unnerving smile, but there was something barbed about this one that put me specifically on edge.

I threw out my hand and blasted his puppet to the other side of the park and pulled one of the many illegal devices I carried from my cloak. His claim wasn't totally without merit—I had taken a few pages from the terrorists' playbook in that it didn't matter what I carried or how many illegal things I did. If caught, I'd never see the light of day again, no matter what I added to my tally at this point. At least, not without having Stavros buried within my hollowed chest and riding my mind.

A shadow hit my cloak and shrieked.

The Department hadn't figured out how to penetrate my cloak yet. But they would eventually.

The ground exploded, and I used the cover to erect my own dome around the park, trying to keep the fight away from the residents of the town, who were spilling from their houses in response to the noise.

The people here would never know what had taken place—even now their phones were dropping, and their eyes were going vacant. The suppression magic would prevent them from remembering, like a vague daydream, and delete any visual evidence on their devices.

But if I let things get out of hand, they would die, and no one from the Department would resurrect them.

I threw out a device to extinguish all lights, then another—one horribly full of fear and flight to force the people to return to their homes. Screams and pounding footsteps echoed the directive.

I gritted my teeth at the changing news reports. We had moved up the First Layer "excuse list" from causing an earthquake to triggering a gas main explosion. The feral's family was going to think he had been killed in a natural disaster, in the same way my parents had attributed Christian's death to an electrical explosion that had blacked out the city.

Fury rose within me.

My cloak whipped out wildly against the shrieking shadows.

I needed fifteen more seconds. Fifteen seconds in which to activate the device that would spirit me elsewhere without endangering the people or the layer any more.

"They will all die," Stavros' voice said, just off my left. "Just like your dear brother. By your hand or by mine, they will die. At least if it's by my hand, the world will have a new and glorious path."

My fury was all encompassing, yet I managed to rein it in at the last moment. Five seconds. Hang on.

Stavros's face flipped into an exact replica of Christian's. Teal eyes beseeched me. "You killed me, Ren."

Black-and-white patterns swirled in front of my eyes, and the sky ripped in rage as I blasted the puppet wearing my brother's face.

Reverberations echoed through the layer immediately and ten more hunters appeared in the street, Stavros's face flipping inhumanly between them. "Oh, dear, did someone get angry?

The device clicked, and a gentle slice tore through the First Layer. I dove and flipped myself through the crack, sealing the slice as I emerged on the other side. Black-and-white patterns slid across my view. I wasted no time, hobbling to where I had pushed the Awakening mage. He was shaking, and lightning was sparking against the warding field I had placed around him.

"What... How... That man made that object fly, and that other shot lightning, and you made the sidewalk wrap around me before sending me under the ground. Please say this isn't Hell."

I touched the field and sent soothing vibes to ease his shaking. His Awakening magic was reacting forcefully, bursting against the confines of the protection field.

"We are in the Second Layer of the world now. Magic is real. That's what you feel rousing inside of you," I explained, out of breath, but without pause. "You will be in danger until it settles. I'll get you to safety. Meditate if you can, put your headphones back on, if you can't."

I lifted my hand and pulled. A portal appeared in the air and spit out the hunter I had ejected from the First Layer. At least he was no longer wearing Christian's face. I shuddered, then twisted the man's life force and rendered him unconscious.

I paused for a precious moment, putting my left hand to my eyes, trying to reject the overlay of the black-and-white patterns that had taken over everything in view, and trying to reject the tumultuous set of emotions that were swirling through me.

"What are you doing?" the boy asked.

I couldn't do it. There was too much.

I pushed the boy back, and paint abruptly spilled from my mouth. A swirling chasm of prismatic color opened on the ground. Lightning crackled in the view.

"What. The. Hell?"

I ignored him and shakily pulled the vortex into a storage paper, then healed the breech the paint had caused. Unfortunately, nothing would grow there for a while, and a corresponding spot in the Fifth Layer was probably experiencing a similar fate.

"Did you just barf paint?"

I put a trembling hand on the forehead of the unconscious praetorian. Kaine's shadows tickled the edges of my fingers and I had to fight to keep my hand in place.

"What are you doing?"

Random bits of information surged through my mind, but also something unexpected. A shape with blurred edges and points.

I could feel Kaine's shadows on the praetorian—feel how they were reaching out toward something in the distance.

"We need to go," I said, wrapping air around my hand and trying to pinpoint how long we had until we were once again surrounded.

Stavros was smart. And giving in to his taunting was always a bad choice.

The Awakening mage looked at the downed praetorian while shaking and flexing his fingers. Magic flowed through him as he tried to gain some control of the new force permeating his body. "Will he be okay?"

"Vermin always creep back," I said darkly as I finished patting the man down, gathering all items from his pockets and putting them in a sealed pouch. "How are you feeling?"

As if the question suddenly snapped him out of his panic, his eyes unfocused.

"I…I can hear everything," the boy said, weaving a little unsteadily. "I can hear the leaves, the animals, the weird wind, like it's the music of the world. I thik' I migh' pass ot'," he slurred as he tilted precariously.

I ducked under his arm and lifted it around my shoulder, then started walking as quickly as my damaged leg would allow.

"W'are yu doig?" he asked drunkenly, and the music accelerated in tempo as it escaped the shield. I used the freed magic to make him lighter, then patched the leak with two b flats that were floating between us. Going through the layers had torn a section of the shield. I'd have to tweak the design again later—get Neph to help me harness the music. I wondered—

I shook my head at my random thoughts and pushed us toward a spot of earth that would do nicely. "We need to move fast. They are coming."

I had used far too much magic in both layers to remain hidden. And whereas I had the slightest advantage in the First Layer, there was no way the Department wouldn't find us in the layer they controlled, especially with Kaine's shadows leading the way. I could feel them coming.

"Nothing makes sense," he slurred, but I could understand his words better now. Magic was patching them and making them whole. Awakenings were wonderful.

My heart ached each time I saw the beauty of one.

"That tree is asking for water." He pointed unsteadily. "And the wind is drumming a marched beat, like it's readying for war."

I picked up our pace. His second observation was a bad omen.

"I can hear the birds...talking?"

I cocked my head reflexively, but couldn't sense any avian conversation. The strength of his Awakening, my lack of auditory talent, and the forced cloaking of my powers, gave him the decided sense advantage.

"What are they saying?"

"Can't you hear them? They said I look like a furemu on its first legs. What the Beethoven is a furemu?"

"Everyone experiences magic differently," I replied. "I know a music conductor who can change the fabric of the air using sound." I thought wistfully of school.

"You can't hear them? Is it because you eat paint? Consumed too much lead?"

My senses were starting to spread far too often to the entire layer system—which was a dangerous path to travel. One wrong sneeze and I could blow First Layer Chicago into Second Layer Antarctica.

It was best not to provide too much information about myself to the newbies, though.

"I don't make mine with lead. I think a furemu is a kind of horse," I said instead. "Like a blue and gold deer horse with antlers and a magic-swept mane. Majestic, I'm sure."

But he wasn't listening anymore. "The music...I can feel it in my blood. Driving the rhythm of my body. Am I dying?"

"You are Awakening. You will get used to magic quickly. A week in the chamber is going to be both fun and very upsetting." I pushed him toward the identified spot.

"Chamber? Week?" He stumbled against me, violin case and backpack—miraculously both still attached to him—hitting against my side and arm. "My family—"

"Will eventually be happy to learn that you are alive," I said grimly, physically propelling us toward the flat bit of empty land, one that would survive for a small bit of time as scorched earth. "What's your name?"

I always had to ask, even though it would likely serve me better letting them remain anonymous like Axer did, not knowing, not talking to them at all—just existing as a strange, brief specter during their entrance to the magical world.

"Liam."

"You can't see your family, Liam. Not for a while." Perhaps never again, though it was the part I refused to say. The counselors who assisted transitions were far better equipped for that task.

"They'll be worried. And my quartet—"

"You are a danger to all of them and yourself until you can control your powers." I swallowed and looked down, fishing one-handed in my pockets for what we needed for our exit.

Ren, you can never go home.

"What's happening to me?" he asked, fingers shooting sparks that waved into measures of music—the color so like Christian's blue lightning—but the magic safely within the shield that was serving to protect him. The shield helped regulate Awakenings—not dim them—and the excess magic was stored in the lining of the shield for use later.

I had been very specific in the requirements in the crafting of the shields.

"Magic," I said, grabbing Will's latest portal pad design from my cloak. I threw it down on the ground as the lengthening evening shadows started to hook their claws and form into shapes.

I had yet to figure out how to evade Second Layer tracking after I used my magic. The problem with Origin Magic was that it was obvious. As much as my cloak hid me from visual view, my magic was a beacon to Stavros and the devices he used to register it.

I'd chosen a bare spot in a neutral territory of the Second Layer. No one would miss the five square feet of space we needed.

The pad started to scorch the earth around it and I tugged Liam forward.

"Time to go," I said.

Kaine, always the first one on site in the layer where he ruled, formed from the darkest shadows of the pit. Liam tried to scramble away, and I had to use a magic-enhanced grip on the back of his shirt to keep him in place. The kid's instincts were good. Kaine was legitimately terrifying.

But Kaine wouldn't make it to us in time. And if he did, he'd be in for a rude awakening. Ever since Raphael had tangled with him in a portal pad, I'd put safeguards on ours. Kaine hadn't tried to follow me in a pad—or anything else of my creation—since our first encounter post-Raphael. Kaine had had some healing to do.

Come and get us. I smiled grimly and tossed Kaine a rude hand gesture as I pushed the kid forward.

"There's a demon. That's a demon," Liam yelled, squirming beneath my magic-enhanced grip. "What are you doing?"

"Taking a long step into a different existence. Welcome to your new world, kid."

"What do you m—argh!"

I pushed us both into the gaping black hole.

Chapter Two

OF MAGIC, NEW AND OLD

LIAM'S SCREAMS didn't abate as the pad spit us into the Third Layer and into a traveling closet.

The pad dropped from the ceiling, its function completed, and Liam swore and leaped away. I scooped it up and stuffed it into the cleaning pocket that Dagfinn, Delia, Will, and Constantine had created through a combination of communication, materials, traveling, and delinquent talents. The cleaning process wiped the pad's trail, to protect the user from being followed.

Not that anyone other than Raphael, Will, and I had portal pads that worked between layers, but it was only a matter of time before remnants of our technology found their way into the Department's hands, and with their vast resources, they'd be able to reverse engineer the design.

A drop of something hit the floor and started steaming.

"Your nose is bleeding, and it's not red," Liam murmured, and a measure of melancholic notes tentatively wrapped around me. His focus turned quickly to the swirling notes and the music soared into a feeling of awe.

I quickly wiped the paint from my nose—a streak of violet this time—and patched the floor before anything emerged.

It would be just my luck for our combined magic to create a musical monster in a closet.

"Come on," I said, pulling my cloak fully around me before I opened the door to the traveling cupboard.

With no other option, Liam followed me as I exited.

Stares followed our progress as we walked through the compound. I pulled my hood further down, and tried to tamp the power that was licking against my skin, waiting to be used.

Always waiting, now.

The shield shimmered around Liam and he bumped into a wall twice while staring in wonder—awe overtaking fear. His attention split between his own magic and the magic happening around him—like the small creatures and mechanical wonders climbing the walls and skittering around us.

As we moved further without attack, he grew bolder and started peppering me with questions.

"What is that?"

"Where are we?"

"Who are you?"

"What's with the blue shield?"

I answered that one. "It's your magic hitting mine." The shields always manifested as blue during Awakenings. Christian's blue.

"Yours?"

"The shield is preventing you from exploding, killing anyone, or attracting the wrong kind of attention."

His eyes widened. "Exploding?"

"Congratulations!" I pushed him toward the lab chamber. "You're magic!"

"That...that isn't helpful!"

He planted his feet in the hall, blue sparks swirling faster under the shield. I tapped it. "Don't worry. That shield protects ninety-nine percent of mages."

He looked anxiously at his arm. "What about the other one percent?"

"Better hope you're average."

"That's not funny."

"Too right," I said, tugging him back into motion. "I need to process you, let's go."

I could see the horrible notions of what that might mean going through his mind.

I nodded and stifled my smile. "There's a grinder and everything."

"What, no! Let go. Are you even human?"

It was an answer that not everyone agreed upon.

I tilted my head up so that he could see my face, and I let solemn promise infuse my voice and connect to the magic of the shield. "You will be safe. You will learn to use your magic. And you can then decide what you will do with your life. Nothing bad will happen to you here, I promise."

He frowned, then nodded almost unwillingly, visibly unsettled by why he suddenly believed a stranger. "Why then did you say—"

"If I can't add a bit of humor to the situation, it sucks twice as much," I said.

Twelve steps down the hall, though, I tugged my cloak tighter.

"They are all staring at you," he said.

"Yup."

"Did you grow horns under there?"

"No."

"Because even that guy with a tail back there—he had a tail—was staring at you."

I didn't answer.

"What are you, some kind of magical messiah?"

"No."

The further we progressed through the tunnels, the more silent he grew and the more his Awakening magic began to react. He flexed it unconsciously. "Where are we?" he asked again.

"We're in the Third Layer of the world. There are five. You will get the run down on all of that soon. Suffice to say, this one kind of sucks at the moment, but that's my problem to deal with and you will be safe here until you get a bead on your power."

I pushed the red button to the chamber rooms.

"None of that made any sense," he said, as I pushed both of us inside the main console area, a somewhat cramped space surrounded by fifteen individual chambers—like an overworked nursing station for mages. Ekaterina, a mage that I had rescued days before, was exiting from her chamber as we entered. Yvette, another new feral, still brimming with the light she'd Awakened with the week before, was reviewing something on the console with Betony, the grizzled lady who ran the ward. Both Awakened mages paused and stared curiously as I pushed Liam toward one of the last two empty chambers.

He started to say something to them, but I pushed him inside. "No time to make friends now. You are going to burst."

I surreptitiously wiped at the paint I could feel pooling in the corners of my eyes.

"That isn't something you say to make someone feel better," he said, voice going high.

"What if you are going to burst with unicorns and happiness?" I asked as I swiped the paint into the vial that was already pulsing at its seams.

"Am I?"

"Let's think positively."

As I started dismantling the shield around him and connecting him to the room and privacy controls, I tried not to think about there being only one empty room left.

The chamber was a neat combination of a stripped-down battle room and containment area. It allowed newly Awakened mages to explore their powers in a safe environment—safe for themselves and for others. In exchange for housing them, the complex funneled and used their Awakening magic. Everything in the Third Layer was reused or bargained for, and Awakening mages required a lot of upkeep, but also generated a lot of interesting, powerful magic.

The chamber was everything I wished that Christian and I had upon our Awakenings.

I pushed aside my sadness, swallowed the paint that was rising in my throat again, and concentrated on the present. "You will be here until you get through your Awakening safely. Lots of others are here to help and you will be assigned a mentor," I told Liam.

I wouldn't trade Draeger for anything—but the human element was important, too. I'd had Will, and eventually the others, to help me with the aspects a construct couldn't give.

Like real hugs.

I rubbed at my forehead as my mind provided five other random tidbits of interest that weren't pertinent. This was why I wasn't a counselor in this operation. "You can request a virtual mentor, like an AI, tailored to you, as well. That information will all be explained in the briefing."

And above all, the recently Awakened mages would be the best source of help for him.

Still, I couldn't help but add, "But if you do try the virtual route, consider letting your brain choose. Never know what's going on up there."

He looked at me. "Thanks?"

I smiled faintly. "Your best question yet. You can have a bright future in the magic world, Liam, regardless of what you've just experienced. Magic is what you make of it."

He frowned. "Is that how it is for you?"

My smile slipped, and I forced it back into place. "You have a lovely talent. One that can make the world a happier place."

I looked at his violin. Now that the shield had been stripped away completely, and his Awakening was stretching its arms, music notes were growing in force, melding together in the air—funneling beautifully around the instrument and his body.

I pulled a strip of ribbon from my pocket that was imbued with three complicated runes and tied it to a clip on the case. I had to reach through his funnel of magic to do it, and the melody was breathtaking—overloading my mind for a moment and tempting me to stay.

I pulled back. "I think you will enjoy magic once you have harnessed it. Good luck."

"Wait—"

"It's best if I don't stay." But I paused at the door with my fingers on the handle. "But don't let anyone treat you differently. You are as much a mage as anyone who Awakened earlier. Remember that."

I slipped from the chamber without looking back.

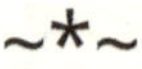

I dropped the device containing the magical packet of information I had gathered on Liam during the rescue—recordings, thoughts, data—into the hands of the console guardian. Betony merely nodded her head, but I could read the thoughts in her expression as her gaze slipped to the final free chamber.

Time. Time was not my ally.

Another drop of paint dripped from my nose, but I quickly pressed a handkerchief hand-stitched by Delia against my skin. The handkerchief was imbued with a collection enchantment that I'd connected to a storage vial in my tower. A nearly full vial.

Visual patterns flashed across my vision, overlaying everything. People veered around me, but they appeared only as tracers of light and geometrics. I needed to paint again—to exchange that which was seeping from me. At the beginning of my exile I'd only needed to paint once a week, then it had increased to twice a week.

I'd last painted two days ago and the need was building within me.

Images of destruction flashed through my head.

I gripped my fingers into fists. I needed to find a remote location to work. Somewhere safe so I could organize all the information that was zipping around my brain and strangling it.

It would grow worse if I did nothing.

The headache I sported was also a side effect. Using Origin Magic was a lovely, lovely feeling in the flow of the moment—the absolute notion that I was doing what I was meant to do. But afterward under thousands of lines of "other code" wrapped in the world—especially in the broken one of the Third Layer—my brain was still trying to sort out what everything meant and to catalog where everything went.

At Excelsine, I hadn't had any of this type of trouble. The excessive amount of magic and connections around me had made using magic effortless.

Painting helped me sort and wrap the data into images. Even if there were...side effects.

I headed toward my quarters, hood pulled low to block out the magic of the people and world around me, with my head bowed to let my nose bleed in some semblance of privacy.

I didn't get far before an official with a bright yellow insignia at the side of the wrap-around collar of his throat stepped into my path and clicked his heels together.

His bright pin stood out like a miniature sun on his black uniform. I liked to call the people dressed in such a way "the bees"—especially now when the yellow blur seemed to be in manic flight. Better than thinking of them in a far more sinister manner, like the Department enforcers with their silver pinned collars. I had no idea why the governments in the Third Layer had patterned themselves in a similar style to the Second Layer enforcers they hated.

"Council meeting, Miss Crown," he said, clicking his heels together again. "They are waiting for you."

Maybe it was just the current fashion trend. Delia would know.

"Miss Crown?"

"Yes, of course." I subsumed the patterns beneath an even more blinding headache, pulled forth "survival mode" for my magic, and set off for the deepest cavern in the mountain. It was like trying to rope and ride a migraine without doing anything beneficial to taming it. But with each step, I buried a little bit more and brought myself back to "normal."

The world wavered. Something in the distance—in my tower—exploded, and the man at my side jumped.

I shut my eyes and pulled myself together.

The massive stone doors creaked open. I gripped the hems on my sleeves, pushed the last of my magic behind the shield I was picturing in my mind, and stepped inside the cavern that housed the council of the Western Outlands.

Even with my safeguards in place, Kaine's presence had me on edge, and I peered cautiously through the dark sloping shadows. I reminded myself that Kaine wouldn't be able to breach such fortifications—not without access to the Second Layer justice magic wielded by the Department that allowed him to slip within the dark cracks.

Kaine was the bogeyman in the night.

But in the Third Layer, in the middle of Outlaw Territory, Kaine's magic would light up like a beacon.

Still, I checked deep in the darkest recesses for Stygian shifts and the edges of the shadows for curling claws.

I let my hood fall back as I approached the forum.

Council meetings had been occurring with increasing frequency, and at each gathering, more representatives assembled. I could see the Ophidians in the section they always inhabited, alongside scores of other Outlaw tribes. Frost Viper, the Ophidian I knew best, gave me a slow nod. The jeweled containers I had given her were shrunken and twinkling in the cuffs attached to the shells of her ears.

Amid the assembly, seated in five large chairs were the council heads of the Western Outlaw Territory.

"Origin Mage," said the imposing and weathered woman of indeterminate years who always sat in the middle chair.

"Ren," I corrected.

The woman tilted her head. "Origin Mage, we were just informed that you brought us another."

"A boy named Liam, who just turned seventeen—"

"That's the fifth feral in half as many days," the woman said.

I curled my fingers into fists. I thought of the last empty chamber. "I know."

"The Department is using your magic to find and activate Awakenings."

"And the Awakenings are getting worse," the council member to her left added. "More children are carrying the tendrils of Origin Magic adjacent gifts."

I felt the rebuke deep within my gut. "With such gifts, they will be powerful allies to you."

"The Department will come for them."

I stepped forward. "Not if we take Stavros out of the Department—"

Murmurs grew.

"You understand little of what you are saying," the council member said sharply. "Although Enton Stavros is the power behind the Department, Second Layer citizens are the ones who give him his position. You underestimate what mages are capable of ignoring in their quest for security and abundance."

"I understand what mages are capable of ignoring," I said softly.

The woman looked at me, her expression sympathetic, but her jaw firm. "Your brother was but one victim. We have thousands in this room. And in this layer, there are millions. The Second Layer has been able to crush us since the Breaking. It has been seventy years since our world was devastated, the magic halved. And in that time, what has happened? The histories detail the truth. The Second Layer wants a man like Stavros in power."

"I will fix this layer. The atrium test shows that it can be done. And the new city will be a success. What was once, can be again." A hologram burst into the air above my palm—a replica of Aurum, The Golden City, that had been destroyed seventy years before. "And then the Second Layer will be forced to look upon you as an equal."

The woman in the center silenced the murmurs and flares of excitement. "The atrium is an incredible achievement. And our scientists are excited about the new city's progress. We understand your power. But understand, Origin Mage, that though justice and flame kindle in our breasts, we are survivors. We don't have the grand desires of some of our brethren in the other territories to own what once belonged to our ancestors. We seek to work with what we have, and to increase our abilities and lives each day in the small ways we can afford. We, too, want security and abundance, just like the Second Layer populace, but most here were born with neither. Finding abundance in a world of scarcity is a tale told to children to give them hope in an otherwise hopeless circumstance. And a way for those in power to blame us when we fail."

"Your world can be fixed. I can fix it. Look—"

"Child." There was a soft rebuke in the word, as the distinguished woman to her right leaned forward. "I near eighty with but half a cycle of moons to go. I remember the Breaking. I lived in the splendor of The Golden City, and only escaped its destruction due to the deathbed visit to my grandfather on the other side of the world the night before. I remember the grand promises of Flavel Valeris and the scientists who flocked around him. I remember his tests, so magnificent. So easy. His dedication to his craft was absolute—his promises for more were without artifice."

"I'm not looking to give more—"

"Everyone looks for more. It is in a mage's nature." She held up her hand, silencing me. "Look at you. You cannot stop your flights to save the Awakened."

"You would have me leave them?"

"They are traps. Traps wrapped in multiple forms. You aren't so blinded to see this. And each time, Enton Stavros comes more prepared. And his preparation is for you."

I lifted my chin. "I have survived each encounter and have saved every feral. I refuse to allow him to take even one more—"

"Child, we do not want Enton Stavros to have your powers under his control, and neither do we desire him to do whatever you think he is doing with the ill-Awakened children. But by running out to save them, you do yourself no favors. Each action you take is reported—reported to Second Layer citizens as the Department desires. Each destination is noted. The Department and their media do not care for the plans and goals you deem worthy. They only care about stripping you of your magic and power, and punishing all who support you. This is evidenced by today's news. With the support of nearly the entire Second Layer Council, the Department is petitioning to attack the Western Territories. An attack against innocent people in the Third Layer who have contributed nothing to the terror in their world."

Murmurs rose around the room, reverberating dread and guilt within me. As interconnected as many of the people of the Third Layer were, the outlaws and people of the Western Territories were solitary survivors, working with what they had, instead of trying to get back that which they no longer possessed.

Everyone in this room knew a Third Layer zealot intimately, but the leaders here weren't the warmongers.

These people had sheltered me, which made them prime targets. I would repay their kindness a thousand-fold.

"They can't touch you." My fingernails pressed into my palms. I inhaled deeply through my nose and let it slowly emerge between a tiny crack in my lips as I looked around the cavern at the gaunt faces and the soft, precious magic that they kept wrapped close, like the last knit scarf they possessed.

"I am working wards everywhere," I said. "With magic that I recycle from off-Layer use. I will protect you. I swear this. And every feral I bring in adds an additional piece to the protection ward. I will protect you."

She smiled. It was a smile that was far older than her eighty years. A smile drenched in suffering and memory.

"We knew when you came to us that death was a possibility and we accepted that risk. Origin Mages have the best intentions. Always. And to bathe in the light, in the hope, even for a small moment, is something that even the most wretched and most pragmatic of us can't resist. But for all their power, all their vision, Origin Mages always forget what it means to be human. To be without."

I frowned. "I will protect you."

She looked at me sadly. "But, Child, how will you protect yourself?"

Chapter Three
OF ANGELS AND DEVILS

I SHUFFLED from the room, far more tired than when I had entered. Puzzling words and blatantly disguised warnings made my head hurt. To be without what? Magic?

My shield cracked, allowing the overabundance of said magic to bleed around the edges and between the cracks.

I could hear hushed whispers curling around the edges of the cavern as the large doors closed slowly behind me.

"She is trying—"

"Frost Viper, you will learn. Learn to balance hope with fear in such times. The more powerful, the messier and faster they end. And this one—"

The door clicked shut.

I leaned against the wall and let the back of my head hit the corner, so I could stare blankly down the long corridor, watching the bottoms of the walls melt into the floor in overlaid patterns. I felt the marble in my pocket—felt the way that it connected to the project that would prove I could fix everything. I felt how my magic reached for the fragments of the world around me. I felt the addition of Liam and the eight other ferals I had saved.

I felt all those things connecting beneath the protections I had painstakingly placed upon the complex. Seals and containers creating a dome and inverting it to be invisible. Flat.

Safe.

I closed my eyes and felt my power. It was a deep well beneath the top layer of abuse it had taken today. But it was there, and I could mend the top, just like I had mended it before.

Why couldn't the Council see what I could? I could fix this world.

I forcefully wiped a new drop of paint from my nose. I could save the ferals. I could do any—

"There she is."

My gaze jerked open to see a mob
of refugees—people from throughout the
Third Layer who had been unhoused and
disenfranchised during the ongoing war
between the terrorists of their own layer and the
authorities of the Second.

They started rushing down the corridor toward
me. Protective magic coiled in my palms
instinctively and patterns sharpened. I had
nowhere to go except through them.

"My village—"

"My town—"

"You must help us—"

"Our people—"

I pulled my hood forward and down as far as I
could and overrode every instinct telling me to
blast bodies and run.

I strode briskly through the press of bodies,
letting my magic nudge them to the edges of
my personal field, and tried not to let their
emotional cries strike like the daggers they
were.

"You—"

"You did this—"

But even worse were the ones who reached out to touch my cloak with reverence as I passed.

"Blessed."

"Blessed."

"Magic's honor."

I shuddered and continued pushing my way through the throng, letting the darkened interior of the cloak shield me in more ways than one.

"You should be doing more," a woman called out.

My cloak brushed my ankles as my steps slowed. A dozen hands reached out to stroke the fabric over my arms.

"You are the Magus Angelus," she said. "You should be doing more."

I gripped my fingers into fists and kept moving. I was almost to the intersection in the hall.

"You are the Magus Angelus," she called out more loudly.

The title brought forth conflicting cries from the crowd.

"Origin Mages bring prosperity."

"Origin Mages bring death."

"Kinsky made the Second Layer stronger. It is now our turn. Our turn!"

"Or it is their turn to die." I looked up to see a woman with fanatic eyes standing at the intersection. "A death demon. Like Flavel Valeris." She spit out the long dead Origin Mage's name like a curse. "She will bring ruin to them, like he brought ruin to us; it is promised in the scriptures of Erthamus, that one will come who will end the wor—"

The woman's eyes went abruptly unfocused, as did the gazes of those around her.

I didn't have to look up to verify who stood behind her. I didn't acknowledge him as he peeled himself from the wall he was lazily lounging against. I stuck my shaking hands into my cloak and turned sharply down the corridor, bypassing the gauntlet of the crowd, who were now looking vaguely confused and disoriented.

His magic—mixed with another warmly familiar one in sepia tones—reached out and blanketed the overwhelming patterns overlaying my vision. The world around me shook for a moment, then settled.

I wanted to reach for him—like a drowning woman being offered a lifeline—but instead clenched my shaking hands into fists and continued walking without acknowledgment. I couldn't allow the bone-deep feeling of relief and longing to settle. I had to hold on to the surge of vexation and worry that was just as thick and overwhelming.

"I prefer the lust version myself," Constantine said, falling into step beside me. "That type of demon is most welcome, especially in the evening when the hours drag by."

"You should be in class right now," I said without looking at him.

"And yet here I am. You're welcome, darling."

"You shouldn't have done that. You shouldn't be here." He should be safe on campus. "I was doing fine. I am doing fine."

I focused straight ahead instead of on the people who were plastering themselves to the sides of the hallway as we passed.
Even at nineteen-years-old, Constantine often provoked that reaction on his own. He held a weird position in the compound—not quite ally, not quite enemy—and was only allowed in because of some deal he had made. I still didn't know what it was.

"Fine?" His voice sharpened from its default negligent state. "You can't hide from me beneath that hood."

I picked up my pace. "I'm not hiding."

"Your makeup is uneven again."

"I'm not wearing..." I firmed my lips and started to scrub at my cheek using my shoulder, but then thought better of it. My cloak was made to withstand my paint temporarily, but it was always a bad idea to push it.

"Even on you, blooded paint streaks aren't appealing," he said lazily.

"Noted," I said stiffly.

He blocked my way, moving silently and quickly. He reached out and tilted my chin to the side, then tilted it to the other—the movement exposing my face fully to the light.

Magic rushed through me, and the paint that had been relentlessly pushing for release finally settled.

"Why do you keep doing this?" he whispered. "No, don't answer. I know what you will say. What caused all of that color to explode with nowhere else to go, darling? You look like a horror movie that got the colors all wrong."

"I got the job done. I saved another one."

He examined me for a long moment, mouth tight, then let his hand drop to his belt. "You need rest. I just used an amount of muse juice that would make a politician weep." He touched a small glass vial filled with sand that was dancing with delicate, spoken movements.

I forced my gaze away from the vial, and with it my yearning. Home was gone.

"I got the job done," I reiterated.

"Did you?"

I created a memory ball of Liam in my palm and held it out to the side for him as I resumed moving.

Constantine looked the memory over, keeping pace once again. "Charming," he said with disdain.

I rolled my eyes, but my shoulders eased at the normality of the statement. I collapsed the ball into my cloak for recycling.

"And the atrium testing is working fine," I said. "As is the city. Will is going to be ecstatic, which he will be without your report because the progress is available remotely.

I stole a look upward when he didn't respond.

"You shouldn't be here," I repeated with less bite. I was far too hungry for the company to deny it when it was in front of me. "It's too dangerous."

"I am a scientific envoy, attending a conference in Ravishkan for two weeks," he said, voice regaining its lassitude. "You, on the other hand, are a terrorist, labeled as such by the

Department. I think of the two of us, you have little to say on the matter of danger."

His feigned lethargy couldn't hide the tight tension coiled within him.

I climbed a series of steps at the end of the hall and stopped in front of the lone door.

"This isn't Ravishkan. You are going to get caught in a vortex somewhere, Con. And they will throw you into a hole even I can't find."

I was barely keeping up with finding the newly Awakened mages. I hadn't even come close to locating the ones the Department had taken before I'd been expelled from campus.

"They haven't caught me yet. Just like they haven't caught you," he said in a blasé manner that contradicted every sharp, pointed feeling emanating from him.

I opened my mouth to argue then shut it with a grinding of teeth. I reached my fingers toward the door and let my magic slip into my self-made lock—a trick the Origin Book, Ori, had taught me the first time I'd manually picked a lock in front of it.

Constantine looked inside as the door swung open. "Ah, the hovel. I've missed it so."

"You were just here. You are always here, like you are worried that I'll disappear if you don't check often enough. And it's not a hovel," I said, entering my turret.

Papers were scattered everywhere, like a bomb had gone off. I checked the wards to make certain that was the only result from the earlier explosion.

"No, you are right, of course," he mused. "It's more like a shanty with a really tall roof."

Ori was crisscrossing the room, flying through the cross sections like a frantic pigeon stuck in a too small space. Upon seeing me, the book dove into a downward spiral. It blasted around my head, making my hair lift in the harsh breeze.

"Charming," Constantine said.

His lip curled further as he glanced at the foot-high, real-time hologram of Axer trouncing combat mages on the practice fields.

Adjacent to Dare's hologram were two others that were currently active. Neph was dancing with the other muses around the flagpoles on Top Circle, a look of sad intensity on her features. Olivia was intently pouring over a text. Will's usual spot held vacant white smoke—he was probably off in the cafeteria, but he'd pop up when he was in one of the designated observation spots, usually with Mike.

All reminders of what I had once, and had no longer.

I had known Constantine was up to something when his figure disappeared from the hologram batch this morning. He was almost always in his lab or with Stevens these days—both places that showed his holo.

"Your vocabulary is shrinking." I locked the door and removed my cloak, shedding it heavily, like the hundred-pound armor it seemed instead of the nearly weightless material it was. "And you created that holo feed of your roommate—created all the feeds—but that one specifically so that I could, how did you phrase it, 'learn new moves'?"

"A constant regret."

Constantine poked Guard Rock with his boot and kept a judicious eye on the ceiling, where the book soared in tight circles again. Guard Rock retaliated, stabbing his pencil through Constantine's boot, forcing the material to expand around the pencil's tip, before the self-healing material shoved the piercing object back out. Guard Rock flipped behind Constantine and stabbed him in the ankle. Constantine trapped him against the wall with his heel.

They had a weird relationship.

Constantine's relationships, in general, didn't fall along standard lines.

"I want you to be safe," I said, resuming the previous conversation.

"Not much use for that on campus if I die of boredom." I heard his boots scuff against the tile and the sound of his heel hitting the floor.

"Don't hurt him." I didn't bother to look behind me.

"He's a rock."

"I wasn't talking to you."

"Charming."

I pulled out a piece of paper and grabbed some charcoal from the mess on my work table. I sketched out some quick mind maps—pulling data from today's Awakening and spreading it on the linen in visual form: where Liam had been found, how he might have been activated based on what I had seen in his magic, what his powers were, and the numbers and attack patterns of the hunters.

Releasing my breath, I let the feelings and magic from the fight reorient through the muscle memory of drawing.

My hand shook. A drop of paint fell and sizzled on the page.

I heard Constantine sigh, and from the side of my view, I saw him punt Guard Rock into the air. The rock flew; arms and legs extended back for maximum air time, then flipped to land on the table. He ran along the diameter line of the table, then screeched to a halt amidst the papers at the end, curling their edges into the air as he assumed a warrior's pose.

Constantine threw him a sharpened pencil. Guard Rock caught it and thumped the lead against the table. The magic shot from the tip along the papers and up into my arm.

My hand stopped shaking.

"Better?" Constantine asked, sounding bored, but tension vibrated along our connection.

I stared at the table. In the live holos, I could see Axer pause, turning his head just a fraction. Neph's hand went to her chest, head bowing forward.

"Yes," I whispered.

Our mutual sharing was something I was still coming to terms with. Constantine now possessed a vial full of Neph's dancing magic. Somewhere in the way that I had connected us all during the showdown with Stavros on campus had allowed us to use our individual magics from afar when our friends were in need.

Constantine could pull on Neph, Guard Rock could channel Axer, I could—sometimes—pull on Olivia's measured deliberation.

Permission-based pulls made stronger by each of us contributing to the community pot.

"It's fine," I said.

"It looks fine."

"It is."

He lifted a shoulder and dropped into a chair. "Fine."

"I'm fine."

"Unarguably."

"You are arguing it right now."

"Debatable."

Ori chose that moment to swoop down again and slice my cheek with the edge of a single page. I glared at it and pressed my finger to the paper cut, healing it.

Constantine eyed the book narrowly. "When did this begin?"

"It is...feeling cramped." I didn't react physically as the book buzzed my head again. It had been doing this for the last week. "I keep telling it that

I can't go off on adventure. I'm getting plenty of adventure already. It doesn't take refusal well."

That wasn't the only reason for the book's reactions, but I kept that part to myself.

Axer's feed disappeared, as it always did when he was done fighting. Constantine had made a quip about hooking his feed up to the showers instead. But Axer was almost always training in some way, and Neph dancing, and Will experimenting, and Olivia plotting, and when Constantine wasn't dogging my steps, his holo always showed him creating something diabolical.

Those five usually surrounded me while I worked, just like they always had—with other friends swarming in and out of view alongside them.

Viewing the holograms made me less lonely, which was sadly amusing, since I was inside a compound full of people.

But the people here were awed and terrified of me, and I wasn't Ren here.

I looked at the feeds from Excelsine with longing. I could no longer go anywhere near campus—even the Midlands were off limits. In order for Excelsine to remain free of repercussions following my expulsion, Marsgrove had been forced to install alert wards against me.

And for their own protection, I had cut communications with all of them outside of shielded areas. No more frequency or armband comms—no friendly or mischievous outside voices in my head.

The book fluttered its pages and Guard Rock took a stab at its binding as it flew past. The book had been keeping just inside the edge of outright mutiny, but it wouldn't be long before it rebelled completely.

Constantine looked and felt irritated as he watched the book, his emotions matching up for once. "Tell it to leave. I'm still surprised it didn't drop you the second you were off campus."

I pulled a clammy hand along my forehead. "I've told it it's free. It feels its debt hasn't been paid."

The line of green was far more in my favor now. Releasing it from seventy-year-old chains made quite an impact on all the bargains we'd made in Excelsine's library.

Constantine reached out and touched the skin in the hollow at the side of my throat, then my temple. "You have a fever," he murmured. "Didn't you paint two days ago?"

I swallowed, pushing the question—and answer—down. "Stavros is going to declare war on the entire Third Layer because of me. He's going to use me as an excuse to collapse the layer. He got praetorians into the First today."

All things I couldn't control, even with all my power. Not yet, at least.

"I know," he murmured, darkness rolling through him, allowing the change in subject—for now. "I came as soon as the first image was shown. They almost got you."

"But they didn't."

"Not today." His expression was unreadable, but his emotions—dark and heavy—were not. "But the praetorians have been given discretion. The Department gave the council edited versions of all your fights in the past two weeks. Damning edits. The vote was nearly unanimous—the timing, no mistake. Even with Excelsine, and the power behind the students there, on your side, the Department knows what it is doing. They have been spinning a negative campaign web against you for months now."

Constantine's father was on the council—at least for the moment—and he was the only one who was remotely on my side. Or more precisely on his son's side. Though, it was hard to tell, sometimes, what his views were from the way he played the political and emotional game in the press.

"They are going to attack this layer with weapons they have been building for thirty years—powerful weapons you can't begin to comprehend—as soon as the trigger they are waiting for is depressed. They are doing everything they can to get you in their grasp and you make their job easier. You risk yourself further every day."

I leaned forward, arms pressed against my stomach. "I know. The territories also want me to remain hidden, to rise slowly with the rise of the layer. They aren't wrong, but I must... I need to save the ferals," I whispered.

Like I hadn't been able to save Christian.

"And I need to save you," he said blandly.

"Con—"

"Do you want to save one mage, Ren, or a thousand? A million?"

I maintained eye contact. "I have to start with one."

He spread his fingers. "But you can't. You can never choose only one. You can never choose to sacrifice just one, and because of that, you lose ten, then twenty. Which is why you lose at chess when it involves live pawns. Put people in place of carved wood and your whole game falls apart. For every pawn you save, you lose a more powerful piece. You can't save every pawn. You know you can't."

He flicked the holo of Axer to the floor.

I retrieved it, then rubbed my thumb over the knuckles of my other hand, staring at the moving images.

"It's only a matter of time before Stavros is given permission to invade, Ren."

"I know," I said quietly. "And I regret endangering the people by being here, but Stavros can't hunt me here. Not yet." I looked at the dense lines of the wards I had looped over the compound.

"You need a permanent place to hide."

"I don't think permanence is an option for me anymore." I tried to smile, determined to lighten the mood. "Good thing I've always enjoyed travel."

"With all your ducklings somewhere else? I don't think so."

Guard Rock nudged me with his pencil and pointed at Constantine with an open hand gesture as if asking permission to stab him.

"Itlantes will open its gates to you," Constantine said, emotions and voice tight as he watched the hologram of his roommate. "And you will find many options there for your friends."

I tightened my fingers into fists. "I'm not putting Axer's family in danger." The Dares' situation was a powder keg already. There was absolutely zero chance that the public would permit either the ferals or me to go there—not with the easy, negative spin the Department could put on it. I wasn't going to start another Great War in the Second Layer.

"The Dares are always looking for an excuse to go to war," Constantine said, all tension hid beneath torpidity. "You would simply be giving them one."

"No. It wouldn't just be twenty countries fighting them this time—they would face every country that believes the Department's spin and believes in Stavros' goodwill."

"I know the Dares. I grew up with their favorite. You underestimate their power and willingness to fight. Especially when they consider something theirs." Constantine looked to the side, expression pulling as tight as the ribbon through his fingers. His expression loosened abruptly, and he rolled his head around his neck. "And you underestimate the Dares' desire to rule the entire layer."

"Axer, running the world? I don't think so." I couldn't imagine him enjoying anything less.

"He was bred to be a warrior and protector, but if you haven't seen how he holds the attention of all around him, you haven't been paying attention," he said bitterly, flinging his ribbon to the table.

I examined him, mystified. "Why do you want me to go there?"

He didn't say anything for a long moment. "Because once you are there, they will stop you from leaving. They will wage the war."

"They would stop me from saving new ferals."

"Yes," he said shortly.

"Then you know why I can't go," I said simply.

He clenched his teeth.

"I can save them. I can save all of them. If all of you are safe, I can do anything," I said, looking at the table. "And Marsgrove is keeping everyone safe at Excelsine like he promised—except you, who keeps escaping."

The dark feelings roiling through him didn't cease, but I could feel him unwillingly shifting within a tide I couldn't see.

"Then you know why I can't go back," he said.

My head jerked to him. "No, absolutely n—"

He stabbed a finger on top of mine, pinning it to the ribbon and table as he leaned forward. "You make your choice, and I make mine."

I swallowed down the "I won't let you" that I desperately wanted to say.

He tossed a device onto the table—a familiar one, already glowing. "You are thinking old thoughts. And disregarding others' feelings for you. There is no shortage of people willing to help."

I stared at the device and licked dry lips. "I used the portal pad today that Will and I—"

"That's not what I meant."

I fiddled with the ribbon on the table, watching the whorls grow as I twisted it in the light.

"I know," I whispered and looked away from him. "I don't want any of you hurt. And I...I want to be the one to save the ferals."

Constantine, for all his polemic leanings, stayed silent while I divested myself of my boots and the last bit of my gear—trying also to divest myself of the admission, the dark secret I had kept clasped to my chest.

"I know that makes me selfish." I didn't meet his gaze.

"You seek to assuage a guilt you should not possess," he said.

"Not guilt. Not.." I shook my head. "I have the power to do it. I am saving them. I've saved every single one since I was expelled."

"And when you finally miss one?"

I swallowed and looked at my glowing hands.

"I care little for these pets of yours," he said, body listlessly draping the chair, emotions tight. "In point of fact, I rather loathe each new one as you trade your safety for theirs."

"I can stay ahead of the praetorians."

"Mmmm. Well, everyone in your little circle is losing their minds right now." He pulled a loop of magic around his temple lazily as if he could hear them. Constantine didn't have a frequency, but he had something more efficient that had never been named. It allowed contact with everyone through means that couldn't be tracked. "And Alexander's putting his affairs in order. It doesn't matter if you don't want to go to Itlantes; Alexander's going to cart you off as soon as he escapes his campus responsibilities. As soon as he isn't integral to Excelsine's stability. He will be leaving, if not legally at the end of the term, then as a fugitive."

I withdrew the toasted supplies from my cloak, needing something else to concentrate on, and started fixing the most crippled device first. "Julian Dare's made that known."

Axer's uncle had tried to grab me, two days ago. He'd followed me all the way to the Third Layer. I had to give him credit for his tracking abilities.

Unfortunately for Julian, the Third Layer's denizens didn't trust him anymore than they trusted Stavros. He was drenched in Department spells, and the Dares weren't known for being involved in anything that wasn't for their benefit. Julian had been unequivocally unwelcome in the halls of the Outlaw Territory tribes.

He would always be a tracking step behind when I started a quest from behind their warded walls. His nephew, however, once freed of campus, would have no problem tracking me anywhere.

"You go to Itlantes with Alexander, not with Julian," Constantine said darkly. "Alexander isn't the one who will take Stavros' place in the new world you seek to flip."

I stared at Constantine.

"Give Alexander the coordinates of the Awakenings. As much as he's an irritant, he is...more than adequate at the things he does well." Constantine grimly watched me wipe another drop. "You worship him for a reason—like everyone else on our blasted campus. Fifteen-minute absences for his merry little band can be covered at Excelsine by Marsgrove and the administration."

"They'll be caught."

"I cannot wait to tell him you said that."

I grimaced. "The Awakenings are triggered, but not precisely pinpointed. The layer feels slightly different around a mage, but it's a large expanse of territory that the difference covers. Which means Stavros can know where a possible mage could be, but not who the mage is. But he has the second most important element in each scenario—time. He is setting off the magic in a targeted area, then immediately looking for grid spikes. So, if he knows he plans to trigger part of the tri-state area, he sends people to the general region, so they can be in proximity ahead of time."

I looked up. "But that is my advantage. I can feel the layer shift as the mage Awakens. I feel it inside of me—I just know where to go, like a thousand points of data converging into an intuitive leap. I have, at most, a five-minute head start, and at worse, none. Axer can't get there before the Department does without me. And having me there would be a death sentence for him."

"But all he needs to find you is a moment of your presence. He can always find you." There was something dark, almost wistful in the words. "And you've already developed something to help, haven't you?"-

I rubbed a finger along a groove in the table, my other hand reaching into my pocket to touch a spelled chip there. "How—"

"Your flaws, while humorous, are always overcome by guilt, darling. You want to save the pawns yourself, but you know their long-term rescue outcome and the stability of the non-magical layer will increase if you remove yourself from the equation."

I shut my eyes tightly. "Don't refer to them as pawns."

"You are a god now, darling. Everyone is a pawn."

"That isn't funny."

"But you can do anything," he said lightly, sending tendrils of darkness curling around me in gentle mockery. "You started thinking those exact words in the hall."

"That's not—" I blew wisps of hair and darkness from my face, then reluctantly pulled my hand from my pocket, curled fingers letting the spelled chip drop like a weight on the table. "The First Layer won't survive the praetorians. I know this. But..."

Christian. Every person like him. One last Awakening pod.

"I know." Constantine's voice was far more understanding than others would give him credit for. He gently pushed the glowing device toward me again. It was pulsing with his magic, waiting to spread its net.

I activated the holotalk with a mixture of sadness, trepidation, relief, and joy.

Chapter Four

REMINDERS

R EMINDERS

NINE PEOPLE APPEARED around the space as if they'd been there the entire time. Maybe they had been waiting—waiting to see if I'd escaped, having seen only the Department's version on the news.

Will jumped to his feet from the cross-legged position he'd been sitting in.

"Ren!"

My shoulders loosened. "Hey," I said softly. I had gotten so used to having them in my head at school that it had been a blow to lose the connection when I'd left. Frequencies were too easily tracked, though. And too easy for the Department to point to for complicity. I'd tossed mine on the second day of my exile for the safety of everyone.

"Did you get him?" Olivia demanded, arms crossed over her chest.

Constantine's magic shaded each crevice. It was a trick of the mind, device, and magic, that each of them looked as if they were in the room with me, but I knew that if I tried to touch one of them, my hand would only encounter a facsimile of flesh.

"Yes. Liam." I settled into my own cross-legged position on the floor. With the device active, the room around us could change into whatever view the participant wanted, but a bare interrogation room seemed appropriate on my side. "And I stickered the grunts."

Will gave a thumbs-up and immediately bent over a square device with Dagfinn and Asafa.

"I almost didn't get them attached this time. The praetorians came."

Silence greeted that pronouncement, stilling the movement in the holo like old tech frozen on a screen.

Then movement suddenly reinstated itself.

"If the tracking doesn't work, we'll tweak again," Dagfinn said, voice assured in the way of someone whose code always—eventually—worked, while dutifully ignoring the elephant in the room. Everyone at Excelsine had experienced the terror of the praetorians on campus, and no one wanted a second meeting in a place where the enforcers had no restrictions. "Someone is going to make a mistake on their side, or we are going to get a hit."

It was a slim hope—that the hunters would lead us to the ferals, or to a secret facility, or to Stavros himself. Julian Dare and his contacts had already checked all the facilities that were known to the public and many that were not.

Not that I would trust Julian suddenly "finding" the ferals. There was no way Stavros thought Julian on any side other than Axer's. And he knew Axer was on mine.

Any discovery of the ferals that wasn't made by us through trickery and stealth was going to be a trap.

"The praetorians have been given emergency powers," Olivia said. "It's all over the feeds. Any time you show up in the First Layer, or anywhere else, they have permission to take you with excessive force. Your interaction today was broadcast throughout the layer and was used to consolidate support for the emergency action."

"Yeah." I rubbed a hand over my elbow, where I'd been hit, then down my leg. "Yeah. I, uh, I think I might ask for help in the rescues."

Some of Olivia's grimness faded. "Good."

Constantine's smugness pulsed in the corner and I studiously looked elsewhere.

I lifted the chip imbued with the spell I'd been reluctantly working on. "I designed a device—where I could appear briefly, then pull one of Will's pads to the position. Like a First Layer GPS locator and portal, but with protections against outside tracking. The receiving side comm needs setting, though."

Dagfinn looked up from the tracking program and motioned eagerly. "It's not something coded directly into your magic this time, is it?"

"No. I got yelled at enough the last time." I flicked the edge of the chip's specs with my fingers, sending the package shooting around the sides of the holoroom, and watched as it zoomed into Dagfinn's palm. He opened the packet and looked through it—Will eagerly peering over his shoulder.

A moment later, Will rubbed his hands together and Dagfinn nodded. "Give us an hour," Dagfinn said. "We can easily do this. Your spells are surprisingly elegant in their chaos, have I told you that?"

I tried to show enthusiasm. Maybe I could sabotage the device on my side.

Olivia narrowed her eyes at me, as if she'd heard my thought, or read it on my face. "I just sent a communication to Dare. He said that his team will be ready as soon as Dagfinn and William deliver the pad and spell."

"Oh. Great. Great."

Sometimes...sometimes the efficiency and genius in my group of friends was not a benefit.

Olivia narrowed her eyes further. "Yes. Great. They are extremely capable of doing the rescuing. And if you leave the scene immediately, the praetorians aren't allowed to be in the First Layer without you present. A benefit for the non-magical population, don't you agree?"

Right. Definitely. And I could...totally leave without participating in the rescues.

Rocks formed in my stomach. "The Department isn't without strong first line resources. Their hunters and thieves are well-equipped with containers. They will give anyone a fight."

I could channel my own magic in the First Layer whereas the others—the ones I would be sending into danger—could not.

Olivia stared at me. "Are you telling me that you don't think Alexander Dare will be able to handle hunters in the First Layer?"

Constantine didn't even attempt to hide his smirk, as he looped one string through another at my side, forming a pentagram.

"Of course not."

"Good. Everyone knows the danger. This is not your war alone."

"No. No, I know. I know." Knowing was different than doing, though. I chewed a fingernail, wishing it was a pen cap. "I made the spell."

Her eyes softened. "We'll be with you soon."

That wasn't something that made me feel better.

Arms wrapped around me and I closed my eyes. The hug didn't include all the sensory details—the one thing the rooms couldn't provide was true physical interaction—but I could pretend. Those were Neph's arms wrapping around me, even though she was a layer away.

I kept my eyes closed and let myself pretend.

"Just another few weeks," she said soothingly.

"Why does Leandred get to be there now?" someone groused. "We all took Individualized Study to minimize class restrictions this term, and are still confined to campus. How does he keep escaping?"

"I'm special. You should already know this," Con said, leaning back in his chair and hooking strategically spaced knots into a thicker rope. He was always doing weird things with string these days.

"Your father is going to be crucified, if you get caught there," Delia said in her blunt, sarcastic way.

"Concerning," Constantine said blandly, not looking up.

"Your magic feels knotted," Neph said to me, gently touching the threads around us which were vibrating. "Not like after Bloody Tuesday, but the edges look and feel the same. Is something wrong with the holomagic?" She looked at Constantine.

I scooted out from under her arm. Neph, of anyone, could gather more than the average sensory data from me—even in a virtual room, a layer away.

"What do you mean? What happened, Ren?" Olivia asked, frowning severely at me and ignoring the byplay that was continuing around us.

"Just tired. You know me, sleep is for when I'm dead," I said. They both frowned. "That was a joke."

"It wasn't funny."

"No." I leaned my head back. "It wasn't, sorry."

"Ren—"

"Don't worry. Everything is working well! The gear was great today. Really took the load off."

"You tried out the new pad?" Will hopefully asked, connecting to our conversation and, thankfully, bringing the rest of the room with him.

I smiled. "Worked perfectly."

"And the traceability pouches?"

"Seems like Bandits Incorporated has a future hit on their hands."

The involved mages did the magic equivalent of a high-five.

"The Department knows where you are, though, traceability be damned," Olivia said angrily. "They can't go after you unless they declare all-out war on the Third Layer—they still have to go through the political arena right now—but it's only a matter of time."

"Way to keep things upbeat, Majesty."

"We aren't under illusions here," Olivia said grimly to Patrick. "Stavros and Kaine can track her. They've been able to track her for a long time. She was safe at Excelsine because she was a student, and nothing had been proven yet. Both of those protections are long gone. The only thing keeping her safe is staying in the Third Layer."

Constantine continued fiddling nonchalantly, emotions relentlessly in contrast to his bored expression.

Patrick nodded. "But even warriors need downtime and fun."

Olivia's expression eased a fraction and she turned back to me, looking over my body and magic.

I wondered what she saw.

"I don't know what Nephthys can sense, but you painted two days ago. And Leandred is there now. You should be fine."

I swallowed, shoulders tensing, and forced my hands to remain at my side instead of going to my nose. "I am."

Her eyes narrowed. "You are lying." She looked at Constantine for confirmation. He blandly looked back. "Why?"

I looked at the floor.

"Ren?"

"I'm fine."

"Are you bleeding paint right now?" she demanded.

"It's fine. I must not have painted enough Tuesday," I demurred.

"You need to paint fully."

"I will."

"You need to—"

"I know."

"It's important to—"

"Definitely." I stuffed a hand under my thigh and wiggled my smallest finger at the holotalk device.

"Ren, you can't keep—"

"Liv? Oh, no, I think the reception is going." The image wavered with the quick movement of my pinkie.

"Ren—"

"May magic be ever at your fingers," I said hurriedly.

The device switched off, and everyone abruptly disappeared, taking much of the light from the room with them.

Heavy silence fell.

"Really?" Constantine stated dryly.

I stared at the device, which was furiously blinking while Olivia tried to reconnect the magic on the other end. I grabbed it, extinguished the magic completely, and shoved the box in my pocket.

"Nicely done, darling. The reception? I will forever treasure the look I'm imagining on Price's face right now. You've given me an inconceivable gift."

I pulled my fingers over my face and didn't respond.

"Good thing you can't get rid of me so easily," he said, his voice as silky as the ribbon he always had in his fingers.

"No, you are a limpet I just can't shake." But my voice was unsteady. Paint bubbled up in me again—as if punishing me for the abrupt dismissal of my friends.

He tapped a finger against the table, and a blanket of emotion crashed over me, pushing the paint back down again. He looked suddenly pale, oddly, as if he had encountered a snacking vampire. I blinked, and he was flush again with health. A trick of the light?

"Tell me about your paintings, darling."

Dark thoughts immediately returned with visuals—darkness, despair, the end of the world. "I thought it was obvious that I didn't want to talk about it."

"Why you think that would make a whit of difference to me, I have no idea."

Affection and relief shuddered through me. I crossed my arms on the table and let my cheek rest on top of my sleeve. "The need to paint is getting worse," I whispered.

"I know," he murmured, and for a moment he almost looked pale again. "I can see the swirling in your eyes. The fever. The color seeping from you." He looked at the specially made handkerchiefs filling the hazard container. "Literally."

"Do you think..." I swallowed. "It was a week at first, then half, now three times a week... Do you think I might...?"

"Turn into paint? If so, try for a tasteful chromaticity."

"You might get grayscale," I said ruefully, thinking of the darkness and despair.

His eyes narrowed. Fingers touched my neck. "Show me what you've been painting."

"No." I quickly pushed all mental images away from his grasp.

"I've watched you paint countless times at school." I could feel someone else mentally join with him, lightly pushing, asking permission. The complicated swirl of Constantine's emotions told me who it was. The one person he couldn't seem to get rid of.

"Not like this, you haven't," I whispered, denying the images to both boys.

"Why?" He watched me, seeking out weakness. "You've painted grim pieces before. But they were all beautiful."

I swallowed with difficulty, keeping the images firmly out of reach. "Not these."

His fingers stilled. "All of them?"

"Each and every one of them," I murmured. "The images grow worse, and it takes more paint each time because I struggle to make something else." Desperately trying to create anything else. "And still, the images form in the same suite of patterns."

"When did this start?" His gaze took in the papers strewn around my desk on mind techniques, meditation, and garments that regulated magic flow.

"Soon after I left campus."

"Let me see, Ren." His cajoling tone switched to a softer one, and that of anything had me pushing up with reluctance.

I closed my eyes and let the images filter through, each growing successively darker and more disturbing.

When I finally opened my eyes, I could see the unease he was trying to hide. An impossible task, since I could still feel it through our connection.

He tipped his head. "You win. Have you tried creating new paints?"

My gaze automatically shifted to the supplies littering the counters. "Yes."

He frowned, and I could feel his mind shifting through data. "But the result is always the same? You can't control your own output?"

"No, and it takes more each time—more of everything, effort, paint, magic. It all just becomes...horrible. No matter what I do. What if...what if I turn into something horrible?"

Like my pictures. Like a portent. A heavy portent of doom that was increasingly trying to gain attention.

"Impossible." He waved a hand, mind still on the problem.

"But you've been here when I clean my brushes." He couldn't follow me if I wasn't there to take him. But he had arrived while I was off painting a few times, and he always waited until my return. Constantine Leandred was exceptional at waiting. "Think about what it took to create those things."

Think of what kind of person made those things.

"Exquisite monsters and terrifying hybrids. A dark Fae Queen working her magic—all wormholes, monsters, missing limbs, and bloodstained teeth."

"The last thing tried to eat three of the workers in the compound's menagerie," I said bluntly.

"I'm certain the menageríer was thrilled."

"He...he asked if I could go back to fire breathing lizards instead of dark matter burping frogs."

Justice Toad was still very much with me in spirit, even if he was in Will's hands on campus now.

Constantine's quick gaze looked around the room, furtively checking for dark matter frogs. "Where are the paintings now?"

I cleared my throat.

His eyes narrowed on me. "Ren?"

"Well...you've seen my brushes. I brought the first painting back here and..." I cleared my throat again. "Well, then I rebuilt the eastern wing."

I felt him sigh. I could feel him adjusting his timeline to never-leave-Ren-alone-again status.

"Which means you can't paint here."

It was more a sorrowful statement than a question, but I shook my head all the same.

Heaviness settled over his thoughts. "Of course not, because fate hates me," he murmured. "Where do you leave the paintings?"

"Er, I don't exactly leave them..."

"Ren."

"The, uh, Origin Book, um, eats them as soon as I finish." It ate them while I sat frozen, staring at the horrors looking back at me.

He said nothing for a long minute before settling on, "Both healthy and wise."

"Yeah." I sighed. "Neither."

The layers only shifted the tiniest bit each time the book ate one, though. Way better than the alternative.

"Why?" he asked bluntly.

"I don't…" I closed my eyes. "I don't want to be a destroyer, Con," I whispered. "But I can't paint anything else. I asked the book for advice. And it…it just dove down and ate the first two pieces, and I just…never looked back."

It meant I never had to look at them.

"Have you asked the book to help before you paint?"

"It doesn't want me to control anything my magic wants to do. It knows I need to paint. That's why it's angry right now. It's a…free rein, might is right, every book for himself type of thinker."

It buzzed my head again, angrily flipping pages as it tightly soared in a clear message to go and gather all my people.

I ducked. We had already had this argument.

He drummed his fingers on the table, then reached over and touched my skin with all ten tips.

His gaze went distant, though it stayed on me. "The magic—it bubbles up from within you. It feels like the whispers the people here utter when they think you can't hear them—like the magic will destroy you. Like you won't be able to—"

"Stop." I swallowed. "Stop reading my mind."

"A lock, a key, a tower," he murmured. "I thought I had been pretty specific, Fate." He leaned back, fingers tapping again, his gaze focused on the bend between the wall and ceiling. "But you need this," he murmured to me, magic wrapping around me in an almost fearful way.

The moment was gone before it was fully realized, and his gaze focused back on me. "Well, where are we off to, then?"

I stared at him. "No. Absolutely not."

His expression was unimpressed. "I'd prefer you stay here for the rest of your days, but seeing as that would mean your days were numbered, we will be making a quick trip. And you aren't leaving this tower without me."

He rose.

"I didn't realize you disliked living so much," I said tightly.

"I like it very much, thank you."

"I'm dangerous when I paint."

"As am I when I'm kept waiting." His smile was sharp.

"You were just advocating for me to stay away from danger. You were practically martial about it."

He looked at me like I was being particularly slow. "To stay away from saving others. This is you saving yourself."

"Con, that's not—"

He leaned toward me. "Are you trapped here?"

My brows drew sharply together. "No."

"Then why do you act like you are, but only when it suits you?"

I ripped my gloves free and threw them on the table, then slammed my palms down. Lightning sparked across the surface. "I blew up three Magi Marts last week—four hundred miles away and a layer down. I just burned a hole into the Fourth Layer that I patched with a prayer and some tape. There were giraffes with canines and hooked nails. Not to mention the closet pinprick into the insanity of the Fifth. And you want me to start slinging paint around you?"

"Perhaps not slinging. A nice set of waterlilies would look lovely on my—"

"I can't paint waterlilies." Lightning sparked the surface again.

"Not with that attitude."

"Not with any attitude. I'd destroy the whole compound probably, if I tried!"

"I would have you pave Tus Onus instead," he mused, barely sparing a glance at the lightning. "Nasty town. And to build a castle upon its banks. I've been playing with a building material for you. Veins of gold and ivory, but not like one of the tacky things you sometimes create when left to your own devices."

He nudged Guard Rock with one of my pencils. Guard Rock stabbed back.

"Constantine, I swear—"

"Please do."

"I'm going to push you back to Excelsine."

He smirked and poked a little harder at Guard Rock, who drew blood with his return strike, his pencil tip razor sharp. "No, you won't," he said, sticking the sliced end of his finger in his mouth. "You like being surrounded by vicious things."

"You are going to drive me to insanity before my magic does."

"Likely. That's what friends are for, isn't it?" The words were blasé, but the feeling from him was not.

All anger drained from me. "I don't want you in the crossfire when I go."

Axer was fighting on the table between us again, but I could see the pinch of his eyes—he was still listening in.

Constantine reached out and touched my cheek. "You forget that you've already imbued me with your paint. And I won't let you go."

He turned abruptly on his heel. "Come, Ren. Stop trying to pretend I don't know what I'm doing. Get that blasted book and pick a place. I hate being the reasonable one."

Discombobulated without knowing why, I rose. "I've picked nine places," I stressed, as I followed him to a rack where he started flipping through papers I'd collected and been given in folders stamped with National Security, Confidential, and Myths. "Nine uninhabited sections of land. They are all craters now. Every one of them."

"Your picking sucks, then. I'll pick."

Our connection threads pulsed as he pushed comfort and determination across them.

Something in me loosened abruptly, because I had touched Constantine with paint before. We'd created paint together countless times, and contact was inevitable. I wasn't the most sterile lab assistant.

But more than that, I had wiped paint across his forehead to heal him. And that had been

Awakening paint. Ultramarine Awakening paint, at that. Powerful, protective paint.

"Let me guess." Heavy, painful relief made my voice shake—because I wouldn't hurt him, and I didn't want to be alone. "Tus Onus. Because you think the shops there have terrible merchandise."

He paused, internally assessing my heady, abrupt, out-of-character relief for a moment, before resuming his search. "I'm willing to list it as a detour. But no, I, too, was listening, when the madman proclaimed an 'Origin Circuit.'"

He said the last part reluctantly. He didn't want me to go near any Origin Magic zone—the feelings were all over him. He was just afraid I was going to damage myself if I didn't.

"I landed in one of the buildings on the Circuit. That's where the book took me after we disappeared from campus."

"And?"

"It's a crater now, too."

"Well, this layer would hardly notice another."

"It's a crater bracketed by spires of death, and it's in the Second Layer which is excessively full of healthy magic."

He paused again. "Endovar?"

"Yes."

I could see him putting the pieces together—the news reports, timelines, and my flight here, which I'd glossed over heavily in mortification

He pursed his full lips. "Of course. that was you. The after pictures were quite...stunning in a certain way. I'm certain they are beautiful death steeples, in the right light. But come, darling, where are we going now?" He looked down at me through his lashes and a strange knot of emotion coiled in me. "Don't make me the voice of reason."

Magic, stoppered up and shoved down, started to seep upward and swirl under my skin. I wiped the corners of my eyes and knew my fingertips would be stained with turquoise.

The book sensed the change—the excitement and dread I couldn't contain—and its tight circles became tighter in anticipation. It narrowed its view on Constantine as it waited to swoop, and I sensed its dark approval.

"So," I said, swallowing the paint down. "Just to make this clear—you want to find an Origin Magic safe house with me so that I can create something dripping with death and destruction? A house probably loaded with booby traps and world-ending magic that will want to devour you?"

He didn't answer for a moment. "Yes," he said with a sigh, flipping open another folder.

"And if I refuse to take you."

"You won't," he said lightly—dark, forbidding promises underlying each word.

I looked at the book circling tightly, felt the edges of my magic, thought of consequences and outcomes and responsibility to those surrounding me. I looked at Constantine—the face of my entire community, brimming with the combined magic of it all.

"You aren't alone, Ren," he murmured, and his absolute trust filtered through me.

I swallowed and raised my arm.

The book immediately dove downward and landed like a hawk on a glove—only I didn't have a glove and the book's taloned corners made its delayed displeasure known.

"The other Origin Mage hideouts—"

The book didn't wait for me to finish, its covers opened, and a complicated construction of color and dimension ejected into the air, like a squid releasing its ink.

"A map?" Constantine asked.

I could tell from his tone that he couldn't read it, but the longer I stared at it, the more the moving picture made sense. The outer edges peeled back to reveal the inner petals of direction—a map of space that wasn't limited to a single layer of the world. This one included space in a way that wasn't of the normal human mind.

My brain stuttered on the image for a moment as it tried to dismiss the notion of abnormality, then I forced myself to take a breath and relax and the whole thing zoomed into something that was more than a feeling. It was a certainty that I couldn't explain using words that I knew. It was like I'd have to invent a new language to describe it, or the way a powerful emotion just owns every thought.

Once I dismissed the idea that I needed to be normal, the extraordinary bloomed.

There were so many places to go. Two sets of points shined so brightly, that I nearly had to shade my eyes from their brilliance. I knew immediately who the residences had belonged to, but those were for another day—one fraught with far more peril. For this journey, I needed one like…that one. A dimmer set, but with a steady hue and some sort of jewel at its center.

Constantine, though unable to read the map, had no trouble reading me. "Where are we going?"

"There." I pointed to a single spot in the jumbled mass, then two more. They were pieces separated in the space of the visual dimensions, but part of the whole in the dimensions of more.

"Specific."

I shook my head at his gentle mocking. "It's the same way that I can't explain where the Awakenings are until I get there—my magic decodes it and sends an…image. It can't be explained in three dimensions. But I can take you with me." I looked at him in chagrin. "It's, er, sort of a leap of faith in that way."

"As are all things with you, darling." He held out his arm.

"Are you sure?" I asked uncertainly. But I wanted him to go now. Now that the buffet had been offered and opened, I was starving.

"I'm here," he said, and for Constantine, that was as simple and honest as it got.

I nodded and tucked my arm into his. Guard Rock vaulted onto my shoulder, and I let the book enfold around us.

Chapter Five

THE WEIGHT OF THE LOST

THE WORLD BECAME a jumble of flipping pages and a mass of data and emotion. I held tightly to Constantine's arm.

When it expelled us into a decrepit front yard, we both stumbled and nearly fell into a gnarled jumble of cacti seeking to impale trespassers.

"That is a horrible way to travel," Constantine said, flicking a vine with his foot. He straightened to his full, impressive height, and looked around in disdain. Beyond the dusty, gnarled vines was a twisted mass of landscape—like pieces from a thousand jigsaw puzzles. I could see the faint tremble in his fingers as he flexed them.

The book swooped down; buzzing his head in what could only be a rude, laughing gesture. "Stupid papered beast," Constantine muttered.

"Whatever, I could feel your magic trying to embrace it." I elbowed him, feeling better already, knowing I was going to release the knots I'd been building. Knowing I wasn't alone. A simple thought, and yet, powerful.

The guilt at putting another in danger was still there, as always, blubbering in the back of my mind, but it was muted. Constantine was a master at sidestepping the emotion as both purveyor and recipient.

I skirted a vine and barely looked at the twisted edges of reality beyond it as Constantine stabbed a trailing plant with the blade end of his long ribbon that had formed itself into a solid shaft. He, too, felt oddly relieved and content—as if he were feeding off my emotions.

"I think I'm becoming inured to normalcy." I dodged another carnivorous plant. "I keep expecting the plant life in the First Layer to reach up and grab me when I'm there."

"Beyond boring, the non-magic world. And my magic was only trying to embrace that blasted book to ensure I survived."

But I had felt him in the split-second journey—he'd held no fear for himself, his trust in me absolute. He was continuously surveying my mental state, though. I could see the thin threads of his watchfulness, and the way he was allowing himself to be influenced by my contentment and fondness.

Guard Rock jumped off my shoulder and flipped onto the ground. He approached the door on small, fast legs and did something complicated with his pencil. The book landed in front of him. Guard Rock stabbed toward the door. The book shook its pages. The stab-shake communication continued for a few more moments, then Guard Rock thumped his pencil and lifted his arms.

The book swooped forward; grabbing an arm in each of its bottom cornered claws, then lifted him into the broken sky. The book took flight across the pieces of sky—appearing in one shard, then another far to the west, disappearing to reappear in another far to the east, winging off to wherever it went when I was otherwise occupied on an outing.

This was the first time I had seen it take off with Guard Rock dangling in tow, though. I didn't know whether to be amused or concerned.

"There's plenty to fear and anticipate without magic," I said, as we watched them go. "You just have to look at the First Layer without a magic eye."

"Boring. That hell-bound volume looks like it's off to cause mayhem, by the way."

"Only boring people are bored. And probably."

"Only tedious people are tedious," he sniped back.

I shoved him, trying to hide an unanticipated grin, and looked at the wards. There were a complicated series of them, which I'd expected. The unexpected part was how old they were.

"The book took your rock," Constantine said.

"I noticed."

"Are you sure? I feel like you might not care if I'm next."

"A sweeper over the ridge looks hungry." I pointed vaguely in the carrion animal's direction. "Watch out." I waved a hand in a dismissive gesture meant to agitate.

"I could be amid a harem right now."

"You said a harem was too time consuming," I said, and turned from him, satisfied that his internal emotions about this outing were positive—anticipation, elation, curiosity, dark excitement—and set to work, pulling magic along the wards while also filtering in some of Constantine's so that he could enter as well. As relieved as I was to have him along, my number one priority was his protection.

The wards were old, but the coded set of magic the book had taught me caused the magic to reluctantly give way under the recognition of kinship.

"It really was." Constantine sighed jadedly, examining the small crumbling house with a critical eye. "You couldn't have chosen a building with indoor plumbing?"

"I'm sure there is a bathroom in there somewhere."

"A single brass pot in a corner is not a bathroom."

"If it's the kind that doesn't fight back, it counts."

We stepped through the door to find a single room. The floor was covered in a thick layer of dust and the room was stripped bare. The structure was more of a small barn, really.

"Not even a pot, Crown."

I laughed, moving inside. The room might have been empty, but a feeling of kinship and magic permeated the air and put a spring into my step. This had been the right move.

"I regret this already," Constantine said behind me. "Forget the harem. There was a beautiful woman looking for zero attached strings back in that base—"

"I saw twelve such women. You could tempt a new one every other hour without having to keep any and stray to harem territory. And those were the ones I saw eyeing you in the halls. I'm certain you could pull far more." I examined the room, looking for a good spot.

"One who was completely willing to—"

"And now let's discontinue this conversational direction."

"—play and had the loveliest pair of—"

I used a sliver of magic to seal his lips together just long enough to stop the flow of words. "I'm going to save us further embarrassment and cut you off there."

He started laughing, caramel eyes twinkling in the rare way he sometimes allowed, and his lips peeled the magic away with a smile. "All you had to say was—"

The dust coating the floor slowly rose into the air, twinkling in the rays of light brokenly piercing the poorly-sashed window coverings.

I heard Constantine sigh wearily in stark contrast to the dark excitement suddenly flowing through him. He flicked the rock on his signet ring and a shield activated around him. It was always strange to me how much he loved watching me use and fight magic, but hated watching me fight the Department. As if he only considered one of them a true threat.

I threw another shield around him, and dove to the side.

The dust swirled into a chromatic tornado and I thrust out my palm, sucking the vortex into my skin and holding it just beneath the surface.

"Don't move your feet!" I yelled and dove to the other side as I felt the world shift the slightest bit. The wards warped inward, then pulsed outward.

Constantine rolled his eyes, but continued to keep his lower body still as he pulled a device from his long coat and held it out. We'd gotten good at these types of defensive maneuvers when we'd first created world-changing paint—before we'd quite gotten the paint right.

I grabbed the device in a sprinting slide, channeled the magic from my palm into the device then cast the device at the floor. Blue lines pulsed outward, mapping each point from where the magic was originating.

A slice of magic cut through the air and I used a puff of air to vault over the top.

I plucked a second device from Constantine's other hand.

"Remind me to record this next time, so your boyfriend can view it," Constantine said, picking a nail with the thumb of the same hand as the magic tried to attack him under the erected shield. "He will be so proud." He lifted a third box from his pocket and held it out in his free hand.

I pulled it from him and used it to capture the rest of the magic event.

The magic was sucked inside in a long intake of sound. I flipped the lid and all sound ceased—the dust motes the only players left in the air. Just fighting the magic had made me feel better—like the enchantments held a dual purpose as a warm-up for an Origin Magic purge.

Constantine looked at me through his lashes. "Now the question is...what are you going to do with that box?"

"Very funny."

"Only to you, darling," he said silkily. "To everyone else, each one of those boxes you fill grows closer to priceless. Just like those lovely little gifts you keep giving each rescued feral."

I looked at the box wrapped in my fingers and felt the weight of it in my hands. "The Department, Stavros, all the ferals' magic..." I looked up at him. "What do you think he is using it for?"

"Nothing good."

I nodded grimly, stepped forward, and stuck the box in his pocket.

He stared at his pocket, like he always did when I gave him magic. He looked up, finally, when his expression was suitably bored again, hiding his true feelings—though they could never be secret from me now. "All done with your feats of glory?"

"Yes, you can stop being the damsel in distress."

"With the shield we constructed wrapped around me? Hardly," he scoffed. He twirled a hand and the shield wrapped around his ring finger again like a living signet of swirling copper and turquoise, then sunk inside.

He lifted his foot and I looked at the floor in front of him.

"Wait!"

He froze. The easy lines of his body were absent for the first time since we'd entered the house.

I bent down and nudged the small beetle to the side. "Okay," I said cheerfully.

He stared at me for an intense moment. "It is possible that I might do the house's job and murder you myself."

I lifted my bag. "What do you mean?" I turned to hide my smirk. "There was a bug. It was innocent."

"Murder, darling." He began checking the nooks and crannies of the place. With only a single room, it didn't take long. "Well, at least it is lacking surprises."

I handed my shrunken portal pad to him. He lifted a brow. "Setting up for success?"

"Just in case."

I considered pulling a table into existence, but the floor was strangely calling to me. I set my bag on the floorboards and pulled out the carefully designed insert Constantine, Stevens, and I had created. It was made of a soft canvas Stevens had provided and Constantine had enhanced. I opened the drawstring bag so that it lay flat on the dusty scarred oak revealing my supplies. I removed the brushes and opened my palette box.

Leaving everything on the drawstring canvas bag meant that I could secure everything for emergency travel with a pull of the string and a swing of it around my shoulder. Everything was designed to be wrapped up quickly, if needed.

I couldn't afford to leave anything behind for Stavros to find. That had been another perk to the book swallowing my paintings.

A thin but massive pocket that was enchanted not to crinkle its contents ran the width and length of the bag and held my specially made paper. I pulled out a twenty by twenty piece.

Constantine had seen me paint before, but I didn't paint in front of people often. There was an unmasking in it. This was me, the Origin Mage, showing my true self without a shred of barrier, showing my power in the most defining way.

I had figured out almost immediately after escaping with Ori that painting did something that nothing else could accomplish after I used Origin Magic. It somehow allowed my mind to reorganize itself and pull the overwhelming information that I absorbed from the universe into a pattern that kept my mind and magic sane.

I looked over to see what Constantine was up to, but he was already reclining on the seat he always carried in his coat—a thin piece of wood angled up his back, and a small curved area to sit anchored it at the bottom, forming a sixty-degree angle for his body, and letting his legs stretch comfortably on the floor. It was exquisitely created, and the two pieces separated, so they fit in the long wool coats he loved to wear—or were easily depressed into a storage paper.

He lifted a brow, fingers wrapping his thin rope polymers in complicated patterns, like he was challenging a cat's cradle to the death. But lines of color and texture extended from every part of him, connecting to me and anchoring me in place.

And he had the portal pad. He could get away, if things went terribly wrong.

Satisfied, I looked down and examined the canvas. What to paint...

Death, destruction, suffering.

No.

But it was still there, on the edge, no matter what I tried.

But Constantine was still there too. The feel of community was still there. Neither removed the endpoint—I was going to paint something horrific. But I'd be okay.

Death, destruction, suffering.

I took a deep breath. I'd be okay. I wasn't alone.

I opened my mind. The world outside. The in-between of the layers. The million-piece puzzle assembled beyond. The way the magic enfolded in on itself and let me push the ferals between layers and into other worlds.

I touched my dry brush to the canvas and let it glide along while I imagined it.

The way I just knew where magic was happening, the way the map looked from the book, the feel of the magic as it arced from the earth—like a well-spring with spread tendrils hooked over the world, waiting to be tapped.

And the other things...the way that Stavros felt controlling me, that hollow inside, the way it felt to have Raphael use the box, how my magic was pulled from me, how I needed to figure out how to overcome that, the memories of Raphael in the Excelsine yearbooks, the look in Stavros' eyes, Kaine's shadows parasitically dipping inside, a distant recording of the Breaking, being inside Kinsky's painting, how the world opened like a million stars zooming in to form constellations of knowledge.

Paint was now on my brush, pulling from me, and it was gliding along the page, bursting life into the nooks and crannies of the canvas, bleeding its message into the cracks and over the statements.

It choked and pulled my brush in madly swirled midnight strokes. Blue, black, purple, brown death. Streaks of white lightning and crimson blood. Creation and life. A nightmare of slashing color and fiber. I'd constructed each of the fibers in this brush with assistance from Delia, and there was always an edgy quality to everything that Delia made—a bitterness with the world that was reflected in the layer upon which I stood.

But that wasn't the only edged thing in my life. Strange dreams haunted my wakening thoughts; dreams of destruction and despair. Gruesome images that spilled out onto the canvas beneath my brush.

Each carefully applied layer of flowers and birds became a disemboweled nightmare spilled upon the blackened grass.

I dropped my brush to the cloth and planted my palm against the canvas. Immediately, flowers bloomed, animals rose, creation unfolded, the landscape lit with life and promise, bursting at the seams. But like all the others, the longer I held on, the longer I pressed, the decay started to occur, and there was nothing I could do to prevent it, except wait for my magic to power the next cycle.

It was a continually looping piece of beautiful creation and horrific destruction, and the endless cycle and unity between the two.

If I let go, it would still happen, just on a slower time scale. I could never stop the cycle from occurring. I could only slow or hasten it. I twisted my fingers, pausing it at the height of creation, then ripped my hand away.

I stood with my head down, panting breaths heaving from my chest, up my throat, and through my mouth. The paint was still there, inside, but when I wiped my lips, I tasted power.

"Well...that was...enlightening," Constantine said.

I jerked around.

Constantine's brows lifted, easing the oddly troubled expression on his face into more familiar lines. "Forgot I was here?" His words were sardonic, but his gaze softened. He motioned. "Come on, then."

I stumbled over and buried myself in his chest. Neph's magic smoothed over me along with Constantine's. It was both a balm to my system and a small shock every time. The sharing was a superior level of trust from Neph to Constantine—a level of trust that had prompted one of the Bandits to mutter the Second Layer equivalent of hell freezing over.

I could feel Constantine looking at the painting. "It's not...completely horrible," he said, as the decay slowly sped up again.

I laughed around a hiccup. "It's horrible."

And the worse thing was it wasn't even as bad as the others I'd done. The creation cycles had lasted longer this time.

"It's mostly horrible, yes. In a beautiful, terrifying kind of way. Did you have to mix everything with so much black for the end?"

It made me think of Raphael's remark so long ago, when he'd been my false art teacher—that there was no true black in nature.

"Do you think everyone has a core of something good within them?" I asked into his shirt.

"No."

At his succinct answer, I curled my fingers in his coat. "No?"

"Some people are rotten all the way through."

"And some people seem that way, but aren't," I said, nudging him with a small amount of magic.

He said nothing for a few moments, then, "Perhaps it is best to judge by emotions that you identify with strongly. Like love. If someone has experienced love, loved someone else, something in them, somewhere, is capable of more. But those born without..."

"Raphael was born with plenty of love. He was tainted, twisted." I gripped harder, letting the comforting magic from Neph and Constantine, along with all the others, increase. "Do you think he could be good again?"

I felt him force himself to loosen from the automatic stiffness his body had assumed. "You test me with such questions."

"If I get taken, if I get turned—"

"You think yourself like Verisetti."

"You know him—on paper, you probably know him better than anyone who didn't know him personally. You've researched him. Without bringing an emotional reaction into it, don't you see the parallels?"

"I've long seen the parallels," he said quietly. "Why do you think I try to keep you from their grasp?"

"Do you think Enton Stavros has a thread of goodness within?"

"I have seen no evidence of such." Unlike the hot rage felt for Raphael, Constantine expressed only cold certainty discussing Stavros.

"But Professor Stevens...she's good." I reluctantly let go, not wanting to suck away all his magic.

"A positive can be born of a negative. And Stevens has her own demons to deal with. As do most of us." Constantine looked at the magic still faintly silhouetting his hand. "I can see why the governments keep the muses chained. Yours is powerful."

"She willingly gives her magic to you."

He didn't say anything for a long moment, face unreadable. "Yes. Your lunacy is spreading."

I patted his shoulder. "You are a good sort."

"I take comfort in the fact that your raw power will soon overwhelm the need to correct your inability to distrust appropriately."

"Hilarious."

He walked to stand in front of my painting again. "The truth is in front of me."

"It is as I said. Death and destruction."

"You feel the weight of the world." He murmured, tilting his head to get a different view of the darkness I had carved into the fibers—a darkness that was shifting and pulling, inviting the viewer inside the tumult. "Literally, as it were. I can see a crumbling globe there with five rotational lines."

I didn't look at the canvas. I didn't need to.

There was something off about his expression, though, as he looked at my painting. There was a tightness and an immense sorrow.

"You don't need to save the world, darling."

"I know."

"Do you?"

It was times like this, right after painting, that I felt I could set all the worlds to rights. That I could truly do anything.

And it was terrifying.

I started packing my supplies into the magic canvas wraps that Constantine, Stevens, and I had created for them. "I have a duty—"

"You have no duty but to yourself," he said fiercely, suddenly, emotions switching from sorrow to fury. "I don't care what the Thirdies try to shame and guilt you with. Or what you feel you owe them. You don't owe this world or the Third Layer anything."

I looked at my fingers—at the power that ran beneath my skin, highlighted even more now that I had given it outlet. "I owe them for taking in the ferals. For taking on the danger of dealing with me. For—"

He leaned toward me, tension vibrating through him. "All I need do is to stride the halls we came from to see the evidence of what you have given them. That structure was a gutted installation, barely serviceable when you first came."

"I didn't fix it by myself. Others came to help."

"Pulled there by you. By the power of you."

I looked at the power in my hands. "And that is a responsibility all its own. People will come. Scientists, societal magicians, architects. My abilities, my...title. Both hold power."

"Mmmm. The way you are speaking is what I've long wanted for you."

But there was a weird coil of something that I couldn't identify in our connection, like Constantine was displeased by his own past thoughts.

"I can fix the Third Layer, Con." Surrounded by its broken pieces and the essence of the break, it hummed jaggedly in my ear every night trying and failing to find its tune. It called to me, to everything in me, to fix it.

Like a jigsaw puzzle that was missing the final tenth of its pieces. So close.

"More than just the Department will call for your blood once they know you've started. Even in a school predisposed to progression, you heard vehement arguments against such a prospect. Seconders don't want to give the magic back any more now than we did seventy years ago when blessed with the bounty. The Fourth Layer will declare war as well. The dwindling people who still live in the Third might want their layer fixed, but they lost the right to that magic years ago. Might makes right in this world, darling. In all the worlds."

I looked up at him. "If that is true, then I have the right, do I not?"

I felt his thrum of shock vibrantly through our connection, before he schooled his expression to contemplate me more closely.

"If you want to rule the worlds, I will not say no." He examined the magic around me carefully. "If anyone can build it into a better one, it will be you. But such a strategy needs a different start point."

"No." I crossed my arms, slumping. "You know I have no wish to rule. But the worlds need fixing. I can fix it. Mendable things make my fingers and magic ache, and I'm tired of the squabbling over what magic is whose."

"Taking the magic back will provoke war. A war between three layers. The non-magical world, at the very least, will not survive that intact."

The same feeling of truth rose in me. I held up my palm and let the magic swirl into the bubbled, recycling layout I had brainstormed with Will weeks ago. Domed cities with safe corridors between efficiently used the magic and recycled it across the entire structure—the layer pulled tightly over the whole like Saran wrap over mounds of rice. Constantine lifted the magic, cupping the image in his palms. He had examined the parts weeks ago.

"It is brilliant," he murmured, then gave a little twist so it whirled back to me. "A compromise that might work. But it won't please the magicists in any layer."

"I know it will work," I said aggressively, compressing the idea and magic back into my skin. "And they can get with the times as I fix this entire blasted layer into something better."

My eyes caught on a sudden shimmer on the floor. I tugged a cleaning cloth from the canvas bag. I couldn't leave anything behind.

Constantine regarded me for a long moment. "Of that, I have no doubt. In that single moment, you will be brighter than anything I've ever seen."

"A single moment, before it all breaks?" I carefully captured the paint in the fibers of the cloth, using a tendril of magic to get the whole drop.

"A single moment for you to choose."

Another drop of paint shimmered a few feet away. When had I gotten so messy?

I wiped a hand across my eyes and crawled over to it. "I told you when we returned to campus after rescuing Olivia that we were going to fix it."

And then I'd done other things for months, pretended to be normal. Look how well that had gone.

"I remember it well. Watching you ride a wave of adrenaline so fierce that you didn't sleep well for days. With that blasted marble in your pocket, then that demon in your chest."

My hand drifted down to rub my chest. I could still feel the hollow Stavros's presence had left inside, like a desiccated hole that I couldn't fill.

"I'm going to kill him," Constantine said blandly.

"I believe Grey mentioned there being a queue for that," I said, trying to alleviate the darkening mood.

I reached over to get the last drop of paint. It was too risky to leave even a tiny splatter point. As I reached it, the drop thinned and spread in a line, slithering along a path. I stilled.

Constantine came to stand next to me and followed my view as we watched the line become thinner and thinner, trying to reach its endpoint.

"Either there is a sudden tilt to the floor, or your paint is on a quest," he said humorlessly.

"I should probably wipe it up," I said, not moving.

"Why spare us whatever world ending event is going to happen?" He didn't move either, but I could feel his emotions and magic gather into a focused point. "It just gives me ammunition against that irritating demolition mage who is always hoping you are in the process of ending the world for him to witness."

"I need new friends."

That sparked a small curve of Constantine's lips. "Unquestionably."

Ten different spells curled beneath the skin of each of his finger pads, ready to be released, whichever spell was needed—held there by a force of will that people rarely realized Constantine possessed. Or rather, the discerning did—and the Bandits knew far better than most—but many mages at Excelsine saw him as a vindictive playboy and nothing more.

I followed the paint drop on my knees as it flowed around one board in particular, then stopped. The trail of paint gathered so that it was outlining the wooden floor board. There was nothing overtly interesting or odd about the board—it was one of hundreds in the room—but when I touched it, I could feel it brimming with possibility. Reaching out to touch the board, I called the magic of the paint to lift it.

I directed the board to the side, settling it on its neighbor, and peered beneath, lighting a small cloud of magic and letting it hover over top.

"There's something in there."

"Of course, there is," Constantine said tiredly. "Human remains?"

"What? No." I reached inside. "Why would you say that?"

"Why would you blindly reach inside a hole in the floor?"

"Yeah, okay. Point." My fingers grabbed the wrapped package inside.

"Darling, you didn't even check for wards."

"I don't sense anything," I said slowly, pulling the package into the light of the room and examining the enchanted burlap and twine. "Except a...vague residue. If I wasn't looking at the spot, I wouldn't even sense that, I don't think."

"Right. You should obviously unearth the death packet then."

"I don't think it's a death packet." The burlap was enchanted, but it was a protection and preservation enchantment curved into the parcel, with no outward spikes.

He sighed, and I could see twelve other spells join his first ten, as he readied whatever he thought he'd need to save the world.

"I could care less about the world," he answered, reading my thoughts. "That is your burden. I merely exist to save you."

I shook my head fondly, not keeping my further thoughts secret either. That is why you helped Olivia, then, I said mentally, as I started to unwrap the twine.

"Lies," he said blandly. But he leaned in to see what the package revealed.

It was a series of exquisitely crafted sketches of the same woman.

Touching the first made the world warp—visually pulling the things close to me, like Constantine and my supplies into macroscopic view, and shifting the rest of the world into a hazy blur. Feelings—deep and crushed with weight—exploded outward, like pollen bursting from an overripe bloom. Emotions and memories fell around me, and I felt the wisp of a woman's ghostly fingers brush my cheek.

Alone. Darkness. Aid.

What do you seek?

"Kinsky did this," I murmured. I knew this woman.

The brush strokes were long and sensual, lovingly curving the frame of the woman's body, her head was just starting to turn, but it was not filled in by detail—as if the artist knew her enough to anticipate her features, but was rediscovering her as she moved to face him.

Like a man painting a memory that he wanted to experience again.

Despair and melancholy and loss.

"He lost a love," I said softly. "Such sadness in these strokes."

Constantine didn't respond for a moment. "I see it," he said tightly.

"It's the same woman," I murmured.

The other images were burned into my brain in a soul-deep way. They, too, had held a melancholic tinge.

Sergei Kinsky was a man who had loved deeply and mourned just as profoundly.

"Yes?" Constantine had stepped away at some point while I'd been absorbed and was looking through the window, curtain pulled back, and magic coiling around him. His cloak suddenly secured around him, transforming him into an anonymous wraith.

"It's the same woman in the portrait at the Library of Alexandria, the same one from Ganymede Circus." I shook my head. "I never found out what happened to that shop."

"And you won't find out today." He let the curtain fall and his magic reached to join with mine, his cloak wrapping him even tighter in anonymous spells.

"Why?" I let his magic automatically connect to mine.

"Because the Department's flunkies have arrived."

I put my hand on the floor and felt the reverberations in the layer. I nodded and sent a summons for paper and wings, then carefully wrapped the small portrait back in its burlap and gathered up my supplies. "You ready?"

"Do I have an alternative to letting that blasted book ferry me back?"

"We could take Will's portal pad," I offered, nodding to his pocket. "It fits two and has an enlargement spell for four."

"The tunnel of death?"

"It's not that bad."

"Everyone screams."

"Most. Most people scream."

"Right. My mistake. Pass."

The book popped into the room, dropping Guard Rock on my shoulder and devouring the painting in one fell swoop. Guard Rock hitched his arm through the strap of my bag, and the book enveloped us from behind when a soldier wearing Stavros's face opened the door.

The house roared, and a giant maw of oak shot toward the man with Stavros's face.

He paid no attention to his death. Magic flitted over his stolen eyes—the scrolling magic that the high-level Department thugs used to see beyond disguises and lies. His gaze was affixed to my bag and a look of deep fury overtook his stolen features along with a sliver of unease.

"You're too late," I said. I didn't know what made me say it as the book's pages closed around me.

Stavros didn't move toward us, nor did he move away as the mouth dove to envelop his puppet. He simply watched us as we disappeared, eyes full of caged fury and cold plans.

He looked at the paint on my disappearing fingers, and smiled as his puppet died.

Chapter Six

OTHER HANDS DO BURDENS HOLD

W E EMERGED in the turret and I stumbled over to the desk. My supplies slid from my bag across the wood. My wrapped painting and the Kinsky sketches stopped near the edge, teetering.

Another death. Images of death and dying whirled in my mind. I was drowning in death's darkness.

I touched the table.

Constantine's cloak zipped from him in an effortless movement. He crouched down, darkly contemplating Guard Rock, who was gesturing something to him. "Your rock says they were ambushed at the 'gate with five arms.'" He frowned at Guard Rock. "The Library of Alexandria? Why the devil were you—"

Magic hooked into my gut, stiffening my muscles as the layer whispered in four dimensions. An Awakening.

I swayed unsteadily, and Constantine was suddenly lurching over to catch me, his palms pressed to my cheeks as he searched my pupils. "Ren?"

Magic soared through me as his expletives grew distant in my ears. I raised my hands and shot the paint splatters on my fingers against the walls to strengthen the wards on the complex.

The wards pulsed. Magic tingled from every pore. The painting session had been...different. I felt more in control, more powerful. I let calm descend and slowly rotated my shoulders forward, feeling the energy course through me as I let the magic pull me upright. This Awakening would be easy.

I rotated my palm downward.

"No." Constantine's voice was dark. He grabbed my hand and pulled me against him. He flicked his finger and my fitted trench cloak peeled from my frame and flew to the other side of the room.

"Constantine—"

"No. It's insanity. With you hopped up on juice and Stavros knowing it? No way are you going. I don't care what—" His eyes unfocused, then a flood of relief filled him painfully and suddenly. "Those idiots got your device into production."

I pulled my hand and body free and the cloak sailed back over to me. I swung it in an arc, shrugging my arms into it.

Magic coursed through me. Power.

"Alexander's on the move. I told him you'd be alerting him momentarily with a location."

"There's no need." I could just pop in, grab the emerging mage, and pop back out. I just had to hurry.

I stepped forward, palm out.

"If you think I'm letting you go, you have underestimated things," Constantine said, magic twining around his fingers; his expression savage.

One of the threads connected to my chest gave a painful squeeze. I fought it for a moment, watching Constantine's face grow darker. An even more painful twist squeezed. Disappointment.

I licked my lips. "I could go anyway."

"You could." Magic coursed through the connections streaming in and out of him and to me—a bright ultramarine and deep brown surging through the others.

I sagged, my hand falling like a shoulder muscle had been cut. "Tattletale."

"I've lost the ability to be evil in the truly great ways. You've reduced me to this existence."

"Fine. Fine. Even though—"

"As soon as—"

"I've got it. You are worse than Olivia." I growled and turned.

His hand slipped down my forearm. "I don't think so." When I looked at him, he was encased in his fitted cloak again as well.

"You aren't coming." This wasn't like painting while knowing he was protected.

"We will simply appear, then leave again just as quickly." His expression was calm, his fury abruptly, carefully tucked away. He rolled magic around two fingers in an unending loop. "Unless you have other plans?"

What if Axer's team couldn't handle the Department? What if the praetorians came anyway? What if—

"If you don't take me with you, I will simply port to Times Square and stand on the sidewalk," Constantine said. "Waiting to see who comes for me first."

He would, too. He was just that kind of asshole. I swore and grabbed his arm. "That's blackmail."

"Far better than tattling. I appreciate your assistance."

I growled at him again, swiped a hand through the air to make a paint-spattered page fall to the ground, and folded us through the fibers. There was nothing quite like painting to make the layers open before me. It was the constant portent of doom I could live without.

I concentrated on the feeling of the Awakening, rifling through the data to ascertain the exact location, and requested the paper spit us out twenty feet from it. Real-time data bloomed, and I could feel Constantine's immediate push.

I gnashed my teeth and forced my mind to send Axer every detail of the location and all the minute pieces of data my senses were spewing.

Even the odd data points, like how strange the ground felt—like it was full of my magic. Miles of it. A girl on the sidewalk stared at her glowing green hands in wonder and fear. Three black cats with glowing eyes slunk under a car, tails curling around the back bumper. Eleven black clad figures stealthily moved through the shadows, around the sides of the buildings in the distance. Magic spiked from the devices on their cloaks.

I moved automatically, raising my arms to blast the forms.

"No," Constantine hissed and stepped in front of me, gripping my wrists with just enough container magic to halt my movement. The ground vibrated beneath us, reacting to the start of my channeling.

I clenched my teeth as I watched the sinister figures moving closer and the girl glowing brighter. Constantine could use my magic, but he'd never be able to match me in the First Layer, if I chose to push.

"I don't need to," he said, squeezing my wrists and reading my thoughts. "You have given me other far more potent weapons—emotional weapons. You said you would leave," he bit out. "You promised Price."

You promised _me_.

But could I live with the girl being taken?

Before I could make a conscious decision, a dark figure swooped in overwhelming one of the hunters then another, breaking one neck then the next. The motions were as soundless as they were lethal.

I sagged against Constantine.

The cloaked figure had taken out six of the eleven figures before the others finally noticed. "Shivit, shivit, shivit! Watch ou—"

A gurgle replaced the end of the word. Then two additional cloaked figures —Ramirez and Greene, identifiable in the connected, shared spells woven in the fibers of all our cloaks—appeared and took out the remaining four. Their faces were hidden to everyone except those of us who wore garments linked through the identity spell.

"Where are they?" Axer demanded in the low, harsh voice that always accompanied him in battle mode, as he pivoted and quickly scanned under the car and around the area.

Dark brown hair shaded deep blue eyes as he visually swept the area and narrowed in first on the girl and hunters, then moved toward us. My magic stuttered a beat as his intense too-blue gaze landed on me.

Axer assessed our body posture, Constantine's grip on my wrists, the way he was positioned in front of me, then he turned and pulled with both hands, tearing rising black clad figures from their feet and new ones from their perches.

The Awakening mage looked up, the sound of falling bodies breaking through her wonder, and I could see the moment fear overtook everything else. Greene moved with careful steps toward the shell-shocked girl, speaking reassuring words to the shaking Awakening mage as he slipped a control cuff around her wrist. I knew intimately and intellectually that the cuff would protect her, but not naturally, not emotionally, not anymore. Why couldn't they let her work it all out in a containment unit like the Third Layer?

My torso pushed toward her, but Constantine forced me back, unsettling my feet and making me stumble.

"Where are the cats?" Axer demanded again.

"Cats?" Constantine's emotions plunged to dread as he said it.

Thick, black wisps drifted from the shadows, as if forced from hiding, and flew straight at us. The cats. Praetorian scouts. Constantine and Axer whirled to face them, feeling from me where the threat was emanating. I raised my hand automatically and power ripped from my fingers—

—then stuttered an inch away from the tips, hovering there painfully—

Two shadows converged on Axer.

One headed straight for Constantine.

I threw more power into the magic and blinding pain crippled me from my toes clear up to my fingertips as the magic was sucked violently back inside me.

Constantine's jab glanced off the diving shadow. The shadow laughed and veered into a tight circle for another pass. I could hear Greene yell something in the background as he pushed the girl behind a car.

Shockwaves of pain vibrated through my body as the magic I'd been channeling shot down to my toes and the earth reached up to secure it—turning it into tempered steel around my feet.

All magic ceased within me. Like a flame that had been abruptly doused.

Breathless and panicked, I made frantic eye contact with Constantine, who whirled to meet another pass of the praetorian.

Greene was throwing devices, Ramirez was fading in and out of the shadows himself, and as a dozen new figures appeared, Axer began lighting the street with colored flame. I could do nothing to help. I grabbed a rock from the ground and hammered uselessly at the steel mound securing me. But it was an inviolate substance created by my own magic.

I tried to pull the location data back to mind, searching for my mistake. The ground had felt strange. I had sent all the information to Axer through the device I had given Dagfinn, and anything registering as my magic would be registered only with my signature.

An intricate trap. Stavros had plenty of my magic. I gave it around freely on campus, and he had been collecting it. The Department oversaw the First Layer grid and safety. He had waited until I was hopped up, like Constantine had said, and laid a trap—one he had obviously had up his sleeve—spreading my magic over the wide expanse of an area that would meet whatever Awakening area parameters he set.

Because of course he knew I would channel magic when answering an Awakening.

I pounded harder at the restraints.

The one thing Stavros hadn't counted on was me securing outside help. I was never going to hear the end of it from the others.

Please, please let me never hear the end of it. That would mean everyone would survive.

I frantically searched for a way to free myself.

Constantine's back was to me as he fended off the shadow again—but he had limited options in the First Layer when not pulling magic from me. As he fumbled for something in his cloak, his right arm snapped under a barrage of spells.

The praetorian thrust a knife into his side and Constantine arched. Electricity lit against the praetorian's neck. A glowing piece of Stavros sparked on the praetorian's deadly shadowed claws.

One swipe with those talons and Stavros would be inside of Constantine.

My arm drew back and with a thousand tossed balls in my muscle memory, I chucked the rock straight into the praetorian's eye.

The praetorian stumbled backward, taking the embedded knife with him. Blood gushed from Constantine's side, but using his broken arm he awkwardly pulled out the box of magic I had given him at the hut. In a less than smooth kneeling motion, he smashed it against the steel encasing my feet. Splinters of metal lifted on winded wings as the crow-shaped shadow of the praetorian zoomed upward, banked then rocketed toward us.

While looking directly at me and seeing through my eyes, he lifted his palm to meet the attack, leeching magic from me through the fingers hanging from his broken arm that were touching my ankles, and up his body into his raised palm. My magic formed a sphere around the shadow as it hit, forming a dark, malevolent ball that Constantine tightly gripped.

It swirled darkly in his grasp. His other hand shook unevenly on its broken axis as it clasped my foot. My magic surged through him to keep hold of the praetorian.

"Don't move. God, your magic is everywhere," he said, voice strained. "It will grab you again as soon as you step free, and I can't do this a second time. Just...just wait." His eyes tightened in pain.

But the arrival of praetorian scouts meant more were minutes, seconds, away. Praetorian warriors who weren't mere scouts.

"I'm sorry," I whispered. His fingers became as immovable as the steel had been, held there by my own magic.

"No," he said, raised fingers tightening around the ball of shadow. "They will be."

Axer, Ramirez, and Greene crushed the hunters with speed and stealth, leaving only two remaining hunters and two praetorian scouts. Fortunately, neither praetorian was Kaine.

"Do it," Constantine yelled to them, his hoarse voice grim.

I looked at him in question.

He shook his head. "Hold on," he whispered to me.

Axer's movements shifted, and rather than repelling the aggressors, he drew the hunters and praetorians closer to us.

As the deadly steps of the combat mages danced closer, I could feel only guilt. They were risking their necks to save the ferals and to save me. And while Camille Straught had thought I deserved a boon for saving campus, I'd probably used it up by now. And she'd never been a fan of feral mages, or any she deemed as less in control.

But following Axer to his grave? Of that, there was no doubt for any of them.

My magicless fingers trembled.

It had been weeks since I'd left campus, since my possessed fingers had tried to kill Axer. But I could still feel the echoes in my hands, where I had gripped the lines of his life and choked the air from his throat. I could hear Stavros cackling about the Dares' only weakness. I could feel Stavros' exultation at finally, finally, getting the Dare scion under his control.

He had wanted Axer's powers for longer than I'd had magic, but Axer had been untouchable. Until me. I was his albatross.

Axer slaughtered the last two hunters, then Ramirez and Greene used their remaining magic to thrust the shadows toward him. Axer grabbed them as if they were rag dolls and flung them into the ball in Constantine's hand.

With the magic in one of his last containers, Axer slid forward and encased the ball in a layer of magic that reverberated through all three of us.

Breathing heavily, he tied the magic and released it.

But he didn't relax. In fact, he appeared unusually vigilant, a strange look appearing in his eyes as Ramirez closed in.

And I could see it—what they sensed as the ground beneath all of us started shaking.

Ramirez immediately became a shadow at Axer's back, watching the street with easy, dark sweeps of his eyes as Greene helped the Awakening mage to her feet. Axer's shoulders tensed. He stared at my neck, my chest, then the hand still gripping my ankle, keeping me anchored. I could feel a single emotion radiating from him that couldn't be hidden—a deep longing to step forward and complete the circle. My heart ached as we made eye contact.

He looked to the distance, then to the ground at my feet, expression pinched as if a set of unpleasant options had presented themselves, and he needed to choose one.

"We need to leave," Constantine said, his grip on me not easing, the three praetorian shadows in his grip steadily growing darker. His gaze met his roommate's. "But not from here."

Something passed between them—a stream of conversation that I wasn't privy to.

Axer reached forward and gripped Constantine's side, knitting it back together then resetting Constantine's broken arm with half a container of magic.

Shadows shrieked in the wind indicating Kaine was on the move. Only this time, the sound seemed to emanate from Constantine's palm.

The magic around me suddenly went dormant. Constantine hissed as my magic flooded him, forcing him to loosen his grip on me.

My freed magic started sucking back down to my feet, reforming chains.

Axer flung his last half-container of magic straight at us.

The world blurred around me, and Constantine's grip shook completely free.

The mist disappeared like fog on suddenly opened windows, and my magic exploded unrestrained. I looked around to see what my freed senses already told me. Constantine and I were forty-two kilometers to the west of where the Awakening was happening, on the edge of a different town. In the distance, I could see people walking down a main street, oblivious to what was happening less than fifty kilometers away.

There was a loud boom beside me as Constantine and the shadowed ball he'd been holding crashed to the ground. Constantine's wrist cracked against the pavement, his open palm scorched.

Magic coiled within me. How dare they.

The praetorian scouts rose, and the entirety of my rage ascended with them. This was my layer. A layer where my magic was king.

Save the town, save the non-magicals, trust in your friends.

I hooked a lash of magic, like a tail behind me, curling around Constantine and grabbing the praetorians and enfolding the five of us into the Second Layer's Death Valley.

Come and get us, I sent to Kaine in a call of magic.

Constantine spun out to a crouch as we slid across the hot sand in the blinding desert landscape.

The praetorian scouts rose, covered in moving shadow, one wearing Stavros's face.

"I'm disappointed in you, Miss Crown," he bit out. "Enlisting others to do your dirty work."

"Too like you?" I whipped sand into my palm and felt Constantine move into position behind me, disregarding his own broken bones.

Stavros's ruthless gaze focused on Constantine, and his smiles turned deliberate. "Interesting. I had thought them your loved ones, but I see that you are fully okay with them dying in service to you."

Rage blew away everything else. I flung away the fingers of magic grasping at my sleeve. I ejected the two useless shadows and flew at the shadow wearing Stavros's face with all the magic within me, clenching it between my sun-struck palms.

I shot the incandescently charged magic straight into it. It shrieked in the full light of the sun, pieces of shadow and Stavros' face falling from it like cracked clay and leaving behind a ragged man. A normal mage, broken and twitching on the hot sand.

My chest rose and fell in rattling heaves, and I stared at the shell of the man who was now absent of a shadow, absent of my enemy's face.

An ordinary man twitching on the sand.

"Ren," Constantine said tightly. "We have to go."

I let out a broken laugh, then shoved my hand out before Constantine could convert on the alarmed actions his emotions said he was about to take. "Wait."

I forced myself to bring forward a careful mental pyramid. To construct something deliberate instead of blindly letting my magic take control. I concentrated, then shoved the convulsing man through the layer and to a point in the distance that Will's super encyclopedia-and-occasional-map labeled a hospital.

Then I shakily withdrew the port paper and enfolded the two of us into the Third Layer.

Chapter Seven

COILS OF THE TEMPEST

I COULD TASTE the acidic burn of paint working its way up my throat. I pressed my hand against my mouth and inhaled deep gulps of air to prevent myself from retching.

"Don't you dare feel bad for that praetorian," Constantine said tightly, holding his broken wrist against his chest.

I took hold of his wrist, turning his palm upward where the burns curled across the skin.

"I can't just..." I clenched my fingers and loosened them in an unending bid to gain control and used the overloaded wards to heal his wounds, checking to make certain no shadow remnants remained. "I can't just do that to people."

Destroy them, not save them.

He said nothing for a moment, as he made circular, loosening motions with his newly healed wrist and recently broken arm and I could feel threads of magic checking me. "No. But not because I give a shivit about some random flunky. You aren't built for the darker emotions." He lifted my palms this time, examining something there. "They will destroy you in the same way Stavros means to."

I stared at his quickly healing skin. "How are the others?" I hadn't felt any lights go out. All my connection threads were still thriving.

"Alexander and his minions? You think they can't take care of themselves without magic?" he asked, somewhat in amusement, though I could feel him searching me mentally for the answers as he knelt down to look at my ankle. "Against fighters who rely far too heavily on being overly-armed? You do remember that there was a non-magic category of fighting in the tournament?"

It was a strange category amid hundreds of events that relied on magic in a thousand different ways.

"Ramirez is the current collegiate champion in all non-magic fighting. Alexander is only second to him by a hair. Don't worry overly much about your pets. Not even when fighting the worst of the Department."

"The Department. They keep… And the ferals…"

He gently touched my ankle with his thumb. I could almost hear the words he didn't say—you can't save everyone.

I shuddered. I could save some, though.

I pulled away from him, and with magic zipping from my fingers, threw the portal pad on the ground. "Get in."

"No." I could feel the hackles of his magic rise beneath his bland response.

"Stavros knows it was you with me."

"Of course, he does. He's not an idiot."

"He can publicly check. He can have the media check."

"And?"

"And?" What kind of blasé answer was that? "He's going to verify your whereabouts then out you as my accomplice. Get into the pad and get back to campus."

I should have pushed him back to Axer's location immediately. I should never have allowed here to be here in the first place.

"I'm not leaping into that thing, especially not to go to campus." He stretched out with his hands behind him on the floor, cracking his neck. His emotions were the opposite of relaxed. "You just shoved me through nine dimensions in forty minutes. Ten is asking far too much."

"I'm not asking. You need to return to campus." God, he needed to get back now. Why was he stalling? My heart beat a fast echo in my ears, overtaking background sound.

He gave me a bland look as he rose. "Do I?"

"Yes."

"No."

"Get in the pad, Constantine."

He slapped both hands on the table, making magic ripple over the top in an echo of my earlier action, and showing his true emotion.

"So, you can go running about on your own? You wouldn't have survived today without us."

"I know. And what do you think will happen next time?" Now that Stavros knew I was seeking help from others? "He'll have plans for you, too. He knows it is you. Knows it is Axer. Once he has indisputable evidence he will destroy both of you."

"He can try."

"I can't keep you safe if you don't let me."

He leaned forward and smiled—it was one of his meaner ones, the kind not often directed at me. "You can't keep me safe?"

"Not if you won't let me!"

"Well, isn't that a pickle."

"They are going to arrest your father. They are going to kick you out."

His smile grew meaner. "They can try."

"Penniless, living on the streets—"

"With my skills, I will always be wealthy. Even if I start from zero repeatedly."

"Thrown in a cell—"

"Doubtful."

"You will be experimented on."

"They could only wish."

"You won't be able to afford the meanest of potions or ingredients. You will have no access to cutting edge materials."

"Now you are just being mean."

"I should never have let the Ophidians allow you into this complex." My voice turned harsher. "Weakness."

Allies, not friends, butterfly.

"Yes, weakness." Constantine's expression sharpened, like he had heard my memory of Raphael's voice, and his palms glowed hotly against the wood. "That's what I think of when I look at your friendship ties."

He tugged hard on the connections between us—stunning lines of turquoise, copper, and violet that were interconnected and beautiful. Then he touched hundreds of fainter ones that the others were channeling through him to me.

They highlighted the choices of both involved parties.

I plucked his, letting the connection stretch. "I remade those, I can do it again."

"And do what? Improve upon the utter certainty that you will never physically harm me or fulfill your threats?" He twirled his fingers, the turquoise and copper threads mixing with violet into a closed fist as he yanked back. "Weakness."

Visions of plunging my hand into Axer's chest at Stavros' command and not being in control of my own actions swarmed my thoughts. And the superimposed image of ripping out Constantine's beating heart while he blindly trusted, made me ill and enraged.

"It might not be me."

"I know!" He said harshly. "That's the whole—"

"Get in." I pointed at the pad, fingers shaking, one second away from pushing him inside.

I couldn't lose anyone else. I couldn't lose him.

He opened his mouth, then closed it—clenching his teeth together and visibly restraining himself from saying whatever was on his mind.

Say it, I challenged mentally—wildly—magic brimming beneath my nails.

He let the threads go with a snap. "No."

"No?"

He took a deep breath and examined the nails of one hand in sudden boredom—the patina of ennui descending over his face so at odds with his caged inner turmoil that it was jarring. "Let me see if I understand your demands. You want me to enter your terrifying, illegal traveling device and return my body to campus, even though the golem you helped me create is at the summit in Ravishkan?"

My surging anger paused, data jarring with already drawn pictures in my brain. "Okay, no, that's—back to Ravishkan, then to Excelsine. Get in."

He leaned forward into my space. "No."

"I messed up the endpoint, fine, but—"

"No."

"Stavros took my brother—"

"I know."

"He's going to—"

He wrapped his fingers into my hair, the movement gentling almost immediately, but palms still firm against my cheeks. "I'm. Not. Going. Anywhere. And neither is anyone else."

A sob started to form in my throat, and I had to look away. Down at his chest where I could see his heart beating and his magic pulsing. To the other connections that were live and strong.

No one thought they were going to die. Yet—

"You can't control that," he said. There was something complicated happening in his emotions, though. "You can just make certain you aren't alone when you do. And your paint is starting to form a monster again."

I ripped my gaze over to where Guard Rock and the book were staring at us. They were perched above the Kinsky sketches and the supplies from the painting excursion. Guard Rock was judiciously poking a glob of paint that was stubbornly trying to slink off a brush and ping-ponging his gaze between us, as if he wasn't certain what required the most attention.

My breath hitched. "I forgot the preservation enchantment."

I tore away from Constantine, from the wild and untamed emotions flowing everywhere—our connection points, the wards, the very air in the room. A deep anger and despair and even deeper love was spiking through him. I quickly strode over to where the book was watching me judgmentally.

I herded the glob back onto the brush with shaking hands.

I'd watched clumps turn into globular monsters of death before. A preservation enchantment would have allowed me to leave their cleaning until I was in a safe zone.

But the Awakening call had come in as soon as we returned. Not a coincidence. Any of it.

Stupid.

With shaking hands, I lifted paint-coated brushes and started cleaning them, so I didn't have to think.

I carefully swirled the first brush in the small cleaning and encapsulating device that Stevens had made for me after watching a different batch—so long ago now—form Daliesque creatures intent on melting everything they came in contact with. Then there had been that time when the paint had ejected round, mysterious stones. And the time when a portal had opened.

The device allowed all those elements to combine, but constrained the product into a more manageable single outcome.

Hysteria rose within me again. Manageable death.

"That praetorian," I said quietly. "And the man at the house without a pot. All those who let Stavros use them... He sends each to die."

"Many men die in service of a general's eyes," Constantine said indifferently.

"As themselves, though." I rubbed the hollow in my chest with one hand, and stuck in the next brush. "Not with his face as the last thing they wear. Why do they let him use them like that?"

The device made a gurgling sound and I wondered what the cleaning device would produce this time with death and destruction underscoring the deep rage that Stavros brought forth within me.

"Don't underestimate the eagerness of men to serve power. And don't feel sorrow for those who choose that path."

That path—but what of others? Like my friends, who were following me down to Hades with their coin already slipping between their lips?

I kept thinking of my friends. Of Stavros's words foretelling their deaths—of them dying in service to me.

I rubbed my chest again. "What if they aren't choosing? What if he burrowed in like..." My hand stilled on my breastbone.

Constantine's entire emotional landscape went bleak and violent for a moment—something deep and dark in the depths—before he did whatever he was able to do to control it. I envied his control. "Then we mourn and avenge them. Not necessarily in that order."

"Bloodthirst?"

"On a less than six-year plan for me this time." He eyed me. "How are you feeling otherwise?"

"You can't tell?"

"I can feel power veritably storming through you, darling. That isn't what I'm asking."

"You are angry with me."

"Incensed," he said mildly.

"And despairing. Why do you feel despair and refuse to go somewhere safe?"

"You misunderstand the cause of the emotion. Why do you feel like you are the only one who fears losing someone?"

I didn't answer.

"You know, back in the fall, I thought for a moment, that you would succeed in resurrecting your brother." He rolled magic slowly under his hand. "It was strange, having hope, something outside of revenge. You didn't succeed, but the hope had already clasped onto me, dug its claws in. Infected my veins."

"I didn't fail," I whispered.

He looked sharply at me.

"I had to…" I swallowed. "Raphael made it so that…" I shook my head. "I let him go. My brother. I let him go."

"Why?" the question was succinct in both word and tone.

"Will. Christian would have…replaced him."

Constantine watched me for a moment in a detached way. "You are terrible at sacrificing pawns," he murmured.

"He's not a—"

"And even worse at letting go of closer pieces."

"I'm not losing anyone else."

"Even with powers like yours, that, I'm afraid, is out of your control."

I turned the brush and focused on the device. "You'd better watch for a rotorsaur. I feel one coming."

It was the name for the insanity that had burst from an earlier brush cleaning. A creature with a snake head and tail, but also with another head—a lion's head—a single human-like arm, three lizard feet and a lizard body.

Constantine grimaced—for once the quick tail of emotion matched his expression. "Even I don't know if the menagerier can handle another one of those. And I'm not sure he is someone who should be uncertain about creatures he usually loves. And you aren't avoiding speaking about your anxieties."

"I'm painting too much."

"You could move mountains right now." The darkness peered up again.

"Or kill people."

Constantine looked at the Origin Book. "Tell me about the places it wants you to go."

"No. You aren't as tricky as you think you are." I watched the container with resignation. "And this creature is going to be deadly."

"I'm exceedingly tricky. You have an unfair advantage. And don't give me this little drama over a creature that half the beings in the Fourth Layer will probably clamor to claim as a pet."

Constantine was shifting with the conversation, as I knew he would, but everything unsaid coiled through him, unforgotten. He would wait and strike at an even more vulnerable point.

"You do have a weird thing for snakes," he said, reading my mind as easily as he always did, and turning suddenly agreeable, an agile viper looking for a better angle. "I blame our first meeting and your obsession with me. Understandable. Aim for something pettable, though, and you will find your adoption rate increases."

"Furry, got it." A smile broke through my turmoil, deep fondness underscoring relief as I felt him loosen his grip on his immediate anger. I twisted the last brush with a little tendril of magic and fur burst from the seams in the container.

Constantine sighed. "That's a Level 10 container. Nothing should breach it."

And here we were, skirting the edge of the topic again.

I fished out the small bundle of fur and paws and scooted it toward him. The animal's hackles were raised, and a low growl emanated between hisses. It could possibly be classified as a cat, if cats came in violet, cream, and electric blue, and had three forked tails and a hundred teeth too big for their mouths.

He stared at it, then at me. "Well, I don't want it."

"It's yours now."

The catlike thing sank its teeth into him and he swore. He tried to shake it from his hand, but the cat's gaze was zeroed in on his and it never looked away even as it curled around his hand, kicking the underside at the same time it tried to tear the flesh from his fingers. Con swore again and magic blasted outward, outlining the cat's skeleton in pure electric blue. Teeth still embedded, the cat gave a noise somewhere between a chuff and a growl.

"It is definitely yours," I said and started to pack up.

The cat let go abruptly and magic sparked. Then, as if it had been its goal all along, it licked a stripe up the wounds it had inflicted and pushed its terrifying head against Con's fingers.

The sharp, sly look in the feline's eyes confirmed ownership as much as the scars disappearing beneath its tongue.

"Vile beast," he said, frowning at the cat at the same time he started petting it. His shoulders relaxed a small measure as the animal's head butted against his palm, slicing his skin only slightly with the graze of its razor teeth while trying to eat the highly magical signet stone on his finger.

Small waves of interest and humor emanated from Constantine as he rotated his hand to flummox the beast. Creating more furry things went on my mental agenda.

"Now, how are you feeling?" he asked, still petting the razorcat.

"Disquieted." I swallowed. Powerful.

"I'm not going back to campus."

"I know." And I am glad—a guilty, horrible thought. "Something terrible is going to happen to you."

"Something terrible already has," he said, feelings coiled and harder to decipher.

The cat curled into the curve of his elbow, leaving slices in his sleeve.

Chapter Eight
REMINDERS OF OTHERS

OLIVIA IMMEDIATELY picked up my holocall—her perfect image sitting primly on the edge of my table with her arms crossed.

"Never hang up on me again," she said.

"Right. Sorry, Liv." I dragged a hand through my hair. It felt like days had passed. Maybe years upon which to put white in my hair. "I painted. Then there was another Awakening."

She looked me over. Some of her embattled expression softened. "Yes. You relinquished control and let Dare's group take it, even if it was a bit rocky. I'm proud. Greyskull said the three made it back and checked out of Medical with permission. How are you?"

"I'm fine. Really." Lies. "They are going to be caught, though. Constantine is going to get caught. You have to convince him to return."

"We are all going to get caught," Olivia said, bluntly. "And if you think anyone holds sway over Leandred but you, they need to check you for fever. What we do before we are caught is what counts."

I shut my eyes hard. "Not helping."

"You called the wrong person," she said mercilessly. "If you want pleasantries and enabling, you should have called Nephthys or William."

"I, yeah. Axer tagged the hunters. Any hits?"

"Of course, nearly twenty. The boys are tracking them now and logging everything. They're looking for patterns and oddities."

"That's good." I ran my fingers along my brow. A step closer. "Axer does it far more efficiently than I do."

"Of course, he does. He was born and raised for this," Olivia said, crisply.

And the Department wanted him. Desperately. They'd do much to obtain him. And knowing he was out there for the taking? How long would it last? How long until the others were caught and tried for treason? Axer, for one, would never be incarcerated in a normal prison.

I tried to cap such thoughts from drowning me. "How's campus?"

Olivia gave a decisive nod. "Fine."

The good thing about my exile was that the Department had to leave Excelsine mostly alone, now that I was no longer a registered student. They had worked too hard at pinning campus events on me to keep pinning anything to campus once I was gone.

Their internal media machine churned on ad nauseum about all the sympathizers I had there, but thankfully it wasn't yet illegal to like someone, so my friends were safe for the time being, as long as they stayed on campus. On the other hand, the Department was aggressively inferring that Marsgrove was complicit in my actions and therefore should be ousted.

Fortunately, Excelsine was under the purview of greater Europa, a collective government that was resistant to Department intervention, and Marsgrove had years of grabbing everyone by the balls.

"Fine, but on edge," she clarified. "The vast majority of students support you, but there is a vocal minority who are doing exactly what you think they are doing. But Phillip gave us...some leeway in skirting the justice magic, even though it cost him. Patrick is having a terrific time."

That gave me a smile. "What about you?"

"I don't know what you mean." Her expression didn't change, but her eyes held a sadistic glow. "Inessa Norrissing is in Medical due to an unknown ailment. I'm studying. Finals are the week after next."

Melancholy tugged at me. It seemed like only yesterday we were studying for winter exams.

"Marsgrove is keeping you safe?"

"Phillip is being a tyrant."

I nodded in relief. That meant Olivia had tried to leave campus and been unable. It was the downside in being a ward of the school—or a muse of the school. Open campus or not, it made it nearly impossible to leave without permission. Such rules were a decided upside for me, though. Unlike Constantine, the slippery fish, Olivia and Neph couldn't just walk off to join me on suicidal ventures.

"How is Leandred?" Olivia asked.

"Angry, but physically fine. You just saw him." Treating campus like the revolving door it was to no one else but him. Campus was open again—students could leave—but no one connected to me had taken the chance yet. Marsgrove had harshly stressed they shouldn't. The Department had eyes on all of them.

Constantine never followed any rules but his own, though. And his father held power Marsgrove did not.

Constantine was also very, very slippery.

She tilted her head. "On campus, he keeps mostly to himself still. Professor Stevens and Dare are the only ones who have continuous contact."

Both powder kegs in different ways, both with unresolved issues.

She continued. "Leandred comes to strategy meetings, but only speaks if one of our plans is going to interfere with his own. And those plans, he never shares, so it is left to me to piece together what insanity he is brewing from the ideas that he strikes down. He has given each of us a number of things, though," she said grudgingly. "Materials, properties, aides, enchantments. William sometimes goes over there to consult. Before he left, I saw Leandred trap a mage in the Midlands who tried to hex William—though William remains as oblivious as always."

"Has Will been targeted?" I asked sharply.

"No more than anyone else, and there are...plenty of people who step in when his head is deep in a book or device. The combat mages, Greene especially, and all the Bandits are fond of him. And people continuously underestimate Michael when it comes to protecting his roommate. Then there's Nephthys to contend with. A muse on rampage thwarts many plans."

The rest weren't a surprise, but—"The combat mages are helping?"

"Including Dare, when he's around, which is even less than Leandred. All for the better, really, since when we have a strategy meeting together..." She grimaced. "They rarely speak aloud to each other, but, it's obvious they are communicating, and well, there's no lack of tension."

I couldn't contain a mirrored expression. "They've lived together for, what, two years, almost three? They work well together—seamlessly—when their goal is common."

They'd be fine. If, in a few weeks, Axer really did leave campus to spirit us away, the boys would be...fine. Everyone would be fine.

I'd be arguing about not going to Itlantes, Constantine would be making evil, veiled threats at Axer, and Axer would probably handcuff us both and do whatever he planned.

Olivia shook her head. "I don't know what happened before you left... But it's like the two of them vehemently agree on one thing, but not something else, and that makes for...tension. A manifested type we can all feel."

I rubbed my chest. "They have issues, and I have a feeling Dare is going to join us sooner rather than later."

Something in the way he had looked at us made me certain of it.

"Good luck."

"That's not funny."

"It's not meant to be. Alexander Dare is as scary, ruthless, and untrustworthy as Leandred, but in far different ways. Lox has been fielding more and more responsibilities on campus, stepping in as the leader. Dare has plans for something. I trust those plans not. But at least Nephthys isn't giving Alexander Dare magic like she always gives Leandred." Olivia looked resigned to the latter.

"You trust Constantine."

"I trust his motives. There's a difference. So, where is he?"

"In one of the rooms off the atrium that we constructed with vortexes, golems, and whatever else he slips to the Ophidians on the side. I sent him to check in with his father and manipulate his golem publicly. I had to make a sealed vow that I was calling you and staying here, though."

If there was an emergency, Constantine could release me from it, otherwise I was stuck during the duration of the vow. It was the only way I could get him to check the golem and keep himself safe.

Why had I ever, ever, let him talk me into creating a golem for him?

I pulled fingers along my forehead.

Because he had asked.

Loneliness.

Terrible life choices.

"Good." Olivia's smile was tight.

"No, not good. Stavros knows he's the one with me," I said. "It's only a matter of time before undeniable proof outs him to the world. Rumors are growing. Wild ones."

"No one ever says it too loudly, but there have long been whispers about Leandred's abilities. Both Leandreds. True Mind Magic is rare, and Constantine was privately tutored until Excelsine, but rumors circulated about his abilities even before."

I frowned. "Yeah, I've seen the ability speculation reports. They are trying to stick the label on him to more easily arrest him and diminish his father's popularity."

"Yes, well, there's no way those ability reports are false," she said bluntly.

I sighed. I knew more than most of what Constantine was capable. "Well, being in the spotlight doesn't help him stay under the radar."

Olivia's expression sharpened. "That he is one of your companions has been a matter of public record since Bloody Tuesday. Leandred was unmasked in Corpus Sun, and the three of us emerged from the Midlands together. Stavros can't do anything other than trail conspiracy theories, though. Not unless something drastic occurs, like Leandred showcasing magic that only he can create. We established precedence during the rescue for all three of us—four, including Dare—that Stavros will implicate all of us in his lies to gain control of you. That the Department attempted to trap you falsely."

"Stavros's traps are getting harder to evade."

And his smiles... Those smiles haunted me—like a man who knew he was going to win. A man who enjoyed playing the cat and mouse game, testing out pawns just to watch them flounder while he baited the trap. I sent her an album of memories: his smugness, his bravado, his traps, his displeasure.

After she examined the images with her detailed mind, she looked up at me, frowning. "You painted and were overflowing with magic. He would have sensed that, so he activated an Awakening, hoping you would make a mistake."

"And I'm going to." I pulled a hand over my mouth. "I feel invincible in the moment, but when I have a chance to think..." The rage was far more concerning, because it was always there, waiting. "I know every new move is a preface to something worse. And I'm playing against someone who anticipates my moves and mistakes."

Olivia leaned forward. "Whatever his magic, this is part of his gift. He rose to power by successfully manipulating those around him until they revolved solely around his gravitational field. His words are as damaging as the magic he possesses. That is the danger of Enton Stavros. That is the danger in dancing to his tune."

I could hear what she wasn't saying, of how her mother manipulated people in the same way, of how she too had once bloodied her feet trying to please Helen Price.

I moved restlessly. "How do I not dance?"

"Everyone dances." Olivia stared at the wall, then looked back at me. "Figure out a way to change the tune. Create a new song." Feelings of love, companionship, and desperation wound through me, and even the holographic interface couldn't dim their projected strength.

I thought of Liam's beautiful music. "The new mages have wonderful gifts. I can't let them be extinguished."

Can't allow them to be left broken and emptied in the concrete casket of an abandoned lot.

"You won't. That is why others are aiding in their rescues."

"I...want to be the one to save them," I said, admitting it for a second time, with just as much difficulty.

"Of course, you do," she said in the brisk way she said all things she found fact, but her holographic fingers gently touched my hair. "And you are. For you are identifying each and sending a team to keep them safe. Focus on that."

"The Awakenings are my fault, in a different way than the media reports claim, but true all the same."

"Any who say so are idiots."

"They aren't wrong."

A pause. "No," she said. "But the fault is not an active one and they should not place the responsibility on you."

I smiled crookedly. "It's ironic how things don't seem to work that way."

"Pay no attention to fools." She sniffed, making me smile for real. "You may not have called your enablers, but you did call your strategist and the most intelligent of our mad bunch. I believe in you."

My throat suddenly felt clogged. "I miss you."

I wish you were here, but I'm so happy you are not.

Olivia looked older suddenly, and sad. "I miss you, too. Come home soon."

"I want to. I want to come home."

"I know," she whispered.

Ori flew in melancholy dips around the room, as if feeling the emotion. Guard Rock's pencil was resting across his knees, rock tilted toward where Guard Friend would be.

We sat there, holographically clutching each other, and I was angry suddenly, so angry that I was here. That I had been forced into this exile, away from that which I held dear.

She clutched at me with sure, shaking hands in the optically counterfeit enclosure of space.

"Don't go out anymore, even if you are needed," she said into my hair.

"I can't not go."

Her grip tightened. "I know."

~*~

There were nine more Awakenings in half as many days. We were far more prepared for them, though, and for Stavros's tricks. With Constantine's help—and a small leech—I used his magic to overlay mine, and I quickly figured out how to decipher the coordinates without even leaving the turret for the last six Awakenings.

All nine new mages were spirited to safety by the combat mages. Even Camille Straught had given me a sharp holographic nod at the smoothly run procedure we were developing.

My guilt over not going on the rescues quickly gave way to the comfort of victory.

None of it assuaged the public's concern over the increasing numbers, though.

A Department press conference had been scheduled to publicly address the increased "trouble" in the layers.

I turned on the news feeds, engaging an enchantment I had learned from Bellacia that allowed me to access ten different feeds and source them for similarities and differences. It was an efficient way to glean facts from opinions and note information that needed further investigation. Front and center was the majority feed highlighting all the points that the ten primary sources agreed on, even if they were couched in political leanings one way or the other—the spell stripped them down to the basics. t Floating off to the sides were the editorialized pieces, ranging from vastly amusing to downright infuriating.

Gradually the printed text and photos faded and a live feed featuring footage of Excelsine rolled in the background.

"With the increased number of mages aiding the Origin Mage at the Awakenings, abettors and sympathizers have been identified within the Excelsine community, and have been added to the Watch List, to which Dean Phillip Marsgrove, former Red Arm of Central Intelligence, reacted with vehemence."

Marsgrove, in all his pinstriped glory stood in front of one of the flags on Top Circle. "To label fifteen students as terrorist sympathizers simply because they were classmates is both negligent and criminal. The Department is using any means necessary to achieve their directive of placing Ren Crown under their control. Take heed, the next one on their list might be you."

The background image then switched to a panel of reporters waiting for the Department press conference to commence.

The news anchor continued, "The statements were met with split reactions among the public at large, and are very much aligned along political lines. Greater Europa, a bastion of progressive ideals—or a fetid pool of anarchy, depending on one's perspective—has sided against the Department's edicts, as usual. But they only carry the support of thirty percent of the other countries, territories, principalities, and domains in the Second Layer. Support is wavering among the middle thirty percent that identifies as intermediaries, especially in light of these most recent attacks and the real concerns that an Origin Mage can upset the balance of our layers and world."

"We will interrupt our broadcast when officials begin the press conference. In other troubling news, the Library Bank has confirmed that four more of its deadliest tomes have been stol—"

The feeds abruptly ended with a sweep of Constantine's hand. "Stop listening to the trash, darling."

"It begins," I murmured, touching the device in my pocket without letting my thoughts dwell upon what it was.

"Or it ends." He twirled his ribbon.

"You need to check your golem again."

"Later," he said blandly.

Other than the half hour I'd talked to Olivia days before, he hadn't left me alone. And he hadn't gone to check on his spells unless I accompanied him—like he was afraid I'd take the moment to run.

"I need to finish this." I pointed at the half-crafted rune in my journal.

"I'll wait."

"You are stretching it on the spells."

I cleared my mind of the device and let only feelings of exasperation remain. He'd been sticking to me like magic glue. I couldn't even have nightmares without him waking up first. "I've been downright boring in the last few days. I'm not going anywhere."

"Same."

I sighed and pricked my finger, rubbing it on a seal near the door. "I swear to remain in this room for the next hour, or until you return, whichever comes first—unless you release me from this promise—I so do vow."

He tapped his fingers together, watching me through narrowed eyes, but the vow was solid. He was hooked into the wards enough to know it. He unfolded from his chair and I felt the brief touch of his thoughts. I reiterated the promise, thinking of the drawings that I needed to do.

He slipped through the door.

I watched the compound's wards and waited for him to descend the stairs, enter the atrium, and call up his first spell, before I activated the device in my pocket that only one person knew I possessed.

The pressroom bloomed around me in full hologram.

Shelle Fanning, the public relations speaker for the Department, was still the PR head, but a hawkish woman named Morven Jance had replaced her on the podium. Shelle Fanning was the softer side of the Department. Morven Jance was the predator, the aggressor stamping out all dissidence.

In the holographic viewing room, Jance watched the reporters' feeds and holos with a combative gaze, daring them to speak against her. "There was container evidence at the scene. The evidence suggests the Crown girl is taking their magic."

A reporter looked visibly disturbed by this—his image flickering—but said, "But why? She has plenty of magic at her disposal already."

I walked my mental projection slowly around the hologram figures, taking in the live images as the magic allowed. It was like being a specter in a manse. I could see and observe, and walk between, but not affect the interactions—all while never leaving the safety of my tower.

"Who knows how a broken mind works. We all know that Origin Mages can't be trusted to know their own minds. It's common knowledge. Fact. The facts cannot be dismissed. The girl is a danger to everyone around her. She must be brought in safely, so we can keep our layer, our lives, intact."

"With all due respect, Secretary Jance, we haven't verified that—"

"Are you saying that you want this layer destabilized? That you think terrorist actions, which hers surely are, are justified?"

"No, of course—"

"We need to return our world to the stable one it was before she Awakened. Terrorist activity rose with her Awakening. It's become a world problem. When will this stop?"

The reporter changed tactics. "Terrorist activity has steadily been on the rise for years. Yes, it rose with her Awakening, but it was already ris—"

"It rose with her. This is an absolute fact that you just agreed with. Next question."

Another journalist jumped in. "If she is unstoppable, how can you stop her?"

"She's a girl. Young. She has powers that are dangerous if left in her hands, but, ultimately, that won't be a problem. She won't stand up to the might of the Department. No one does."

"So, is she powerful or weak? You do understand your message is confusing, and one might say that you are using political tactics that—"

"Get her now—contain her—we all win. Let her continue her destruction, all will suffer. I hear every day from people who are scared. Mages who want the suffering to end. Everyone agrees. Next question."

Jance was relentless and unwavering in her condemnation of me, mowing over all who began to express an opposing viewpoint.

"Not good, dear roommate," a new voice lilted.

I looked to the side. Bellacia's specter was standing next to me. Media spells were interesting when connected to frequencies. She and I had set up a weekly chat—with me using the frequency feigner in my pocket that identified me as Burt Watson, Second

Layer Inspector. We had met twice in these holographic press conferences where privacy spells allowed anyone to be a fly on the wall.

"I wasn't sure you would be participating," I said. "I am here for the...pain of it, I guess."

"Daddy has me on other, more devious assignments. I need to separate myself from the appearance of misjudgment. But I plan to be in the thick of it soon, when I see the way the wind blows."

My fingers tightened into fists. The direction was decidedly not in my favor. "I thought you'd want to be the one blowing the wind."

"There's a time and place. Timing is so delicate. And right now, war is brewing, Ren," she said.

"I'm not the one brewing it."

"No. But you are the one in the thick of it, and that's a powerful and dangerous place to be. What will you do?"

I looked at the crowd. Stavros and his press secretaries had many of the media personnel already under their thumbs. But they didn't have all of them.

"I don't know," I whispered. I was out of my element in this way, spinning webs and manipulating events. "What can I do?"

She looked at me, cat eyes slitting. "There were others with you at today's event."

I didn't respond.

She hummed. "If your magic registers in the First Layer, Prestige Stavros has received permission and been given emergency powers for the praetorians to be there as well. There is no reason for him to end those powers, and every reason for him to extend them." She walked around me, scenting prey. "They are blaming you for the event. But it's fascinating that I noticed a blip in Alexander Dare's presence on campus just prior to the event. I didn't report it, of course, and most people don't have my observational skills, but do be more careful. Though they are so very careful, combat mages have a certain...style they can't hide."

I closed my eyes in resignation.

"Quite a burden, my observation, because it would make a strong story—the defection of powerful mages who were pledged to the safety of our layer. But with Camille caught in the crosshairs... And, you. You are such a thorn sometimes, dear one. With the scent of the strongest story dangling from your precious fingers. The other must be relegated to a piece for the right time."

"And you'll choose the right time."

She shrugged delicately. "You need me to choose. Deceit is not your skill."

Pictures of all the feral Awakened mages in the past six months flashed on screen—the ones I had rescued, and the ones I'd had no chance to save. "I just want to help."

She tapped her curved lip. "I know your intentions. The problem is that only those who have been touched by you do."

I looked at the hologram of Stavros giving a refined, fatherly speech about protection and action. Protection and action against me, the world's ultimate villain.

"But if we bring her under our protection, think of the good she could do. She needs guidance and a firm hand controlling her magic," he said paternally. He was a master of grandstanding and self-promotion.

Bellacia watched his speech, switching her sharp gaze back to me. "You possess the ultimate story. You are where the lines lead. What headline will carve your epitaph?"

I watched Stavros's talented dance. I had no answer that didn't end with the world.

Chapter Nine

WHEN IT ALL BREAKS

DARKNESS, death, destruction.

I sat straight up in bed, pushing the covers to the side. My breath heaved in my chest, and I flailed for purchase as I unconsciously tried to call socks to me.

My socks hit me in the face as the world ending magic between the layers drew inward like a sieve, spilling its dream sand onto a single point. Adrenaline fought against the grogginess of four hours' sleep. I called my cloak with a flick of my wrist. It smacked against the wall and disappeared into the bed crack.

"Another Awakening?" Constantine looked up from where he was fiddling with a drawing, legs crossed at the ankle on top of the desk. "That's the seventeenth. Rather boring, this same tune."

His shirt was open and rumpled, his hair looked like his fingers had passed through it one too many times, and he was barefoot. If I posted this image of him, I'd be rich in a week. I frowned as I shoved my hand between the bed and the wall, grasping the priceless garment with sleep-numb fingers.

I sent the coordinates to Axer. First Layer Botswana was about to have a wild ride.

I looked up into the early rays of light pouring through the windows above, unhampered by anything in flight. Ori had been disappearing for longer periods of time. Guard Rock was gone, too. He'd been leaving more often, the more I'd been allowing others to do my duties.

I looked at Constantine. "Have you been up the entire time? No sleep?"

The first few Awakenings had been riddled with traps. But the last few had been surprisingly free of them. The simplicity of the rescues had increased everyone's tension.

Constantine hadn't been immune.

"Don't cast stones in a gravity field, darling."

I pulled a hand over my body, concentrating on the battle tested clothes I wanted to change into and subsequently on where I wanted my nightclothes to go. A moment later, one arm of my t-shirt flopped from the drawer it was supposed to be neatly tucked into.

"Go back to sleep," Constantine said, eyeing my clumsy result. "Alexander and his minions will handle this one just as they've handled the other ten. The Awakenings are getting positively boring for them."

"I know, and that's what worries me." I tugged at the awkwardly hung trench cloak encasing my shoulders, and moved quickly to secure the spells I'd need. "I just like to be prepared."

Dressing for battle had been a useless task since the combat mages had taken over. But...being prepared just made me feel better.

I was especially jittery tonight.

"I'm fine," I said.

"As fine as you always are," he said, one brow lifting at how shoddily I had dressed myself.

"What's that supposed to mean?" I tugged my boots on quickly and manually. There were some misplaced dressing spells that weren't worth the pain, especially during battle

He surveyed me, sighed deeply, then waved a hand over his own frame. His own version of a battle cloak settled perfectly upon his shoulders in response.

"You can dress yourself better than I can." I pulled my last boot all the way up. "Congratulations. I can make it so that you're glued to that chair for the next two days."

"And deny the world two such glorious buttcheeks? Besides, you give obvious tells in your connections. I know what you are going to do—"

I shot a stunning bolt before he finished, and he grabbed it from the air, coiling the magic in his palm. He looked at it, smiled, and turned the magic into a blue iris, which he then pressed into his skin. "—before you do it. Thank you, darling." He stroked his connection threads in his mercurial way—in a combination of contentment and irritation.

I grabbed the last device I needed, slinging the band around my frame, and stepped into the hall.

Constantine closed the door behind us, and followed me toward the room I used as a port. "Come, darling, do we really—"

My heart stopped beating for one second, two, three, and waves of panic swept through me. My knees buckled, and I pressed a hand against the wall to keep myself upright. Constantine was next to me instantly with a hand tucked beneath my arm.

"What is it?" he demanded, all playfulness and antipathy gone.

"Another. Another Awakening." My brain focused on the energy swirling around the layer system schematic in my brain to pinpoint the location. "It just started in Honolu—"

Pain. This time, only Constantine's grip held me upright. "Ren," he growled.

"Samoa. Madrid. Niger." I looked up at him, clutching his arms as he held me up. "Too many." Horror and overwhelming guilt brought me low.

He read my face. "There's never been more than one First Layer Awakening in a two-hour period. You can't get to them all," he said grimly. "Send the five coordinates. Alexander's unit can split to two sites. I can bribe three of the Ophidians to take a third. Dagfinn, O'Leary, and Price can alert Marsg—"

"There are twelve," I whispered, new information overlaying each previous piece in milliseconds of upending, changing data.

He breathed in sharply. "Twelve?"

"All over the globe. The magic...the wards on the layer are stretching. Too much is happening beneath them. I don't know if they will hold." I sent the entire packet of data to everyone connected to the location device, including the fact that I was going to the second one, since the combat mages were already on their way to the first.

I pushed aside the panic I could feel from everyone, and concentrated on Constantine who was contemplating the consequences of knocking me out and tucking me away.

"Strategically spaced?" He narrowed his eyes and I felt ghostly fingers align to pinch my consciousness. I wrapped my hand around his wrist in soft warning and charged defense.

"A trap. I know," I said. "But I'm going anyway. Twelve feral mages, Con."

"One Origin Mage, Ren."

I whistled, and the book flew through a black-and-white patterned hole in space a moment later with Guard Rock dangling from its lower corners. Guard Rock dropped onto my shoulder. The book looked on edge, but it opened its pages, awaiting instruction.

"You don't need the book to travel." Constantine's mental fingers released me with difficulty, like an arthritic grip letting go, then hesitating on the edge.

"No." I swallowed. "But if it's a trap, the book can help." I tucked Guard Rock into my hood.

"So can I." Constantine slipped his arm beneath mine.

We blinked and a moment later we were standing on a beach in Honolulu. Swirls of wing-shaped magic swept upward on a sweet plumeria breeze. A girl with aviator sunglasses perched on her crown and an airplane logo embroidered on the breast pocket of her shirt, reached toward the sky.

The tip of her finger was extended as far upward as she could manage, and I could see magic swirling down to her, as if the cosmos was stretching toward her in response.

Behind her, wicked delight painted the face of the hunter who was lifting the device that would incapacitate and drain her magic.

I wasted no time concealing my presence. I shielded the Awakening mage with a pull of magic and shoved her into the Second Layer at the same time I blasted the hunter into the ocean.

Magic rippled outward in a hungry wave.

"Ren—"

"No time." I looked at Ori, grabbed Constantine, plotted the coordinates in my mind, and skimmed the layer to Botswana.

Fallon Lox, Mars Ramirez, and Camille Straught looked up sharply as we appeared.

They were surrounding a young girl overflowing with warmth and fire. Her magic reminded me, achingly, of Sari Tarkovar, the girl I had saved on Bloody Tuesday, who made everyone around her feel warm and secure.

I darted my gaze between the attacking units—even the Department mages were being influenced by the new feral. Even they were throwing kinder magic—nets and capture spells designed to incapacitate rather than kill.

There were more Department mages here than at any other Awakening.

I reached out a hand and curled my magic around the glowing fire and warmth of the girl, ready to push her through space—overwhelming magic jumping to my command, as if starving from the absence of its use in the past few days.

Constantine grabbed me, twisting the magic and cutting it off.

The layer rippled out again, causing everyone to wobble on their feet.

The three combat mages didn't wait, they used the distraction to open a vortex that looked surprisingly like one of Constantine's, and, grabbing the girl, the four of them jumped inside.

I considered pushing Constantine in with them, but the layer was wobbling again, and I grabbed the fabric of it, smoothing it and sucking the two dozen hunters into the holes as I knit it all back up.

Constantine was suddenly in front of me.

"Ren." Constantine cradled my cheeks in his palms. "You have to calm down. The First Layer—"

But too many communications were streaming through at once—everyone jammed over one comm like the world was screaming together.

"Everyone in the Department who handles First Layer concerns and hunts has been mobilized to respond to the Awak—"

"Samoa and Jakarta have been secured by allies—"

"The Asunción mage was taken by hunters—"

My fist curled at the loss, and I blocked the rest of the broadcasts. Seven to go.

I grabbed Constantine's arm and ported us to Xi'an.

Axer was already there, by himself, protecting a boy with purple-stained fingers and the blank, internal mixture of joy and terror that Awakenings produced.

"Get her out of the layer," Axer demanded furiously, whipping a tail of magic that cost him half a container. One hunter collapsed, another hissed as a slice of crimson nearly cleaved him in two, and a third barely made a headfirst dive behind a car.

Constantine's fingers slipped from my wrist as he threw an exploding marble at a hunter aiming at us. The hunter was knocked off his feet, but another lobbed his own magical grenade in our direction. Axer lifted the dirt around it as it landed and threw the wad of earth and explosive back at the man.

Spike. The long chain of Awakenings squeezed like a set of stomach contractions. I clutched my stomach, feeling like it was rupturing.

"Something's wrong with one of the Awakenings," I gasped. "Worse than the others."

I grabbed Guard Rock from my hood and threw him at Constantine's back. "Help them."

"Ren." Constantine pivoted sharply as Guard Rock latched onto his cloak. His hand reached for me, and I saw Axer's magic fly my way.

In one fluid move I shoved my bag into Constantine's hand, deflected Axer's magic, and opened space, concentrating on the point that called, and folded myself inside.

I could feel the end of Constantine's shout. But I couldn't think about the fury and terror I could feel from him. This Awakening felt worse than all the others. Like something terrible had already happened.

I appeared in a hallway in Santiago, and the timbers of the sidewalls splintered.

There was nothing there, though. Strange. In each of the previous Awakenings I had ported next to the mage. What had I done wrong this time? I concentrated and pulled the location to me again.

Little zips of magic pulled into view, traveling along the blue and silver damask of the wallpaper, and connecting to a bedroom a few steps away. I carefully opened the door.

The Awakening mage was slumped over, cradling a tawny haired boy against her chest. Magic was zipping around her—a tempest of electricity.

The boy wasn't breathing.

A zip of magic traveled slowly past my face as time stopped and I stared at the scene for an eternity. I moved forward, and the zip snagged onto the timestream, disappearing in a blur. I touched the girl.

Her head jerked up, and translated Spanish spilled from her lips. "I killed him! I killed him! I don't know what—"

I pushed a packet of knowledge straight into her brain. The magic looped back through her system and shot from her skin into the boy's. He heaved forward, taking a deep, hacking breath. Her arms shot around him, and the magic flew more wildly.

I stared at them as they gripped each other. Siblings. A strange feeling worked its way up my throat.

Shadows emerged from the edges of the room, coiling inward and upward from the baseboards and floor like smoke. No. Choking sorrow turned to rage. I tore open the first shadow, and destroyed the second. The third smiled, opening its arms.

I flung the portal pad out and whipped it around the girl and her brother, then sealed the edge around me.

We landed in the same Second Layer Death Valley location I'd chosen previously. Magic, like anything else, diverted to the familiar by default.

Almost immediately, shadows rose from every direction.

I reached for the sibling pair. We'd go to the Third Layer, where the rocks joined the—

My hand hovered motionlessly in the air at the sight of them.

The boy was seizing, staring blankly at nothing while the girl shook him like she could stop his second death. Powerful magic swirled wildly around her. "Carlos, Carlos!"

I had made a dreadful mistake.

The boy was from the First Layer and he wasn't a mage. He didn't have the magic to mentally navigate a world drenched in it. Not without dedicated exposure.

I shot a bolt at the first diving shadow, then at the second. But this was the praetorians' playground, and they smiled manically as they shot into the sky, then dove again.

The boy couldn't survive the Second Layer, so he wouldn't be able to survive the Third—

The girl turned to me, desperate and angry. "Help m—"

I enveloped us again, dropping us into the busy emergency ward of a hospital in NYC.

I grabbed the girl before she could react and forcefully pulled her away. Immediately, the hospital staff started running to the boy spasming on the floor. An earthquake rumbled beneath our feet.

The girl strained toward her brother. "Let me go, let me g—"

"They'll take you both, if I do. I'll send someone to help your brother," I said, already slamming Marsgrove with the request.

I folded us back to where I'd left Axer and Constantine in mainland China. They weren't there. A quick check said they were still in the First Layer, together, but now just to the southeast, in Taiwan. Greene and Ramirez were in Africa again.

"That's good," I said out loud, blankly staring at the charred ground of the battle. "There are five—" I felt the light of one extinguish. "Four more, now," I said numbly.

A little whine in the back of her throat was the only warning I had before the girl started sobbing. Heaving, world-ending sobs.

"Mine was like that, too," I said, voice detached. I didn't bother asking her name, I just drew on Constantine's magic and plucked it from her mind. "Rosaria. Huh. Rosaria and Carlos, R and C. Me too."

"What?" she asked brokenly. "What are you—?"

"That's a good question," Julian Dare said, appearing out of nowhere.

I stopped his net before it landed on me.

"I think not," I said coldly.

"You are not in your right mind," he bit out, eyes icy and calculating. "And the world suffers."

I could see every atom of the world swirl around him, opening the universe's secrets to my view. "I am fully in my mind."

I could pinpoint every single atom that I could use to bring him down if he tried to stop me.

"You need to be neutralized until we can use you."

"You can try."

He smiled and magic shot from him in a crystal-clear wave.

"Julian!" Marsgrove yelled, appearing out of nowhere and knocking aside whatever Julian Dare was attempting to do to me.

Magic shot sideways, and the skies cracked open.

"Get out of my way, Phillip."

I didn't wait to hear the argument as another of the Awakenings dimmed. My hand wrapped around Rosaria's palm and I pulled the more overwhelming Awakening magic from her, fixed the sky, and folded us through space.

The feral in Niger was safe—Greene and Ramirez had triumphed—but the feral in Madrid was gone, confirming the dropped link in the chain. A body-shaped burn mark was the only thing left in a crater of white rock when I arrived.

No allies were at the tenth Awakening in Weber, New Zealand...but the Department wasn't winning.

There was something a little...touched...in the Awakening boy's eyes. Like he hadn't lived in the real world for a long time and had no feeling for anyone who did.

The boy reached out for one of the hunters who came to close. The man's hand dropped, eyes going glassy.

"You are looking for a powerful leader to follow," the boy said.

He reached over and touched me, and I could feel a connection trying to form—a silver blue line—stretching from the hunter to the boy to me, and through me to Rosaria.

I pushed gently at the connection to the man, pushing it away before it fully formed.

The boy—the name Samuel Bly whispered in the loosened connection—cocked his head. The hunter's eyes were still unfocused, the thread shimmering in the air between them.

"That isn't the way I work," I said softly. "We choose our connections."

Samuel cocked his head to the other side. "He wants to make this connection. He just doesn't know it."

I shook my head. "No, thank you."

"It will benefit you both. I can feel it in the way that you both feel. It will benefit the four of us."

I looked at the powerful magic surrounding the boy. Muse magic manifested in a slightly different way, but there was a similarity to his. "I have a friend who can help you harness and control your magic and these feeli—"

Before I could complete the sentence, swirling figures moved into view. With a rush of adrenaline, I threw a shield around Samuel and shoved him into the Second Layer. Talking was for later.

Everything shuddered around me.

The Bogotá mage, the eleventh Awakening, had vanished. Taken between one breath and the next, another Department triumph.

In Taipei, I found Constantine and Axer.

Axer had twisted a protection field around the twelfth Awakening mage, who was staring at her hands, just like every feral seemed compelled to do. He adhered a device to her back and activated it. The petite girl disappeared to the pre-programmed destination. I didn't know to where.

He took out two hunters, while Constantine incapacitated a third.

The book soared overhead, protecting them, like I knew it would. Guard Rock was actively darting between them, stabbing and twirling. Constantine's cat and Axer's paper guardians were pouncing and swooping.

With the girl gone, both Axer and Constantine seemed to relax a fraction, but they argued vehemently as they blasted magic at the dozen remaining hunters, and, occasionally, at each other.

"We need to find her," Constantine said.

"What a stunning deduction," Axer said sarcastically, shattering one man's leg and breaking the neck of another.

I cocked my head and looked down at my chest and the silver blue coating of magic there.

I could hear the two of them arguing, even though their lips weren't moving, and I had no frequency in place anymore.

"You let her leave," Axer said. He viciously slashed a man's midsection without a shred of expression showing the mental battle he was fighting with the man at his side.

"Right. Because I have so much control over her. Like a chidog leashing a feldragon." Constantine was moving and ducking smoothly through the fight, dropping anyone his hand touched.

"You don't, but you can't seem to accept it."

Constantine sent a blast of magic at Axer at the same time that he threw a bolt at someone sneaking in from the right. Axer caught the blast with an unamused look and threw it into the chest of a hunter trying to rise.

I looked up as the world swirled and the dawn sky darkened to unnatural night once more—far too quickly a day cycle. I gripped the hand held tightly in mine and knelt down to touch the ground.

"The mechanisms that can hold her are in the hands of people we don't want using them. We should be searching out those devices."

"To control her. To limit her." Axer snapped, hitting him back and neutralizing two others that were circling Constantine.

"To stop her from constant magical suicide."

"You can't stop her," Axer said grimly.

A dozen freshly cloaked men ran down the street. With a forward motion of my right hand on the pavement, I sent a wave rolling down the street, throwing the reinforcements to the ground.

Both boys swung toward me.

"Er, hi?" I gave a small, useless wave with my non-dominant hand, at the same moment I realized why I hadn't used my left. Rosaria was staring blankly, crouched beside me, as if everything in her world had been turned on its head. Her hand held a death grip on mine.

I found mine wasn't any less clutching. I couldn't make myself let hers go.

Constantine immediately headed our way, absolute fury smoldering under a blank expression.

"My brother died when my hands sparked," Rosaria whispered, oblivious to the undercurrents, looking at the destruction around us. "Is this what magic does?"

I gave her hand a squeeze. "No. He's going to be fine. It's not all...death."

Axer swung his hand and emptied an entire container of acidic magic into a man's face.

Chapter Ten

CRACKED PIECES OF ICE

I CRINGED. "Mostly."

Rosaria's face filled with horror as she watched Axer wipe through the remaining soldiers as if he had been warming up before, and now was finishing a workout. There was a reason he was feared. A reason people always said with hesitancy, "But he's on the good side."

It reminded me a little of watching him decimate a hundred opponents in Freespar on Will's tablet that first peek into the magic world.

But I had also seen him rehabilitate and heal the most fearsome animals and opponents he fought, and restore the landscape, always making certain it contained magic.

I pulled magic into my palm and thought of Christian. I tugged at the light connection already formed between Rosaria and me and touched her feelings for her brother—the mixture of love, frustration, and the devotion that they shared—and pulled it into the magic I was creating through the layer and grid.

A butterfly clutching a rose unfurled in my hand and I placed it in her free one.

Guard Rock climbed to my shoulder and flipped into my hood, watching her from his favorite spot.

"It's what you make of it," I whispered.

She stared in wonder as a lush garden bloomed around us with alyssum, asters, and liatris, and dandelion seeds lifted into the air like fluffy stars. Her gaze met mine and she gave a stuttered nod.

"I am so angry with you right now, darling, that there isn't a synonym violent enough to describe my fury," Constantine said mildly as Axer finished off the remaining hunters.

I cringed. But the wonder on Rosaria's face and the feeling of my power was too much for regret.

"I needed to save them," I said. I touched the ground as the layer cracked another small bit at the overwhelmed points. Far too much magic was exerting itself on a layer bound to non-magic.

The shaking world steadied and stilled, but the extra magic used around the layer that was pulling into my body was filling me almost uncomfortably. It was a heady, curious sensation.

"You are the one you need to be saving."

I had no time to unpack the pieces of that, though, as praetorians suddenly surrounded us. And with them was Kaine.

Power surged through me. I opened the layers with my mind, clasped both of Rosaria's hands in mine with a whisper of "It will be okay," and shoved her to the same place that held Samuel with his connections and the girl reaching toward the stars.

Freed, I held one hand out toward Constantine to return him to the Third, and the other to Axer to send him to the spot where I had sent the ferals. But both were already in motion—Axer sidestepping and Constantine slipping around me before I could connect to either of them.

The praetorians swarmed, and like the shifting tile magic in the Midlands, I used the magic I had already channeled to flip the entire section of First Layer city pavement we were standing on into the Second Layer.

The fifty-foot patch of Taiwanese street shone starkly in the massive Saharan desert.

The praetorians rose, shrieking, and their shadows grew long and uneven along the dunes.

The first shadow hit the salt circle Axer threw and was sucked into the sand.

Kaine smiled and dove toward him.

"No," I gritted out, and threw a paper from my cloak. I layered a shimmer of nasty enchantments over it as it whirled—the same wards that kept the portal pad safe from Kaine.

Another praetorian flew into its path.

The sacrificial praetorian screamed as the paper touched him, and his shadow cloak sizzled, leaving behind a normal mage, broken and twitching on the hot sand.

Axer thrust a sword through Kaine, then twisted his body just as a shadow pierced the air where his back had been, skimming the edges of his cloak in slowed motion. But Kaine's shadowed fist pierced Axer's other shoulder as he turned.

I took out the praetorian trying to clasp a metal gauntlet around my wrist, but the action left me unable to help Constantine as a praetorian ripped away his protective shield. Constantine hissed in pain and tried to block the shadow as it pierced the diminished magic of the cloak and reached for his face.

I whipped toward him, but it seemed that I was moving in slow motion as well. No, no.

Magic blew through me like a thing of smoke and fury, and a stream of glowing, ultramarine paint ejected from Constantine's forehead onto the shadow. The shadow hissed and sizzled, flailed and staggered, then seeped into the dirt like the Wicked Witch after being doused in water.

My brain scrambled for a moment, but there wasn't time to think. Four praetorians swooped toward Axer as Kaine thrust another shadow spike toward his chest. I used the magic gushing through me to pull the paint from the fibers of the anti-Kaine paper and cast them out in a splatter of Pollock-like flare.

Kaine evaded it, but the other shadows dropped, twitching to the sand, their human forms convulsing as their shadows coiled and attempted to seep inside their hosts again. Another four took their comrades place, and four more swept behind.

"There are more, Origin Mage. There will always be more. You can't defeat the shadows even in the sun."

"We'll see."

"Excellent," a horrible voice said from the man on my right, features dripping to form another set. "Cast out the weak, Origin Mage. Thin our forces to only those that deserve to be my guards."

"Sacrificing people is your gambit." I shot viridian paint at Stavros's host. The body dropped but Stavros's face appeared on another.

"Our gambit soon, I think."

Kaine and Axer moved at uncommon speed. Their fight was almost too fast to process. Three shadows were swooping around them, waiting for their chance to attack. Constantine was trying to help, while not moving from my side. But even I wasn't certain how to help without taking both out.

"I have to thank you, Miss Crown, for your lovely hand delivery of three ferals. The first, trussed and waiting for us with stars in her eyes."

Chilled water rushed from the top of my head down my spine to settle ice cold in my stomach. "No."

"And the boy with such a special skill set—one that we might not have secured without your help according to the eyes I had on scene. He will make a formidable ally, if I twist those skills and decide to let him live. And the girl who killed her brother. Power there. And so much emotion. Delicious, it will be to digest."

Constantine's hand wrapped around my elbow, alarm striking through him like a lightning bolt, as he channeled our entire community. I pushed away the group magic like I was swatting a fly, focused only on Stavros's parasite.

A media report resounded through the air.

"The Department has rescued six of the twelve Awakening mages. The Department secured three of them at the site where the Origin Mage illegally and irresponsibly pushed them, likely planning to consume their magic later. The damage toll—"

I pinched the report dead with a shake of the layer. "No."

I had assured Rosaria it would be okay.

Stavros smiled. "You have a particular affinity for returning to the same places over and over. Do you seek solace? Comfort? Home? Weakness. Makes tracking you disgustingly simple. But you think yourself powerful enough not to worry. And what do a few ferals matter?" He shrugged. "Not at all. A winning mindset. I must say I'm pleased."

Unwittingly, I had shoved them right into the Department's net. The hunters had probably stood there waiting for the next to appear before trussing, tagging, and taking—or disposing—of them. Like they had with Christian.

The image of the siblings clutching each other blighted my view.

"We'll get the girl's brother, too. She might survive a few days' more in her present circumstances, and watching us work over her brother—well, mental torture is the best kind."

Blackness swirled inside me.

"No." Darkness, rage, certainty.

Stavros smiled. "Oh yes."

I thrust Constantine through the air and into Axer's chest with enough magical force to send them both skidding fifty feet away from Kaine.

"Ren, don't—"

Then sent the ground beneath them whirling through flipped space—taking Axer and Constantine far away. The book dove between the layers as the layer broke and shifted around me. Beneath my feet, the sand shifted and trembled. Fifteen shadows dove at me simultaneously, and I pulled.

The Second Layer Sahara was nothing like the Fourth Layer Sahara—overflowing with nightmarish creatures living under the sand and creeping through its individual particulates to invade new hosts—but it held a few nightmares that the non-magical desert did not.

And no longer was I limited to dealing with a single layer. Not anymore.

I smiled grimly and flipped a section of the Fourth Layer into the Second—like a Midlands tile that was being reordered.

A giant lizard with wings erupted from the tiled dune, roaring and diving toward a praetorian, then another hit the empty sand near Kaine, who swirled into the shadows of a cactus as the lizard gave chase.

"Is that it, Origin Mage?" Stavros appeared on the face of another praetorian. "Is that all you have?"

"You will die," I said. "I will not let you live."

I pulled at the layer again, making it wave along its axis, pulling the bright spots the wyrm dragons called home in the Fourth Layer toward our position. I couldn't call the animals to me directly, but I could influence their environment—the magic upon which they relied, and the paths upon which they traveled.

Wyrms gravitated toward the hottest sunspots in their wretched desert sands to coil and nest. A few showed up occasionally in the Midlands and Axer had long ago taught me about them. Run from the hottest points in the sand, as those are always nest markers.

I pulled the heat signature. Home is here.

The wyrms immediately followed the magic.

And as soon as they were within range, I obliterated the bright spots, turning their feeling of home into feelings of rage. Someone had taken their nests, and I had pointed them straight at us.

They burst through the sand in a flurry of terrifying teeth and horrible shrieking sounds. Razor-blade scales ripped through the concrete as one grabbed a praetorian, then another was caught in the teeth of another.

Stavros face flipped from one screaming guard to another, and with each one, I remade the layer—leading the wyrms on a rage-filled quest to devour the intruders.

The rage ran through me as I took out each one.

A decrepit, delighted sound emerged from his throat. "Do you think I inserted my soul? Only the naïve think that giving their soul will return something lost to them," he said with a pointed, cruel smile.

No, not death. I'd unmake him.

Tiles from landscapes in each layer of the world lifted and flipped in a blizzard of destruction—trees ripping from one, water and sea creatures splashing from another, desert vistas churned, skyscrapers broke, memorial buildings collapsed inward, four-headed beasts, creatures, beings, and plant life swirled, all with living mountain zephyrs fueling the surge.

Strands of hair swirled around me in lashes of brown and red as power cascaded everywhere in electrified bolts.

The regular praetorians fell before Kaine, whose magic fed all of them, and one by one they were sucked into the tornado of tiled change as I pulled sections from each layer to destroy Stavros and his puppets of death.

Kaine, in shadow form, flew between the bits and pieces of debris—flying against the world-ending current—strangely riding the currents. And when each remaining praetorian flew by, he opened his shadow-encased maw and swallowed the shadows coursing with my magic.

Energy rippled through him, making him grow, not in size, but in presence with each consumption.

It was horrific enough to pierce my veil of rage.

A stone statue struck him, cracking an arm, and Kaine fought to right himself, smile growing, as he landed unsteadily. "Soon, I will have enough of your magic to make me an Elite. We will have real fun then."

Stavros flickered across his features. "Rafi was always such an astute pupil."

"You don't get to call him that," I said tightly, opening my palm. A remnant feather of the hummingbird tattoo Greyskull had given me fluttered fiercely across my skin.

Stavros smiled. "I can call him whatever I want. He's mine. As you will be. Friendless, overpowered, and alone."

"Like you?" I flipped our positions, disgorging myself into the layer space behind Kaine, and plunged the tattoo like a knife into his back.

He shrieked, and shadows spewed from his mouth. Rage and pleasure filled me.

The separating shadows dove toward me.

I grabbed the tile before me, spinning it downward to trade with the first point that came to mind—because what difference did familiarity make now?

It made a lot of difference, I discovered a half second later when Axer and Constantine reappeared on the flip side of the tile. I stared at them in horror and channeled magic a second too late to flip them back. The two were already diving for me.

"No, no, no!" I said, trying to twist and bend, to whoosh them away—stirring the blizzard into a tornado.

Bursting with malevolence and power, Kaine converged on them from behind. And I could see the moment where Axer was forced to choose—from hiding his magic signature to giving up the ghost. He rotated in the air and shot Kaine into the tornado as Constantine tackled me to the ground.

"Ah, Alexander Dare. With a logged signature. Lovely, lovely to see you here, my boy," Stavros said, grotesque features alight with pleasure, his decomposing face whirling through the tornadic destruction attached to Kaine's breaking shadows. "Aiding the Origin Mage in destroying the world. Probably with the goal to take her to your island for a bit of experimenting. What a Bridge Mage could do with an Origin Mage..." His voice was filled with pleasure. "I'll know soon. Just as I know the powers of all Awakened mages."

Rage. White and blistering. "You killed my brother."

"An unfortunate occurrence in one way, and yet at the same time—look at you. Do you think you would have achieved this type of power if you hadn't stolen it from your dead twin?"

Nausea rose swiftly, and paint bubbled up from my throat and over my lips.

"Oh, poor thing," he said with perfectly executed, false empathy. "Archelon got the whole sad story from dear Rafi when they merged. Do you prefer to think that your brother gave you his magic? His magic remade you."

"He's lying," Constantine yelled harshly in my ear.

Stavros smiled. "Am I? I Awakened your brother. And I killed him." He leaned forward. "You're welcome."

The world turned black.

Symbols flashed across my vision. I grabbed for one and broke it. Paint—every drop of it that had been gathering inside of me—burst forth, coating the world. Stavros would die.

Two sets of familiar hands banded around my wrists. Magic flowed through Constantine and Axer to me—magic from our entire community—but there was something broken in it—as if the circuit was almost complete, but not quite, and that meant their magic and manipulations couldn't stand up to mine.

"No, Ren. Revert it," Axer commanded, his normal ready state overtaken by urgency. His cloak started to sizzle as paint ate through it.

"I will end him," I spit, yanking at the hands and magic holding me.

Stavros smiled. "Commencing the first part of the operation."

Axer threw back his head, throwing off his hood, and his ultramarine gaze, uncloaked completely by the loss of the magic protecting his identity, bored into mine. "And with it the world. The world is breaking, Ren."

He pressed a paint streaked palm against my forehead and I could feel the agony beneath his skin. He had a dozen shadow-filled stab wounds and necrotizing magic was eating away beneath.

"Look."

I looked around me, and it was as if I were seeing the devastation through new eyes. The sign of a First Layer home flipped by me—257 Maple Avenue. We had a Maple Avenue around the corner from my high school.

A tiny mote of horror seeped around the edges of my rage.

But my horror was not enough to assuage the deep blinding hatred that had been building in me for months and those emotions separated—breaking out and away. My fury was a living, livid thing in the tornado of hell exploding around us. My magic wanted Stavros to die. Even if it meant that everything else followed.

I didn't know how to calm such fury. I had accepted the death of my brother. Accepted that he would no longer be with me in this life. But his murderers...

The ones that were murdering ferals? They had to pay.

"You will kill us all," Axer said calmly, eyes the same hue as they'd been the night my brother died. He pushed the images of all my friends across a connection that he was pulling from Constantine—a connection that had never been stronger. Alexander was weaving the connections into a thick rope instead of a multitude of separate threads. "Rage has a price."

I sobbed.

"You have to decide."

"Weakness," Stavros spit. "Your friends will be the first thing I rid you of."

Constantine looked at me calmly, resignedly, like he had long anticipated this and was ready for this death. The edges of the tornado sucked in closer, licking at his skin, pulling at it, ready to deconstruct.

The sob caught in my throat.

I didn't know how to stop what I had started. But there was something that did—something that was removed from my emotions.

As soon as I pulled, Ori came streaming through the whirlwind—papered wingtips catching the edges of all the tiles. It looked down at me, then looped backward and dove sharply through the funnel, pulling the entire storm down with it, open pages flaring skyward as its spine angled toward me, sucking magic from me in a violent pull.

Reverse.

It drew each tile, animal, and piece of the world that I had mismanaged against one of its page tips, mixing it with a splatter of paint, before casting it like a whirling frisbee through slits in the layers that opened like scattershot holes blown through a target.

Crelobsters plunged into blood red oceans glimpsed through a resealed tear.

Wyrms dove into the boiling sunsands to rejoin their offspring.

Banyontees replanted themselves in starlit glens.

The Great Pyramid reconstructed itself.

The Conservatory of Ten sealed shut.

A possum backflipped neatly onto a branch.

The book pulled harder in the sucking whirlwind of a storm, pulling on my magic—my very being.

Flipping each tile back into place, resetting each section, each animal, each magic, reading me and reversing the way that I had pulled it.

"No!" Stavros shouted as the book returned everything to its rightful place.

Except for me. For I had no place to go.

And I was... God, I was dangerous. Too dangerous.

I readied myself to release the boys. To do whatever I needed at the end. Guard Rock dove down the back of my cloak, embedding himself in the spells woven too closely around me, and I brokenly regretted that he was too close to send to safety.

"Flip the tile, Ren," Axer commanded. Their papers and protections pulled into their cloaks.

I couldn't. I had to end this. To be here until the last pull of the book signified the end. "Let go," I whispered.

"No." Constantine threw a cat's cradle at Kaine's reaching hand and his shadows shrieked as the strings ignited around his shadowed fingers, tying them together.

I couldn't flip the boys without taking myself, too. There were too many ties between the three of us for me to separate us this close.

I could feel the pull grow tighter—the book was almost done. I could see Kaine again, wearing Stavros' enraged face as he watched the book undo all my terrible work. He looked at me and held up Kaine's shadowed hand.

"Let go!" I tried to shake them loose, but my magic was under the book's control, fixing the world.

Brilliant ultramarine, turquoise and copper connections bored into my heart. "Flip. Us," Axer demanded.

Black magic jetted toward us as Ori sucked in the entirety of the tornado's whirlwind. Parchment burst around us as I pulled both boys and the imperial leather spine into my arms, and forced us through the earth.

Chapter Eleven

COMMENCING in 3...2...1...

W E LANDED in a knotted mass in the atrium of the Western Territories' compound with a crack of at least one broken rib a piece.

Five layers of the earth shuddered, then stilled.

An object cracked the stone floor next to me. Five pieces of burnt paper fluttered down next to it. Ori lay dormant on the ground, pages splayed in the least regal way I had ever seen from it.

Its pages were blank.

"No, no, no."

Tears falling, rage irreparably broken, I fought halfway free of the boys and pulled the book toward me.

I pressed the healing magic I had stashed in the wards over the past few weeks against the book. But the abundance pooled on top.

Empty. The book didn't stir.

Healing magic flowed from my hands, and pulsed everywhere around me. Patterns and paint and possibilities appeared, but my mind was blank and broken on how to use it to fix this. I pressed my hands against the book, dragging my fingers down its pages, trying to inject the fibers. But the magic simply spilled over the edge like water poured over wax.

"Not that I don't enjoy your body pressed against mine, darling, but I'm going to require a stomach transplant as well, if your kneecap continues carving it from my body."

I disentangled myself completely, wheezing as I completed the cracking of another rib in the process. But as soon as I was free, I turned shaking fingers overflowing with magic against Constantine's fibula and the fracture I could feel there, as well as Axer's broken ankle. The magic reached into the air like a mushroom cloud, spilling down to fix their ailments.

Axer gently cut off my flow of magic to him before the magic touched the multitude of stab wounds he possessed.

No, of course. Why was I trying to...? It was dangerous healing Kaine's strikes, as one risked sealing the shadows inside.

My thoughts jumbled, and I turned the entire flow to Constantine, who was a mass of bruises and internal ruptures. His eyes were shut tight, and he was mentally walled, as if he was thinking unpleasant thoughts.

He cut off the healing magic from me with far more force, making me stutter on the cold floor as the magic abruptly curled into the air, sparking, with nowhere else to go.

I couldn't be trusted. Magic whispered from every corner about all the ways I could use it.

I clutched the book. Untrustworthy.

Axer was unsteadily pressing a cloth against each stab wound. Each time he pulled the cloth away, another shadow pulled free, snapping to the cloth where they wriggled in a half-Velcroed fashion.

Infected because of me.

"Does that get rid of the shadow entirely?" It hurt to speak, but it hurt more to think about the infection eating him away from the inside. I held the empty book against my midsection, magic pooling uselessly around it and me, like a cape of curling smoke.

This was why it was better to fight alone.

"Yes." He winced, as a shadow the length of a sword popped free. "Worth the time we spent developing it spring term." The words weren't just addressed to me.

I looked at Constantine "You and Axer?" I wheezed.

Constantine jabbed two fingers against my sternum. "Fix your ailments. So help me, I'm going to murder you." Magic sucked from the cloud surrounding me to the point of contact, then through my sternum out to my ribs.

My ribs knit back together, and I took a gasping breath. I felt him grab something in my brain—a point that controlled healing—and set the rest of the channeled magic free in a whirl that swirled out all the way to my hair, fingers, and toes, fixing everything wrong in my body according to some health map that existed in my subconscious mind.

"Trying to fix everyone else while you sit half dead," he said darkly. "Trying to save everyone but yourself." Lips tight, he fished out a bottle of elixir and drained it. He shuddered as it did whatever it was supposed to.

Trying to save everyone? I had nearly ended the world.

I sat with empty hands clasped around an empty book, restored to empty, full health.

Axer stuffed the shadow-writhing cloth into a Level 10 jar and sealed it, then let both the jar and his head fall against the floor as he painfully healed the rest of the injuries, closing each in turn, fingers pulling magic from the compound through the channels he had clearly identified as mine.

A cat meowed, and I could feel Guard Rock digging around under my fitted cloak, trying to inch his way out. Safe. The book would have been happy that Guard Rock was safe.

I looked at its blank pages, wiping my eyes against my shoulders.

"Breaking News" appeared on hundreds of holos lining the walls.

"Today, the Origin Mage tried to destroy the world," a reporter announced.

With Ori cradled in my arms, I stared numbly at the wall. I stared at the millions of atoms of magic that made up every piece and component of the compound's wall.

"With little regard for life or order—"

Numb anger pulsed, filling the emptiness in a rush, and I stared at the magic around the reporter which telegraphed a location in the Second Layer. Tweak the ochre line two degrees left, push the apricot square into a hypercube, flip the ginger spiral, array it all to black-and-white...and I could make a sand wyrm appear next to her.

I could make her eat those words.

The book fell from my arms and I dove to where Axer was rising to his feet. I grabbed his cloak.

His arms wrapped protectively around me as we crashed to the ground.

I thrust my hand into pocket after pocket of his form fitting cloak, frantically searching for what I needed. He stilled my motions—clasping both of my wrists in one of his hands. He stared at me for a long moment, then slowly withdrew a heavy cuff from an interior pocket. I squirmed free of his hold, grabbed the cuff, and snapped it painfully around my wrist. Magic immediately dampened, taking everything with it.

My forehead hit his shoulder, and I stared blankly at a singed patch of his coat while the world dulled.

"You can't wear it for long," he murmured.

"We'll see." My shoulders shook as I blindly pulled the empty book back to me.

"Stupid girl." Constantine's fingers splayed over my spine and magic from a dozen familiar, precious sources started to flood me—a different type of healing. There was a lot of emptiness to fill. His cheek dropped to my crown as the magic started winding through me faster, physically bouncing back to me from each of them. The heavy cuff gave me no power to push it away.

Which was a relief, because I didn't deserve it, but I wanted the comfort.

I gripped a torn piece of paper in one hand, cradling the book against my chest as the three of us huddled in the hall listening to reporters along the walls argue and speak over each other trying to deliver the news.

"At first, the apocalyptic event just affected the First Layer with the Origin Mage using Awakened ferals as the lodestones to break the seals on the wards holding the magic in place—or the magic out of place, as it were. Then when the Department shored up the seals, she began breaking pieces of all the layers." A dozen recorded events rotated around his hand with each delivered point. "Even the Third Layer, home to terrorists and dissidents, expressed shock and dismay, as they, too, were targeted."

The First Layer problems hadn't been caused by me—not at first. But I had enveloped it into my revenge—I had enveloped everything into my rage.

The broken red threads to my first home fluttered untethered in the air between my knees.

Check on them, the threads whispered.

I closed my eyes, refusing to act on the desire to seek out my parents—suppressing the feeling with long practice. The wards on their house had been one of the first things I had checked after my expulsion from campus, doing so from far afar, on a deliberate route elsewhere, in case I was followed. My gaze had swept across everything for twenty miles, so that a sweep across their house wouldn't register as anything pertinent. The wards were intact. I had to trust in them. In my own work, in Olivia, in Raphael and Marsgrove.

I had seen enough movies. I knew that the moment I went there with fear driving me, they would be found. Staying away was the best protection I could give.

I pressed my chin against the top edge of the book's cover and turned my head just enough to focus on one of the reports.

"Two hundred governments have condemned the Origin Mage's actions, with thirty already declaring war against her, after her magic was shown coating every affected site. The Origin Mage has extensive knowledge of wards and protection enchantments. She is dangerous, and should not be approached. She is being aided by Third Layer terrorists in the Western Territories. All information should go through the Department terrorist-alert frequency. Any information you have should be given immediately, no matter how small. Any tie that can be made could save—"

Another newsfeed on the wall showed a panel of people involved in a vehement argument. I recognized one of Bellacia's reporters arguing against another.

"The Origin Mage destabilized the entirety of the First Layer," the other man said. "Every non-magical felt it, and the suppression spell hasn't entirely been able to erase it. Diplomats are working feverishly to blame it on changing environmental factors."

"She stabilized it again though, John," Bellacia's man said.

"Maybe. There is a lot of cause to doubt that. And, frankly, who cares if she restabilized it. She destabilized it! That she can do it at any time verifies that Prestige Stavros was absolutely right when he declared last month that this would happen—and he announced minutes ago that this will happen again."

"Prestige Stavros wants Priority Five invoked. It's no secret. And Priority Five is dangerous."

"Dangerous? Our way of life—our very lives are under attack! And you are worried about losing a few freedoms? It's being reported by the Department that all but one of the feral mages were killed in the Awakenings. And outside reports are that the praetorian guard was wiped clean by the Origin Mage. That only Praetorian Kaine survives. The guardians of the Prestige wiped clean."

"But Origin Mages don't kill people—"

"Excuse me? Does your small mind not recall Flavel Valeris and the millions destroyed? Or countless dark ages across layerkind? This is an executed attack. She knows she must take out the Department—our last line of defense—to ruin us, and this is her first step. The longer we go without bringing the Origin Mage in or putting her down, the closer we are to total annihilation."

"Is there anything we can do?" another reporter asked.

"You can vote on Priority Five."

A murmur of discontent cascaded through the newsrooms aligned along the feeds on the walls.

The first man held up his hand. "No one wants Priority Five. But want and need are two separate things. What needs to be done to save our world?"

"What's Priority Five?" I asked Constantine and Axer woodenly.

"The Department's ability to hook into any magical signature in the layer and lock it down," Axer said, voice dark as he finished healing himself and used tender muscles to bring himself further upright without dislodging me.

"What, like they can find any person and freeze them in place?"

"Then they take you, process you, put you away. Or they let you go, of course, if you are innocent," Constantine drawled from my crown, and I could feel his dark emotions swirling through all of my other friends' in the cocktail he was feeding me. "Nothing to fear for people who are innocent, as they say. Without considering that the people driving the policy might not be."

The options for misuse of such power in the hands of someone with ill intentions...

I looked at my hands shaking around the book's spine, and the heavy cuff circling my wrist. What were my intentions?

"Stavros tried to get it passed twenty years ago using Alexander's mother as fear bait, but Stavros was careful to always separate himself from the action. If you watch the memories, he always sounds regretful. Highly regulated, no misuse," Constantine mimicked, and I wished I could see his face. "Another politician took the political hit when the public reacted negatively."

"So, they already have the system?" I asked, voice as hollow and strange as my emotions.

"Yes. However, a few politicians made it so that the regulation of the 'button' to instigate the system is under a mile of red tape. Only an emergency action pledge on the part of two thirds of the voting countries will unseal the policy vow—which was magically bound. There is nothing Stavros can do without those votes. Priority Five is as useful as a dream to him without the unsealed vow."

"Constantine's father is one of the premiere votes in the block." Axer touched my knee, then my hand, sliding down to my fingertips. "Give me the book, Ren."

I hugged it closer. "No."

"Ren."

"It's dead. I killed it."

Constantine's fingers tightened on my back, and he abruptly spun me a half turn so they were both in view.

"No," he said, pointing his freed finger at me.

"I wanted revenge," I said. Constantine's gaze tightened.

This wasn't like Rosaria's Awakening magic accidentally killing her brother. I had whipped the world into a frenzy on purpose.

"My revenge did this. I did this. The book died cleaning up my mess. I would have ended the world to kill Stavros. I don't want this power," I whispered, staring at the cuff.

Axer's hand darted out, and I looked up to see him clasp it around Constantine's wrist abruptly. Axer's gaze was steady on me, without looking at his roommate, whom he held immobile.

"And yet you chose the world over your revenge, when it was pointed out to you, a mage of seven months. You figured out how to fix it."

"At the expense of—"

"Maybe the book is dead. Maybe not," Axer said calmly.

My heart skipped a beat. "What do you mean?"

"Magical books aren't the same as magical creatures, beings, and mages. The enchantments imbue them with life—real life. But if their pages and knowledge are left intact, they can enter dormant states. Bringing them back is something best left to a bookspeller or spellbook."

I let the book fall open, pages still blank. Whatever was needed of my magic, I'd—

Constantine bared his teeth. "Absolutely n—"

Axer's hand tightened on his wrist and Constantine made a strangled sound, then shook himself free, lips tight and gaze firmly on the wall.

Axer held out a storage paper I'd made for him, gaze never leaving mine. "Books that magical don't have a ten-minute limit. One day or fifty doesn't matter. And we have far larger problems to circumvent first. Like the matter of your freedom."

"But—"

"Put it inside," Constantine barked angrily.

I put the book in the paper and Axer folded it and carefully tucked it into my fitted cloak pocket.

"It will be okay," Axer murmured.

"Will it?" I asked numbly.

Constantine's eyes slid closed, then snapped open to focus narrowly on the crowd of people who had gathered down the hall.

"Come on," Constantine said, lifting me to my feet, dark gaze ahead.

We started moving through the gathered crowd and I tried not to flinch at the fear and awe that pulsed from both sides of the hallway and every open door.

I had earned those looks this time.

I looked at the boys, who were getting their own fair share of looks. I could stop those, though. I was toast, and I would take responsibility for my actions, but the boys could return to normal life away from my dangerous company. I just had to disentangle them from me.

There were ways. I flexed my fingers and looked at the cuff. If I was careful and thought through the magic... For the good of—

An emergency alert pealed across the newsfeeds.

"Breaking news coming in from the Department Pressroom. And this one is a doozy, folks.

Two mages have been identified as complicit in the Origin Mage's actions today—Alexander Dare and Constantine Leandred. Proof of involvement is being transmitted to all news outlets."

My legs gave out beneath me, and only Constantine's grip kept me upright, as the media showed pictures of both their faces.

"Alexander Dare just won the All Layer Combat Competition for the second year straight, and is classified in the most extreme threat level that the Department maintains."

A montage of Axer obliterating opponents played beneath.

"Awakened in the one percent of stirring mages at age ten, he has been watched and tested consistently for the Bridge abilities of his mother. The Dare family was unavailable for comment and their island home of Itlantes is under port lockdown from ingress and egress per Prestige Stavros' instructions. Under no circumstances should Second Layer citizens approach the Dare scion."

The way to contact the Department was again displayed with a place to automatically connect to the frequency.

I'd lost him his home? Nausea overtook me, making me lurch.

"Constantine Leandred is the prodigious only child of Senator Stuart Leandred. He Awakened at age ten as well, and was the winner of the Science and Magic Olympiad at age fifteen—the only year he entered. He has twenty patents to his name. One of the most troubling is a maelstrom synthetic, that if unchecked, could destroy everything in a four-mile radius of its unleashing without damaging the mage holding it. Adding to the troubling reports, sources at Excelsine University say that the Leandred scion is vicious, reactionary, and unprincipled. Senator Leandred has been quick to deny all claims against his son, but recent investigations by the Department have shown that Senator Leandred—"

"No, no." I looked around wildly for anything that could help—numbness setting into my limbs and making my actions heavy.

There was no surprise on either of their faces. Grim acceptance and a bit of dark pleasure showed on Constantine's. Axer was the blankest I'd ever seen him.

His hand wrapped around my cuff before my fingers made it to the metal latch.

"Let go," I said, struggling against his power which easily overwhelmed mine beneath the cuff's field. His far larger hand blocked the latch beneath his palm, and there was no way I could overpower him physically.

"No," Axer said, quickly taking my arm in his other hand and putting me into motion as he and Constantine shouldered me through the hall of blank, staring gazes.

Their homes, their freedom, Dare's family—the ties to which I could see pulse just as brightly as mine once had. This was why I hadn't wanted help. This was why I hadn't wanted anyone risking their neck for me.

"Disavow me," I said, trying to peel his fingers away. "Anything. I'll do anything."

People flattened themselves against the walls when the "shoulderings" started to be accompanied by electrical shocks.

"I know," Axer said. "Paradoxical thinking, given that you wanted to give up your abilities a moment ago."

"That's not... I'm poison," I said, struggling. Because it was true. I had automatically reached for the cuff to save them, I still was trying to peel Axer's fingers away. I would do anything for people I loved. And when that "anything" turned to actions that would impact the world, there was a big problem. "I'm poison."

"You are speaking to the wrong person if you think that makes you something to avoid," Constantine said, nearly lifted me off the floor to keep me moving—a sack of potatoes between them.

The news reports kept going.

"This is just the beginning. There is a dark history of what happens when Origin Mages are left to their own devices. When our entire existence is predicated on the goodwill and good judgment of a single person, we risk much, for what if that person falls to the dark?"

The live feed switched to a woman holding a baby. A man stepped up behind her and put his arm around her shoulders. The woman stroked the head of the baby, pulling him close against her chest and tucking her chin against the fine hairs at the top of his head. My god.

"Where will you be when your magic is taken? Will you be at home? Work? Will your children feel the choke of magic when you are unable to reassure them that everything is going to be okay? I'm here to tell you, it won't be okay—not unless we do something about this threat. Not soon, not when, <u>now</u>, before everything and everyone you know dies. Before she—"

Axer yanked the entire grid of magic from the wall with a curl of his free hand and everything went blank. He crumpled the magic in his fist and let it drop with a crackling thump. People screamed behind us, causing me to crane my neck back to see, as the ball of magic bucked and sparked like a firework with multiple fuses flopping around, deciding which way to shoot first. Panic erupted behind us.

"And I'm the one who gets called an asshole," Constantine mused, dark pleasure undercutting the words.

Axer's magic saturated everything in sight as we walked, testing and weighing strengths and weaknesses in the compound. The bravest residents continued to watch with inscrutable gazes darting between the three of us as we passed.

"Ten minutes, Origin Mage," called one of the elders at the end of the hall, bringing my attention forward. Judgment and darkness painted her face.

The other elder—the one who had lived in Aurum before it had been destroyed—stood next to her, and she looked at me in sadness as we passed.

Such commands had always preceded unpleasant meetings. I couldn't imagine what kind of town hall I was facing now. If there'd been a target on the complex before, there was a huge bullseye in the deepest crimson painted on it now.

Their home.

I looked at Axer's thick family threads, which were blazing hot, like they were being tested in fire.

"Your family," I said to him, reaching out with magic, then curling it inward, shaking.

His fingers tightened momentarily on my arm. "I accepted this event long before today."

I felt like I might lose whatever lunch I had eaten the day before. "Your family—"

"Knows exactly why I am doing this." His gaze never left mine and I could feel the heat of it straight to my toes. "And what is at stake."

He deliberately let go of the cuff.

Without looking away from his locked gaze, I touched the latch. I hesitated, then let my hands drop to my side.

He touched my neck, warmth gathering beneath his touch. "It's going to be okay."

Constantine opened the door to the turret and slipped inside.

Axer's quick, discerning gaze took in everything about my workspace even before he entered.

The way the slopes and angles were slightly askew—deliberate choices—making it look ramshackle when it was anything but.

"Mbozi would never let you get away with that corner angle," he said, deliberately light.

"Then he hasn't the vision I credit him with," Constantine said, tracking his roommate's progress with dark eyes, and unleashing a packing spell for his things—hundreds of items that had been steadily collecting across my work space.

Apparently, only Constantine could call my turret a hovel. And apparently, he was leaving.

I looked down, and swallowed. I should feel relieved that he was finally leaving. Yes. I was relieved. My stomach asserted that it was as hollow with relief as my magic and my mind.

Guard Rock inched out from my cloak, then hopped to the table. He looked at the pocket containing the storage paper, then into the empty air of the turret's ceiling—an open question in the actions. I swallowed heavily and shook my head, touching the pocket. The book was gone. And it was my fault.

Guard Rock's pencil drooped, then he straightened his rock, thumping his weapon down. Vengeance on our enemies.

I touched the top of his rock.

Behind him, Axer's gaze was firmly fixed between Kinsky's sketches and my world bending painting. He looked from them to me, fingers curling into his palm instead of touching either, eyes blazing with some sort of hunger.

"Why are you standing there?" Constantine demanded, making me jerk. His gaze was fixed on me as he piled everything movable by magic onto a flattened, open drawstring sack. "Pack. Alexander is taking you to his cursed home."

My brows pulled sharply downward. "What?"

"When things inevitably disintegrated, as was always going to happen," Constantine bit out, throwing himself onto a stool to reach items on the back of a worktable that couldn't be moved with a packing spell. "You would go to Itlantes to hide. We agreed."

Axer looked down at the paintings again, fingers drifting to his chest. "We can't go there," he said, voice even, but for a moment he couldn't hide the flash of pain and regret. "Not anymore."

"What?" Constantine exploded off the stool, packing spell exploding with him. The stool hit the stones. Papers littered the floor in fury.

"Itlantes has been locked," Axer said, and the sudden fiery red glow illuminating his family threads made me nauseous again.

"Yes, my ears work just fine," Constantine bit out. "But you expect me to believe that a government lock means you can't get in?" he demanded.

Axer looked at him dispassionately—a mask for something else. "I can get in. We can physically find our way there and under the wards, but the Department will know within the hour. And Pri—"

"I know what bloody Priority Five means."

Axer slapped his hands on the table between the paintings and Constantine's growing pile and viciously leaned forward. "They'll get the signatures immediately if she steps foot in Itlantes. Think."

"They are going to get them anyway," Constantine answered, just as savagely. "You can't tell me that your father doesn't have measures against it in your wards. I know he does."

"Of course, he does. But then we are stuck there. With Priority Five in place that means permanently—while the rest of the world burns."

"Let it burn."

Axer laughed without humor, straightening back up. "You never grow up."

"And you don't prioritize your friends."

Axer's nostrils flared, jaw tight, and gaze fierce. "No? Not all of my friends reside in this room. You are the one who has given yourself a single link in the world."

"The best choice I've made," Constantine said viciously. "You don't deserve her."

Axer's magic flared around him before he did something internally that visibly buried the anger.

Axer took a deep breath. "We aren't going to Itlantes," he said, voice even, but firm. "The governments have to go through emergency measures, and the Department has to get buy-in. We need the governments to calm down, not to obtain the long-awaited evidence that the Dares are finally taking over the world. Taking Ren there will consolidate the governments under Stavros. We need them separated and questioning."

"You will always protect your family over everything else," Constantine spat.

"You were once part of that family," Axer said tightly.

Energy angrily zinged between them.

"Go," I said. Magic slipped unheeded from beneath my heavy cuff and pushed toward them in command before I even realized I'd channeled it.

Constantine pivoted sharply, slicing his hand through the magic and shattering it. "Your asinine desire for that cuff... It won't stop you. Not even a null cuff will—it will just cause your eventual, utterly splattered death when your stoppered magic destroys everything in its attempt to escape."

I touched it. "I know. More reason to—"

"To what? Leave you?" He magically tore the thought from my mind, leaving a blank space that quickly filled with the same reflexive cogitation. "Before you embed it in your thick skull that you are better off without us, no one is going to believe we aren't with you or that you are without us now. There is nowhere to go."

I had nothing to say to that that didn't include a sob, so I pressed my lips together.

Constantine grabbed his head with both hands then wiped them outward, magic pulsing and flinging a wrench across the room so hard it stuck into the wall. "Stop! The only thing to feel guilty about is your stupid, self-sacrificing ways!"

There had to be a way to fix this—a fix without using magic—

A ribbon of magic lassoed around me, sealing my arms against my body as he towered over me suddenly. "If you go anywhere without us again, I will end you," he said furiously.

Overwhelming streams of input from those still at Excelsine abruptly lit the air around him—becoming visible as they crashed into him in crazy waves and made his gaze wilder.

Axer's spike of surprise at being included in Constantine's spontaneous statement was nothing next to whatever emotion made him narrow his eyes at the magic streaming wildly into his roommate. He reached out a hand, but Constantine jerked backward. The lasso around me abruptly released, as Constantine prioritized getting away from his roommate's concern over making his point.

Axer's hand fell limply to his side, and he took a deep breath. "Death threats aside, we need a few days. The Department knows we are here without a doubt—they will know, eventually, wherever we go in the magic worlds—but this is a secure facility. I can fortify it further." I could see his magic flaring out and touching different places in the wards, as if tagging what areas to strengthen first. "The First Layer is the only one that might truly hide us for a while—if Ren can stop herself from doing magic."

Axer tipped his head at me in question.

I looked at my trembling hands and the cuff that was even now causing me a dull ache. "No," I whispered.

He nodded, as if fully expecting the answer. "You are already part of these wards. They can sustain a few outbursts. We—"

The complex started to shake. Axer and Constantine instantly layered shields together five deep with me squashed in the middle.

But this wasn't an attack from without. It was from within.

I felt the magic in the complex start to shift. With regret and understanding I unlatched the cuff and connected myself to everything in the room—allowing my hungry magic to shift everything as a unit.

I had given the elders power over the complex. Given them the power of the wards I had put in place—even against me.

When they had said ten minutes, I thought that meant the time I had until they flayed me in a meeting. Naïveté.

I understood exactly their reasoning in this move. I closed my eyes and held onto the edges of my overwhelming magic.

Colors whirled, and I landed heavily on the ground, Guard Rock slamming against my stomach.

Axer and Constantine were immediately on their feet on the spiky grass, backs to each other and to me in 120-degree angles, magic ready.

The magic of the room formed an invisible dome around us in the bleak, unfriendly landscape of deep Outlaw Territory, but the dome would only last for half a minute.

Small additions of magic dotted various areas of the dome in small bubbles—apology gifts from two of the residents.

I closed my eyes and with the hand not holding the cuff, I fished a storage paper from an interior pocket and held it up. I hesitated for a moment, but there was no rage left within me, only sadness. Sweet bitterness curled, and I let calm descend over my hesitation. The dome's magic abruptly swirled and funneled into the paper, pulling the papered edges inward to form a small, tightly folded cube. The action dispersed the dome's hold on everything within, including the extra bubbles. Their contents fell to the ground with everything else.

The worktable shook, then broke, scattering the projects and items Constantine and I had been collecting. Unnatural lightning blasted in the distance, then steadily began rolling closer in a 360-degree circle around us.

I looked at the barren landscape and the drooping, unfriendly skies, then at the eager death shift tumbling toward us from all directions. Even Guard Rock looked resigned to fate.

"I'll kill every one of them," Constantine vowed.

Chapter Twelve

RUNNING

R UNNING

I PULLED EVERYTHING I could into the enchanted sack Delia, Constantine, and I had created on campus a week before my expulsion. The Third Layer death-shift thundered closer—only about three miles out now. I slung the bag around my shoulder and clutched the loose cuff with shaking fingers.

Swallowing, I nudged the layer, slowing the shift's roll.

Magic leaped toward me from all directions, painting the broken sky in twisted patterns.

In front of the shift, Third Layer vehicles of all sizes flew toward us from multiple directions, dodging the jaws of the total shift with long practice and focused intent.

"No one good is on those transports." I held the cuff, breath coming in small heaves. Panic was pulling my vision into spirals. I could see a new world at the end of the spiraled tunnel.

But it wasn't our world.

If I followed it...

"No one in this blasted layer can be defined by that word," Constantine spit. "We will be penned in one minute."

He looked at my cuff and his fingers twitched as if to take it from me, but then he reached out and clasped it around my skin, muting the feelings of power. "She can't do it. Pave this layer," he said viciously to his roommate.

Axer shrugged out of his damaged battle cloak, and flexed his arms. Offensive magic, without a lick of the defensive magic inherent to wearing the cloaks, flowed in spiral designs down the skin below his black t-shirt as he calculated the distance of each caravan.

In response, the vehicles immediately zoomed sideways, in less distinctive patterns.

Axer smiled. "That won't help you," he whispered to them, and the spirals increased speed along his skin—pulling into devastating patterns that I recognized. The death shift increased speed commensurately, as if anticipating such Pyrrhic victory.

"Weren't you the sane one of the three of us a moment ago?" I asked. Adrenaline suppressed unhelpful emotions while the cuff suppressed the overwhelming feelings of infinite possibility. I fished Will's portal pad from the collected mess in my bag. Safety first, guilt and despair after. I quickly nudged the passive spell component that expanded the pad's size parameters.

Axer cocked his head, gazing back at me from the corner of one eye, attuned to every change when in such a state. His magic immediately coiled back, spirals zipping up his arms, and he scooped up Guard Rock as the fitted cloak draped itself back around him.

"Sanity doesn't mean I can't revel in unavoidable provocation—just that I can recognize a better alternative when given one."

He released the collected magic with a snap and the death shift responded by aggressively eating a few vehicles whose drivers weren't quick enough to dodge.

"The drivers better have magical insurance or some really good protections," I said, sparing a quick glance around the horizon.

Constantine's face was carved from granite. "I will destroy every one of those Western Thirdies." Darkness and certainty rolled through Constantine's emotions like the shift through the bleakness in the distance.

Tuning the pad with quick movements, I said, "I think that's a pejorative term." Delia had never liked the term, that was for sure.

"I will pejorative their blood vessels. I will pejorative their children. You built that complex, you imbued it with your magic, you gave and gave, and they shoved—"

The pad opened to size. I grabbed Constantine—Axer's hand already wrapped around my arm—and stuffed all of us through.

The layer shift violently increased speed and rolled over as the portal pad suctioned closed.

Tus Onus was the programmed destination. Popping into an active troop encampment outside of it was not.

"—shoved you from the very place you conceived. That you—"

"There they are!"

I jolted as shouts and spells zinged toward us. Axer threw up a shield as the three of us fell to the ground simultaneously.

"—conceived. That you—"

I flared the used, narrowing pad outward like Constantine's ribbon, draping it over us. A tunnel of darkness and flashing light spit us—as well as a section of the ground that had been around us—into the bright desert, and into a legion of armed brigands.

Axer's shield was the only thing that saved us.

"—built. That you—"

Constantine didn't stop speaking, but he grabbed the edge of the shrinking pad and furiously tugged it around us again.

We emerged teetering on the edge of a waterfall streaming over a rocky gorge.

A water dragon broke from the surface, and a rider with skin the color of the sky was balanced on its back propelling a spear of white toward us.

Axer spun the three of us as the spear whispered past, then pushed us into the pad once more.

We flopped on the hard ground of a wooded glen in a recently devastated section of the Fourth Layer. Ley circles spread before us and golden light sparked as my finger touched one.

"—made invulnerable."

Two men in tattered robes emerged from the trees, eyes lighting manically. "The Origin Mage."

A spell pit broke beneath us, sending us falling.

"Even better—"

A trap set for someone or something else was still a trap we couldn't afford to be caught in. I forced the pad below us with a blast of magic.

Horns blared, an inhuman roar ripped through the air, and the men above swore. "They are coming! Hurry, grab her!"

We fell into the pad and instead of hitting the bottom of the pit, we were pitched out onto the hard pavement of the Third Layer city of Fawn that I had used more than once for transit.

Stavros was right—and not just about a pre-programmed pad—I defaulted to the same paths. It was a weakness and a habit I had to break.

I was unfamiliar with the two places the boys had chosen—both Fourth Layer spots—but suffice to say that we were either picking poorly or we were being tracked quickly.

"A bit of both, I think," Axer answered, as all the people visible on the sidewalks slowly and cautiously backed away from us, some touching the skin beneath their ears. "We have twenty seconds. See if you can give us forty on the next one."

"I'll give them forty years," Constantine said darkly. "Of flooding, of famine, of—"

I twisted the pad's parameters to a place I had never been, but one I had starred on a mental map as a possible place to transport ferals to in the future. I tugged Axer and Constantine inside as Third Layer terrorists appeared.

We emerged in the wasteland, outside a small, dead space in the Third Layer.

Easily manipulated with minimal magic and not subject to shifts in the same way, dead spaces were scattered around the Third Layer. Each was a tiny oasis in the treacherous landscape—the paths to them known to the outlaws who traveled the badlands. Frost Viper had made certain I knew them all by the end of my first week in the compound.

I pushed both boys into the dead space as the shift spurred by our arrival rolled over the landscape. In the Third Layer, shifts were a constant constraint.

"I will make them rue," Constantine said, barely stopping his continued diatribe for a breath.

As angry as he was at me for leaving him with Axer during the battle, then pushing him away from Stavros and Kaine, Constantine's fury was pinpointed elsewhere with true rage. "You brilliant, stupid, empathetic girl—giving them a way against you. I know ways around your designs. And they will rue this decision. Ungrateful, backstabbing ingrates."

Axer's gaze was analyzing and accounting for everything around us—the dead space, the apocalyptic shift now happening outside of it, and the contents of the supply bag. At some point during the madness, he had tucked a small device into his ear.

"I think the fact that three separate Third Layer terrorist leaders—including Vincent Godfrey's son—are heading toward the compound at high speed might have something to do with our expulsion," Axer said, tone mild, gaze anything but.

Vincent Godfrey had been killed trying to destroy campus on Bloody Tuesday. I shuddered to think of his son's aims.

"No reports yet on this location," Axer said, tweaking a buckled device on his cloak. "We have at least five minutes. Well done, Ren."

Five minutes? I picked at the cuff. We were already exhausted from the earlier events of the day. We couldn't sustain this madness.

Constantine's eyes grew darker. "With Ren's wards, that complex could have repelled whoever they sent. No, the elders had this planned—long before the news hit the frequencies about the mass Awakenings. I guarantee it," Constantine said darkly. "Insipid, panicked, backstabbing shivits."

Axer spared him a glance. "You give too much credit to their ability to ignore ties that were woven long before any of us was born."

I looked at my broken home ties—both sets of them. The people in the Western Territories compound weren't terrorists, no matter what the Department tried to spin, but the intertwining between factions across the Third Layer were rich, horrific, and complex. The many terrorist fronts had been demanding my release to them for weeks, but had been kept in check by the Territory elders and the long range plans we had collectively been spinning.

I was reminded of something the elder who had lived in Aurum had said to me:

"We are human, with all the fierce love and destructive hate that comes with it. While many clasp the hope—soft and gentle—that your magic could provide better lives for all in ten years' or twenty's time, others have a fiercer hope—the kind that rubs flesh with revenge, pride, and courage—now or never, a brasher and more desperate emotion."

With my new status as the highest enemy of all states, it would pit anyone who had me under their roof against all others.

I was dangerous.

Constantine stepped toward Axer. "You know, this looks nothing like your island paradise—the one with overwhelming excess magics that the governments are always trying to sanction—with its ruminating bench where you can pick apart the motivations of people far and remote in the safety of your physical and magical separation from the rest of reality."

There was a world of subtext strumming beneath every word—lies, liar, lying, hatred, loathing, pain. The two had been at detente for the last few months, revolving around a single common ally, but detente was different than forgiveness or friendship. Nothing had been solved between them—the giant morass of whatever was in their past still lay before them.

A giant pile of twigs, leaves, and tinder awaiting the dry season.

"After that lovely series of jumps, I don't need a bench to know that going to Itlantes would be an end game for all of us right now." Axer was slowly rotating, gaze taking in every point in the distance. His shoulders were tight. For as little as he cared for nameless faces in a crowd, he was never unaffected by his roommate. "How many more hops can we make in that thing?" he asked me.

"Will's design makes it unlimited as long as the recycling unit is engaged." It was a joint project he and I had done with Loudon, Kita, Patrick, and Asafa. "But that doesn't help us with the tracking issue."

The Department could easily track the magic in the Second Layer, as could anyone in the other layers with a device designed for tracking travel magic.

Axer split his focused attention between his roommate's continuing rage—Constantine was now doing something with a cube he'd pulled from his pocket—my gathering of the pad, the broadcasts he was listening to on the small device in his ear, and the landscape at large. "It's a marvel of between layer travel, but it's not made for stealth."

"Not yet," I conceded. "I don't think I can do better than this spot."

Not if anyone in the Third Layer figured out a pattern—and patterns, unfortunately, came instinctively to me.

"We can't sustain ten-minute jumps for long, even if we could achieve them," Axer murmured, head cocked, listening to something. "And though I have little sympathy for the people hunting us, unless we really do want to pave it—and possibly ruin the other layers at the same time—we can't repeatedly churn the Third Layer. It will destabilize before we complete ten more jumps."

I could probably do something about the destabilization—and probably kill us all in the fourth attempt with how controlled I was now—but jumping around with ten minutes' lead and having to stabilize every time would make us sweeper snacks within a day. I looked up, expecting to see one of the vulture-like animals circling.

"Our arrival here was just noted." Axer's expression turned grim. "As of this moment, you are listed as kill on sight in the four other layers, if the murderer can transfer you to a Checkpoint in ten minutes' time. They are even handing out single use permitted First Layer Checkpoint transfer devices—like the one we used to transfer the ferals—free to anyone who registers. Anyone transported by one is taken straightaway to a detention facility at the Checkpoint." He paused briefly before continuing, "And Ren, if you end up at a Checkpoint, you will disappear into Stavros's hands immediately and will be out of our reach forever."

I expected Constantine to start swearing again, but he had gone unusually still, furious temper cooling into something colder and harder to chip at.

Axer looked at him, and I could see the slightest bit of unease run through Axer at whatever he was reading on his roommate.

"So, we..." I couldn't even finish the statement. Hide? Run every ten minutes—waiting for someone to take us during a last stand?

"The Third Layer isn't going to want to give you up to the Second. I had thought maybe a particular spot in the Fourth..." Axer shook his head. "But we should stick to the Third. If you are taken here, we still have the chance to find you."

And vice versa—the more important point, to me, until I could safely absolve them from my fugitive status.

I touched the marble I always kept in my pocket. The marble that was far emptier than it had once been—still pulsed.

"Most of the places I've been to have been tracked and noted," I said.

"Death." Constantine looked out at the landscape, lips pressed tightly.

I looked at him. "I know you are furi—"

"Ours," Axer said.

I stilled and looked at them.

"We need somewhere they won't look. Or somewhere they can't look." His blue eyes pinned me like he already knew my secrets. "Make us disappear."

"I meant you do it," Constantine snarled, turning to him.

"They will search all the homes and installations of the allies I have made. We need those allies later. She can do it."

"I know she can. But you would make her? Like this?"

"Yes." Axer's expression was hard. "She learns quickly. Even more so under strain when given a small amount of recovery, then another, harder challenge."

"You would cause—"

"Don't deny her who she is."

"I never have."

"But you will," Axer said, intensity in his gorgeous eyes. "She won't last in a gilded cage."

"I know. Or she'd already be there," Constantine said savagely. "You are ignoring the ramifications. This is a farseerstorm that you wish on your enemies but one you don't want to see captured by a Level 10 container."

"You, too, want her to be who she is." Axer's gaze was mesmerizing. "Your fear can't deny your desire."

"Fear can deny any desire," he spit, and there was a loaded exchange of meaning between them. Communication that I was never privy to in their method of unbreakable communication.

I touched the marble again. It wasn't ready, and I had almost ended the world already today, but...

I looked at the boys, knowing that I was now responsible for their safety. There was no room for fear or failure.

"I can do it," I said quietly, putting my hand on Constantine's arm. "I won't...I won't end us. It will be creation. I can keep control."

For their safety. For Rosaria and Carlos—Ren and Christian.

Constantine looked at me for a long moment. "Darling, I'm not one of your spineless Thirdies. You can ravage a thousand landscapes and twist everything under the sun into swirled lollipops and I'll just mock all those who forgot to bring their own stick."

"I won't—"

Constantine rubbed at his temples. "Stop talking. I swear you were born with enough guilt for both of us. Just...don't stick us in Flavel Valeris' palace."

"I won't." I breathed in deeply, feeling my other emotions bury themselves beneath. I could do this. I could be better than I'd been. I had to be.

I ran my right fingers along my pocket and left fingers over the cool marble, and let my fear join the other unhelpful emotions underneath.

Death. I looked at the drooping sky. What would Ori do in this situation?

It would lead a merry chase.

I pulled five small paper dragons from my kit. They fluttered excitedly.

I paused over the latch of the cuff, then unlatched it. Power flooded through me—all the greater for having been stoppered. I grabbed onto the lashing tendrils, but it was like roping a storm. Axer's warm hand slid under my unbound hair and the power dimmed, siphoned away just enough for me to grab hold.

I knelt and concentrated. No rage, no anger of any kind—I submerged it all. Melancholy. Kinship with the layers and magic that flowed between all of them.

"First you." I imbued the first dragon with a hefty dose of magic, and the broken layer crackled around me in response. If anyone hadn't known where we were, they did now. "Then you."

The next dragon had less magic, and so forth, until the last of them held the barest amount. I then pulled out a sixth dragon and pulled the siphoned magic back, overloading the paper, pulling the freely extended magic from both boys, then encapsulated all of it in two vibrating fields around the distended creature.

I held up the first five. "Activate only when your predecessor is gone and your spell triggers. After that, you are free. Become a flower in the landscape, fly to new pastures, find each other—whatever you desire." A small bit of trickery under their own control.

"Except you," I said to the sixth. "Do you understand your task?"

It vibrated with swollen excitement.

I tuned the portal pad, imbuing it with timing parameters for six jumps. Each jump was spelled to one of the dragons.

"Three minutes," Axer said, eyes fixed on a specific point in the landscape. "They'll be in view soon."

"Okay." I swallowed. "Here we go."

I activated the pad outside the dead space and the first dragon dove inside. The others followed, grasping the tendrils of each spelled jump. The last, bloated dragon eagerly zipped inside at the end, taking the pad with it—suctioned through the layer—our only external emergency escape.

We waited in agonizing silence as the layer shift rolled over and around the dead space, then

Axer nodded. "Bait accepted. All crafts have changed course to the first of the pad's points."

A minute later, I felt the pop in my mind, and the layer rumbled. "Second jump initiated."

I latched the cuff back into place. Immediately, Constantine's dark emotions, and the crazed feelings emanating through him from Olivia, Neph, and the Bandits, dimmed.

Dimmed, but not completely absent. I could feel the brushes of the second dragon's activation as the pad did its work at the second site a minute later.

Axer touched the metal. "A Level 9 suppressor cuff. It won't last." His fingertip touched a small, burned hole.

"I know," I whispered. My very sweat glimmered with color these days. And paint had eventually eaten through every cuff I'd ever worn. "I'll work through it."

I shakily lifted the small black box that had splayed out with our supplies—a bubbled addition gifted from another source of magic in the compound as we'd been expelled—feeling the weight of it in my hands. I set it down on the uneven ground.

Constantine narrowed his eyes. "Is that—"

With a press against the sides, a large vehicle activated into the space in front of us. It was loaded with supplies and the inverted shielding wards I had helped create for the Ophidians' vehicles during free moments I had in the complex when I'd been trying to learn people's names and trades, and to help with whatever I could to make their lives better with the magic that I had.

Frost Viper—thank you.

"It is." Constantine's darkness lifted the minutest measure with his own answered statement. As if his complete kill count had split to kill and "maim" counts instead.

"It's a non-magic way to get us to where we need to go as long as no one is following."

I walked unevenly to the front of the bike, mounted the driver's seat, and mechanically checked the gauges. All magic, fluids, and evasive enchantments were topped. The spine of a manual on recycling spells peeked from the side of the vehicle where it was tucked.

Recycling spells. I'd become adept at the enchantments out of necessity at first, then interest later.

Still... I looked at the landscape outside the dead space, and touched my pocket again. Feeling his gaze, I looked at Constantine. He looked at the pocket I kept touching, then back at me, not even needing to read my mind, he knew me so well at this point.

"I'm driving." He moved with purpose toward the front of the single, long seat.

"I can do it," I murmured.

"I'm. Driving."

"Do you remember the way?" I scooted backward, feeling stupid relief curl. I touched the control cuff. The long drive would require a constant touch of magic through the recycler.

"Every crater, Charybdis effect, sand wyrm, and siren-weed of it," he said darkly, long leg lifting over the front.

After threatening the Ophidians with a bomb and instant death, his trip on a similar bike had been less than kind.

As the single passenger with Frost Viper, the best driver in the territories and the Ophidian leader for a reason, I'd had it easy. The ride had been amazing.

My mind shifted, looking out at the broken landscape.

There was something wistfully sad about fixing the entire layer. The outlaw vibe, killer animals who spun shifts, and jagged skies of death...

The sky crackled with green lightning outside the dead space, as if in answer.

"What if what I did makes the sand wyrms go extinct?" I murmured.

Constantine stopped checking the gauges, and Axer paused his task of fitting the rest of our supplies in the trunk compartment in the back.

Their heads slowly turned to me and both boys stared for an extended moment.

"What?" I asked.

Constantine narrowed his eyes at me. "Are you trying to cheer me up?"

"I got rid of the wyrms' homes—"

Axer's face changed, understanding softening the hard lines of it. "And they were all returned. Your book—"

I laughed without humor. "Exactly. I promised the people here that I would fix the Third Layer." I touched my pocket. "And I...what am I doing? What do I know about fixing the world?"

"Quite a bit," Constantine said darkly. "I'm pretty certain I saw my nightstand from the manor fly by in four separate pieces disconnected by threads of reversion magic."

"That's...that's not helpful."

"I never liked that nightstand."

Axer motioned and Guard Rock ran up the side of the vehicle and flipped into the small recessed space between the trunk and seat that Axer had created.

I saw Constantine look back at them and his fingers twitch.

"Don't you dare," I said.

"I'd never leave your rock," he said blandly.

Guard Rock allowed himself to be strapped down, gaze already stretched to the distance—our small lookout to the rear.

I felt Constantine shift, and I pinched his side. "Don't you dare," I hissed.

"With a few additional words, that sentence could be perfect."

The bike shifted as Axer settled in behind me. Trapped between the two, I became instantly aware of the precariousness of my position and where to put my limbs.

"And, by the way, darling," Constantine said, looking at me over his shoulder with a bland expression. "Just to be clear... If you push me to another location while you remain at a battle site again, I will tie you up and drop you into a dark hole," he said, starting the engine. "Then I'll fish you out, make certain the bindings are still secure, then drop you in again."

"Not handcuffed in the tower?"

"The oubliette," he said darkly.

I let my forehead fall against his back, securing my arms around his midsection, Axer's thighs hugging mine.

School trips, science class, death, destruction, antipodean portals... I tried to think of a popular song that had always been playing on the radio—the one Christian used to hum then try to deny what he was singing.

A small bit of comfort crawled under my skin from Axer and from Constantine in response to whatever emotion I was exhibiting. I closed my eyes.

Chapter Thirteen

ERSTWHILE COMPANIONS

I SLIPPED from the seat and flopped onto the grass six hours later.

We'd found a single patch of green in the middle of the endless wasteland—one with a giant tree—and Constantine had headed for it at speed. Only two sand dragons, a lizardgator, and a rabid Stygian phoenix had interrupted that side trip.

Our plan would have been toast without someone along who could fight without using magic.

Axer was possibly the only one having fun, using the weapons the Ophidians had stocked—a new one each time—challenging whatever monster or pitfall presented itself, as if performing a training exercise.

"Adrenaline junkie," I muttered.

He could fight a sand chimera with a spoon, but even he was starting to tighten up without using his magic.

The whole trip might have been a grand adventure under different circumstances. Under normal circumstances, we'd have been sharing magic between us in a continuous circuit and not worrying about using any of it for such stringent concealment. But it was too dangerous to freely give in to that desire while there were so many mages tracking us. And while wearing the cuff, I was a sharing liability.

Without it, though...

I'd spent the last two hours trying to swallow down paint after Axer made me remove the metal band. Only a concentrated effort had made it possible.

The bike allowed for a thin sheen of recycling between the riders and the machine, but like everything in the layer, it was thin. Each of us had been working overtime on keeping the paint that had started creeping up my throat contained. Throwing up a portal to the Fifth Layer would immediately end our anonymity.

Each of us had to use the containers strapped to the bike that the Ophidians used on such trips. But where the Ophidians were used to such constrained circumstances, none of us were. The three of us were privileged Second Layer mages—even worse, Excelsine mages—where abundance was taken for granted.

It was like having words flashed and being told not to read them. Reining it in was exhausting. Without the cuff, an explosion was imminent. And with the cuff, the magic buildup was just getting worse.

Axer was literally vibrating with constrained magic as he dismounted. Constantine had jumped off the bike and was crouched some fifty feet in the distance, doing who knew what. But I could feel his own unspent, forcibly capped magic coiling in bigger whorls.

"I'm driving next," I said. Sandwiched so tightly between them I had barely been able to move, let alone defend us.

"This isn't a dream, darling," Constantine called.

"No," I said quietly. It was sort of the opposite.

I had felt the last of the dragons activate three hours ago, scattering his papered seeds within a hurricane wind and destroying a large section of barren wasteland; prompting an intense global debate over the possibility of our deaths. Axer and Constantine had relished in a dark sort of pleasure in repeating some of the commentary from the communications they were still receiving.

We were listed officially as dead in twelve countries. But that left hundreds of countries that were still searching for us.

We were existing on borrowed time. Eventually one of us would use magic, and a chase worse than the last would begin.

I rotated my shoulders against the earth to ease the clogs and tightness in my neck and back, feeling my aches. This must be what fifty felt like. Mom had been sniping about it for the past year.

"At least we found an actual oasis for a few minutes' respite," I said.

"This isn't an oasis," Axer said, slowly rotating his muscles, letting the vibrating magic simmer into a continuous thread that rotated across his skin—a world class athlete pulling his body back into peak shape. For now. He made his own magic bow to his control, thinning it into the loop easily, unlike my fledgling efforts.

"But we need you not obliterating the landscape," he said. "And if we hit another sand vortex, you were going to say screw it and start remaking the layer right then and there."

His statement wasn't...incorrect...and the earth did feel like it was moving beneath me. I shook off the mesmerizing sight of his magic and looked down.

The ground was moving, all at once, like shifting tectonic plates. A horrible, enraged screech split the air, and rotating blades spun in my peripheral view.

"Um...?"

"Death tortoise," Axer said, not sounding at all stressed about an animal with death in its name and spikes of saw blades rotating along its sides.

"Is it going to eat me?" I let my eyes slip shut, feeling the adrenaline of the last half day start to drain. "I feel like I might let it."

There was something cathartic about traveling through a landscape where everything wanted to eat you because it was hungry, not because it could use you for world domination.

And maybe because you deserved it.

"Not today."

Thinking about fault made me go down darker, unhelpful paths, and I had to forcefully corral my emotions. Control. Control, Ren.

"How do I not become…" I shook my head. "How do you do it so well?"

"What, control my desires?" he said lightly.

I regarded him from the ground—or, from a death tortoise shell, I supposed—looking up as he was haloed by the light. "Balance your abilities," I corrected. "How do you forgo the emotional path?"

He crouched next to me. One finger lifted a lock of hair that had blown into my face and tucked it behind my ear.

"All choices are about emotion. It is how you use your emotions that make the impact of the choice."

I swallowed. "I have lost my balance."

"No. You haven't lost it, you simply have yet to fully gain it. You see balance in me, but I was trained from birth to hide all that I am. I've never been allowed to be all I can be." He raised his hand and I could see a phantom of magic coil there—a wisp of illusion that held a deep crimson hue. "Because of fear. Even my mother, whose powers are known, restrains her abilities to appease the masses."

He cocked his head. "But now there is you—you who can wipe entire worlds from existence. Sending ten armies to fight you means nothing, for a single assassin would have just as much luck—for the only way to win would be the element of surprise. You have an ultimate power. And no way to hide it. You can use that."

"Might makes right?"

"Even under a benevolent rule, might always carries the edge. You have a clean slate, in a way, because everyone already knows. They already fear you outright, instead of just fearing the possibility of your power. You have the chance to use your abilities without the firestorm of discovery," he said, intensity underscored by deep desire. "For the firestorm has already come."

I watched him. "You suck at motivational speeches."

He smiled. "I'm not trying to motivate you. You see balance in me, where I see hidden, inactive potential. I see freedom in you, where you see fear."

I touched his hand. "I don't want you here. Either of you. For your own safety."

"I know."

"But you won't leave," I said, somewhat wistfully.

"No."

I stared at him as the sky moved with the lumbering gait of the turtle, and the deadly spikes whirred. "I'm a weakness for you. For all of you."

"Yes." He curled a lock of hair around his fingers.

"They will get to you, and your mother, through me."

His eyes tightened. "They will try."

"Stavros has already used me against you."

"And he failed. He will fail again," he said with certainty.

"I want to believe that. But that means..."

"Yes. It does."

"Your turn to drive," Constantine said flatly to him, as he folded elegantly next to me on the other side and stuck his hand into one of the baskets that had been attached to the bike and withdrew a sandwich.

I let my hand drop.

"Vine mayonnaise?" Constantine made a face, and Axer rolled his eyes as he pushed himself to his feet. "Who puts that on caperly bread?"

I felt around the grass, then raised my hand around a stick, offering it to him.

Constantine's sensibilities were overly offended by the suggestion—roiling over him in a quick, visible wave. I started laughing, some of the tension in my muscles easing.

Not accessing simple magic was slightly hilarious in certain instances—such as watching

Constantine's eyes narrow in on the offending sauce and how he was going to get rid of it without calling magic down upon us or using a stick to scrape it.

I was going to have to thank Frost Viper for more than just the supplies.

Axer grabbed several things from the basket and headed to sit behind the tortoise's head.

I sat up and accepted a sandwich of my own—some strange meat substitute and pseudo-vegetable combination that Frost Viper had included—concurrently checking the passive magic of Will's encyclopedia bracelet as we began rolling back and forth across the landscape—like a giant pirate ship in search of rabid world-eating sardines.

"So... It says death tortoises dive into the sand. Should we—?" I rolled a hand back-and-forth.

"I put a compound on its neck that prevents it from being able to put its head in its shell," Constantine said, carefully using one of his recycling containers and touching a rod to the mayonnaise. The tiniest stream of magic from the rod inched the offending sauce onto a leaf held next to it. "It stops it from diving."

I stopped mid-bite. "I already checked torturing the wildlife off my agenda."

"It's a temporary and reversible torture," Constantine said, removing the last drop of sauce, like every bit was a poison that would kill him. "Furthermore, it is in the animal's best interest to have you survive. The corporatists hate them, and anything that infringes on their profit-only views. Look at this beautiful landscape on which they could construct luxury homes," he said, pointing at the deformed wasteland of pits, traps, and decay that we were currently tromping through. "Besides, Stavros has never shown a love for anything non-mage... I can guarantee the animal's demise if the Second Layer gains control of you and somehow completes their plan of folding the Third Layer into the Second."

It was a reminder that I wasn't the only terror-inducing mage in this game.

Constantine's expression remained bland, thoughts dark. "In exchange, it will move us to our destination—albeit slowly—without alerting any of our five billion enemies. You can give it half your sandwich, if that makes you feel better."

I tore a section and carefully set it to the side. "You are sure the compound will wear off?"

"I'd never hurt an innocent soul while you are holding my leash."

"That's not funny."

"He's not joking," Axer said, not turning from the spot where he was nudging the tortoise to keep to its path. They were both oddly tense.

I cautiously poked around. All connection points were still opt-in and strong. "There's no leash anywhere," I said carefully. "And if there is something—"

"Metaphorical only," Constantine said nonchalantly.

I frowned at him.

Axer took a drink, gaze quickly traversing the landscape. From another saddlebag, he had dug out some of the special goggles the Ophidians used, and was watching the perimeter with enhanced vision, occasionally dropping chunks of some orange plant into the turtle's mouth in the type of peace offering I was used to him making with outrageous wildlife.

He scratched the underside of his arm. Magic sparked under his skin, even in the internal loop he had set up.

The magic was unattached to either Constantine or to me, but it occasionally reached toward both of us before he could pull it back.

I looked over at Constantine and could see the same thing—but somehow even worse—with magic from far away seeking him out in bursts.

I watched the jagged sky. They were dangerously close to overloading. More so than even I, which was beyond strange. Comparatively, I'd been in a far worse condition when we'd started.

Each of us had already expelled involuntary bits of magic—like the involuntary act of breathing. "Random" patrols had started to inch closer to our location in response to the spikes.

"Are all of us going to blow up when the magic becomes too much?"

Constantine, finished with his food in the way that all boys over the age of thirteen made it disappear, was sketching out something in his long pencil strokes that could later be converted to magic. "Probably. We are too accustomed to intermingled magic. We too often get the sustained pleasure of using each other as outlets in a situation where no other outlet is available."

We'd had a few of those situations in the last few months, but they'd all been short. Who knew how long we'd be on the run?

Guilt, shame.

In a magic rich environment, they could jettison the magic and use it, recycling their own system with the room wards—but here...

I looked between them.

The tension that had been simmering between them since we'd all started working together had been far lower in the past weeks than when I'd first discovered they were roommates.

But it had never gone.

It was almost a different sort of tension now. Like two broken ends of a string that were alternately trying to reknit or shred the other.

With as drained as I was, I strangely didn't seem to be in the same imminent danger that they were.

I swallowed and chewed the last bite. "How long are we riding this death trap?"

"For as long as we can manage."

"This is a good exercise," Axer said, without looking back. "I work with either no magic or with unlimited resources. Having to keep it so close and share it between such thin parameters is a good exercise in control."

"Control is your drug," I allowed.

"Don't worry yet," Axer said. "We're fine."

But by the second day of travel it was obvious that they weren't.

We had avoided two caravans and five strike teams by the edges of our fingernails. And the best warrior of the age had needed to do everything he could to hide every part of himself that wanted to fight. He was brimming with enough magic to shadow a sun.

Constantine's magic, on the other hand, looked dark and sick.

Even Axer became tight-lipped when he looked at his roommate's magic. "If you continue this way, you'll put yourself into a coma."

I watched Constantine with a frown while stretching my limbs skyward trying to move around the aches where magic was forming overfilled blocks. Pressure needed release. It was the thing hindering us the most—the three of us were veritable signposts of magic, especially together. We were on borrowed time in more ways than one.

"We can try the field," I said.

"No," Constantine said bluntly.

"You could do your roommate thing. You should do your roommate thing." I frowned.

Roommates—especially ones who got matched due to a level of overwhelming magical sympathy that dwarfed personal hatred—had connections that others did not. They shared magic across layers during the combat competition without breaking a sweat.

"It has been offered," Axer said in a clipped voice.

"No," Constantine said blandly.

"Martyrdom suits you ill," Axer said to him.

"I've been balancing Ren for weeks," Constantine said, and the snap of his emotions couldn't be contained. "Two days..." He waved a hand.

"Weeks that involved ample outlets and frequent returns to campus. Calling continually on the others without those outlets still gives you their powers, but at the expense of your own," Axer said. "I can feel the strain."

I frowned, looking down at my magic, then at Constantine's. Appalled, I scooted away from him.

"I'm wounded, darling, I have a very nice spell set to prevent cooties."

"That's not funny," I said harshly. "Have you...?"

It was strange, in retrospect, as to why he had kept returning to campus when he always seemed so incredibly irritated to leave—like I was going to disappear while he was gone, but he had to make the trip anyway.

Because he'd had to. "No. I refuse to let—"

"My choice, not yours," he said lazily. "Is it not?"

"Your magic looks terrible," I whispered.

"Never."

"Let Axer fix it."

"No."

"I will cut you off, if you don't." I touched the threads. "My choice, is it not? You can heal on your own, and so can I."

Constantine didn't answer for a long moment and I felt the spiking of different emotions before they settled into the more even ones that he had mastered in the past few months. "Fine."

He grabbed the device we had perfected, and draped the field over them. The conduit opened—a thin beautiful, complex weaving of magic between them.

I stared. Constantine's magic blossomed, the sickly gray cast disappearing like a shadow hit by a burst of sunlight. Even under the careful magic exchange allowed by the shield, it was glorious. What would it look like, freely flowing between them in waves?

I had seen highly sympathetic mages do magic together thousands of times at Excelsine. Mike and Will's lovely, steady hum, and Patrick and Asafa's compatible bursts of frenetic energy and soothing slides entwining into a thick net. Sari and Bess with their enchanting single hum of overt goodness. Neph's magic with nearly anyone.

It made me wonder what my own magic looked like when intertwined.

"She's going to the Department over my dead body," Constantine said. I looked up to see he was addressing Axer—something passing between them that I couldn't hear—their bond especially tight when linked.

"I know." Axer's gaze remained connected to his, a grim set to his mouth—for as soon as he took his hand away, Constantine's skin started to gray again.

I didn't have to hear their conversation to understand that there might be a path littered with our bodies before the end.

Chapter Fourteen

BODY OF THE SUN

THE DEATH tortoise—full of picnic food to last it a week—swam through the sand to the south, then dove beneath with a screech.

I watched it disappear, then moved my attention back to the scorched remains of Corpus Sun.

Peering over the edge of a dune, we watched the factions of terrorists, soldiers, settlers, and scientists move in an uneasy detente under the thin dome I had erected over the entire site in my first negotiations with the Western Territories.

"Lovely. This looks like just the spot to start a revolution," Constantine said amiably, a direct contrast to his true feelings, as usual.

Axer carefully miniaturized the supplies using the devices' own internal magic, and slung the bag already containing the miniaturized vehicle across his chest as he began scoping out the perimeter with Guard Rock. Constantine's cat sat at the base of the dune, grooming itself in boredom.

I stared at the cat, then at Constantine—who shrugged in response. We resumed our vigil in tandem.

"Not a revolution," I murmured.

"Darling, your entire existence is a revolution."

My magic was still all over the site that surrounded what had once been Corpus Sun. A thin dome—a facsimile of the one that Constantine and I had tiptoed through months ago—covered the remains of the city. It kept out shifts and recycled a finite amount of magic within.

But the real jewel was the thick containment dome at the city's center. An impenetrable layer of magical Saran wrap pulled an opaque dome over what had once been a five-block radius of shambling buildings, inaccessible at this stage to anyone without the key. A mystery that the Third Layer scientists and engineers on site had been pretending to chip at for months.

I touched the marble, girding myself. "We'll need to deactivate the appraisal wards."

Constantine's eyes narrowed in on the Third Layer scientists' tent, locked down with wards between the exterior and interior domes.

"Are you sure about this?" he asked, looking sharply at me. "This is your test case. Your results may be tainted by our presence."

I pulled my lips between my teeth, wetting them. "What difference does it make now? It should hide us for a bit in a place we can use magic. Maybe for two days? And we need that." I tried to smile at him; tried not to let my gaze slide to the sickly gray tinge of his skin.

His complexion was responding less and less to each influx by Axer—two people sharing one, emptying oxygen tank. I swallowed.

"The site already flags my magic," I said, trying harder to smile. "And authorities from both layers have combed the site outside the inner dome a hundred times and turned up nothing. We might even make it out alive."

Inessa had spouted the information last term during an effort to taunt me.

"...the evidence against you that Daddy's troops are currently searching for in Corpus Sun."

Inessa had taunted me, hoping to scare me, but what she'd done instead was give me a heads up that the Legion was trying to access the site. The problem with Inessa's declaration was that the Legion's search was illegal. And even Legion troops had to proceed carefully. Second Layer forces caught in the Third Layer would technically be considered a declaration of war that Second Layer politicians hadn't been ready to commit to months ago.

A few whispers in the right Third Layer ears had upped the Third Layer presence immediately. The Second Layer hadn't resumed their poking—unless they had been very, very careful about it.

The problem with a global police force in the Second Layer that answered to a vast number of politically disparate countries was that they weren't war sanctioned for any but the direst of circumstances. They could be sneaky and underhanded, but they had to get permission from the Council for acts of war.

That was the reason the Department hadn't been able to openly come after me in the Third Layer. Until they got a declaration, they had to be covert. Or they had to lure me to the Second Layer.

With current events in play, we were on shakier ground. A quarter of the Second Layer countries had already signed documents of war while we'd been turtling. It was the holdouts that were keeping troops out of the Third—hampering Stavros just enough to give us time we might not otherwise have. Axer had been right.

"Traces of the two of us and Price are already established here as well. The perfect camouflage." Axer crouched down. He pointed at nearly invisible blocks of green near the external dome, then similar ones around the internal dome. "Trackers. Multiple types placed by multiple factions. They will go off as soon as someone tries to cross the beams. They need to be disarmed with something that can dissolve, then immediately renew them. But that shouldn't be a problem, should it?"

He looked at Constantine in challenge, eyes dark, and withdrew a thin tube from his cloak pocket.

I cringed. Constantine had used something like that on the wards at Excelsine, when letting Godfrey and his men onto campus, then sealing up the wards later. And he'd taken it as a challenge since then to make something less detectable for future ill plans.

But even though we'd be using his discoveries to help us, it still didn't remove the thorn between them that Constantine had put the entire campus in danger—a population Axer zealously protected.

Constantine withdrew a vial filled with a vibrant green liquid and shook it lazily without looking away from the challenging stare of his roommate.

Axer frowned, halting his motion in lengthening the tube. "Is that all of it?" He looked at the ground between our dune and the dome, then at the tube, and the liquid in the vial. He sighed and retracted the tube, placing it back in his cloak.

"Well, I didn't exactly pack for storming castles," Constantine said. "This is plenty."

"And what are you going to do with it exactly, throw it?" Axer said evenly. "Might as well just announce our presence by tossing Ren with it. There are fifteen scouts watching this section of the barrier."

"Find the prettiest scout and lure her—or him—over to the barrier with your muscles while I deactivate a sliver in the field," Constantine said lazily.

I cringed.

Axer stared at Constantine. "That is a stupid plan." He was already pulling devices from the secret pockets and buckles in his cloak.

"And yours is...?"

"It was to drip it through the distribution tube, then walk through the opening like we belonged. But without using magic, the amount of potion we have will never spread that distance. So, Plan B. There's a flarelizard nest fifty meters from the border on the far side. As soon as the scouts move, you move too."

We both looked at him like he was insane. Flarelizards spit lava.

"You can't use magic," I said. Fighting flarelizards was one thing—I'd seen him fight dozens of things without magic—but mobilizing them? We were going to be a crew of two sooner rather than later.

He shrugged and rolled his shoulders, his own magic tighter than I'd ever seen it. "I'll be fine."

"They'll know we are in the internal field as soon as she opens the seed," Constantine said, disregarding the imminent death of his roommate and going to the next problem in the plan.

A flash of gold lit the crowd in my peripheral vision, jerking my gaze to the people roaming just inside the external dome. I scanned the crowd, gaze traveling to the right, looking for the source, unease spreading through me. Scientist, settler, two men haggling over some bit of magic, five soldiers sharing a canteen, a small crowd peering at a broadcast, two more scientists, three terrorists, five men in territory clothes...

"They'll know something is happening, but not exactly what," Axer said.

Another flash of gold made my gaze jerk to the left of the crowd, search turning more frantic as the boys continued bickering.

"It's a pretty easy guess."

"But it will still be speculation. They can't gain entrance. And every Third Layer faction will try to keep it secret from the other layers. They'll cite previous problems at the site, if there are any spikes. We'll make certain there aren't."

"You were the one worried about being trapped," Constantine said languidly, chipped darkness beneath each word. "I'm relieved to see that burden lifted."

"We won't be trapped." Axer was staring at Constantine in challenge as I looked back at them.

I wet my lips. Gold meant only one thing for me in dangerous situations. "Listen, I think—"

Constantine narrowed his eyes at Axer, ignoring me. "You will burn her out."

"A phoenix burns with new life."

Subtext underscored their words, but I didn't care about any of it at the moment. "Seriously, we need—"

Constantine smiled tightly. "Well then, I guess that's settled. All we need is for you to create a distraction and die with glory."

"Pirate scum!"

We all whipped our gazes to peer over the dune as voices erupted from the settlement and my unease turned into full blown panic. Five men were fighting in front of the scientist's tent, and in front of them, the external dome had thinned so significantly as to be a dewy membrane—wobbling on a leaf, waiting to fall.

"Oh, no," I whispered.

"Someone deactivated two-thirds of the wards in the exterior barrier," Axer said, eyes narrowed and searching the crowd.

"The recycling magic is still active," Constantine said, body tight. "But the apprisal spells were turned off."

My gaze narrowed on a man on the edge of the fight circle gathering outside the scientists' tent. Hat tipped rakishly low, the brim tilted just enough to let the sun catch the gold cuff hugging his ear. I couldn't see his eyes, but the edge of his lips curved into a smile, as if he could feel my gaze. A shimmer of a hummingbird rose in the air above his lazily circling hand, then he pivoted and blended into the surging crowd.

Raphael, who was always plotting far in advance.

I murmured the politest swear word I could think of for this situation.

Both boys looked at me. "What?"

"Raphael is here."

Constantine's head whipped back in the direction of the fighters.

"You saw him?" Axer asked calmly, his gaze dissecting the surging crowd. He turned the device in his hand up a notch with a flick of his finger. It was indicating all lifeforms within a one-mile perimeter around us and highlighting the details for each life force.

"He's not a participant, but he started the fight. He disabled the barrier." I was certain of that.

"He knows you are here."

It wasn't a question, but I answered anyway. "Yes."

"And he disabled the barrier." Axer tapped a free finger against his thigh. He looked at Constantine's magic, then mine, before meeting my gaze again. "Can he enter the interior dome? Once you activate your creation?"

I shifted uncomfortably. "I can't unequivocally say no. He has fewer resources than Stavros, but knows me better. But I haven't felt a disturbance in the surrounding wards. I'm the only one with the key." I touched the marble.

Axer's tapping increased as he surveyed the fight, his body tense—then stopped. He tucked the device into a buckle notch. "We risk it. Let's go."

Constantine gaze whipped back. "He'll try and take Ren."

Axer tipped his head grimly. "Then you get your chance to do all that you've desired."

Constantine stiffened.

Axer was already moving and I scrambled to follow. "He gave us an opening. We need recovery time and the magic. Even if it's only for an hour. And we need to contact the others. We'll deal with Verisetti, if we have to."

A firework burst, and people began streaming toward the fight from all directions. Guard Rock swung into my hood.

Constantine scooped up the cat, flat gaze on his roommate. "And your proposal—"

"Walk right through the crowd."

We scrambled over the dune and ran down the slope as if we were scouts joining in. The thin barrier was barely a brush against my skin, but the available magic inside was not, and it called to me. Once in the surge, we began moving sideways. That part was oddly easy. Keep my head down, stay to the edge of the crowd, inch closer to the dome, don't use magic.

We reached the edge of the interior dome quickly. Under a recycling dome, magic that was not our own was available to use in a way that it hadn't been in the shift-happy outlands. Axer put his back to us and began skipping tiny devices along the ground and into the crowd. With each flicked device, the emotions of the crowd waved and were manipulated along with the trajectory, focusing the eyes of the crowd to each endpoint. Enough additional mayhem and attention focused elsewhere for twenty seconds, maybe.

Constantine crouched over one of the tracking wards, holding a pair of oddly shaped tweezers I recognized from his lab. He slowly extended the tweezers and carefully scraped the edge of the magic, then quickly repeated the action along a three-foot perimeter.

He tapped the magics into the vial and capped it. Jets of bubbles rolled over the magic, reacting slowly at first, then with more vigor until the only thing left was a chartreuse mixture.

Dipping the rod in the vial, he withdrew it and carefully, but quickly drew a pentagram in the air between the polar points of the three-foot area. The pentagon in the middle of the design flapped inward. We stepped through the flap carefully and quickly and Axer ducked behind us at the last second.

Constantine pulled the shimmering flap back into place in a reversal of movements.

My breath caught to see Raphael leaning against a tent directly opposite our position. Face half-hidden beneath the tilted brim, he smiled. The hummingbird buzzed his lazily circling hand.

My view of Raphael disappeared with the rest of Corpus Sun's outer frontier, and the lack of magic inside the containment dome gripped me immediately.

It wasn't like a control cuff, where magic was still available, just hard fought. This was like a null cuff—a null zone without magic at all. Even my ability to feel the boys was absent, even though they were right next to me.

I gripped my panic tightly. Raphael was outside; we were trapped within without magic. Keep going, keep going, Ren. I unhooked the control cuff, though it didn't matter here whether I had it on or not. The null air around me provoked a numbness, like I'd never feel part of myself again.

The null field wasn't like the wards meant to alert others of our presence. No magic could be created within it. However, it was just that, a field—an unwanted dressing spread thinly on a sandwich, and we just needed to pass through it to find the deliciousness beneath.

As we approached the inner dome, light flashed around us in a sudden intensity that was stunning and purposefully disorienting. A barrier, thick and dangerous, swirled in front of me—full of magic, but not part of the zone.

I swallowed. You can do this. You _can_. Calm. Creation. Creation with purpose.

I opened my palm and let the rays of light touch the cradled marble. Let the touch unlock a light-filled doorway on the other side of the field. We quickly stepped through.

Into paradise.

Magic whooshed back fully into my control and immediately reached for the boys in a debilitating, almost violent relief. The control cuff slipped from my fingers. Axer caught it and me before I hit the ground.

After two days of travel with limited magic means and in such close quarters, my freed magic immediately sought the two of them and vice versa—filling me in on all the things I'd been missing—then spread to the world around us, already filled with my magic and bits of theirs.

A soaring sky rose in the center of the immense dome, the edges of the clouds and sky tapering gently downward to the ground.

Inside was just as I had imagined it in the pushes. Plants lush with new life spreading their fingers in all directions. Mushrooms and vegetables sprouting from the soft ground. Insects rising with the soil—awaiting predators.

It was a silent landscape, but one brimming with life and possibility.

Once opened, birds and small magical animals would migrate here. Then bigger animals. Then humans.

An Eden waiting to be filled.

The magic in the marble grew more vibrant, pushing against its constraints. I released the last vestiges of all that I had been collecting inside of it.

Magic rich with life lit every surface, glistening on the leaves and vines; on a beetle's wings.

Guard Rock leaped from my hood, and the cat landed on a synthetically-sunny patch of green.

Axer smiled, shook out his triceps, and let the magic he'd been holding inside slowly connect and recycle with the city dome in a long, slow exhale.

Constantine shivered and whispered my name. For once, his emotions were calm, not raging, as he, too, connected to the magic. Aching wonder and bitter triumph mixed with sadness. The dinginess that had been gathering along his skin—forming a muddy gray aura—peeled away.

I let relief override the unease I still felt over Raphael's presence outside the dome. I let relief overtake the sorrow of what would happen now that the dome's magic was activated—of what I had set in motion—this event spurring several others that I hadn't disclosed ahead of time.

Let anyone try and take this relief from me now, though, I thought fiercely, watching the health of both boys renew along with their magic.

"How did you progress this far?" Axer asked, taking it all in with calculating eyes.

"The paintings. I'm not in full control of what I paint, but how it happens...well, I learned how to speed forward the natural cycle within the creation. A day in a minute, a week in an hour, a year in a day." I let the marble roll around my palm as it spread its light on a sunflower growing, wilting, turning to seed, then growing again with a dozen companions, then a dozen more. Creation. The opposite of destruction. "I now just need to slow the flow. Bring it back to normal." Root out the destruction.

If only I could do the same within me.

"Speed the natural cycle." Constantine shrugged in feigned indifference. "No problem. Create a whole new world. Easy."

I looked at the beetle. "But with the same materials. In the same vacuum that creation first encounters. You gave me those parameters." For the Second Layer and for the First Layer.

Axer crouched down and dragged his finger through the earth beneath. "If you use too much oxygen or too little nitrogen... You could get dinosaurs. Giant insects. Fish-like beasts."

I smiled at the marble, holding it up to the light of the sky—a reflection of the real one outside, bending around the null void. "Maybe we will in one of the domes. Couldn't that be marvelous?"

"No," Constantine said shortly. "And I knew the moment you had me give you the composition of Excelsine's elements, what you planned. That doesn't mean I think you owe any of this to anyone."

"You said you didn't promise anything, was that incorrect?" Axer asked, voice far too mild.

I watched the marble flicker as it released its last gusts. I let my hand slowly fall—memories and bargains swarming me.

"Show us, Origin Mage, show us where you have started."

Half-formed sentences were immediately on my lips—it had only been a month, they should take the kids anyway, humanitarian laws should apply, I was barely more trained than the kids I was bringing in each day, why did it fall on _me_ to save the world?

I held each tumbled, unsaid word in a breath against the roof of my mouth.

I opened my palm, letting magic swirl above the whorls in bubbled domes connected by lightning fast magical routes. "I propose this."

I looked at the nearly empty marble, not Axer. "I never had to formally promise. I was going to fix everything. A little here, a little there. Steady. In a way not even the Second Layer could object. The Western Territory scientists have been monitoring the external progress here. I wanted to...prototype the internal before I showed anyone. Needed to know if I could do it. And with the layer shifts able to hide small things it seemed... Opportune."

I let my shoulders slump. "Worrisome thoughts."

"Your prototype is perfect." Constantine felt heavy with a relief that wasn't just due to his magic being able to relax and connect without control.

I tilted my head at him. "I didn't think you were that excited about this project. You never seemed to care about fixing the layer outside of the scientific."

"I care even less now," Constantine said. "You mistake the source of my relief."

He narrowed his eyes on his roommate as Axer sunk his fingers into the dirt—streams of magic flowing out as the vegetation bloomed from his magic—relieving him of all the overflowing excess. Guard Rock shadowed him, watching Axer poke around and examine each particle of magic, sometimes copying his motions. Shoring up wards in ways that I hadn't thought of, accelerating habitats and making them lusher, coaxing the bees to do...something—shimmering magic imbuing everything.

"Are we playing house?" Constantine asked.

"If you paid attention to the bees on the Fourth Circle versus the ones in the Midlands, you wouldn't be asking," Axer responded mildly, pointing at Guard Rock to repeat the motions with another hive.

Constantine narrowed his eyes and pulled out the two sleek boards of his traveling chair. Then pulled out another set of chair boards for me.

"We're here. Call Price," Constantine said. "She's been going out of her mind without an open link, and one of us is going to need a lobotomy after this."

I frowned, sitting in the chair next to him. "We don't have a—"

He touched my temple and pulled a thread of magic downward into my palm, his eyes slipping closed for a moment in bliss as he shivered, in full control of his abilities once more. He cupped his hands underneath mine for a long moment before slowly pulling them away, still connected by the wisps of whatever mental magic he had done—flush with power once more and skirting the impossible.

I blinked to see our room at Excelsine form in my hand.

Olivia was alone, scribbling something ferociously at her desk. The heavy, heady relief at seeing her nearly flattened me.

My side of the room looked untouched—though I could see the indentation on my bed that someone hadn't smoothed out all the way. Olivia sleeping there, or Neph.

I swallowed and looked back at my roommate. The wards were reaching down toward her, but there was a stretched feeling, like too many strings pulling in opposing directions.

"Our wards are still in place," Axer murmured from somewhere behind me, seeing where my gaze was focused. "But it won't be enough soon. Not with the three of us expelled now. She'll be forced to get a roommate."

"Of course," I said quickly. "She needs one. It's okay. And..."

Sadness mixed with irritation all over Constantine's emotions suddenly as he cupped the back of my neck with his palm—his other hand still holding the threads of the window to my room. The irritation was standard, the sadness was unusual. "You'll find Price again. And you can be her wonder twin once more and have sleepovers."

We could make cookie dough and eat it all. Or quiz each other on the latest regulations, legal constraints, and parliamentarian procedures.

Or argue about the portal I painted on the ceiling that dropped stardust on her hair at inopportune moments.

Even if, by that time, we weren't roommates anymore.

"She could do my nails," I said half-heartedly. "And I could do her hair."

Constantine paused in the magic he was sending to me, expression disturbed, as if the image of Olivia Price painting nails—or me knowing my way around a hairbrush—was alien to his worldview. "I meant your kind of sleepovers—weird debates and cantankerous cheer. Not a delusional kind."

Olivia looked up suddenly, as if realizing something was amiss. Her head shot toward my side of the room and naked, pained relief made her sag for a split second before she held out her hand. A glass ball zoomed into her palm, and suddenly I was looking at her eye-to-eye in mine.

"Where are you that you are calling like this?" she demanded. I could feel her magic reaching for mine, and vice-versa. But it was a thin, distant connection under the null zone surrounding our Eden. It was like having a video chat through a pair of old tablets instead of the extended ultra-reality of our hologram visits. "I can barely feel you, though this is better than the alternative of nothing."

Her accusatory gaze went to Constantine, parked next to me with his hands over his lap working on his string manipulations once more, as if he had picked up knitting and was casually engaged in the hobby after a day at work.

"We are in Corpus Sun," I said.

"Where?" Olivia's voice went flat.

"Corpus Sun."

She narrowed her eyes and touched beneath her ear. "I see that the Third Layer underground verifies that possibility. They are sending twenty units to apprehend anyone who exits the sealed dome in Corpus Sun. Quietly."

"Well, here we are. Safe!" Completely surrounded! I cleared my throat, searching quickly for another topic. When looking at Constantine, flushed with health, I couldn't regret our destination. But I'd save up telling everyone our insane exit strategy for later. "Where is everyone?"

It was rare to find Olivia without her own comforting force of people when she was waiting on news.

"Everyone is fine."

"I asked where they are," I said slowly. "Not how they are." None of them had been involved in the Awakenings. There shouldn't have been a status needed on their end.

"We had some mishaps." She narrowed her eyes. "Why there? You'll ruin your secret test case."

I blinked.

"You aren't subtle. Neither is William." She waved a hand. "Why are you no longer in the Western Territories' complex where you built a fortress? I've been trying to break into Leandred's mind for days. All of us have." She looked at him. "Repeatedly. And the Western Territory leaders are being tight-lipped, but all feeds confirmed you left two days ago. Neph has been trying to cut ties with the commune—renouncing her musehood—trying to get off campus ever since."

I swallowed, tears choking me. I concentrated on Neph's threads and sent everything in me through the tiny straws the null zone surrounding the city allowed beneath. I felt her shock, followed by a severe return of desperate emotions.

A tear slipped down my cheek. "Don't let her do that."

"We are, all of us, half-sitting on her, and half encouraging it to see if we can do the same," Olivia said grimly. "Marsgrove locked down campus. The Department is trying to get campus turned over again, citing the lot of us as accomplices. Only Marsgrove has been able to keep Neph here, invoking death contracts. No one is pleased, not even him. Why are you there?"

"We were kicked out," Constantine said, lounging back in his chair, wisps of magic still connecting his hand to mine, even as he worked.

Olivia's brows drew together, then straightened. "Ingrates."

Constantine absently motioned to her, then to me, in a way that said "exactly."

"How long can you stay there?" she asked.

I looked at the magic around us, already seeing the wilt at the edges of the world that would happen when it was breached; a world that wasn't yet ready for mages. "Two days. Maybe less."

"Ren put in a safeguard against herself in her lovely test case that allows the scientists to enter once they chip their way through," Constantine said idly, gaze on his project. "Just like she did with the compound. She is such a thoroughly helpful enemy of the state."

Olivia looked as furious with me as Constantine felt.

"No. It's my turn," I said. "Don't think that I've been sidetracked either. What mishaps?"

"There was a faulty retrieval. It doesn't matter. I just pinged their frequencies, so a few should be here soon. I have some troubling news, though, if you haven't seen the reports." Her brows pinched together. "Alexander Dare is missing. He shut off his links, even to the combat mages. We think the Department might have gotten him."

"Unfortunately," Constantine drawled without looking up. "Not so much."

"He's with us," I confirmed, crossing the arm that wasn't holding anything across my chest as if it could save me. "We couldn't use magic. I guess he shut down that system. Not that he's a robot—I mean, he's good at control—I'm not, but I promise to try not to end the world again—but not a robot, and he knows how to save up, and he had to use some of it to save Const—"

"Darling."

"Right," I cleared my throat. "Anyway, he's with us."

Olivia stared between the two of us, then she looked slowly around the space she could see in the warped view of the glassy ball. I raised and tilted my palm, and I could see when she finally spotted him.

I pulled my cupped palm back to rest against my stomach. "The three of us are...on the run?" I said, still unable to make statements without question marks when I knew they would disappoint.

She focused back on me. "No."

"Yes?"

"No. In my reality, this type of thing doesn't happen."

That cracked a reluctant smile. "Yeah. It's, um, a little messed up."

"That's entirely unfair, darling. I haven't killed him yet."

"Dare's going to bring you more trouble," Olivia said, as if she too understood that volatility was more perilous than cold dislike.

"You know, Price," Constantine said, leaning back even more, his roiling emotions calming more than they had in hours. "I think, someday, I might not dislike you."

"Whatever, Leandred. If I could peel you away from Ren, you'd already be sticking to a waste receptacle somewhere."

"Likewise."

For a moment, they both felt oddly serene and in entire accord.

I could feel Axer doing the mental equivalent of an unamused eye roll, and I sent him a feeling of concordance.

Olivia pinned me with her gaze again. "What happened two days ago? I know only what I've seen reported—which might as well be the screams of terrified Tremming rats—and what I got from your tracker." She watched me as she said it, reading into every twitch and wince I displayed.

"Stavros taunted me about capturing the Awakening mages, then about my brother, I got angry, tried to kill him, didn't succeed, tried to end the world, Kaine ate the praetorians." I rubbed the back of my neck. "The Origin Book—"

"Kaine ate the praetorians?" Her gaze went to Constantine's for confirmation. "The news said you killed them. There's blurred footage."

Blurred footage of you trying to end the world, she didn't say.

I rubbed my hand along my throat. "No. Kaine ate them, like Raphael ate Kaine."

"I want memory balls of everything," Olivia said, posture tense. Raphael mentions made her tense, too, but for different reasons than Constantine. I decided against mentioning that he was probably a few dozen yards away. And that he had maybe helped us for unknown reasons.

No, silence was probably best here.

"Footage, Ren. Kaine eating." She made a tense motion.

I shuddered as I pulled the memories to the front of my mind. After trying a few things, I could shoot miniaturized representations around the hologram in my palm. Axer reached over my shoulder and touched the magic, pulling a duplicated thread before moving back. Olivia looked at her own copies with an expressionless face, then carefully put them into a box to revisit.

"I don't know what Stavros and Kaine are doing"—it had kept me up thinking about it—"but the praetorians—"

"Will surely show up again, somewhere else, pieced together in an even more horrific fashion," she said grimly.

Golems of shadow and malice pieced around human flesh instead of clay. I shuddered again. "Kaine said something about being an Elite soon."

Axer stiffened mentally in concert with Olivia's body. I grimaced. I had obviously forgotten to retell that part.

"He said that?" she demanded.

"Yes."

She grimaced. "Origin Elites are mages capable of manipulating existing Origin Magic in small amounts. The Triumvirate, the ones who handle

Origin Magic tweaks for the Second Layer, are all Elites. There are five in the Department currently—three handling the magic at any one time—mages who fix and tweak the layers. Think of them as people who apply Band-aids and ointments versus you, a surgeon. They are highly regulated and tracked. It is not a position one seeks lightly. The Equilibrium Society...”

She tapped a finger against her lower lip. “Let me do some digging. The society isn't pleased right now, and are tentatively putting you back on the hit list, but knowing that Kaine is trying to become an Elite might change their tactics. The Praetorian Guard, destroyed, was enough to move a segment of public view against you. But if we could blame it on the soulless Shadow Mage who seeks to control the layers—”

Will, Neph, Asafa, Patrick, Loudon, and Dagfinn stumbled into the room. Relief fully bled through me. Neph dove toward Olivia, fingers curling around hers on the viewing ball and I clutched mine closer to me like it had physical form.

“Delia, Mike, Lifen, Kita, the others?” I asked desperately, using my shoulder to carefully dab away the paint that suddenly formed at the corner of my left eye.

"All accounted for," Saf said gently. "They'll be here soon."

"Brilliant." Loudon breathed out the word, like they had run a long distance and he was still catching his breath. "You had it. I could see it—the end of the world. I couldn't stop smiling as they ques—"

Will elbowed him sharply. "Sorry we were detained, but we are here!" Will's smile was a little too bright. "The others will be here soon, too."

"Detained how?" I frowned, unease turning into something else. "Who questioned—?"

"What did you find, William?" Olivia asked him briskly, cutting me off.

Loudon gave me a double thumbs up, pointing at his grin and some mark on his arm. Then mimicked electrocution, tousled curls shaking.

"They tortured you?" I asked in a too-high voice.

"What? No!" Will's eyes were too wide though. "Marsgrove would never let that happen on campus grounds. They simply threa—"

"With a baton!"

"Put fifty thousand munits on the guy with the scar," Patrick murmured to Asafa, and only because of their position behind Olivia, could I hear it. "Open market hit. I don't like what he said about Givens' and Tasky's families."

I started shaking. Constantine immediately put his knee against mine and I felt a giant pull from the combined force of his connections through me—magic that seemed to have grown since his forced refusal to use it these past days few days.

Will stumbled over his words. "We still don't know how the Department Awakened one mage, no less twelve at the same time, but we did gather data. A lot of data. Ren, you can't imagine the data. I've been luxuriating in it for days, the numbers—"

I started to collapse the ball.

"Tasky, shut up," Patrick said abruptly, walking into the front of the viewing frame, eyes narrowed in on me. "Crown," he barked.

Neph put a hand on Will's arm and I watched numbly as the rest jostled each other with hissing whispers.

"Crown, I'm only going to repeat this once," Patrick said.

"I'm a danger to everyone. I know. I want you all to disavow me," I said sharply.

Patrick smiled tightly. "And if you don't listen," he said deliberately, as if I hadn't interrupted. "Then I will magically reinforce it." I felt a twist along our distant connection.

"Campus has to be freaking ou—"

"Campus knows that though you do stupid things you are not hunting ferals to kill them and steal their magic, as per the Department party line. Campus knows that there is something rotten happening in Stavros's playpen. Campus remembers quite bloody well how he tried to kill all of us to get to you. Campus remembers that you saved us twice."

"Okay okay." My breath was coming in panicked waves. Neph looked like she was gripping the viewing ball so hard she was trying to figure out a way to dive inside. Her fingers were scrabbling, like she couldn't figure out how to get to me. "Silent support! But you don't need to—"

"We are in this together," he said darkly. "My stupidly thick connection lines tell me that this will be my grandest adventure—maybe the end of the world as Ludes wants, maybe the saving of it for the Queen. The bonds and ties of community, something bigger than all of us. You can want to keep us out of it all you want—we will defy you."

Olivia stepped back into the front of the view. "You leave us out, we'll just do it on our own, but without your aid or protection. How do you feel about that, Ren?" Olivia said, voice steady, connection lines visibly pulsing with Patrick's next to her.

"Manipulated."

Constantine's dark satisfaction nearly overwhelmed me for a moment, drowning out all else.

"Then we feel similarly on this." Olivia showed a bit of teeth. "But since we are coming at it from the same protective angle, let's let it pass without apology and move on, shall we?"

"People are going to die," I whispered, but let the connections in—a jumble of emotion. "I don't want—"

"None of us do, and yet, we all understand that if the underbelly of the Department gets their hooks into you, death might be the best outcome. The public might be hoodwinked by the head of the Department right now, but we haven't been so fortunate."

No one said anything for a long moment. Neph bent her head over the viewing ball and I felt mine tip toward hers in aching reflection.

"So..." Will cleared his throat. "The Department targeted particular areas of the First Layer—close antipodean points, all—with a goal in mind. Not a good one. Something to note after a good long look at the data; it is possible that you may have saved the world by breaking it completely and resetting it."

Olivia frowned. "Send me that data. Few will swallow the idea, but I'll get it to Bailey."

Will nodded furiously, tapping something on his arm.

"The Origin Book saved the world," I murmured, touching my pocket. "Not me."

Will looked up, and his gaze softened at something he read on my face or in my voice. "I'm sorry."

Next time the sacrifice would be me. I'd make sure of that. Neph's head popped up, expression fierce.

"One of the Awakened mages in their custody is still alive," Will said gently, touching the back of Neph's hand in the way that I had seen her do to him a hundred times, without taking his gaze from me. "Rosaria Ricardo."

My breath hitched. The faces of the other mages flew through my mind's eye. I could feel them, my magic clinging to them in some form still, though I couldn't locate them.

"Two others I touched are still alive, too," I said.

"Ren..." Will trailed off, looking at me worriedly. Neph clasped her hand over his, and they gripped them together. "The Department displayed the bodies of the feral mages they captured aside from Rosaria, claiming all of them dead by your hand."

Rage blew through me, but I grabbed it and held it instead of letting it have its way. With the faces of my friends in front of me, I clasped the edges of the supportive emotions that Constantine was feeding me from them and let those fill me instead. Then I examined the rage, understood that it was there, and let it settle to a simmer under a shell of hard acceptance.

Constantine stared at me in shock.

I looked around the sphere in my palm, charting expressions. The grimness in Olivia and pain in Neph and Will stood out most starkly, while sadness, high-strung anticipation, or darkness swirled in the others.

"The Department is lying," I said calmly. "At least about the two I touched."

Will nodded quickly in solidarity, eyes soft. "I believe you. They can say whatever they want about the others, but they couldn't publicly get away with saying Rosaria was dead. Reporters were on scene by the time you pushed her there and they saw her arrive alive—they showed it on live feed."

"Good," I said, a bit relieved.

"However..." Will rubbed the back of his neck, a sure indication of more bad news. "The Department is saying Rosaria will expire by the weekend due to the core magic injuries she sustained during the Mass Awakening."

"Likely so they can sweep her under the rug and take her to wherever they've taken the others," Dagfinn muttered. "Then to Villain Plan Next: Grab More."

"And we still haven't figured out how they do the activation." Will shook his head. "I still don't know—"

"Stavros knows how to use Origin Magic," I said, flexing my fingers. "Maybe even without his Triumvirate casting it. And he is using mine."

I could see them exchanging loaded glances.

"We can't handle twelve more Awakenings," Will said quietly. "Without your direct involvement, we couldn't have handled the five we managed. And elite squads in multiple countries have pledged to help—they are flexing their muscles in anticipation of you returning to the field."

Part of me pulsed, wanting to flex my own.

"Stavros whittles each new plot to a sharper edge and we scramble," Will said.

A step ahead. I thought of Raphael's smile. I thought of Dagfinn's muttered comment. I thought of all the pieces we had in play, and all the pieces that were still to be placed by Stavros and sacrificed.

"We don't scramble anymore. We let new Awakenings go," I said. I swallowed down the sacrifice as invisible pieces were knocked from a newly visible board.

Both Constantine and Axer stilled, then their emotions split in opposing directions. Coiled anticipation, battle lust, and overwhelming approval from Axer, unease and an even frailer hope emanating from Constantine.

Olivia drew in a sharp, alarmed breath and I felt her tugging at our threads, so far away. "Ren—"

"And we don't free Rosaria."

The not so invisible piece hurt even more. Constantine's frail tendrils of an emotion I didn't often feel in him grew in strength. The emotions from Excelsine were a steady drumbeat of alarm and panic.

"Ren—"

A step ahead.

"Stavros has us on the run. And he'll keep us here. We can't play to two tunes." I let the emotions come and coil—shame, anguish, guilt. I felt Axer prowling behind me. I let the coil change to acceptance.

Determination.

I blocked out all of them and let the magic flow from me in patterns that turned into painted visions in the air. Like a facsimile of the walls of my room before their destruction, figures fought in the air, lab creations were made, and creatures rose up.

"We need to make our own composition." I plucked Liam's musical notes from the ether and the drums of a battle hymn began. "We go after the labs. We figure out what Stavros is doing with the Awakened mages and their magic."

Save the boys' reputations by exposing Stavros's... Save the rest by putting down the monster before he could hurt them. I tapped my arm, eyes mechanically locked on Christian's bracelet—mended by Will so long ago in an enduring sign of heart and friendship.

"We use the data we gather," I said, swirling the painted air into new patterns. "We find the already Awakened ferals—lying in a cell or on a slab somewhere—we root out Stavros's plan, then we wipe him from the board."

"Ren—" Olivia's voice cracked. "You—"

"Stavros knows how to trap Origin Mages," I repeated evenly. "And the world knows the danger I pose. My firestorm has come." I looked at Axer. "Running is no longer an option. I will be running for a long time, unless I fight for my freedom now."

And for theirs, for they were tying their freedom to mine.

I felt Axer move.

I felt Constantine's frail hope—whatever it had been—crash and burn, consumed by an amalgamation of emotions so chaotic and thick, that I couldn't separate them.

"You still have a choice, and despite your lovely words and support, which I will always treasure,

I urge you to divorce yourself from me. Things will only be getting worse from here on out. This life has always held an end for me," I murmured. "My freedom has been a ticking clock from the moment I saw magic spark."

Olivia's expression drew itself into argumentative lines. "Ren—"

"What I do with it before...that is what matters."

"Before what?" Olivia asked sharply.

Rosaria, Samuel, the girl looking to the stars...their images wavered in my palm, no longer blank names on a page. Anger wove together with an inexorable need. Constantine's knuckles were white.

"Before the end," I said quietly. "I'm going to find the ferals. I will expose what Stavros is doing to them. And I will take him down."

"Absolutely not," Olivia said. "I won't allow it."

Some of the overwhelming tension in Constantine released.

Axer stepped from behind me, sliding into the frame like a panther about to strike. "Don't you wish her to be the cat, Price?"

Constantine stiffened again—so severely, that the magic keeping the others in view wavered for a second.

"Shive! Is that Dare?" Patrick asked, reflecting the shock I could see on the rest of their faces.

Olivia's throat worked. "I wish her to be neither animal in such a scenario. Stavros will never be the mouse."

"Then let her be the dragon," Axer said with a glitter in his eye.

Protecting my hoard. Home, protection, need.

I didn't have to ask, but my gaze sought Axer's. He tipped his head and I felt his answering emotion. He was absolutely on board.

All emotion from Constantine went terrifyingly blank, and the view of the Bandits disappeared as he crushed the magic in his palm and rose from his chair.

Chapter Fifteen

THAT WHICH IS UNBEARABLE

"**W**HAT ARE you doing?" Constantine asked coldly.

I rose to face him. "We can't live like this." He was flush with health now, but I could still see the underlay of gray that had been crushing him.

"What, in a garden of bounty?" He waved his hand angrily around us.

"This is only temporary," I said softly. The vibrant greens were already starting to brown, the magic working free of the decomposing elements and lifting to re-energize us.

"You were already working on how to recycle it. It will be easy with you now inside to figure it out." He grabbed some of the magic and twisted it into a vicious looking flower.

My view grew watery. "It has nothing to do with the recycling. It's only a matter of time before the engineers break through. And as soon as the dome is breached from the outside, the magic will cease to exist in this manner."

"They aren't breaking through your creation."

I winced.

"Ren," Constantine said, voice dangerously dark. "Did you give those scientists a way in?"

I winced harder. "For when the dome would eventually be activated... Of course, I put something in to allow it."

He cursed, then cursed again. "Get rid of it. Right now."

"I can't. I set it up to be free of my control." Like I had with the compound.

Constantine looked like he was contemplating murder again.

"We will not be here when they break through, I have a protection for that, just like with the compound," I said quietly. "I would never have allowed you in here otherwise. But we can't stay here. And hiding doesn't stop the Department from kidnapping and killing people, or from them herding us to them like sheep."

"So instead of running to the First Layer, where you have some modicum of advantage in saving your ferals, you are going to run to the Second Layer, into the belly of the Department's facilities, and save them there?"

"Saving them at their Awakening was a Band-Aid." Saying it hurt, but made it no less true. "I need to stop the root of the attacks themselves."

Constantine started laughing, and I felt Axer shift into a more alert position. "We just spent the better part of two days running away from anyone with enough firepower to capture an Origin Mage. Anyone who can put together a team is coming after us—special forces, mercenaries, bounty hunters, pirates, brigands. You are vomiting paint like it's exhaled air. This dome is going to collapse at any time, and you want to enter one of the most secure facilities in the Second Layer—a layer that is trying to lock down on your magic before taking you in for testing?"

I swallowed. "Yes."

Constantine was suddenly looming over me, his palm pressed to my chest with magic. "Do you remember this?"

A deep bone-numbing emptiness invaded me; cold feelings of darkness, rage, and certainty that weren't mine spreading through my chest making it hard to breathe.

Axer ripped his hand away from me, fingers digging into Constantine's wrist, and though he immediately tried to shake him off, Constantine never looked away from me.

"Do you remember that?" he demanded.

"I remember," I said stiffly. I couldn't look at Axer as I recalled Stavros's feelings of pleasure and triumph when he used me to kill him. "You know I haven't forgotten."

"Then why in the hell would you—"

"Christian was killed in this sadistic game that Stavros is running. That Raphael and Kaine are playing. Rosaria killed her own brother during her Awakening. Because the Second Layer is run by an evil man who made certain that when she Awakened, she did so violently. And each newly

Awakened mage, as well as every citizen in every layer, is in danger as long as he has power."

Constantine shook free and leaned in toward me again, his handsome face contorted. "Stavros is going to take you and he will change you into something else. And there is nothing I will be able to do to save you."

I looked up at him. "He won't stop at me, Con. Something worse is coming. Maybe more mass Awakenings. Maybe the collapse of the First Layer. Maybe by me, even." I looked at my hands. "I have power. I have might. I have the will to drive out the enemies of those I love. And I will not be stopped in that. They aren't wrong—those who claim I'm dangerous. I am. I have emotions just like anyone else and I make mistakes. But my mistakes can be world ending. It's my fault the ferals were taken."

"And you think that going after him will fix anything? He wants you to go to him. He's baiting you. He is flushing you out."

"Flushing me out, boxing me in. It doesn't matter. This affects more than me, and I'm behind. I've been behind, playing catch up, since my brother sparked lightning between his palms. I'm not waiting for Stavros's next maneuver. I'm not waiting to pick up the pieces."

I couldn't. The pieces were too painful. Moving forward, moving ahead, was the only way to stop the shattering.

"You will be caught. You have almost been caught each damn time."

The dried leaves around us caught fire. Guard Rock jumped upward. The cat vaulted and caught him midair in its teeth. They landed beyond the ring of flames. Smoke curled from Constantine's fingertips, furious sparks firing his brown eyes.

I smothered the flames licking the edges of the garden with a swipe of my palm. "So have you. How many times did you travel between Excelsine and the compound? How many trips did you almost not complete because you were nearly caught?"

"No one cares about me. You get caught by Stavros and you won't be you anymore," he bit out, then laughed bitterly, stepping back. "But you are going to do this regardless of what I say. I can feel the strength of the thoughts running through your mind. I'm going to lose you, too. Out one day, never to return."

"That's not—"

"I let you in." He reentered my space, as if he could do nothing else. "I let you get close, so I could get closer to Verisetti. Stupid."

"And here I thought my power was half the draw," I said evenly.

"Your stupid sense of loyalty. Your stupid trust. Your brilliance. You are my weakness. And I thought I had gotten rid of those." He laughed bitterly, but not before his gaze slid to his roommate who was standing stiller than still. Looking at Axer only seemed to make Constantine angrier, though. He turned back to me, more furious. "And all these shivits are going to follow you gladly. They are going to let you die. Be taken to the basement, be implanted with something not-Ren. Become nothing of the person you are. Gone. Left. Leaving."

He stepped away. "Everyone leaves," he said, tone abruptly detached from his emotions.

And I could feel an old reaction from him—his emotions trying to curl around and sever the heavy, girded ties between us. Leaving first before someone could leave him.

But he stepped physically closer again, as if he couldn't bear to do it.

I took a step into him and grabbed his cheeks with both hands, forcing his head down. "I'm not going anywhere." I gave him a shake, then let my fingers mirror the same motions that he had done to me days before, repeating the same sentiment back. "That's what you said to me. I'm not going anywhere either."

He looked down at me, motionless. "You will have no choice. Just like you do with the ferals, with your brother, with your friends—you take on the struggles of those you hold dear and leave nothing for yourself."

"I have to stop whatever Stavros is doing," I said quietly, without releasing him. "The world depends—"

"I. Don't. Care. About. The world." He ripped away from me.

"But I must. It—"

"If you say it's your duty, I swear this dimension will no longer remain standing," he said savagely. "And you." He spun, transferring his anger to Axer, who was watching and listening. "You are encouraging her. You are willing to let her die in some quest to save humanity. Just like you are always willing to do."

"She can't be hidden, Constantine, no matter what either of us do."

I wiped the side of my mouth, removing the paint I couldn't swallow down.

Constantine's magic worked for a moment in the way that said he was planning to do something harmful with it.

The only tell was the slightest stiffening of Axer's jaw muscles. "Yes, I already know how you feel."

"You know how I..." Constantine struggled with it for a moment, before pulling his arm back and propelling a ball of sickly gray at him. Axer caught it, drained it, and formed the nucleus into a bright blue ball of coiled energy. He let it drop and it burst into a liquid on the ground. The liquid surged forward until it reached Constantine, then ran straight up his body and made him pulse with life.

This only seemed to enrage him more.

Axer seemed aware of the consequences of his action, as his body arrayed in the lines that prefaced battle. "Someone needs to remove Stavros. You know it must be done. She will never be safe until he's gone. You can feel the way the world is turning. Your father knows it, too. Something terrible has been brewing."

"Not her," Constantine hissed. "You. You go after him with your bloody mother."

Axer's jaw ticked. "You know that isn't enough."

"I won't let it happen."

"You can't stop it."

"Stop what? Her becoming a fugitive? The face of death? Too late. That carpet has flown. This is about far worse things. They'll kill all that is her. They'll never let her live—not as anything other than a vacant puppet locked away in a cage."

"Then we break the cage. Like we were unable to do before."

A tree uprooted behind Axer and flew faster than I could process. I threw up a hand to stop it, but my magic only succeeded in stripping layers of bark, one after another—the inner particles breaking free each time with force beyond my anticipation—the center of the magic not stopping until a thin dagger of core wood hovered a foot from the back of Axer's head, held there by his own magic without movement from his hands.

"You won't have your protections anymore, if you kill me now," Axer said tightly, staring at Constantine instead of turning to address the imminent death hovering inches from the back of his neck.

Constantine pulled, and the particles wavered in the air, coming closer to Axer's neck. Axer's fingers came up—the only thing showing his strain.

"Fuck you, Alexi." Constantine was shaking and pale, magic vibrating from him oddly. Once more, the tangled ball of connections running through him pulsed.

"You can barely stand," Axer murmured. "How do you think this will work? You can't keep this up."

"I will be able to soon."

"By doing what? Sacrificing yourself? To do what? Hide her away? To deny her free will and yourself a life?"

Constantine gave an ugly laugh and the wooden dagger moved an inch closer. "Deny her free will? This from you? Who denied us both?"

"Yes. A mistake at thirteen that I won't repeat at twenty." The words were heavy with meaning.

The wooden dagger dropped, and Constantine took an uneven step backward, eyeing Axer like he was a venomous snake who had just said he would cut out his own fangs. Whatever was between them, it seemed to include the ability to detect truth from lie.

Constantine took another step backward, keeping us both in view like he was preparing for an inevitable strike.

Axer stepped sharply around him. "You trusted me once more. You said so, in our room."

"Because I have to trust you. You are what she wants."

"Not all that she wants," he said, again scenting blood. "And I don't think you are being truthful."

Constantine turned abruptly on his heel. "I will go along with this stupid plan, because I can't bear doing otherwise. Stavros, Kaine, or Verisetti will get her over my dead body." He started forming the magic to connect to Excelsine again. "But I know how this will end."

For once, his inner and outer feelings were mirrored, lining up directly as truth.

We reconnected to Olivia and the others, all of whom looked like they'd had their own tense discussion.

"You disconnected," Olivia said to Constantine, gaze piercing.

"Minor blip in the magic," he said languidly, shrugging and giving every visual indication that nothing else had happened. "Everything is shored up now."

Olivia looked at me and I shook my head. Her eyes narrowed further. "You are fully committed to this plan?"

"Yes."

I needed to get evidence on Stavros. I needed the boys to be able to return to their lives free of my taint. I needed my friends who were supporting me to be able to do the same.

She nodded. "We discussed options while you were having your minor 'blip.' We are all fully committed." She looked at me sharply as I started to respond. "We are doing this, Ren."

"Okay," I whispered. I looked at Will. "Will, you said you know where Rosaria is. Why can't I locate her, even though I can feel her?"

I let my magic slip out again, but it felt like a skate slipping too fast over ice I wished to look through.

Will looked furtively between Olivia, Constantine, and me. "She's in the highest security ward in Crelussa Sanitarium," he said, sounding apologetic. "That's why you can't locate her."

Patrick shuddered.

"She'd have been given a nullifying cell, too," Delia said darkly.

I lifted a reference article to Crelussa Sanitarium from my bracelet. It was a high security facility that processed Awakening mages from across the Second Layer. Run by the Department, it catered to a broad spectrum of mages. It wasn't the only place to Awaken, but it was by far the largest.

Will raised a brow and sent a schematic zooming around. I sent him a grateful look—he'd already had this at hand, knowing what I'd choose—then looked at the design.

"So, we're doing this?" Dagfinn asked tentatively.

"They'll expect us," Axer said, looking over my shoulder. "And if we destroy anything while freeing her, it will look to the world like a terror plot."

"I know," I murmured.

My tone must have indicated a signal, because Dagfinn started excitedly punching codes into the air, fingers flying like a conductor directing an invisible score, and Patrick, Loudon, and Asafa high-fived.

"The highest security programs, in a known facility. Finally, a challenge," Dagfinn said with relish.

On the other side of the connection, the others leaned in and immediately began offering suggestions and knowledge of the building and wards.

"You can't use your magic there," Axer murmured to me. "The risks..."

"I understand."

Fury suddenly drowned Constantine's other emotions, and even his carefully crafted facade couldn't withhold the expression.

Olivia watched it all without comment, expression on the verge of cracking into something that wasn't as dignified.

Her lips pinched together. "This is a terrible time to do this."

"There will be no good time," I said quietly. "Sometimes...sometimes I think you just have to do what you can with the time at hand."

"We could let the Dares do it. I know they have plans beyond this," she said darkly, glaring at Axer. "He wouldn't be there with you otherwise. And the combat mages have gone suspiciously silent since his disappearance—saying they can't help because the amount of scrutiny they are under would only harm any plans we have. They are all plotting something."

I could feel Axer's amusement, dark and molten beside me, even with all the emotions stirred by his argument with Constantine still beneath.

"You know I won't, Liv."

She watched me, grim-faced, then glanced at the thread connecting her to the school. "Marsgrove won't let me leave. He has every legal right and ability until break to make me stay."

"I know," I said, not even trying to contain the relief. "And I'm glad. I want you to be as safe as you want me. All of you. But...I can't stay safe."

I couldn't come home. Not yet. But I could find a way.

Pain rolled through her expression. Because she understood the same thing I did—all ways led directly through Stavros.

She took a deep breath. "Fine, then. An assault on a creepy sanitarium run by hundreds of Department mages, it is!" she said with a grimness that didn't befit the exclamation. "William, send everything we have. Ren is on the run, forces arrayed against her, checkpoints set up on all ports—"

Dagfinn rubbed his hands together. Asafa cracked his knuckles.

"—and her magic the most recognizable in the world now, with one of her companion's just a hair behind. Sounds great!"

I cringed at her tone.

Olivia pinned Constantine with her most intense gaze, and her expression morphed into something almost like worry when he said nothing. She looked at me and I slowly shook my head again at the question there.

Her gaze switched harshly to Axer. "Don't let us down, Dare."

"I'm not one of your minions, Price."

"Excellent. I've been told I can't kill those."

Chapter Sixteen
PLOTTING

ON THE CLOCK as we were, it took us most of the morning to gather information and start to prep.

A large topographical hologram splayed around us. Axer methodically shifted it smaller and larger, while walking around it.

"Mountain fortress. Guarded by five ward fields. Mostly meant to keep people in rather than out."

"Because no one in their right mind would go there unless someone made them," someone groused.

Axer reached over and tapped the schematic. "But easily accessible by non-magic means. They have a sophisticated notification system, but if we can start in the interior of the first field, we'll have no problem manually scaling the mountain. Entering the facility isn't the problem, leaving it quietly is."

I stared at the path he was drawing with his finger up the lengthy side of a steep cliff. "Easily? What in the world do you think that word means?"

"You'll be fine."

"You've been looking at this schematic for like, zero minutes," I said. He had looked over everything, lightning-fast, and zoned in on the maddest entry route, then moved onto interior defenses and blueprints. "Maybe, you know, maybe there's another way in that doesn't involve our bodies being scraped from the valley below."

"There are lots of ways in," he said with a small smile. "The door from the east, with its hundred-warded security, would take the three of us about an hour to crack, but we'd already have two dozen guards on us and the alarms raised by minute two. The tunnel from the sixth basement level, is a possibility, but it is protected by a magic generator that would attach and subdue us. We could get around it with the proper preparations—precautions that would take us a minimum of two days to create."

His finger pulled down the schematic. "The loading docks have half a dozen points of entry, but are highly secured and actively monitored by three different towers. Their sole job is monitoring authorizations. Guards are constantly looking for unauthorized people and shipments coming through. They have defenses specifically made to target Port Mages, and your magic is too comparable to take that chance. We could get past the electrical substations with little trouble on the third shift change in twenty hours, but that leaves us too little leeway on time."

His finger stopped and tapped the first path again. "This route takes the least amount of time and magic. Both of which we can't afford to waste. I won't let you fall."

Everyone was silent around us.

We had figured out how to get simulated holograms working again for a limited time, by linking through the worms I had brought with me to populate the city. Of all the things I would have thought to use, worms weren't even in the top hundred on the list.

Axer had picked one up during the discussion on reinvigorating communications and Dagfinn had gone silent, then nodded reluctantly.

"Worms leave trails in the earth," was all Dagfinn had said before he'd gotten the system up and running.

It never paid to forget that Axer was an elite combat mage, and what that meant for the quickness of his mind and decision-making skills.

"Did you just...seriously glean all of that from the schematics in ten minutes?" Patrick asked, voice subdued.

The smiled slipped from Axer's face and he was looking at Patrick like he did pretty much anyone who wasn't in his intimate group. "Yes."

"All of that—"

"Infiltration training and commercial warding aren't exactly non-standard arts. Crelussa isn't a military campaign that will take weeks to plan and put in place. How do you think we fight on the field?" Axer answered, somewhat impatiently, when the others still looked doubtful. "By sitting down and strategizing? You either train yourself to notice openings quickly, to pinpoint all the exits and threats, or you die painfully, repeatedly. Disemboweling curses are love taps in training."

No one said anything, then a muttered, "And you say I'm the dark one."

"You want to debate military campaign strategies," Axer said, piercing Patrick with his gaze. "Then start looking at how to get around triple-weave security. Because I guarantee we will run into it down the line."

I stared at the mountain path again. "Magic carpet?" I asked hopefully.

He flicked a finger against my unbound wrist, making the magic beneath ripple. "Too much magic."

I grimaced.

"How do we get to Crelussa from here?" I searched my knowledge of travel and layer magic. Getting inside the first field would probably be as easy as letting Constantine have at it, but getting to the site required travel, and we were strapped by time and secrecy. A new portal pad was out, even though Will had two more.

"Priority Five is still being hotly debated, but the Department has most layer transportation locked down and your signatures have been entered into the system as Class Five felons." Will looked regretful. "Ports won't work. And the bounty..."

"Right. Everyone is looking for us. People smarter than us, too."

Will straightened. "I wouldn't go that far."

"People with more experience."

He blew out a breath. "People with setups already in place. Give us a few years and we'll be unstoppable. But right now, we are still in Bandit beta mode. Our devices, wards, and machinations work, but we have holes everywhere—especially in security and cloaking."

"We have Alexander Dare." I thumbed at him.

"And his magic is being tracked as hard as yours is," Olivia said pointedly. "He has amassed quite a following in a short amount of time who want to be the ones to say they brought him down."

I looked at Axer, whose eyes glittered in anticipation. I grimaced. "Great."

"I feel crushed that no one is directly after me," Constantine said laconically. "I'll have to try harder."

Olivia looked at him without humor. "You've got your own personal fan club of a type that makes it worse. Ren has the government, Dare has the adrenaline junkies, and you have the bounty hunters."

Constantine narrowed his eyes. "Ren's bounty is the highest."

"No. The Department is offering bounties on each of you, but they are a pittance compared to the personal one that your father placed on you. Twenty million munits and a lot of political favor to the person who returns you to him intact."

Constantine's expression closed.

"Ren and Dare are off limits for a return of any kind. But you might get out of this with permanent house arrest. Your father is your greatest weapon." Will said it earnestly, as he did all things, not noticing or feeling the way Constantine or Axer stiffened.

"How fortunate," Constantine replied with his own glittering gaze.

"This personal discussion is riveting and all," Delia said, looking between everyone darkly. "But I know a secure way to get from the Third Layer to the Second only five miles from Crelussa. A water mirror—a natural doorway—part of the underground movement when plans were less...political. My source also mentioned that there is an entry path through the tunnels under the mountain Crelussa sits upon, but that the path is far less silent than what you need. But, one of the tunnels could be a possible exit route."

No one wanted to touch on how Delia had gotten that information with a ten-foot pole, or why a "source" had scoped out a high-status target in the Second Layer.

"Not that any of this will matter when Ren is caught in the middle of Crelussa Sanitarium," Delia said darkly. "And the two of you are tortured to get her to do what Stavros wants."

After Olivia and Constantine, Delia was the least excited about the scheme.

More than one person grimaced.

"We are in this until the end now. And the plan won't work without her," Patrick replied. He pointed to the boys. "And they go where she does."

"Could we bribe someone to do it?" Asafa said, rubbing his chin slowly. "A guard? Set up a device?"

Patrick shook his head. "The princess has to lay the spell. It's an unfortunate side effect of the whole gambit. She's got to key the girl's location into the layer. None of us have that ability. Origin Mage tricks." He shrugged.

"This is madness," Delia said bluntly. "They will be caught."

"Optimism! If it all goes tits up, we'll just have her flip the whole sanitarium somewhere else!"

"Let's do that now, then," Delia said darkly. "I know more than one person who would be thrilled to take that place down."

"Cutting the ties in that way would break part of the Second Layer's security system, which would be highly thrilling," Loudon said cheerfully. "Take the whole grid down, the good and bad. Instant chaos. I'm on board."

"No," Olivia said grimly.

Asafa tapped the schematic Dagfinn had pulled up. "The wards are tied together. People keep thinking of Ren as a bulldozer, when they should be thinking of her as a surgeon. Sure, she can take a sledgehammer to it, but there would be dire consequences."

"Getting back to the plan..." Olivia said pointedly.

"Right." Patrick clapped his hands. "They have a maximum of four hours in which to be in position—"

"Midnight tomorrow."

We all looked at Dagfinn, who was listening to simultaneous feeds from around the layer and painting the air with magic as he flipped between them.

"The Department is coordinating something at midnight tomorrow. The head of the press is sending notices, gathering people together to coordinate a statement at that time. The timing…"

"The Department is going to force Rosaria's 'expiration' from her injuries," I said grimly. "Make a show of it for the press."

"Or they are roping us in, so they can make a statement of capturing the three of you. It's a trap," Olivia said grimly.

"It's definitely a trap," Axer said, turning the schematic and setting up additional forces in strategic places. Our "chance meter" in the upper left key decreased slightly. "But it doesn't matter. We'll lose our opportunity if we don't successfully convert either Plan A or B. We can still do both."

"Or Plan C, where we all leave campus in a bloody burst of glory," Patrick said, "We can do a Five Man Act—"

"No," said four voices in concert.

Patrick frowned. "I've always wanted to do that one, with the Treacherous Don as a setup. I'd make a great one."

"Sure, Trick. In fact, let's just do all three of the nearly impossible trifecta while we're at it."

"Nearly imposs—"

"Can you get in with the press?" Will asked us, ignoring Loudon and Patrick as they started arguing in the background.

"No. Not without killing three of them, and I don't think that's the kind of count we want added to our tally at the end of this. We can use them as a distraction, though, if we cut it too close." Axer said absently as he moved magic around. "We'll need pretty tight communications."

Olivia turned briskly to Constantine. "We need to activate the device you gave Dagfinn."

Constantine tightened his lips, but gave a short nod, and walked to where we had stashed our supplies.

Will and Mike were debating signature blockers. "The heaviest magic signature blocker should go to Dare. No one is really questioning whether he can defend the three of them against an assault—pretty much any assault. Blocking his signature is the most important thing—he can field all the magic as they escape. Ren wears the cuff Dare brought since she can't be caught doing magic there."

"Hey!"

Mike turned to me. "You are just along to set the locator."

"No one thinks that I will be able to stop myself?"

"No," came the chorused reply.

I grudgingly sat back. "What about Constantine? He gets nothing? Why aren't you worried about him?"

"Leandred never uses magic without reason. He's not going to freak out and do magic because he experiences emotion. It's doubtful, anyway." Patrick shrugged. "Before you showed up, I would have told you he was dead inside. Maybe if you are dead or all of you are dying, he'll use magic, but at that point, we are past worrying about detection."

Expression bored, Constantine tossed a small device to Axer, ignoring everyone else. "Key yourself in."

Axer lifted it, his magic caressing the edges, seeking the spells inside. He said nothing for an extended moment. "You didn't think you'd be returning to campus again," he murmured. "When you left for Ravishkan."

Constantine said nothing.

"You didn't tell me."

"You'd have figured it out quickly enough," he said shortly. "She was going downhill."

I pointed at myself. "I'm right here."

Constantine's bored gaze connected to mine. "You were going downhill. When was the last time you spewed paint?"

"An hour ago. When was the last time you looked like you were wearing a full body gray mud mask?"

"Six hours, at least."

I touched the dirt and drew up a lotus. I tucked it into the crook of his elbow. "You have reason to be angry with me, and I'm sorry for it," I murmured. "But don't hurt yourself."

He looked at the flower then me, gaze bored, internals conflicted. The flower wasn't doing what it was supposed to do. I frowned at it, then on impulse pulled in a bit of Axer's magic and mixed it in.

Light immediately filtered over Constantine's skin. His expression didn't change, though the shock and panic beneath did.

"How do you look so bored but feel everything so strongly?" I asked, touching the flower and imbuing more mixed magic.

"Practice," he said, disengaging my fingers with some difficulty.

I watched him try to pretend to work again. "Will you forgive me for these choices?"

"Constantine Leandred doesn't let go of a grudge, didn't you know?" Axer said studying the interior blueprints again, keyed device on the table. "Not for anyone."

Well, there went the mixed conflict. Constantine's emotions straightened into a singular line.

"Most people aren't worth it," Constantine bit out. He turned to me. "Sacrifice someone to save yourself, then I'll forgive you."

I gave him my most unimpressed look.

"Sacrifice him." Axer thumbed at his roommate. "That's what he's planning anyway. Everyone wins."

"You'd like that plan," Constantine said darkly.

Axer didn't outwardly react. "And yet, you're still sitting there, intact."

"Yikes," I heard Saf mutter.

"It's like a telenovela. I need popcorn," Patrick whispered back.

"Shhhh!" Dagfinn sounded like he thought Axer was going to reach through and end them all.

A ping sounded above us and we all looked up. I winced.

"You need to stop allowing people ways to control your creations," Constantine said harshly at the reminder.

"No," I murmured. I walked to the edge and pressed my hand against the magic. Those outside were still many hours, days, away from cracking it, but they would. "I'm giving people ways to skirt around my magic in case someone else gains control of me."

He looked sharply at me. "You are plotting. You were already plotting."

"Preparing, Con. Preparing." I let my forehead rest against the barrier. "I, too, know how this will likely end."

I let my head tilt to look at Axer. "So, if we were doing a military campaign..."

He looked at me steadily. "I only said Crelussa wasn't one."

I nodded slowly.

"Great," I heard Mike mutter while Constantine started cursing. "Just great."

~*~

The media was playing the same news songs on loop. I hadn't missed listening to the news reports while traveling, and I much preferred the boys' selective updates. Still, it paid to be aware of what was happening, so Bellacia's favorite news spells were being put to work.

Thus far we had been correct to assume that the Third Layer would keep the news of the dome's activation under wraps. That didn't mean there weren't other things to report in the search for us.

"A joint task force has been formed linking the intelligence agencies of fifty countries in the Second and Fourth Layers with the Department and Citadel. The Fifth Layer has an active loop to capture any mage who enters. On advice from the Department, the Fifth Layer has closed its borders completely, though sources close to the Department worry that the Origin Mage will find a way to supersede those measures, if motivated. However, her age and inexperience give us hope that she will be brought down quickly."

Closed? I flexed my fingers.

"No." Axer didn't pause in the spells he was weaving on his cloak, but his magic briefly wrapped around me, then released. "Finding Stavros will be easier than subverting the Fifth Layer magics. One impossibility at a time."

Constantine shifted angrily, head bent over the eye lenses he was enchanting.

Excelsine was having a campus-wide, mandatory meeting on Top Circle, so the three of us were alone for the first time since Constantine had activated our communications, and so instead of having their chatter in the background, the news was repeating instead.

A reporter interlaced her fingers solemnly on the feed. "All but one of the feral mages have been killed in the Awakenings. Our layer—all layers—mourn the loss of lives just born to magic."

Axer extinguished all the feeds with a clenching of his fist.

"The other two..." I cleared my throat. "They are still alive." It was a sticking point for me. Stavros's thieves had switched tactics sometime after Bloody Tuesday. They'd started taking the Awakening mages alive.

Bloody Tuesday was the day Stavros had discovered me. It was in no way a coincidence.

But far too late for Christian. If only they'd taken him alive, if only there'd been no body to bury.

I closed my eyes tightly. Unhelpful thoughts. Forward—forward with what could be changed, and who could be saved. I thought of Bellacia's path. "If we can get recordings of what is happening—make people see—"

Axer shook his head. "Stavros won't admit his crimes on national newsfeed. Even the minuscule admissions you got for Bailey the first time in Corpus Sun aren't repeatable. Not with the defenses he has put into place."

"We could find a way around them."

"He doesn't make the same mistakes."

I chewed on my lip, fingers caressing the thin spine of a war abstract that had been in Frost Viper's apology gifts. "Maybe he could, though. If he thought he'd won."

Axer examined me closely, suddenly intent. "Do you know what would have to occur for him to think he's won?"

"Terrible things," I whispered.

"Nope," Constantine said, dripping a compound onto a rune-filled slide.

"Helpful," Axer said, pushing his cloak to the side, eyes still narrowed on me as he mentally worked new plans.

"At keeping her from being a mindless automaton?" Constantine carefully dropped three twigs into the cauldron, then twirled an unused stirring rod before folding the spun magic into the new mixture. "Agreed."

"I have to do the unexpected." I knew what that meant, in the abstract, in the same way I knew what sacrificing someone meant. Nightmares and unreality.

"Can you?" Axer asked.

"I don't know." I forced myself to maintain eye contact. "Maybe it's not a can. Maybe it's a must."

"Absolutely not," Constantine said blandly.

"The easy play isn't available," Axer answered ruthlessly, without looking at him. "It's all hard choices from here until the end."

"Oh, there are a few easy ones," Constantine said, far too pleasantly.

I tapped my pen against the table, mind churning over data. "My brother, and all those before him. All the Awakenings that have been covered up over the years, with the feral population dwindling to such a low as to be almost a myth at Excelsine. The hunter in Spartine Prison who killed Christian—he had orders. Those orders changed. He received both sets of orders. Maybe that's our in."

Constantine examined me—pushing aside the lenses he was crafting and giving up his pretense of not paying attention too. "Do you want to confront the man who killed your brother?"

Yes. No. Yes.

"That would...that would probably not help my rage problem."

He said nothing for a long moment, hiding his feelings deep beneath the lingering anger he was using to shield himself. "You dealt with it earlier, I noticed."

"Yeah, best not to push it by throwing my brother's murderer in the mix." I pulled a hand down my ponytail. "Besides, we are already breaking into a high security facility."

"What would be a second?" he asked in an entirely too off-handed way.

I closed my eyes, pushing aside the alluring thought of facing one of my brother's killers.

He leaned forward, eyelids dropping to shade half his eyes. "Revenge...I know its tune. I know its lure and bite. I know how it whispers in the midnight shadows. How you string it along to feel the teeth linger."

Axer's fingers tightened.

Constantine leaned back. There was still a lingering anger in the actions, but it was as if an avenue of revenge sated some of the bloodlust. "But as much as the old demon in me incessantly calls upon me to pull you down to my level—so much easier than traveling the opposite path—I wouldn't tempt you to follow this lure. I would deliver your revenge for you, should you desire it."

"What did Idami Senturten steal from Ren?" Axer asked grimly.

I looked at him in confusion.

"Who?" Constantine asked apathetically—gaze still on me, the smallest wave of dark satisfaction in the vibration of his emotions.

A sinking sensation settled in my chest. It was the type of response from Constantine that always meant he was to blame.

"If nothing else, you are consistent," Axer said grimly.

I only knew about Idami Senturten peripherally, but Delia relayed gossip like she was the only water bearer at an ultra-marathon, so I wasn't unaware of the talk surrounding the older girl. Idami had disappeared in disgrace before the end of winter term—in her last year at Excelsine—after an anonymous packet of devastating evidence had been given to the board revealing a plethora of illegal activities.

I also remembered passing her in Constantine's living room fall term during the first few weeks we had been working together.

"She used you?"

Irritation and, strangely, lazy satisfaction filled him. "As if I would let someone use me. Mutual use is an understanding."

"What did she do?"

I touched our connection threads, as if to look for non-physical wounds. He paused at the touch and some of his lingering anger drained, leaving a deep sadness behind. He patched the feelings up quickly with hauteur.

"She stole a dozen secret designs from students around campus, using her wiles, however few they were, to scam her way inside and copy, then profit from them." He twisted the ribbon around his fingers. "She went beyond the understanding we had and stole one of your designs that you left on the table. A doodle, not fully formed, but enough to sell after she realized its worth—and yours."

He wasn't even trying to be coy about turning her in anymore, his emotions all clogged up.

"Don't get revenge for me," I said quietly, answering both queries on the matter.

"Never fear." He smiled at the ribbon, head tilted back, eyes barely visible beneath suddenly heavy lids. "Revenge is a dish best served personally."

I watched him with unfocused eyes. I thought of all that I knew of Constantine's past. And of all the documentation that had appeared so suddenly—everywhere in the media in the last few days to prove that Constantine was my companion in terror.

"Revenge always has consequences," I murmured. And Bellacia had truly outdone herself.

"Sometimes the consequences are worth the satisfaction," Constantine said with a lazy smirk.

"And when does vengeance end?" Axer bit out, leaning back. He called his cloak to him and his clenching fingers mirrored his closed expression.

Constantine's emotions went dark. "When I say it does."

Axer began mending another intricate spell and laughed without humor. "Idami Senturten was one of many in the winter. And yet spring came, and you left Verisetti alive."

"A mistake I will rectify."

"Will you?" Axer's gaze settled weightily on his roommate. "Or will you turn from revenge again and make the choice to pursue other emotional paths?"

Constantine's emotions turned darker still. "What difference does it make to you?"

"It makes a lot of difference," Axer said quietly, returning to his work and leaving his roommate in tumult.

Hidden in a small copse of trees, I slid into the empty hologram after darkness set outside and within the dome, making certain I didn't carry any parts of Corpus Sun with me. Constantine had set the connection up for me, so I could call the Bandits without him being present.

He would not have done so if he knew who I was calling.

"Trying to end the world again. Tut, tut, lovely." Bellacia watched me from a reclined position, like I was the best cat toy in the store and she was contemplating its delicious destruction. "What were you thinking?"

I'd been carrying the negative certainty for hours, and wasn't going to discuss anything else first.

"You gave up Constantine," I said tightly. "They had Axer. But there was no evidence of Constantine's involvement. You provided it."

She smiled tightly. "And it gained us a stronger position. Our papers and feeds are back on top. Back in the saddle, in the middle of it all. And you need me there."

I clenched my teeth. "He's more than ruined. He'll be killed—or worse—if he's caught by Stavros." I didn't let her respond to that. "Is your bitterness satisfied, Bella?"

Her eyes flashed, but then she smiled. "I suppose it should be," she said tightly.

"You don't touch him again in revenge."

She didn't answer for a moment, then, "Fine."

I grabbed the vow from her, wrapping it around my pinky. "I will hold you to it."

"I know you will," she said, watching me speculatively beneath heavy eyelids.

I tucked the vow away. "I need to figure out how to clear Constantine and Axer. To separate them from me. How do I do that?"

Bellacia just laughed. "Clear them? No. Their fates are now tied intrinsically with yours. They will sink with you, or rise with you."

"There has to be a way."

"Hmmm....well, I suppose you could use the layer dynamics and impose a grid on all the layers to make people forget." She spun a finger cleverly in the air, cat eyes half-lowered and watching. "Force the public to your will."

I stared at her. "Tempting."

"No? But it will solve so many problems for you."

It might. Then again, mind magic had never been my forte. I might amnesia the entire planet or brain damage our entire species.

"I wouldn't know where to begin," I said.

"Oh,"—she sidled up to me—"I think you would.
Even if you needed a bit of...help. All those holes
in that pack of hunters' minds in December.
How exactly did their memories get erased?"

Constantine had done it. He had used my
magic and the suppression spell to modify their
minds.

Bellacia smiled slowly. "Won't you try it? For the
good of your lovers?"

"They aren't—" I took a deep breath. "No. I
will not. Besides, you'd keep a report of the
magic and blackmail all of us later." And that
wasn't even taking into consideration about all
the texts and tomes and books like Ori who
had living memories and couldn't be memory
wiped with a suppression spell. "I'll find a
way—another way—to clear their names."

"Good luck, lovely. Now what do you have for
me?"

I held out the recordings I'd made.

She took them, quickly soaking in the contents.
"Damaging, but Enton Stavros appears in none
of these."

"He's not stupid. He won't fall for that trick twice. He has a deliberate curse field against me—made of my magic—when I try to record him now. Or when Constantine tries. Everything goes to static. Or worse, it shows me doing something terrible instead, like a reverse perception."

"Are you doing worse?"

I shifted, and she narrowed in on the motion. "You aren't entirely blameless then," she mused, sharp eyes working. "And you think you will be ridiculed if you show the footage because you are pushing the lines of what is acceptable."

"I—"

She held up her hand. "Ren, my dear overpowered magelet, it's called editing."

"Right," I deadpanned. "Because you always have my best interests at heart."

Her laughter tinkled around me. "Come, give the other recordings to me," she wheedled.

"No. Can you use those?" I pointed to what I had given her.

She tapped them with her fingers. "I can release these in two of our smaller markets. But it's not enough. And dripping small pieces of information to the public is the death of true shock. Give me something big."

"The Department has secret labs."

She laughed. "Everyone knows that. Five of my competitors will sanction it as the only way the Department can combat you successfully. You will change no minds with that."

"Are you going to the event at Crelussa?"

Her eyes narrowed. "No. But one of our reporters will be on scene."

"The Department is manipulating the crime scenes and magic of the Awakenings—they have been collecting the magic for years, for purposes unknown. The girl they have at Crelussa is going to die precisely so the media can be silenced, and she can be moved."

"Your proof?"

"Well there are two choices as to who is Awakening them, and I'm not it," I said darkly.

"You want me to run with your word against theirs?" Dark humor drifted across her features.

"It's the truth."

Bellacia shrugged daintily. "The truth, it may be, but I can't spin it on just your word, especially now. The public needs safety, and you aren't providing it. You are a terrorist. Sympathy for the devil on the devil's word? I'll lose my credibility. And you need me to be credible—and against you—when the time is right. No one with brains believes you dead. But your disappearance has calmed some of the immediate panic. Try not to do anything stupid, but give me something more."

"You need me to record them killing magicist babies?" I said tiredly.

She leaned forward. "Get me the truth. Get me evidence of what Stavros is planning, and I'll slit his belly with the claws of the press."

Chapter Seventeen

THAT WHICH IS FREED

I ALLOWED the hologram to collapse and carefully made my way back to where the boys had set up our sleeping gear in a sandy, desert area under the stars. After two oaks had crashed and sprouted four tall saplings within an hour, then eight midsize trees, then sixteen sturdy giants—a copse growing at an abnormally accelerated rate—it had been a unanimous decision to avoid fertile ground for sleeping purposes. With the way the dome was evolving, it would be just our luck to be crushed by a palm or to have one sprout then stab right through someone's rib cage.

"You shouldn't trust her."

I jumped, hand going to my heart.

Axer was slowly rolling a ball of blue magic under his palm, while watching the Eta Aquarids' meteors fly in the mirrored sky.

"How long have you been awake?" I tried to slow my pulse as I sat between them.

"You aren't subtle." He gave me a look from the side of his eye. "And you weren't sleeping."

I looked up at the sky. "I am kept awake by the choices in my future as they stretch before me, dark and dangerous."

"Night is when all fears come to rest. In the silence of decisions made and choices yet to come," he said, a smile curling the side of his mouth. "Minor issues."

I looked down at Constantine splayed out on his front, one hand wrapped around the pillow he'd called into existence. The dark circles under his eyes were telling, but his features relaxed in sleep in a way that they didn't when he was feigning boredom. A gentle white noise spell was wrapped over him to aid rest, and I noticed that it wasn't of his own signature.

"I never thought Constantine would be the one fretting." He'd been wrapped in a barely coherent tension for weeks, really. The kindly placed sleep aid was possibly the only reason I wasn't in an oubliette right this second.

"He doesn't do fear well." Axer tossed the ball into his other hand and began the same hypnotic circles with it on the other side. "And he's exhausted. He's been trying to regulate your magic, pulling in dozens of threads and weaving them into yours—being your muse when your real one is far away, while not calling upon me but in the direst of circumstances."

"I know," I whispered. "I don't want—"

"If you think he's doing it out of a sense of misplaced guilt, you can curb that thinking. Constantine does what Constantine wants. And only that."

Bitterness coiled under his words.

"What's with you two?"

"Old story," he said dismissively.

"Funny, he didn't want to talk about it either when I asked."

He tapped a finger against his thigh. "I'm surprised."

"What, that Constantine doesn't share his secrets?"

"No. But this one would be a good play for him. I am the decided villain of the piece."

I watched him. "You were friends."

"Yes." The corners of his eyes tightened. "Our mothers were close—his mother was one of the few souls who sought friendship with mine. We spent our childhood attached at the hip. He Awakened within an hour of me. We shared adjoining cells, and magic can sometimes...bleed. Ours did. We were ecstatic. It was like a secret club none of the others on the island could join."

"We both had powers that needed to be hidden, but they ate at us, wanted to be used. We got into a lot of trouble. Wanted to do and experience everything." There was an almost wistful look on his face before it was wiped clean. "Simpler times."

I could see them in his mind's eye. Eleven-year-olds running around town together and getting into mischief with their newly-Awakened, powerful magic.

And then they spent their late teen years as enemies. I had thought on the cause before, but it seemed even more apparent now.

"You were at Salietrex with them."

He didn't say anything for a long moment.

"I was the reason we were there at all. An outing hastened by a stir-crazy boy and his ever-indulgent friend, and accompanied by said friend's even more indulgent mother."

I touched his shoulder. Christian and I had been out the night of his death because of his own shenanigans, but how many times had I cursed myself for not swaying him to stay inside? Wondered if I had been the one to have put us into the hunters' path that night...? It didn't bare thinking about.

"We were barely there an hour when terrorists took the city protections down."

"One of the ferals Verisetti was using was turning the people of the city against each other. Sashia had a lovely power. A softer mind magic. One that encouraged others to be better. In a less kind soul, such power could be a threat, but she was one of the kindest, softest souls I've ever met. People wanted to please her because they felt better about themselves and the world around them. Extremely empathetic—and the feral grabbed onto her right away. Flipped her mentally before we even knew what was going on. I grabbed Constantine who was trying to get to her."

His head tilted back, staring at the ceiling. "I've gone over that day with a fine-toothed mental comb. The number of small things that would have made a difference. Things I should have seen."

"If I had used my powers, I could have absorbed the powers of the mage that Verisetti was using to turn the people of the city into murderers, and maybe the other mage who was shielding them both." He turned the ball of magic over in his hand. "But instead I shielded Constantine—we had long ago combined our shields—when Verisetti turned his attention to us."

The ball moved in an overly-controlled circle over the planes of his chest. "He snapped her out of the mind control, for just a moment, and she used her last bit of free magic to convince

Verisetti's feral to flip us through the only exit, to safety. We never saw her again—outside of the feeds of the event, which they played repeatedly in the kind of detail that I'm certain Constantine has never forgotten."

I shuddered, thinking of how I would have reacted if I had seen the replay of my brother's murder. It wasn't pretty, and I'm glad I didn't have those memories.

"She saved you. Both of you. Instead of herself."

"Yes. Of course, she did." He closed his eyes. "She would have done nothing else."

"It's not your fault."

"There is no rationality on anyone's part when it comes to Sashia's death," he said quietly. "And I am not without blame. In the instant that I could have made a choice, the only thing I could hear was what had been drilled into me from birth—that I could never show my powers."

"Constantine knows." About his powers, there was no doubt.

"Yes."

I thought about it—about their age at the time of the Salietrex Massacre. Axer had turned twenty in April, and it was hard to think of him as anything other than solid and mature—quite frankly he was larger than life in a way that was almost unreal—but at thirteen, and in a moment of chaos?

"What happened after?"

His face twisted. "Stuart was already there—he'd felt his own connection with his wife snap—and he took Constantine. With Sashia's death, Stuart Leandred lost the thread that had connected him to the light, but we didn't know that in the moment. Several terrible things happened at the same time, and... If one of those events alone had not happened—things might be different. But they weren't, and they aren't." He rubbed absently at his chest, as if chasing a phantom pain. "Constantine broke everything but the most fundamental bonds between us before the week was out."

It was rare that I ever saw Axer as anything other than godlike—he always seemed above mortal problems and emotions. But the vulnerability that flashed through his eyes said something else. A hurt at thirteen that had scarred them both.

"But you ended up together at Excelsine."

He slowly slid the ball around his other palm. "Bonds, especially early ones when magic is forming in a mage, are hard to break, and so it was a less than happy day—though not an unanticipated one—when we ended up in a room together the very first day of school. But it was almost like meeting a mirrored version of the boy I'd known. He was focused. Manipulative. Hardened."

"He was already planning to kill Raphael."

"Yes," he said simply. He looked at me. "And if he could have survived it, me too. The bonds you have now will be very difficult for you to rid yourself of."

I touched them. I had no desire to get rid of any of my bonds unless I became a danger to the others.

He looked back skyward. "Luckily, you have enough power to secure them both ways, otherwise you'd be strongly open to being taken advantage of. It's one of the problems ferals encounter, and the reason why before Stavros started making them disappear, opposing forces tried to grab them early. First bonds, and strong bonds, never truly die."

I ran my fingers over my own bonds. I saw Axer's eyes drop down to the ones connecting us, as if he could feel my fingers upon them. His eyes shifted to the middle of his chest, then he looked back up at the sky.

"I am kept awake at night by the choices of the past," he said. "The ones that have driven me to who I now am. I promised myself that I'd never let another be destroyed who could be saved—that I'd anticipate events before they happened so that promises sworn to in infancy could be kept intact. To hide a single ability so that I could walk among the public, so I could save all those who couldn't save themselves. That is a test I take every time I go out."

The magic in his hand flashed teal and sapphire. "And I made certain never to make a connection with those saved. Not until a First Layer girl tried so hard to save her brother. Giving you my magic was the easiest choice I've made. And now... Perhaps it is time for a revolution." He pushed the magic into the ground and flowers bloomed in long undulating paths toward the walls.

I looked at Constantine, dark circles underlining his closed lids even in his boneless sprawl. "He never told anyone. About your abilities." He couldn't have, or else Axer's powers wouldn't just be speculation. When Constantine wanted it to be, as the case with Idami Senturten showed, his vengeance was thorough.

Axer didn't reply for a long time. "No." He looked at the flowers and they flashed violet. "He never has."

"Just like you've protected his abilities, an even more closely guarded secret, even though you can't stand him."

Secret keeping was less surprising on Axer's end—whatever their split had entailed, it had resulted in one with obsessively tight control and a savior complex, and the other with highly destructive tendencies. The former traits were not ones that lent themselves to flappy jaws, but still, maybe if pointed out...

"Why is that, do you think?" I asked gently.

"Goodnight, Ren."

~*~

I woke oddly slow.

Some of the Bandits were arguing in one of the steady hologram feeds we'd set up to stay in contact. A necessity so that as soon as we were discovered, everyone would know.

"They should go in with a Five Man Act," Patrick argued. "It's versatile."

They had obviously been arguing for a while. I frowned as I sat up, wondering how I could have slept through the ruckus. A time check had me scrambling. There was so much to do.

The remnants of the white noise spell someone had put on me broke completely beneath my movements and I stared at the dissipating spell in outrage. Axer was nowhere to be seen, but Constantine was at our makeshift desk working on something. His only acknowledgment of my waking was that he pushed out a chair on the other side of the table with his foot.

"Old Man and a Fireband would be better," Loudon said, as he looked up from where he was building the second of three recycling explosives. A long trail of soot ran down his face and colored a quarter of his short golden curls. "People will cheer the show for at least a minute before they realize they should be screaming."

"Both too flashy." Dagfinn shook his head. "Just let me darken the site."

"Yeah, because that won't cause any alarms, the entire grid block of Crelussa going out." Asafa snorted and helped Loudon carefully wrap a band around the second explosive—his own hair even spikier than usual after the electric shock he'd received wrapping the first.

Dagfinn shrugged. "Blame it on the lingering shifts. Hi, Ren."

Glances skittered my way and I waved as they chorused their hellos.

"The Layer Equibs are getting fretful enough as it is," Patrick said, continuing the argument.

"I thought we made a pact with them?" Loudon said.

"Yeah. But they are antsy little shivits. I've half a mind to level them, but the Queen'd be pissed."

"Old Man and a Firebrand would take care of that," Loudon said in a singsong voice.

"Five Man Act," Patrick insisted.

"Three Man Sneak," Constantine bit out without looking away from his work. "Now stop speaking."

Patrick snorted. "Three Man Sneak only works when you don't have overwrought sexual tens—"

The feed blinked out.

I looked at Constantine, and away from the piece of trap paper I was withdrawing from my portfolio. "Really?"

He threw the used magic into the recycling container we were using. It bulged at the seams, making me eye it for an extended moment before concentrating on him once more.

"Olivia's going to kill us for hanging up," I said. "How long have you been working on this?"

Long enough to bloat that container.

Constantine wadded up another spelled chunk, pressing it into a small fingerpad mold. "I'm close. And I switched them to Alexander's feed. He's in the untamed wilderness somewhere." He motioned carelessly at a path of flowers leading to the thicket of trees, which were even thicker and closer than when I'd fallen asleep. "He can deal with your friends. I might kill one of them otherwise. And we unfortunately need them."

"They are trying to help in their own...special...way."

"We have the great Alexander Dare planning our glorious heist. We don't need a two-bit con. Old Man and a Fireband, useless," Constantine muttered.

"What is—"

Constantine shoved a piece of rippling magic in front of me. A list of confidence games scrolled endlessly along with tiny moving holograms illustrating each.

I studied the list, catching one out of every five or so names as they passed—small descriptions popping up with each then fading like airplane messages in the wind.

Constantine noticed my absorption, because he shoved a small device that popped up an even clearer list. I figured out how to slow the list and increase the size of the holograms. There was an interactive portion that allowed me to add in my parameters and the skills and sizes of the figures, and it would manipulate the odds of a gambit working, as well as to suggest the best one based on the mages involved.

"This is awesome."

"That device sells for a half-million munits on the black market and only works when the purchaser is alive and within ten feet. An O'Leary made it." He gave me a look, as if to say that this should make me wary. "The family excels at the hustle. Never underestimate what they will do to gain what they want."

I smiled. "I think that's why Olivia likes him."

"Only because he likely understood your potential straight away and played the good-fun con. Price would have known what she was up against immediately, and the bargaining chip she possessed. The O'Leary's are excellent judges of power, and feared for their malevolent trickery. Even their youngest, dear Patrick, who appears so delightfully affable."

"Like you?"

"I think even you calling me affable is a stretch."

I laughed. It was a release I hadn't realized I needed. "You know what I meant."

"You trust too much."

"I like thinking the world is full of possibility."

"Extend that possibility to include that someone might betray you, and see what you think."

"The possibility that someone can become more."

"O'Leary's family is a problem," Constantine said resolutely, working on the next mold.

"Olivia—"

"Knows this already, and is stupidly competent most of the time. Which is why I hardly care. Still. Never forget what people will do for family and love. Desperation is an emotion many live to regret."

I looked at the way his fingers were clenching the string. I touched the back of his hand and felt them loosen.

"I'm sorry."

"Of course, you are."

"I know you don't like the idea of going after Stavros, but I didn't think you would agree with Axer, of all people, concerning the parameters of the Crelussa plan."

Constantine hadn't even raised a single protest amidst the flurry of "you're going to do what?" responses from campus.

"You don't argue with a person who has spent forty thousand hours perfecting a craft. You don't have to like the person, but when he clearly sees a path, arguing only makes you look belligerent and stupid. You don't see him in here micromanaging me, do you? Touch this one."

I looked at the delicate fibers he was weaving together—work that would yield success or death.

I touched the pad he indicated. When I lifted my finger, the pad stayed stuck to the table. "Um…"

He indicated the next one. That pad lifted a small measure with my finger before falling. He nodded, then reached over to his bubbling brew. Pulling out a bit of the molasses-looking material, he crafted another mold, imbuing it carefully with spell materials.

The next pad stuck for half a minute before falling from my fingertip. He smirked and began working in earnest, the solution unlocking before him.

"By the way, that is for you." He pointed to a new cuff on the table.

I lifted it, examining its parts. I could feel the echo of the field covering the dome. "You made a null cuff?"

"Layered between two other fields. Try it."

I swallowed and wrapped it around my wrist. I could feel where he had delicately placed the magic to soften the feeling of the null. But it was still a null cuff.

I could see him watching me, though he was pretending not to.

"I'm fine." I smiled.

"As fine as you ever are," he murmured.

Two hours later, my jitters had increased to the point where I was nearly vibrating in my chair. A small testing device was strapped to my upper arm, securing a light field around me that pinged when magic was occurring.

"Try that one," Constantine said. I pressed my finger into the seventh iteration of the mold, and it wrapped easily around the null field and adhered my finger to the table. Neither of the previous two iterations had sparked as magic, but they'd also failed to keep my finger stuck. "How did you get the pads to spark so little magic?"

"The mountain rats," he said. "Someone did a paper on them years back and detailed how they move."

"You remember details from a paper you read years ago?"

"I'm a genius. And motivated. I started working with all sorts of things this term. Knowing."

Knowing that we would end up this way. But he didn't have to be—

"Shut up, darling."

"Stop listening in then. Did you build little winged boots, too?"

"If I had, the Department would shoot us from the sky," he said idly.

"I'm surprised we aren't riding a...death pegasus, or something."

"Anything magical larger than two meters is pushed back by their fourth ward field."

"Worried some Awakening mage will fling themselves over the edge trying to catch a ride?"

"Yes." He twisted a filament. "Getting in will be easy. Once we are in there, if we don't disable the fifth field, we won't get out."

"That's where I come in," I said, my leg jittering up and down on its own.

Constantine snorted. "I don't think that's the plan."

"It is not," Axer said.

I swiveled to see him standing in the trees, watching us. Something passed between the two of them, barbed and jagged, before Axer brushed it aside and walked forward.

He reached for my magic, checking my levels.

"It's been a little over two hours and it is still okay," I said, touching the cuff. But we could all feel the backlash gathering beneath.

"Three hours maximum, then," he said and removed the cuff.

Absolute relief took me, making my entire body feel limp. A cough bubbled up and I grabbed a storage paper, cupping it around my mouth. Paint splattered inside, and shrieking could be heard—like demon souls screeching from hell.

Constantine's mouth pinched. "If she gets separated from us—"

"Then we deal with it."

"We"—Constantine pointed between them—"can take care of this without her."

"Now wait a minute—" I pushed the edges of the paper together.

Axer's gaze never wavered from his roommate. "This doesn't work without her. You know that."

"It can."

"Can it?" Axer's voice was methodical.

"Told you." I could hear Trick whisper through the mental feed Constantine had engineered, forgetting that Axer walking into the room meant they were back with us. "Too much ten—"

Constantine pinched and twisted the end of that thought and Trick swore. "Dammit, Leandred, I swear that—"

Constantine crushed the communication in a shaking hand, leaving the three of us alone.

"If she is separated from us—"

"Then we find her," Axer said.

"She is all I have," Constantine said, head tilting down to his chest.

My breath caught, and the paper crumpled in my hand as I tripped toward him, grabbing his forearm in both of mine. I tried to say no, that he had all the Bandits, too. He just had to reach out.

"You have more than that," Axer said roughly. "You just don't want to see it. You didn't want to see it after Salietrex, and you don't want to see it now."

Constantine stepped into his space without dislodging me. "Oh, I still have you, do I? Where were you when good old Stuart was ripping my life force from the inner fabric of our ancestry? Flaying me within an inch of my life?"

"I was at your door, trying to gain entry. I felt what he did to you. You know I did."

"But you didn't stop it."

"You barred me. I beat my hands and magic bloody against your shiving door. Only you could have barred me from entry."

For one shining second, I could feel Constantine's truth in his reaction to Axer's words. I could see the gaping hole where Constantine blamed himself. Where he blamed himself far more than he blamed anyone else.

"You thought you deserved it," I whispered.

He scrambled away from me. "No."

"Con." It was agonizing, the feelings he was trying to bottle. And I could feel Axer do something—ripping the bottle away so that Constantine was struggling to reach it.

"You aren't to blame," Axer said. "Verisetti was to blame. Stavros. Your father for his misuse of your trust and life. Me for not stopping Salietrex. Not you."

"Of course not," Constantine said stiffly. "I fully blame you, and I always have."

Axer stepped forward. "Not you."

Constantine crossed his arms. "Of course not. Don't be ridiculous."

But Axer, like the hunter he was, had caught the scent of blood. "Have you blamed yourself all this time? How did you hide that?"

"You gave me up," Constantine said, attacking again.

"You forced me to," Axer replied, but he was prowling now.

"You replaced me."

"You left me. Broke every connection that wasn't permanent. I spent a year trying to right things, throwing myself at every door. Do you know what that felt like? It was agony. I had to move on. My family forced it upon me until I realized the truth myself. And I was still absurdly happy for about five seconds when I saw you at the dorm's door."

"You've always been stupidly optimistic," Constantine sneered, but it was the response of a wild animal backed into a corner.

"Have you blamed yourself all this time?"

And something shifted and fell in Constantine's soul. "No. I have not. Because then I would have nothing."

Pain, anguish, ceaseless self-loathing bombarded our connection. My palm hit my throat as I tried to hold back my rising sob.

"I blame myself too," Axer said, stepping closer still. "For her. For you. For not knowing what your father would do. For letting you push me—drive me—away. I hated you. I hated the mental torture you inflicted each time I reached out. I hated not having you there."

"You let my mother die," Constantine said, like a desperate man.

"And you tried to give up mine." Axer's own face darkened. I caught flashes of it through my connections to both, the images and memories forming a triangle. The Department coming for Dare's mother. A young Kaine trying to subdue her on one of her clandestine visits outside the island. The nature and timing of such visits were only known to the island's inhabitants and to Constantine. "You didn't succeed, but you tried. You willingly did that."

"Of course, I did. She stopped my father."

And I could see his memory of it—Axer's mother, who I'd only seen in memories and feeds, taking Stuart Leandred's magic until he could no longer connect his rage.

Constantine laughed without humor. "He was so very sorry after, too. As if it excused any part of it. As if I wasn't actually at fau—"

"You weren't at fault." Axer's voice was grim. "No matter what he made you believe. Your only failure was in pushing away the people who wanted to help you."

"How could I look at you?" Constantine said bitterly. "Whole in a way that I would never again be. It's taken years to shed a portion of the damage from the life hooks."

Magic rippled over him and I inhaled sharply. A set of crisscrossing patterns twisted across Constantine's face in a mass of disfiguring violet blooms. I remembered those patterns. Back at my birthday celebration in the First Layer where we'd been attacked, one of our attackers had thrown something at Constantine that had caused them to appear. They had been worse then, rawer, but they were still there.

Physical scars?

"Those wounds are far deeper than physical, darling," he said, answering the question I hadn't asked out loud. "They make a lovely reminder when I need one, though in the face of your stupidly dogged determination, I have forgotten too many times to keep them fresh."

He said nothing for a moment, then, "It was you, wasn't it?" he directed at Axer. It was more a statement than a question.

"Yes. I let him know what would happen if I ever felt your life force being ripped apart. And then I cast upon him the closest equivalent of each spell he had triggered on you before anyone could stop me."

He said it casually. As if he hadn't just admitted to torturing Constantine's father.

"And it was while fixing the wounds I gave Stuart that my mother realized what else she could fix, and that I realized what I could become, if I wasn't careful. What everyone fears."

"We can do this alone," Constantine said abruptly, standing straight. "You know we can. We don't need Ren to go."

"If anybody is staying, it's the two of you," I said in disbelief, pushing against whatever was forming inside the crumpled paper. "I'm going."

"What would be worse—her being a thousand miles away, or a room over?" Axer never altered his gaze from Constantine. "Which do you think will be less trouble?"

"Hey." I frowned at him.

He turned to me. "You have the capability to be more powerful than anyone on this planet right now. Paint drips from you—opening portals and remaking life." He gave the storage paper a pertinent glance. "You grow more powerful every day with fewer outlets available to process your magic. Recognizing the outcomes if Kaine and Stavros find you is not an aspersion on your character."

"Yeah, okay."

"But she can't use magic," Constantine said flatly.

"Neither can you," I said grimly. "We are all wanted mages now. We'll all show on a scan. A bullet point in favor of leaving you behind and me going it alone."

"The difference is that I can stroll through an orphanage without needing to do something," Constantine said, pointing at me. "You'll be in a place oozing with magic. You'll want to use yours. Something will happen, we'll get in a bind or someone innocent will, and you'll turn on the fireworks."

"I won't."

He closed his eyes, then as if closing the conversation, he pulled another batch of magic from his bubbling cauldron and resumed communications with the others. "You always do."

Chapter Eighteen

THREE MAN SNEAK

T HREE MAN SNEAK

IT HAD TAKEN an additional twelve hours to prepare.

Another ping sounded, and I looked at the dome. "They are close to breaking through."

When next I entered, this small world would look nothing like this. The dome would be swarmed, and the magic twisted into something else.

"You'll make another," Constantine murmured.

Our supplies and personal menagerie were assembled, and the three of us looked nothing like ourselves. We now wore the downtrodden forms of three mercenaries who were far beyond their prime.

"Ready?"

I gathered them close, then took out the marble and threw it into the air. A shimmering field fell like a released curtain, and we stepped through, into the scientists' empty tent—empty, since all hands were working on the dome.

The marble that I'd kept in my pocket for months cracked, expelling a cascade of spells. It had been designed that way—as a one-way trip that hastened all other spells, but it still felt like the loss of a lucky totem.

"We are in! We are in!" Came the excited and fearful calls of the men breaching the dome.

There was no flash of gold, but I knew Raphael was out there.

We drove the Ophidians' vehicle to a tense rendezvous with hooded combat competitors from the Second and Third Layer who replenished the weapons combat mages normally carried, then drove to an even tenser meeting with members of Patrick's extended "family," who provided us with additional supplies we would need.

We had then navigated through the water mirror on a harrowing trip which stretched far deeper than I'd been led to believe, and were finally at the "easy part."

Right.

I wiped the dripping sweat on my brow along the cuff of my sleeve, and hung on for dear life to the edge of a mountain.

I wasn't used to being the worst at something. Socializing, maybe, but I felt that was improving nowadays with me smiling and nodding and generally keeping my mouth shut.

But as Constantine reached for another good hand hold way above my reach, I sighed and resigned myself to making two moves to his one with a quick scramble not to be left behind.

"You coming?" he said lazily, right fingers tucked into a healthy crack on the face of the mountain we were free climbing without the aid of internal magic. The null cuff glinted on his wrist as his knees bent in an upward lunge, right hip pressed against rock, left fingers hanging loose at his side, waiting to extend skyward.

"You suck," I said morosely, through the passive, closed-loop, silent communication that he had set up between the three of us while we climbed. Even the mountain rats couldn't hear us speak, though one was eyeing me judgmentally as I resignedly looked for my next hold.

Constantine looked down, eyes glinting silver with the spelled lenses he'd made that allowed us to see in the dark. "You're short."

His amusement over my vertical predicament seemed to have eased the last of his anger.

"You're lazy," I shot back. "I'm doing twice the work."

"Efficiency is more than a state of mind, darling."

My right toes slipped as the hold crumbled beneath my shoe and sustained weight. Constantine's spelled eyes widened, and his right fingers let go to grab a memorized hold further down as his left fingers reached to grab me. My reactive magic surged against the barrier of my cuff as I scrambled to shift my weight.

A palm caught in the dip between my shoulders and pushed me pancake flat into the rock.

"Ow." I scrambled to get my big toe tip curled atop another even tinier hold; cheek flat against stone, magic rebounding painfully.

"Try not to die," Axer said, hand leaving my back, already looking up and mapping out the next twenty holds—as good at climbing as he was all things physical.

The mountain towered so far overhead with juts and overhangs that I couldn't even see the top through my spelled lenses.

"I think we are still doing this the hard way," I said, mouth moving over too-smooth rock.

"Yes, flipping universe space would be easier," Axer mused.

"I know!"

He looked down at me.

"It would be," I said.

He hid a smile, poorly.

"Con poured super grip glop on my fingers to keep me attached to this blasted rock, and this still sucks."

I pushed with my toes and extended my hand upward, pinching my fingers around a small bit of rock. "Neph would be good at this." With her shimmying, graceful moves, and super strong legs. And better height. "My fingers are made for gripping pencils."

Guard Rock, secured in my backpack, jabbed me with the tip of his. He extended it upward as if to signal that I was moving too slowly.

"Why can't you climb, and I can ride in your backpack for once?" I said to him, knowing he'd hear, as Constantine had stuck a small tag on him, too, at the last minute.

He jabbed me again.

"We aren't even using ropes. Because we are all mad. Do you really want to jab me again?"

He did. This time purely for amusement.

"I should have just strapped you to my back," Constantine said, still climbing, but staying closer to me like he did every time there was a slip. "Like a pocket fairy."

"You aren't funny." I pulled myself up another two feet, undulating upward while hugging the mountain's face. "And I'll totally do that. At the next landing. I have duct tape in my bag. The good kind. You can call me whatever you want."

I rotated my body to grab a series of three more pinches. Both boys doubled my distance. Then tripled it as a series of cracks were the only holds available to me in between the easy ones they could reach without problem. I stared at the paper-thin fissure that my lenses were helpfully highlighting—a spelled addition courtesy of Constantine and based on some popular mountain climbing frequency.

I would need to stick the tiniest tips of my fingers into those fissures—areas that they'd both been able to skip entirely with their greater reaches.

"Come on, Ren. We have to make the lower cliff edge in the next forty minutes."

I pressed my cheek against the hard stone. "Just...just leave me here. This is the end."

"Killed by shortness."

"You will pay," I said, lips against the stone.

"Tallness does not become you." And now his amusement fully drowned even his lingering resignation.

"So much paying."

~*~

We took a break on a ledge near the top so that Axer could attach small devices that would help Dagfinn keep track of movements inside. I let my legs dangle over the side and tried not to think about what awaited us at the top.

"Someone is making me magically taller before we get to the crux."

"The crux of this climb is no harder than the other five you had to do that we didn't," Constantine said.

"I hope your fingers get stuck in a fissure," I said.

"Harsh."

I smiled unwillingly, rubbing at my wrist.

Constantine immediately retrieved a stoppered bottle from his coat. He took my wrist in his hand and dripped a drop on top of the cuff. It sizzled and spread along the material, nullifying the burgeoning magic and making what was underneath even more painful. I winced.

He looked sharply at me.

"It's fine," I said.

His lips tightened. "It's not fine."

"Con, I almost died like twelve times on this rock and haven't used magic. I won't use it to save myself."

"That's not—" He took a deep breath. "You never use it to save yourself," he said grimly.

He looked at Axer, who was steadily looking back. Axer tipped his head in response. "We'll figure out an alternative next time."

The pain got worse every inch nearer to the top.

I watched the null cuffs glint on their wrists and the magic that neither could use flit under their skin. Their magic was also stoppered beneath the field that Constantine had created by combining our shield-field with a sliver of the null field surrounding Corpus Sun.

As soon as we pulled ourselves over the edge of the last overhang, the castle loomed up through the dark clouds.

Lightning crackled around it—feeding off the energy inside as well as the forces without.

"Okay, not forbidding at all," I muttered, shaking off the cramps that had started to build.

Guard Rock hunched into position, ready to spring.

I had seen pictures of the facility, so I knew that even though the sanitarium was supposed to be a place of healing and holding, it was a creepy castle in the middle of nowhere. It held a lot more of the "holding" feeling than one of "healing."

If Excelsine were a lovely and strange mountain in the middle of Europa, this was its opposite—a fortress of rock and stone positioned above Siberian desolation.

There was no time to scrutinize the desolate view, though. Axer was pulling out containers and Constantine was withdrawing vials. A drop of sweat rolled from my hairline down my cheek.

I looked at my cuff and the time, then took a container of magic and slid it beneath my belt.

Constantine handed me a vial, and I upended the contents on my crown. The magic slid down, connecting with the container. Only then did three more containers join the first—combining to make my magical signature a mixture of the three mages whose identities I was assuming. They had been carefully chosen to ensure access to any part of the compound—a technician, an enforcer, and a console assistant. The boys each had the same combination of disparate identities. Patrick—or rather, Patrick's family—had provided them.

How they had gotten the magic, I didn't want to know.

Constantine affixed another small circle of magic beneath my ear, and as if my thought on Patrick, instead of Constantine's pre-made magic, had connected the others into our closed communication loop, Dagfinn said, "You are certain the identities are solid?"

"Are you questioning the illicit deeds of my illustrious family?" Patrick asked idly.

"No. But the sneak only works once."

"Then the three of them better use it well."

The Three Man Sneak involved assuming the identities of people already at the target destination—for us, the employees at the Sanitarium who had the access we needed. With magic involved, it made the whole ruse a lot trickier, but Patrick had given us ID pods to switch identities as we went.

"Each pod grab lasts fifteen minutes. Don't try for more," he warned again, as we dragged three newly unconscious mages into a closet.

Fifteen minutes didn't seem like much time, but detailed blueprints of the facility were a matter of public record, and most of the Bandits had at one time or another graced these halls, making it simple to take the most direct routes to our single, concrete goal.

"They'll have Rosaria in the high security wing. But you must watch for anyone in the cells around her. The most privileged mages get sent there. It's considered a boon. So, it's far more likely you will encounter magicists."

"Where'd they keep you, Ludes? Where's the lowest security?"

"Very funny."

"Shh! They are entering the main quadrant. And chatter is why they didn't hook us into the climb phase. Let's not make them slip now," Dagfinn said with his normal, paranoid edge.

"Ugh, it looks just like I remember," Kita said distastefully, ignoring Dagfinn. "I hated that place. Worst two weeks of my life."

A grand industrial space filled with ordered magic opened before us. Ten by ten-foot containers were arrayed in a block-like grid on one side—sixty-four up and sixty-four across, easily seen from a central command station that managed them. Magic zipped around each cell, and a single figure aged eleven to fifteen inhabited each one.

It reminded me nothing short of a very large prison.

Movement was happening within most of the four thousand plus cells—new mages practicing their skills, learning to control their magic, yelling, screaming, kicking, fighting—though almost all the movement was in the lower half of the grid. I lifted my gaze to the ones in the top half who showed less movement—to a one they were meditating, sleeping, or staring creepily outward.

Okay, maybe looking at the command station was a better option. Five mages worked the grid, flipping spell switches and allocating resources in different directions. Two of the cells flipped positions as one mage seemed to settle, a zen look overcoming his expression, while the other grew more agitated.

The cell containing the more agitated ferals shifted downward.

Two cells at the top abruptly winked out. Two others shifted upward to take their place. A pattern was forming. The cells moved to accommodate the flow of their inhabitants' emotions and control. Suddenly two new mage cells appeared at the bottom from a holding station somewhere below.

Magic flowed from the grid out into the tubes that led out of the complex, presumably to whatever defensive spells the Department maintained.

It wasn't completely unlike the Third Layer's setup for Awakening mages. There were cages in both settings, but there was something a lot more personal about the ten cells in the Western Territories' compound. The circular shape made it possible for everyone to see and communicate with each other if desired, the caregivers were no more than ten feet away and interacted personally with each of mages, and there was an ability to exit after a certain point in the process. In contrast, this was a more astringent, inhuman manufacturing design.

It was also notable that each mage here wore an unbreakable cuff—already regulated to stay beneath the level their Awakening could create. The complex here would skim that magic right off the top.

The mages in the Third Layer got to experience the full feeling of Awakening—over-extensions of their magic included.

In one of the brand-new ground floor containers, a thirteen or fourteen-year-old mage in the most awkward stage of physical life banged against the reinforced glass and shouted something as we passed. I shot a quick look at the console station mages, but they ignored him and us. The two dozen mages who were standing in the open space of the room taking notes in the air while watching the cells and sending commands to the console mages, ignored him as well—or at least gave no empathetic reaction to him. He was just another dog in the mass kennel.

"Worst two weeks," Kita repeated. "And initiatory day beat the other thirteen days by a mile in misery."

Magic ruptured in bursts from the newly initiated boy. He hunched over his cuff, then started banging on the glass again, slipping painfully and slowly down to the floor.

I veered toward the command console, and only Constantine's hand wrapping around my wrist stopped me from going to destroy it.

"You can't. You'll kill them all. And _we_ are going to be caught if you don't stop gaping like a tourist," he said across our restricted three-person loop.

"What, Awakening in a cage wasn't the deliriously nationalistic event that magicists like Straught declare it to be?" Patrick responded.

I looked at Axer to see what he thought of the attack on his teammate, but he was paying attention elsewhere. "Camille is fiercely loyal," he sent across the same restricted channel. "She will defend all which is around her, and she grew up to think nationalism equaled loyalty."

It was always a mistake to think he wasn't paying attention.

"Where does the energy go?" I asked the group at large, watching the magic fly through the tubes and conduits as we continued our long trek through the room.

"It goes directly to the Department's warding and defense system, to be used to defend the layer against threats both internal and external."

"So, they can use it at their discretion, as long as it is used in defense of the layer?"

"They are susceptible to audit by the council and a writ at large. But the accountants know how to manipulate the accounts. There has never been a speck of impropriety. The necessary amounts of magic go where they say they are going, while any excess is stored for emergencies or public works. It's a popular program. Giving back magic to the world," Patrick said derisively.

"You are lucky you are from Antioch," Kita said to Patrick. "They let you Awaken at home."

"We still have to pay the magic tithe and the Department always audits."

"Better than this."

It wasn't just inane chatter, I knew. They were trying to keep communications light and nerves at bay—just like they did during intense gaming sessions.

"Or you can do like the Dares, and not give back their full share," Patrick said as we turned into a wider corridor. "Itlantes—always so suspect."

I looked at Axer.

"We tithe the magic, but we don't allow auditing," he said. "Everyone thinks we are stockpiling."

"Can't deny the truth," Loudon chirped.

I didn't bother to ask if it was or wasn't the truth. It would only make sense to someone always as prepared as Axer to have stockpiles, and no story about his father had made me think differently about Maximilian Dare's goals either. "How did you get that to happen?" I asked Axer.

"War." The severe expression on his borrowed features hid the amusement in his mental voice.

"What about you, Leandred?" Patrick asked with a grin in his voice. "I know you didn't join the riffraff in the sterile cells here."

"The same," he answered briefly.

"You Awakened at your manor?"

"No," he said. "I Awakened in Itlantes."

Silence descended over the spell feed, then—

"Seriously?" Mike said in a deadpan voice.

"Mother was especially fond of the warm seas that time of year," Constantine said languidly.

"Holy shivit, you two were friends?" Loudon exclaimed.

"Not in the slightest," Constantine responded.

"What about in the strongest?" Patrick said, homing in on word choice and trickery.

"We've reached the first interior," Axer said, cutting off all further questions.

This quadrant was smaller. Eight by eight cells. The mages inside were also a lot more focused than the others had been.

"The final stage."

When a top cell winked out, it would appear in a small area where the mage was freed, then monitored for another two days before being released to his or her caregivers.

Further in were the cells to hold the highly volatile. Those mages who Awakened due to trauma or whose magic had repressed itself or gathered in a different way, coming online at an older age. That was where we would find an eighteen-year-old girl.

Where we might find more than just her.

Mages passed us—Department mages with their buckled collars and straightforward stares. And others were standing in the center slice of the room taking notes and conducting magic while watching the cells here as well.

"There was a girl at school who talked about Awakening naturally," I murmured in our mental loop. The girl had argued with Camille about it.

"That just means she didn't get an inhibitor cuff at ten. A few countries have rules against early cuffs, but the majority use them. It's considered an antiquated notion to Awaken naturally. It puts the rest of the layer in danger." Olivia's discourse sounded like a rehearsed speech. "Regardless of what happens, everyone still has to submit to Awakening in an approved facility as soon as abilities are shown. Failure to do so results in huge penalties, so all countries in the Second Layer comply."

"Or are made to comply," someone grumbled.

"We have rules for the good of society," Olivia said brusquely. "Allowing a rogue with too much power to roam free is something that has always concerned the masses."

"And what is the alternative for a person who wishes to be free?" I asked, looking at the tubes and the overwhelming magic flying through them.

"Don't be a rogue," she said curtly. I swallowed and looked at the mage inside who was staring vacantly while magic flew around him. "Or be a rogue so powerful, that they can't touch you."

"Might makes right."

"Always." I could feel Olivia watching the boy in the cell through my spelled eyes. "But there are other forces that can prevail," she said softly.

I didn't get to ask her what those were, as the automatic door I was walking toward remained closed, barred to the stolen identities layered over the three of us. I nearly slammed into it.

Constantine grabbed me from behind and whirled me against the wall.

"Shivitty shive!" Patrick and Dagfinn started swearing.

Axer veered left, walking down the forked hallway away from us in his older guise, as if that is what he had intended to do the whole time.

Constantine leaned in and curled a piece of my false hair around his finger. "We should do lunch instead," he said, entirely audible so that the whole hallway could hear.

I blinked at him.

"You've been working too hard and these brats will still be here. I'll treat you." He leaned in, bringing the lock of borrowed black hair to rub against his lips.

"We need to finish our tasks," I said aloud, swallowing nervously and trying not to watch as another person passed us. She rolled her eyes as the door-magic scanned her.

"Are you certain I can't convince you?" he asked me, somewhat lasciviously.

"Maybe...maybe after?"

Constantine's hand thrust out and gripped the closing door, his finger sliding over the edge deliberately. The door opened again. His gaze never left mine. "I'll hold you to that."

"I don't know, Trick," Loudon said cheerfully. "Seems like—ow!"

I let out a long breath as we slipped through.

The cells inside were of a superior build to the others—stronger and more difficult to escape from. The tubes running from them were also reinforced with additional magic.

One cell stood apart from the rest.

The interior flashed with streaks of lightning and a girl was standing in the middle of it, eyes white with overpowered light. Lightning shot from her in all directions, like she was a plasma globe feeding the energy around her and forcing hers upon her environment.

We had found her.

I felt paint shift up my throat.

I swallowed—only the dwindling effects of the cuff allowing me to swallow it down like the worst sort of heartburn—and concentrated on one of the containers strapped to me.

A group of adult mages had their heads together, gazes flitting between something in their hands and the girl in the cell.

I pulled the facsimile of a hologram screen into the air, pretending to take data with my right hand instead of the runes I was sketching at my side with my left.

Constantine did the same—looking bored and world-weary as he pretended to type out his hundredth report. It gave us a reason to be standing in the middle of the room, surreptitiously scoping it out.

I joined my runework with his and let him slide the conjoined magic across the floor.

"Where are you?" I sent to Axer.

"Found a better spot," was the only thing he sent back.

Five console mages worked here, monitoring and tweaking and sending status reports. Another man, whose demeanor indicated he was likely in charge, paced back-and-forth, staring darkly at the cell.

"Director, we can commence in two hours. Safety precautions will be at their maximum."

The man nodded sharply. "Have the cell made ready for transfer and call up the pod blocks. You've double-checked the specifications on the explosives?"

"The blast will be contained to this area and will not affect the Awakening mages in the regular grids. The Department will be conducting the inquiry themselves, so we don't need to worry about planting anything. Additionally, if there are mages you think will be a future problem, we have permission to...pursue collateral damage."

"Absolutely not," the director said, lips pursed.

"But—"

"We are a facility that operates for the goodwill of the public. Philosophers, scholars, and dreamers can debate our methods and how we handle Awakenings, but I will not have our mandate questioned. We are a safe facility for the Awakening members of our society."

The director only paused to point at Rosaria. "A compelling argument has been made for this mage to be hidden. For the safety of the layer as the Origin Mage hunts the rest down. If we are asked to do more, I will be questioning it. Doing anything like you just suggested is a step into a regime I want no part of, and neither should you." He stared at the other man.

The man bowed his head. "Yes, Director."

The director nodded sharply and strode into another area.

"Ugh, I hate it when people on the other side sound reasonable," Trick said.

Three of the console workers resumed working, but the two minions who had spoken exchanged looks above the others' heads. Unease prickled along my shoulders. I disengaged the recording I had started when the director started speaking.

"Something's not right," I murmured.

"Agreed."

I looked up to see magic seep down from the ceiling. No one else in the room seemed to have noticed it yet, but I surreptitiously watched it, knowing that Axer was on the other end. The magic split and seeped into the corners of the cell, under the green edges. I immediately sent my runes onto the path he was creating—slipping them inside the cell.

I looked to the console to make certain no one had noticed and did a double take. My breath caught. A painted woman stared at me from the wall beyond the console, watching. I'd know that style anywhere.

The woman's head tilted, gaze never leaving mine as if she'd been waiting for me to notice her. She reached for a pocket of paint, bringing a piece of paper to life.

A starred symbol twinkled on the paper. The woman slowly waved me forward with the fingers not holding the paper, gaze intense and glimmering with the faintest bit of hope. I stepped forward.

A hand clamped my wrist.

Constantine looked at me in warning, following my gaze with a pinched frown as he pulled me back. "What are you doing?" His demand curled through my thoughts. "Have you both gone mad?"

"Is everything okay?" one of the technicians asked out loud, following my gaze, frowning at the way one of us was holding the other back. It was one of the two techs who had acted the most suspiciously.

"Very. Thank you," Constantine said aloud with just the right amount of obsequiousness. "She's had a grueling day. Shift's over in ten, thank magic."

Constantine pinched me, and I tried to shift my eyes away from the painted woman who was urging me forward with more force.

"Don't let him touch that button!" Dagfinn yelled.

I ripped my gaze away from the Kinsky portrait to see the technician's fingers inching toward an alarm button.

The technician next to him suddenly surged forward, knocking the man's hand away as hers moved quickly over controls and magic. "We have unidentified—"

"Sir, there is something strange moving—"

"You're going to have to take them out," Olivia said grimly, as the console lit up with activity.

Constantine had already dropped my arm and any false servility from his face. Magic was darkly dripping into his palm.

"Personnel! All personnel!" A voice blared magically, echoing through the room. "Red Alert. Repeat, Red Alert!"

Chapter Nineteen

ASSAULT ON CRELUSSA

THE TECHNICIAN jerked as holograms bloomed all over the console area. Alarms blasted and the mages taking notes scrambled to collapse their devices and run toward the console.

"Sanitarium breach from the tunnels," one of them shouted, fingers flying with magic. "The wards have been tripped. Three sets, now four. All targeting and repressive spells have been deactivated. We can't obtain magical signatures."

The Bandits were swearing in mass, scrambling to get eyes on the rest of the sanitarium. "Son of a... Where's Dare? What's he doing? The sneak is over. Exit point A has been closed. Exit B is closing. We are in deep sh—"

The alert technician threw a spell net toward us, which Constantine absorbed in one of the papers I had given him. Constantine smiled darkly as the man's eyes widened.

"Emergency functions at the Sanitarium have been activated, 01," Dagfinn said tightly, using codenames. "That means immediate removal of—"

I didn't wait, moving swiftly toward the cell and pulling out the rest of the spells from the container that we had pre-prepared. Lightning and chaos sparked inside, and I hurriedly threw everything we needed for the plan to work. The sneak was dead, but we could still achieve our aim.

The console technicians were shouting over each other, drowning out the single technician who was trying to alert the others to our presence. Constantine prowled slowly toward him through the madness, container magic in his palm.

"They—" Another technician's arm collided with the first man's as he tried to push a button.

"Hands on magic, Gormly! They are right outside. Defensive magic engaged. All signatures inside locked for defenses."

"No! They are right h—"

"Hostiles gaining entry."

The magic on the door to the chamber burst, shaking the room.

Still working the spells, I spared a glance for the intruders and looked directly into the eyes of Vincent Godfrey's son. A savage look entered his twenty-five-year-old gaze as magic filtered through his pupils and he pointed at me. "Grab her!"

I dove at Constantine, who opened his arms and spun both of us behind the console.

In the mayhem, two of the console technicians spared me a confused gaze, but the terrorists were already streaming toward our position, and since we were dressed as technicians, they rapidly turned their attention away from us and toward the intruders.

Wards and defensive magics began illuminating the room as more bodies streamed in over the top of their quickly falling comrades.

One blast targeted our putty, identifying it as dangerous and blasting it through an airlock.

"The terrorists are trying to free the feral! Remove the cell now! Now! It doesn't matter if all the permissions aren't in place, go!"

I would have smiled at that excellent assessment, if Vincent Godfrey Jr. hadn't tucked his dive, sliding around the console and into view.

One of the technicians went down at our side, then another.

I heard Delia swear, distantly, in my head.

Godfrey's gaze affixed on Constantine, raw and bloodthirsty, and without any doubt that he could see though the enchantments we had hidden ourselves beneath, since the enchantments only worked on people already spelled into the system here.

"You," he said to Constantine, raising his hands. "Will die slowly."

I was already scrambling to push us both around the console's corner. Now was probably not the time to point out that Raphael had been the one to murder Vincent's father permanently—Constantine had only temporarily killed him.

Killing magic released from Godfrey's hands, and I threw myself in front of Constantine, pulling a shield up from my shoe to eat the incoming blast. Constantine's defensive blast curved around me. Still hampered by the cuffs we hadn't removed, Constantine's strike was easily batted aside, and though the shield worked, it was destroyed by the hit and Godfrey had already sent another.

A ceiling beam dropped into the path of Godfrey's killing strike, and Axer dropped from the ceiling, magic swirling around him, blanketing the room as he spun, and taking out everyone standing.

"Level Ten demon!" one of the technician's yelled.

"I will pay TOP MUNITS for that signature fabricator," Loudon said, with a bit of demand as the room responded to Axer's fabricated magic signature as if he was truly a demon from hell.

"Not sure you can pull off the panache," Patrick said to Loudon, mental voices as ragged as if they were audibly out of breath. "Exit C back in business. Working on Exit D. Real life Freespar. Look at him kick the shivit out of them."

"Secure the Origin Mage," Godfrey yelled out harshly, now tucked underneath the console we'd abandoned. "Blast open the feral girl's cell. Kill Dare and all the Second Layer scum in this compound! But Leandred's mine!"

"Someone has a crush!" Patrick crowed—mania in his voice.

"Seriously, now is the time to shut the chatter!" Mike yelled.

Multiple voices were freaking out and combining in my head—pointing at all the different aspects of horror that were happening.

I narrowed in on Olivia's voice and Neph's forced calmness and pushed all the others to the rear of my mind. Axer stalked toward the console, simultaneously blasting magic around the corners of the room.

"Three seconds, 01," Olivia said grimly to me, changing to codenames. "Two. One."

A grinding noise tore through the air. My head jerked toward the cell. Rosaria was staring straight at me—eyes ablaze with white—her hands on the glass, reaching toward me. The locks popped one after another, then the cell dropped through the floor.

"The feral's cell has been dropped to the transportation level of the sanitarium," Olivia said. "Spell still in place. Locking mechanisms secured. 3, 2, 1. She's gone. Comms?"

A tense moment passed, then Dagfinn said, "Arrival at Keating Glen. Transfer to Level 1. Transfer to Level 2. Transfer to Level 3—Darpin Sloughs. Conspiracists guessed that one years ago. Transfer to Level 4—I knew it, Level 4 is in Fels Hollow. Level 5. Dear Magic, are we going to get—no." He swore, but it was without heat, voice giddy that we'd traced even that far using conventional means. "All outside spells erased. R—I mean, 01?"

It was the moment of truth, and the feed went silent with it.

I closed my eyes, feeling the magic and connecting to the kernel I had so carefully placed. "Got her," I whispered.

Two other life forms snapped together. "Got three." I sagged. "I've got three. Same location. Found them." Maybe all of them.

I almost couldn't process the idea—something that I'd been working on for weeks that was now within my grasp.

"Transmitting details." I sent the amorphous block of mental data through the link we had established to decode travel parameters for Awakenings.

Dagfinn crowed. "Verrange. A sea town—it isn't even listed in the conspiracy threads. Starting the parameter match now to identify the exact site, but we got them. Verrange. The Level 5 labs. Hell yes."

"Now, get out," Olivia said tensely.

Patrick swore. "Exits C, D, M, and T are gone, and one of the terrorists is activating a Level 8 ward killer and bomb on the transportation level."

Swearing echoed across the comms.

"The transportation level holds all the stored Awakening magic. Vats of it," Saf said, too calmly. "Held together by layer wards. Igniting them will kill everyone in that facility and take down the security of the Second Layer in one stroke."

"We have to stop them." I was already moving. Constantine made a sound that was somewhere between a growl and a sigh as he dove after me.

Axer simply wiped his hand in an arc, clearing our way at the expense of two spells striking his back. He was already peeling them out of his cloak and throwing them back as we skidded around the corner and out of sight.

"Ren," Olivia said.

"Queenie, she's right," Patrick said, voice oddly tense. "She has to."

I lunged for the other corridor and shot off two spells—just enough to give cover as Constantine followed. I narrowly avoided a direct blast and twisted into another corridor. The walls to our right crumbled under another blast.

The Bandits had given up all attempts at being quiet, but instead of the loud commentary, they had become eerily focused.

"Stealth mode was fully disengaged," Dagfinn said with dead calm. "Now it's my turn. Go left, 01 and 02. I have you covered."

We veered left. Bolts of magic shot from the surveillance spells running along the ceiling, taking out the mages behind us. Dagfinn, freed of concealment restrictions, began activating one system after another.

"03, rendezvous at point five-one-one, repeat, five-one-one," he said to Axer. "I can route System 2 to cover you."

"Comms, switch views and jog incoming streams." Asafa's voice was calm as he gave orders—the master coordinator of their gaming group. "Leader, find the terrorist's point of entry. Troublemaker, jolt ward eight-two-five. Courser, keep the magic flowing."

"I've got visual contact, Balance," Kita said—codenames fully in use now that we ran the risk of being compromised from the outside.

"Troublemaker, rally that hall, then take out the next two, and the one behind. Comms, leave a trail."

I skidded around the corner as magic flew from the spells lining the hall, targeting everyone but us.

"They are closing in on our burrowing points," Patrick said grimly. "You have less than three minutes before they seal us out."

"03 is kicking the utter crap out of Godfrey Jr. on his way to the rendezvous point. But Godfrey just yelled, 'Destroy the painting.' What painting?"

My breath caught and the only thing that kept me from returning was Constantine's fingers gripping my collar and tugging me back into motion.

"The Kinsky."

"There's a Kinsky painting?" someone asked, confused. "I never saw one."

"It's in the secure ward," Loudon confirmed. "They hung it after his death. His last vetted piece. Big kerfuffle over it back in the day. Thought it might be unstable."

"Chatter," Constantine hissed.

The feed went silent for a second. Constantine wasn't usually the one that chastised anyone for talking.

"If they are targeting it purposely... Maybe one of you should prevent that. Get to it first? See why—"

"On it." Axer sounded out of breath.

We were almost there.

"03 heading back to the main room, and it's refilling with hostiles. We can take out half, but we need another exit for him," Asafa said grimly. "01, we took out all the terrorists in the loading dock, but I can't do anything about the box. Turn left, Re—01. On your right."

We burst through the loading dock door. The mountain vista spread out like an inverted Excelsine, taunting me. Loading transports lined the bays. A hundred vats of shimmering magic were encased in reinforced wards. Bodies littered the floor.

A spellbox bright with white light—a moment from bursting—vibrated beneath a ward box containing the connections to dozens of similar boxes. The shimmering vats blinked atop them.

I grabbed at my nullifying cuff.

Constantine's fingers wrapped around my wrist, trapping the cuff. His other hand was already raised, his wrist bare.

"No," I said. "You'll be—"

But his magic was already spreading out like a pair of giant wings, throwing the storage paper I had given him fall term toward the spellbox. It wrapped around it at the last second, and a muffled boom burst the paper into confetti.

"You're going to have to make me a new martini set," he said, almost idly.

"Your magic." He had just sunk his magical signature directly into the mountain.

"But not yours. And let's see my father try to cover up this one with the government," was the vicious response.

"Move out, move out," Olivia shouted. "Incoming."

I could see a shadow shrieking along a mountain in the distance. One bad event on top of another.

"It's Kaine," I said. Constantine swore.

"That's not all. Department reinforcements just arrived on the summit. Shoot, shoot, shoot, you've got to get out of there."

The building shook.

"I have no idea how you are still alive, but a terrorist got through 03," Dagfinn said tightly. "Direct hit on the Kinsky."

"Forget the Kinsky!" someone yelled. "The Department and praetorians will take care of the sanitarium—get out of there."

The layer began slowly grinding.

Kaine's shadow suddenly shot faster than I'd ever seen it, shooting straight up to the room we'd just left.

"The Kinsky took another hit! It's related to the sudden layer instability!"

"We just lost 03." I could hear the fear in Dagfinn's voice. "And all surveillance on that level."

Constantine swore again.

We didn't bother with id spells, doors, or assistance—Constantine simply lifted his hand upward and pulled down with his unbound magic. A hole ripped through the floor above, then the floor above that, tearing a large, jagged pathway. I grabbed a carpet from the transport dock and we tossed ourselves on top and shot upward.

The reason for Axer's silence became apparent as soon as we flew into the destroyed room. Our own comms sputtered and broke under the cloud of spreading shadow.

A few of the Awakening cells had been split open in the fire and their mages were either splayed on the floor or walking around in a daze, magic sparking off them in devastating waves.

The rest of the Awakening mages were alert in their cells, and they stared in terror. The walls separating the Awakening areas had been demolished, so that every Awakening mage in a cell was now in crumbling view. The magic that ran along the sides was sputtering.

The cell grids weren't going to hold. And the combined shockwave of four thousand Awakening mages and their magic springing free, without direction, would be devastating.

"Come to join the fun?" Kaine smirked at us.

He and Axer were dueling in the center of the unnaturally enlarged room. Terrorists were taking potshots at them from the side. Kaine's shadows lifted one after another from the ground, breaking their necks midair before dropping them to the floor. "Mustn't let the terrorists win." A shadow sliced toward Axer and he dove and returned fire.

"I will finish my father's plans and the greater ones that I've been given!" Godfrey said viciously, trying to destroy them both.

Five more spells were shot from the sides, and both Kaine and Axer took precious time to deal with each while trading their own blows. Axer's cloak was smoking with the number of hits it was absorbing. There were only so many killing blows it was going to be able to absorb.

Everyone in the room was throwing killing magic. Our carpet taxi took an immediate hit and Con and I tumbled off. I raised our best shield to cover us. Constantine shoved me behind a terminal and began ripping apart a massive cat's cradle he pulled from his pocket, string coiling in his grasp. He twisted three strings together then threw them outward. A net opened and secured around four mages—two terrorists and two Department security officers.

He nodded grimly and grabbed the cat from his coat and an enormous handful of string. "Everyone out there but the hero is an enemy," Constantine said viciously, then shot all the string in a magically enhanced arc straight at Axer. "Go!"

The cat bounded into the air, three spade tails flapping in slowed motion as it hit the first net with a clawed paw, then the second with the middle tail, and a third with a back foot, rotating in the air like some weird bluish-purple cat ninja as it punted each net toward a different section of foes.

"Wha…" I couldn't even finish the word as the cat flew along the thrown arc, past a ducking Axer, tumbling as it hit its final targets.

"I have serious problems," I mumbled, raising another shield behind Axer as a mage took aim, and another in front of us as we were targeted too, all while watching my creation secure the forces around the main show group by group. "And so do you."

"I accept your gift. Thank you, darling," Constantine murmured. The cat streaked across the floor, spit acid at one of the mages targeting us, then dove into Constantine's open cloak. The string maneuver would only work once. The rest of the forces—the best of them—were already tweaking personal shields to account for it.

Axer got in a shot on Kaine, sending his shadows shrieking, and our communications returned for a moment.

"Watch to your left, 01. Forty unaffiliated soldiers incoming from the west. One hundred from the east. Fifty from—"

"Ren, it's Helen! Transport room! They aren't there to save—"

Kaine yanked Godfrey Jr. into the path of Axer's overpowered killing blow, then swirled into smoke.

I frantically looked at the spread of the smoke to see Kaine in front of the Kinsky. He gave me a taunting wave. Behind him, the woman closed her eyes as if in great pain, and a parcel ejected from her hands as Kaine swirled into the painting.

The painting pulled inside of itself with an unnatural crack. Axer's spell hit the wall a split second too late.

Patterns bloomed, spreading like a plague along the wall. Rumbling started from deep within the layer. The walls and floor began to shake. I stared at the ejected parcel at the base of the wall and held out my hand.

"RUN!" multiple voices screamed.

"Full destabilization has occurred. Readings marked and logged for posterity. Enacting Order 5376.15.94 under power of the Prestige," Helen Price ordered from far below, her command running through the systems and blaring into the air due to some predefined security measure.

My gaze was on the patterns expanding along the floor as the Kinsky parcel zipped toward me. I heard Olivia's soft, unnatural, "No, that's not, no."

"Olivia?" I asked. "What—"

"No."

My gaze shifted downward almost unwillingly, through the break in the floor, not allowing the jagged rips and beams to hinder my gaze.

Helen Price stood below. She looked up and met my gaze, and another face flickered in dark amusement over hers, before she ducked into a transport and was gone.

The parcel from the Kinsky hit my hand and a series of clicks and magic clanged in succession.

And as if she was next to me, Olivia's breath went uneven. I could feel her channeling magic hundreds of miles away, screaming, "No!'

Below, ten of the large storage vats of Awakening magic disappeared in a flush of magic. Then another twenty, then all the rest. In a blink of an eye, they were all gone.

The other Department mages disappeared—hopping on transports, heading in different directions.

"The layer will be destabilized," Mike said, shock threading his voice. "The Department didn't even try—"

"All Second Layer troops are withdrawing," Will said in equal shock.

Voices were overlaying each other on the comms.

"Leaving only the terrorists in such nice, spread apart target zones," Dagfinn said viciously. "Courser, look at this buffet. We never get such clear shots in game. 03, conserve your containers. Target colors set. Courser, you're on that one, that one, those three, Troublemaker has five, Balance has four, Destroyer got a block of six, Traveler gets three—"

"They took the magic," Delia said tonelessly through the sounds of the Bandits using the surveillance spells to fell the terrorists still standing.

"The code. Emergency procedures," Mike said, shock turning to grim certainty as the last terrorist in the room dropped. "The only way the magic from the Awakenings can be relocated is through an Act of War or if the structure destabilizes beyond repair."

"This wasn't a trap set just for us," Constantine said grimly, helping me up to meet Axer, who was walking toward us. Constantine looked around the devastated room filled with bodies, then up at the Awakening mages whose cages were flickering out. The layer cracked and shifted again. "This is a sacrifice."

"I can feel their terror," Neph said. Silent until now, her voice was numb.

"And they have it all immortalized on recorders they set up," Olivia said, voice scarily even. "The reports and several selective bits are all over the newsfeeds already—they claim they had to take the magic to save as much of the layer as they can. They are already reporting that a cataclysmic event is about to occur, and the sanitarium will be lost as well as the stability of the Second Layer. Because of Ren. The only thing they don't have is your magical signature,

Ren. They have Leandred's, but if they get yours... Their footage even looks like you are working in tandem with the terrorists."

"Which begs the question—how did Godfrey Jr. get here?" Constantine walked over and kicked his dead body hard.

"Revive him for questioning," Trick said immediately.

"There's no time," Dagfinn said, voice going tight. "Structural integrity of the building is declining rapidly. Seventy percent—sixty-five percent—Sixty—"

Axer whipped out a storage paper I had given him long ago. It was the paper that had once housed a dozen different terrorists. Magic shot around the room and pulled Godfrey's body inside, along with a slew of others.

"Godfrey will remain temporarily dead in suspended animation until we need him," Axer said grimly. The ten-minute timeframe was paused in the paper—a bit of temporal physics that I had done by accident and been hoping to recreate on a medical scale someday.

The layer cracked again, and it snapped the overwhelming patterns back into a normal view. I shoved the Kinsky parcel into my cloak.

"Can you do that to everyone in the building, Dare?" Olivia asked sharply and hopefully.

Axer looked at the over four thousand mages staring back at us. He looked at me and I shook my head, lips pressed against the horrible emotions rising in my throat. "No," he said grimly.

The building sparked and started teetering. I could feel it shift—shift to slide down the rock, down the cliff, crumbling into the ravine. I had climbed this mountain. I knew how far the canyon lay below.

I looked at the grid of mages in their various states of Awakening—the coherent ones staring back—four thousand plus mages about to die as part of Stavros's bigger play.

One of the mages near the bottom put her hand against the glass, gaze fiercely connected to mine.

The foundation cracked. I let my cuff fall.

"Ren, you will be blamed," Olivia said sharply, seeing the motion through Dagfinn's hacked surveillance.

"I know." The building tilted.

Axer's cuff fell next to mine. Constantine looked sharply at him. Axer raised a brow then looked deliberately at Constantine's already bared wrist.

I closed my eyes and reached out with my magic and froze Crelussa and the Second Layer in a mile radius around Crelussa, using the knowledge I had gained from creating the bubbles in the Third Layer.

"Signature logged," Olivia said tightly. "The stories are already being spun."

"How long can you hold the radius?" Axer asked me, gaze switching lightning fast between weak points in the structure.

"Five minutes, maybe. Without consequences."

Axer turned and shot off a spell so suddenly that I jerked. Two techs rose, struggling, from the floor in his remote grip.

"Please, we can help," one of them said, flailing at the band around their throat. "We can give you more time. Fifteen minutes, at least."

He set them down, and held his hand palm out to the side. A spell flew from Constantine to Axer's hand and Axer twisted it before lassoing it around the techs. "You betray us, even in thought, and you—and your next closest kin—die without the ease of death that falling from this mountain would give you."

The first tech shook her head in terror, then ran to the controls. "We don't want the Awakening mages to die. The Department pulled the magic offsite. Why would they do that? We are dead without it."

"They are sacrificing you," Axer said, turning away. No longer constrained by a cuff or container, his fingers spit another spell at the floor which spread rapidly in all directions. "Revive any of the others you need. But each person you revive will be under the same death spell until we are physically gone from this site," he finished without watching as the other tech paused in his scramble to revive two of their coworkers.

The tech revived one, but set a coma spell over the other. A good choice, as the other was one of the techs who had acted suspiciously.

"Can you flip the mountain?" Axer asked me.

"Yes, but I can't guarantee the results." I swallowed. Possible cataclysmic repercussions. Crelussa was full of magic. Even with the vats gone, the magic of four thousand Awakening mages and the slew of linchipin wards that survived and held the Second Layer safe equaled the combined force of multiple nuclear bombs. I couldn't anticipate the repercussions.

There were so many pieces in play. The book had hit the reverse button for me, but this destruction wasn't mine. It wasn't one person's alone—no thread that could be followed.

I shook my head. "But we can save this spot. Build it anew."

"Remake Crelussa?" Olivia asked sharply.

"Brick by stone by ward by line."

"Can you do that? You have to get them exactly right," Loudon said, all seriousness for once. "Crelussa is tied to so many things. Do you understand that, Crown? Exactly. Or it—and anything connected to it—goes boom."

I licked my lips. "Yes."

"You might not save them. And you will be blamed," Constantine said. "You will still be hunted."

"We have to try," I said quietly.

"I know, darling," he said, and opened his palm, motioning to me, already knowing what I was going to do. There was a sadness, resignation, and surrender to his emotions that I didn't understand.

I pulled out the box I had been safeguarding since leaving campus.

"Is that the campus magic?" Patrick asked sharply. Without waiting for a reply, he and Olivia started barking new commands at others apart from our feed.

It was the campus magic as well as the Department's destructive magic that we had all flipped with the field Con, Stevens, Mbozi and I created.

"What are you going to do?" Mike asked softly while Will contributed to whatever Patrick and Olivia were doing.

I felt Neph open herself up to me, her emotions muted in sorrow. I couldn't even imagine what she was feeling from all of us.

"We are going to recycle this site using the mages and magic already here," I said, looking at the cells. Determination and confidence was strumming through me.

I opened the box on top of Constantine's palm and withdrew the end of a long satin ribbon. I connected to the magic of the box and pulled.

This time the canopy of gold and silver satin opened outward like a parachute—throwing the magic into a shimmering net around us, then pushing like an expanding balloon to cover the entire building and site.

"Standing by," Olivia said. "We are with you."

"I know." I could already feel them. Feel Excelsine waking up. The connections were too entangled to identify—an interconnected web of support connecting into an impenetrable field.

I adhered the edges of the canopy to the layer and pulled the community magic that we had engaged.

Constantine's breath stuttered next to me, then his fingers gripped the box and his mouth firmed.

I connected to the wards and the magic, nudging it to reveal its previous state, then hooked those together. Then the next set, then the set after. Ten, twenty, fifty.

Like starting a roller coaster ride, we initially sailed forward. But all too quickly we hit the uphill climb. Everything was still building toward an end, but the car was slowing and clicking louder. It was becoming harder and harder to get the magic to do what I wanted. The edges of the wards kept slipping away.

"The magic is backsliding. Like it's trying to go up a slide, and keeps slipping to the bottom," Saf grimly agreed. "What is happening?"

"It's not enough. The magic isn't enough," Olivia said.

A surge of magic powered through the canopy, and I started knitting again, faster this time. But intertwined with the surge of power came a sickly, terrible feeling.

The feeling became worse, and the copper and turquoise and violet threads that had hummed with life since Constantine had stopped hiding them started dulling, thinning in my hands. I tried to inject them with life, but as it was with the Origin Book, once the magic began pouring in one direction, it was something I didn't know how to reverse.

I looked at Constantine. At his graying skin and resigned expression.

And I knew with a sudden, horrifying certainty that he was dying.

"No, no, no," I said, lower body scrambling, upper half elbows deep in a magic I couldn't stop.

"Neph just passed out!" Mike said from far away. "Will, Olivia!"

"How could she pass out? What pathway was she...oh, no," Liv said.

"Shoot, shoot, shoot, Leandred was expelled," Kita said. "Why did no one think about that? How has he been channeling the magic? Just through Nephthys? What have the two of them been doing?"

"Sacrificing themselves, obviously," Mike said grimly. "Bau is not a surprise, but what the hell, Leandred?"

The color was seeping from Constantine so rapidly now that I couldn't even identify a shade that wasn't gray. I tried to physically tear my hand away, but his grip became steel around mine. I stared at him in incomprehension.

"It's okay. Your muse will be okay." With his other fingers, he softly touched my hand that was gripped hard in his. "And forty-five hundred for one is a tolerable trade."

I couldn't stop the magic and I couldn't get out any words.

"No," said Axer's voice, without inflection, from behind me at the same moment he grabbed the back of Constantine's neck with one hand and mine with the other.

And then Axer's magic reached through mine. I felt it pull hard, taking control and pinching the connection from Neph and campus to Constantine.

The building started to slide again. The techs and mages cried out, useless in these last moments of terror.

"Dare's stopping the play," Olivia said grimly. "He'll get them offsite. We need to see if we can save any of the Awakening mages in or after the fall. Crelussa is going down. Get ready."

"Understood," Dagfinn said. "We are going to prime the—"

Then Axer grabbed the entirety of my connections and pulled. The Bandits all hissed.

"That's not stopping! That's not moving offsite! That's—"

He pulled from Constantine, too, but a different pull—he had taken control and was funneling Constantine's abilities. I knew the feeling of this pull. I knew what Axer was doing. I felt Neph yanked back into full alertness and health. I felt Constantine revive fully on a gasped breath and abruptly flushed cheeks.

Constantine was staring at Axer in shock and disbelief, both of us half-turned to look at him.

"I would still choose to save you. I accept the blame for that," Axer said quietly. "I always have."

A combination of incomprehensible emotions overcame Constantine's expression. Then he closed his eyes, and their connection burst open.

The pulls zinged a hundredfold—bursting outward with added deliberation.

"Do you all feel that?" Will said in wonder while the others shouted.

I felt Neph stroke our connections, then offer up the entirety of her muse community ties.

"How is he doing it from so far away?"

"You know how."

"Dear Magic. He's a Bridge. And he's using Leandred's magic and the connections he is still holding. He just copied one of my thoughts—I felt it."

"Not just those connections either."

I couldn't look away.

Watching someone who had hidden a talent for so long—shaky at first, then growing stronger and stronger until flares of gold and blue were the only things I could see.

Axer used the combination of Mind and Bridge Magic and pulled from the mages in front of us, then the ones behind us, taking over their connections, searching and grabbing the ones that directly led back to Excelsine, then the ones that led to those, then to others, connecting them into a web that not only pulled on school, but that also pulled on the four thousand mages overflowing with power before us.

And he funneled it all directly into a container he was touching—me.

The thoughts of thousands of different mages were incomprehensible, but their feelings ground me. I knew exactly what to do with a streaming red room, and I had been schooled every day at Excelsine in how to handle chaos for a finite period.

Neph's magic swept through the pathway created just for her—and soothing magic fell upon the entire chaotic web.

Axer was looking down at me, and suddenly, it all seemed easy.

"Give me everything anyone knows about Crelussa," I said, and opened myself completely.

And he used my magic to stretch effortlessly across the layers, pinpointing each mage through the connections already set, like our very own Priority Five. As soon as the point touched, he created bridgeways into their magic, and Constantine pulled the thoughts from their minds and Neph soothed the roughest edges left behind.

We took from all the techs, the workers, and mages who had graced these halls here and at Excelsine.

And I absorbed it, like the book had, like the red streaming room at Excelsine demanded, and knitted the experiences and knowledge together.

One of the revived techs looked at us in wonder and terror—and in absolute certainty that she was only temporarily discarding the latter as she extended her hand toward us. Connections bloomed across her palm and we grabbed them. The brightest one whispered that it connected to one of the engineers in charge of Crelussa's ward maintenance. And Axer pulled that connection into the bridged web, then pulled another dozen attached to that engineer, then a dozen more—while Constantine copied the knowledge from their minds.

I could feel the shock and fear as each person's knowledge was given to me. But a weird thing happened in the seconds that I started to rebuild Crelussa. Like the tech, there was a moment of stunned silence, then everything became a whirlwind as people actively began pushing anything they knew.

Excelsine was first. Always. They had hardly taken a moment to feel shock before they were joining in with everything they had.

The mages in Crelussa—both the Awakening ones and workers left behind—had joined in the terrified way that anyone seeking life sustaining aid would—completely and unreservedly. There had been little conscious choice at first.

But when they seemed to realize what was happening, when they saw the tech extend her hand, the actions became deliberate. People began shoving their parents, their families, their neighbors, anyone they had ever touched into the mix.

It was those people that took the longest to grant full, unrestrained access. Not all of them did grant access—some had to be forcefully taken—but the majority contributed all that they could.

We had ten seconds counting down as we pulled the last stone on the mountain into place, but it felt like an eternity had passed.

I could feel the paint stirring in my blood, the blood seeping from my nose, and the secrets of the world sparking the air around me.

Axer let out his breath, his eyelids sliding shut and his hands loosening. It was the pose of someone who had done something so utterly satisfying that they didn't know how to express it. Like every stoppered urge held for a millennium had been finally relieved.

Constantine was staring at him like he'd been asked a question for which he didn't know the answer.

"Congratulations," Olivia said grimly. "There's now a tie for the most terrifying mage in the world."

"The bounty on you both just tripled." Loudon whistled. "Niiiice."

"Are you okay, Neph?" I asked desperately.

"Yes," Neph answered softly. I felt her stroke the pulsing connections. I closed my eyes and clasped them gently.

"She is lit like a sun flare. The entire campus is pulsing. Now repeat what you just did and delete everyone's memories," Olivia said grimly. "Including ours."

Constantine was already reaching back out.

"No," Axer said.

"Dare—" Olivia tried.

"We aren't hiding anymore."

Constantine's hand was hanging in the air and he was staring at Axer, that same incomprehensible look on his face.

"There is no way anyone will let the three of you live freely after that," Olivia said grimly.

"We'll see," Axer said, never breaking eye contact with his roommate.

"Leandred?" Olivia asked sharply.

"I'd like to see someone try at this point," Constantine said, but his voice lacked its usual languidity, as his hand slowly lowered.

I looked down at the complicated magic web in my hand, then walked to the tech who had opened her hand and connections first. There was no feel of Stavros on her—I'd gotten used to identifying the mages he had implanted. And none of the successfully revived techs had it. The initial techs had picked well after the evidence of Axer's death spell had become apparent.

She backed away as I approached, her hands open downward in a "don't shoot me" mage gesture. I grabbed one of her hands and looped the ward structure around her palm.

She looked at it in shock and terror. I was surprised she still had the capacity to increase both emotions.

"This one controls the entrance wards," I said, indicating the bright yellow in the web. "Don't let anyone enter the facility until you have assurances of safety from the countries with Awakening mages here—from the engineers and security forces—not the Department. Tell all of them that the facility will fall unless a contingent containing a representative from each country that has an Awakening mage here is present to step across the threshold."

She swallowed and nodded shakily.

"Will it?" Delia murmured.

"No," I said solely through the connection, so that the tech couldn't hear it. She needed the ability to voice that statement as truth.

"Sending that detail to Bailey, as well as the surveillance recording of you saying it," Olivia said. "Going live wide in 3, 2, 1, done."

"Department security forces securing the perimeter were just stopped by outside military forces," Asafa reported.

"We are at a twenty million spread for the news. Thirty million. Sixty," Dagfinn said.

"Twelve delegations already indicated arrival in ten minutes, 01. One hundred delegations. Two hundred."

I looked at the tech. "Each Awakening mage gets a representative."

"I understand." And she looked like she really did.

"Opening Exit AH," Dagfinn said. "I can't believe you crassetars got all the way through the alphabet, then down to H again."

"I can't believe Dare made us create fifty-two exits, and that we've exhausted thirty-four." Kita sighed. "The only thing that sucked more than planning all of those was watching all of them disappear."

"We can use that exit to get us to Verrange," Axer said.

I inhaled and nodded.

"Now?" Mike said sharply. "We aren't going to regroup?"

"All eyes will be here, on Crelussa. There is no better time. And one of the natural routes Peoples shared can get us most of the way there."

It had been hard for Delia to give those routes to Axer. I could feel the lingering uncertainty in her. She wasn't the only one who didn't trust him.

"You've got the site and coordinates, Comms?" Patrick said.

I reached for the lights in my head that throbbed with their presence.

"Yes," Dagfinn said. "Five hundred feet underneath a nondescript office building for a children's toy company. The building schematics aren't going to be of much use, but I've got a program running over them. Hacking into all dark site alternative schematic plans for the town that might hint at what is hidden beneath."

Axer unfurled his fingers and I saw the magical compass in his palm, pointing assuredly west with whatever coordinate Dagfinn had remotely input into it the second the identification spell worked. I saw the phoenix dragon tattoo under his cuff, surrounded by a crown, a sword, and the elements of the universe. I touched my wrist, certain that I would find the same tattoo upon mine.

He looked at me. "We will find all of them now," he promised.

Chapter Twenty

SECRETS OF A CANVAS

"THERE IS NO doubt that it was the Origin Mage who was at the site today. Even the conspiracists cannot deny it, as her active magic was registered all over the site and <u>every</u> detector in the four magic layers of the world indicated her exact position. Furthermore, surveillance feeds show her giving the wards of the Crelussa Sanitarium to—"

I took a deep breath as the small boat pushed away from the broken dock. We had to be dark on comms for this initial portion of the journey, but Constantine had set up a small passive feed to receive news as we navigated the extremely swift underground river that traveled a natural path from Crelussa to a small ski town where we'd find our next transport.

"Also, it was definitively proven today that Alexander Dare is a Bridge. In a stunning and terrifying display, he and the Origin Mage connected the site to thousands of minds in the layer."

I looked down at my fingertips. "I'm sorry."

Sorry that I hadn't been able to do it on my own; that he'd been forced to reveal himself.

"I'm not." Axer was holding steady to the spell that commanded all the oars while surveying the river banks. Defensive spells were ready on his fingertips, hidden beneath an identity signature stolen from one of the techs on our way out. He was multitasking our real escape as paper butterflies carrying wisps of our magical signatures flew south.

"But you—"

"You don't like to risk others," he said softly, looking at me. "It is a testament to your caring nature. But this is a fight that was already in play before you were born, a fight you didn't design, a fight where all of us were already at risk."

I fought tears and looked at Constantine, who was mending a string and pretending that the cat sitting on the floor of the boat wasn't watching the actions with mesmerized eyes. He'd gone from wide-eyed shock in Crelussa to blankness by the time we'd hit the tunnels.

"You had that whole speech about the orphans. And you were the first to drop your cuff. You were going to sacri—"

"You are obviously a bad influence," Constantine said darkly, but at the same time he stroked the bond that was all the brighter between us. "And you"—his gaze lifted to Axer—"I don't know whether to murder you or run from you. What in the scarping whole of the Second Layer were you thinking?"

"That finally, finally I'm free."

"Free? You have never been more chained. You exposed us both. After years of hiding."

Axer shrugged, gaze on the shoreline, as if a life changing event wasn't being discussed. As if he could hide the tightness of his shoulders. "They will blame me. They will say that the powers of a Bridge are even worse than anticipated, or they will say that they are worse combined with gifts from the other side of my parentage. They will say that I caused so much duress that people simply gave me their knowledge."

"Why?" Constantine demanded, shaking with rage and something more complicated.

Axer looked at him finally, gaze zoning in. "Because I don't want to hide anymore. Today just made the choice easy."

I remembered the look on his face back in fall quarter, back when he was facing down the Bone Beast. He had been ready to expose his powers to save campus, but his expression had been resigned. There was none of that resignation now.

Constantine seemed to sense the same thing, tense in a way I hadn't seen him before. "Why?"

"Because hiding has felt like acid eating away at my soul since Salietrex. Because I am caught by regrets that even time hasn't softened. Because even though I've long wished to feel any other way, I will always try and save you," he said quietly. "That was the one thing I never regretted about Salietrex. Even when I wished that I had been the one left behind instead, and in the bitterest years afterward."

Constantine looked away. "With you in his possession, Verisetti could have wrecked the whole of Asiatica. Farther even. And you'd already be Stavros' pet, because Verisetti is careless with his toys." Constantine tried to shield his emotions, but not before I could see the ones he couldn't visually hide. "And you've saved a million others since then. Mages who would have died without you being free."

"But I didn't save the first," Axer said, gaze connected. "Nameless faces, but not the one I knew, not the one I cared for."

Constantine's jaw worked. He closed his eyes, then something—some weight he'd been carrying—dropped, along with his shoulders. "Mother understood. She knew what would happen, should either of us be taken. She wasn't a powerful mage, just a...good one. She understood the stakes. And she wanted you safe. Us safe. She always wanted that. She always chose loved ones over herself. She was never going to leave either of us behind." Constantine's fingers worked over the string almost blindly.

"Why did you?" Axer asked quietly.

Constantine's fingers curled, then he looked at Axer. "I knew something fundamentally had broken in me with the use of the hooks and the sustained mental torture. Something that disconnected me from humanity. You kept trying to share it. You kept trying to share my pain. It was for your benefit as much as my own to break every tie I could."

"But after—"

"After Sera healed me, with you fretting behind her and providing most of the magic—I hated you. You, always the knight triumphant, except this one time. You, trying desperately to reconnect the bonds. You, my only tether left. Seeing myself in a broken mirror of what I used to be as I looked at you. It was utterly, blindingly obvious—you had to go. And it was easy to blame you. You accepted the blame without a thought otherwise."

The memory played in their minds—Constantine spitting out the words you killed my mother, get out—so vividly that I could see it. "You still accept the blame," he said. "When it was quite obvious who was to blame."

"Verisetti."

"Right."

"Con—"

He closed his eyes. "Revenge is easy. It was always easy. Not having connections is easy. Not having to deal with losing anyone else. Not needing anyone else again. Especially not anyone as close as you."

"I would have shared all of it."

"I know, and I hated you all the more for it. Broken toys don't understand they are broken." He looked down at himself, streaming with connections, and gave a sharp laugh. "And now look at me. It's like a tingreal infestation, once she gets her hooks in you."

Gratitude and love, fierce and sharp, pierced me from Axer. I blinked, slightly dazed, uncertain if I should be apologizing to one or hugging them both.

"And here you are again, and I can feel the bonds reconnecting, I let them reconnect, and it's just my fate to be in the same position yet again," Constantine said bitterly. "For I know how this will end. Losing the people closest to me. For all that I protected myself from it."

Axer did something cautiously with his magic that made Constantine close his eyes then slump forward abruptly, chin dropping to his chest.

"I hate you," Constantine said, but I could see the way he was pulling Axer's magic into him, like a man who'd been starving for years.

"I know," Axer said softly.

"I refuse to stop."

"That's fine."

"We are cursed." Constantine's voice was resigned. "We are all going to die."

"Or we are saved," Axer said softly. "And we will all live happily ever after. That was always your ending. Better than my bloodthirsty vengeance."

"I was a stupid child."

Axer reached over and touched his forehead, slowly swiping his thumb across it in a mimic of what I'd unconsciously done on the Bloody Tuesday battlefield so many months ago. Ultramarine paint bloomed beneath his skin, and the scars beneath faded further. "We can be smarter adults."

"Is that what we are?" there was the tiniest bit of humor underneath the resignation.

"It's possibly too soon to tell," Axer said, with the duplicitous earnest playfulness I never saw outside of when we were alone or with his inner circle.

It was funny. By exposing the scars between them, they had ripped away at the scar tissue. And while everything between them was red, raw, and inflamed, it also sought some sort of resolution.

The broken magic swirled around them in a different way than before. Before, they had been completely cut off from one another. Now they were two halves of a broken whole—the ripped edges on one side a match for the other's wounds.

"Stavros will be there," Constantine said. "In some form. He'll know when we get to the ferals."

"Yes," Axer murmured. Wards burst from him, connected through and with Constantine, layering around us. He looked at me. "What did you get from the Kinsky, Ren?"

I touched my cloak and pulled the burlap wrapped parcel free. Examining it, I carefully stuck my fingers inside.

"Darling," came the resigned sigh.

Even Axer was looking at the burlap with a carefully controlled expression that couldn't hide both censure and excitement.

"Wait until she sticks her hand into rotting floorboards," Constantine said idly to him. "You can't hide that spike of adrenaline and anticipation. Death wishes, both of you."

"There are two alarm wards in the twelve you have going between you," I murmured, fingers running against the material inside. "I can feel each of them." So easily, the way they were pulling from each other and layering their powers together. "What could go wrong?"

"Are you kidding me?" Constantine demanded.

I smiled, and stroked the connections which were inching closer together. "Yes."

Though the outside of the case was scratchy, the inside consisted of a soft, protective coating. Stevens, Constantine, and I had created something similar in the lab, but there was a marker here that was different. Kinsky's magic instead of mine. It hummed harmoniously beneath my fingertips.

I pulled the object free to reveal a portrait. It was not an unexpected find, but I frowned at it, fingers moving carefully under the frame. "She's looking elsewhere in this one."

"The same woman, though," Constantine murmured. "Always the same woman. No one's ever known her name."

I looked at him.

"Kinsky's Muse. Artistic use of the word, only, as far as the world knows—nothing else was ever substantiated."

"No one knows what happened to her or who she was," Axer said. "I searched."

It wasn't a surprise that he had searched for anything Kinsky related. He had given me a set of Kinsky's papers after all, and a deep well of knowledge surrounding Origin Magic from an outsider's view. And he had been collecting and defending against it specifically since we'd started working together.

He'd just pulled my paint forward in Constantine.

Origin Elite—I wondered if he would pass that test, too, after today.

I thought about how Kaine had disappeared inside the other portrait a split second after the woman had ejected the portrait. It bothered me that Kaine could travel that way—a way that I had thought solely mine.

"Kaine hardly bothered with us really—he was almost solely focused on the painting," I murmured. I tilted the portrait, watching the paint shift. The profile of the woman inside tilted back the slightest amount. "He sped up when it was being targeted, then defended it specifically. Defended it over grabbing us."

"The Kinsky, the storage vats, the ferals, Stavros's plans... The ties are here," Axer said.

I regarded the portrait, trying to figure out what it was about this one that was different. The woman was standing in an empty kitchen, head turned away and barely moving as she seemed frozen in the motion of looking toward the window. It was the embodiment of an eternal sigh; the last turn as you watched your love leave.

In all the others I had seen, the women had been facing the viewer, and each had gone into motion at seeing me, waving me forward or offering something. Though this one was different from the full-on invitations of the others I had seen, spoken to, or traveled within, there was something similar in the feel—the promise of something more, something hidden beneath the crests of paint.

I touched the edge of the frame and the taste of the sea and feel of despair burst upon my senses. The tones encasing the woman were earthy and melancholic. The lost love. The earth maternal. A breeze dotted with salted tears came through the open window to her right, to the direction she had started to turn. There was the barest hint of a tormented sea beyond the Cornish field through the open frame. The curtains moved inward in the breeze, washing over the side of the woman's face in her frozen turn.

It was an odd juxtaposition—the woman moving in small twitches versus the living scene around her. Like she kept trying to turn, but was constantly being pulled back by a gravitational force acting from the exterior paint of the portrait.

There was no sign of a turn, of her holding forth a piece of paper, like the other Kinsky inhabitants—the portrait at Ganymede Station, that I hadn't had the chance to explore, and the portrait in Alexandria, that had asked me where I wanted to travel and giving me the first taste of an Origin Circuit.

This one seemed too small to travel through, though as a mage I had learned quickly that being thought constrained by non-magic physics was a disability in thinking.

But there was something about the painting that felt small. That felt...contained. Like it was specifically created, not a full experience.

Looking at the woman, I thought of my brother. Of how even though I was past the immediate grief, I was still taken by it sometimes, in the dark, when other things bled from the forefront of my thoughts. Lost love, lost family. I let the barest hint of sympathetic magic spiral through my fingers as I caressed the corner.

The woman's head tilted toward me just the smallest bit in real time, like she was checking her peripheral view, then the fingers of her turning hand reached back to the lower, opposite corner and pulled the edges of the painting around her like a cape.

I reached forward automatically as the picture changed with the swirl of oil.

In the woman's place was a chest containing a miniature portrait of the woman on the decorative latch. The background was bare as a Vermeer white-washed wall, and equally as complicated in its devious simplicity of muted tones and shadows of light.

I reached toward the latch, and the chestnut and mahogany colors started to swirl. My lips curved a tiny bit automatically. It was still thrilling to watch art come alive, even after months of doing it myself. And this was a master's work—like seeing the Mona Lisa finally open her lips to tell me her secrets. Thrilling.

I touched the oil, which turned slick beneath my fingers, then thrust them inside. The metallic latch was cold under my fingerpads, and the woman watched me in miniature—as if in this incarnation she could only be captured in small scale.

She said nothing, made no movements to help or hinder me, and offered no items, but there was an anticipation in the way she watched me—her weariness washing away with the displacement of paint. So, I lifted the latch and carefully pushed back the hood of the chest, watching as the oils shifted and moved, and as she disappeared from view.

Inside the chest was a single item, a hand-bound book. I was reaching for it as soon as I consciously understood what it was.

I pulled the volume out and as soon as it was free, the picture swirled and warped once more, and an empty table stood in its place. The woman's peasant dress flowed freely around her legs as she walked across the field toward the sea, visible through the still-open window in the stark room.

I stared at her steadily disappearing figure until she lifted her arms and was carried into the sea-swept vanishing point. Freed. Liberated. Unbound.

I turned my attention to what I held without opening it. The leather-bound volume contained twenty or so pages, each thick and uneven opposite the binding. A book made from separate but deliberate pieces, not a blank book filled in haphazardly.

Kinsky's mark—a bird in flight—was stamped into the lower right corner of the cover.

My hand shook in realization. This was likely an artist's journal. Sergei Kinsky's artist's journal. Given to me in desperation, and unlocked with emotion.

I looked back at the portrait, but it was no longer a portrait—the woman was gone. The only animation in the otherwise empty room was a breeze blowing the hem of the curtain. Everything alive about the painting now came from outside the inner frame.

I carefully lifted the cover of the journal. Magic puffed from the pages, like dust from a forgotten tome on a forgotten shelf. The dust swirled and hovered above my hands.

The pages were thick, and zings of twilight magic drifted along the fibers as my fingers caressed the edge of the first page. Kinsky's magic was a world of vibrant and muted grayscale. But peeling back the layers of each picture showed a shocking amount of color hidden carefully beneath. I was looking at a full, vibrant hidden world stuffed beneath depression. The grays were rich in tone, texture, and variety, and it was hard to tell whether Kinsky was saying that it was the default state he was trying to highlight, or the secret of it.

Five of the pages lifted upright and vibrated. Paint, pastels, and charcoal flew from their canvasses and into the air in front of me, coiling together in broad and small strokes to show moving images of an event. I reached out and let the magic wrap my finger and the taste, smells, and sounds of the event swept over me, pulling me inside. I gasped as a woman with smoky eyes beckoned. I knew her. She was the woman from every portrait. I walked forward in anticipation—no, Kinsky walked forward with anticipation—I was just experiencing the memory.

The memory swirled, and the woman's once beautiful warm skin was unnaturally blanched and sweating. Dark circles underlined her eyes as she reached up with stuttering last words...

I pushed away at the sudden realization of death, but the magic held me tight, and I saw Enton Stavros in an immaculate suit present himself at her funeral along with a man I didn't know—Oler Mussolgranz—an imposing man with cold, dissecting eyes. Stavros could give me back what I had lost and more. He could shield me from all those who would hunt me. He knew what I had long suspected and hid about my abilities—abilities only Priyasha had encouraged. Always Priyasha.

Stavros was building a place for rare mages. The Zantini Institute. He wanted to help fix what had been lost in the Third Layer and create a think tank for the future. His offer was generous, but I felt unease at this man with the soulless eyes. Nothing like my Priyasha's warm, honest, fiery gaze—a woman who lived in the sun and loved the salt of the ocean.

But Mussolgranz touched Priyasha's dead hand and I could see her soul—the inner fire of reds and yellows and deep earthy golden browns that always swirled around her—hover above her cold lips. That light of life had gone out the moment she had breathed her last—taking all the wonder of life and my future with her. And here was a man, telling me he could bring her back.

And I said yes. Always, yes.

I broke away with a heaving gasp.

"Ren," Axer said sharply, both he and Con were holding me up as the story world dissipated.

"He promised Kinsky he would return Priyasha. His love. Her name was Priyasha. She died." Paint spewed from beneath my fingernails, sizzling on their cloaks where I gripped them. "He lied. He lied."

"Who?" Axer brought my gaze up to his, making me focus, even as he spread a palm above the sizzling patches on their cloaks.

"Stavros. Mussolgranz." I had heard the latter's name before. In the Ganymede Circus art store. The snobbish magicist woman had said that it was the only kind of Kinsky she would purchase—one made under the direction of Mussolgranz when at the Zantini Institute.

Axer sat back on his heels, mouth going grim. "The Zantini Institute started as a think tank for rare mages. Oler Mussolgranz ran it."

"It started as a think tank, then turned into what?"

"The Institute became part of the Department when Stavros became Prestige. Renamed the Chamber, it was a laboratory and research base just as the Institute had been. They were always making great strides," he said. "But their methods were...questionable."

"What, that's...is there no one with imagination there?"

Axer frowned, then touched my neck, fingers lightly brushing my skin. "Ah. Translator. Basement, Department, Chamber—all those names are far more complicated in their original language." He smiled. "I like your translation better. Better to make them simple. Simple can be defeated."

He leaned back. "Mussolgranz died with Kinsky, and the Chamber died with him. Stavros survived..." He twisted his hand. "And the Basement was born."

I looked at the path ahead of us. "Time to see it first-hand."

Chapter Twenty-one
GENESIS OMEGA

WE CAUGHT UP with the Bandits through our comms at the edge of Verrange after traversing three more natural paths through roots, streams, and rock veins.

"Bailey has been working overtime," Olivia said, giving a short report. "She was remarkably prepared for the event. Her reporter recorded some excellent footage. Thousands of the Awakening mages and their families, as well as a surprisingly large number of the tech personnel on site, are adamantly claiming that you three saved Crelussa. The Department can't close the reports fast enough."

"Er, right. Yay!"

"Ren."

"Yes?" And my lambasting was going to happen in 3...2...

"I'm glad you got Bailey on your side," she said quietly.

I softened, aching. "I miss you, too."

Neither of us said anything for a few moments as I exchanged remote hugs with everyone—made all the easier by the connections that had been so freshly used.

With shadow cloaks engaged, Axer, Constantine, and I navigated to an underground secret entrance beneath the nondescript toy company in Verrange. Dagfinn had deduced and located it while comparing on-file schematics and accountable magic space. There was a lot of unaccounted space beneath the office building once Dagfinn put magic tracers—all illegal—into play.

"Approaching the gate," Saf said, tracking us.

The gate was a ten by ten magical barrier, connecting to the tunnel. In its center was a circling stream of patterns that began moving faster and interlocking the more I stared.

I looked at Axer and Constantine. Both shook their heads.

"That's why this lock design is used. I can see only the barest pattern, and that's only from having been so tightly connected to you," Axer said.

"Found enough intel to get you through the five blocks after this first one," Dagfinn said. "But it's only you, 01, who can access this gate without a key."

The elaborate patterns shifted, zinged and circled, then parted on an answer that I knew. I knew this pattern—had solved it before. "Got it." I let the answer bleed through the comms so that Dagfinn could work up a skeleton key that I could imbue with the magic for if there was ever a next time.

I inhaled calmly and touched the locking mechanism on my cuff.

Axer stayed my fingers and smiled. "We can remain hidden a bit longer. I've got this one." He held up a sphere that I knew intimately—a puzzle box of the same design that I had solved last term—and inserted it into the pattern. It engaged the lock, combining the two sides to form a whole that was then turned.

The barrier dropped.

I blinked at it, then looked at him. He raised a brow. "I told you that practice was for saving the world."

All those puzzles he had given me to solve had sharpened me. I had recognized the patterns when Ori had first started training me.

"I did, like, sixty of those for you," I said slowly.

"And now we have sixty ways to proceed without you doing any more," he said with a smooth grin, slipping inside.

"We need to get those," I heard Loudon whisper.

"Dammit, Ren," Olivia said.

Axer raised the barrier when we were on the other side and pulled out the key.

"Activating remote trace on the tunnel gates. I can get you clearance through the next five," Dagfinn said. "03, sending you the path."

It had been implicitly understood by everyone that Axer oversaw anything that might involve reconnaissance and fighting.

Which was good, because as we made our way through the twisting corridors it allowed me

to connect all the talk about Stavros and the Basement, the Chamber, the Institute, the little bits and pieces in Crelussa, Helen, the vats, and the timing.

"Liv, I need to know what Genesis Omega is."

She inhaled sharply through the comms.

"When Helen jettisoned the units, you suspected something." When she didn't respond, I said, "Liv?"

"Yes. I know." She seemed to be trying to get herself together. I sent a reassuring squeeze her way.

I heard her swallow. Heard the deathly silence in the rest of the comms.

"Tell me," I said softly.

"Yes." Her voice became certain. "Genesis Omega was a series of population control measures given under the guise of puzzles and tests that Great Grandfather made all the Vanator children do. Phillip and my mother included. Ways to rewrite the political system from within."

"Population control, like, you can only have one child?"

"Like a culling," she said bluntly, and I could feel the emotions ripple through the others as the chill ran through me.

"Culling the non-magicals?"

"That was Helen's plan," she said in distaste. "But it wasn't everyone's. The Vanators created world-breaking operations of different types. Population resets. Temporary dark ages. Using different ways to do it—extraordinary mages, convergences, the captured force of disasters—but Helen's plan used the Awakening canisters, specifically, as a start."

That caused a flurry of reaction over the comms that I forced myself to ignore.

"Are you telling me that they are planning to wipe out, what, large swaths of the population? The layers?"

"I don't know."

"But Marsgrove knows?" I remembered the strange conversation he and Grey had when Marsgrove thought I was "asleep." He had sounded frustrated more than anything. "Why hasn't he told the world?"

"He has been in a flurry since the Department took the canisters. Believe me, there are going to be some major happenings in the next few days. And maybe it's not what I fear, but the canisters..." She broke off. "And no, Phillip didn't know. Nothing concrete. I went through his files. I went through those files using three decryption puzzle boxes that Dare gave us while he was still on campus—dammit, Ren, stop solving puzzles for people," Olivia said grimly. "Phillip only knew Helen had been up to something, knew Stavros was using her, but not what for specifically."

"A new dawn," Mike murmured.

"Yes. There have been whispers—there are always whispers. When Kinsky was alive, I was told there was lots of talk at the parties, in the shadows. The regular things—that Origin Mages destroy as often as they create—that a new dawn was coming. The normal conspiracy theories."

"Raphael knows something," I said. I was sure of it.

"Yes," Olivia said grimly. "He spoke to me of it in roundabout ways. He wants to kill Stavros for his own fervent reasons, and Verisetti's been lost to insanity for years, but he said multiple times that humanity would benefit from his killing of Enton Stavros. That he, Verisetti, would take those involved down and leave those of us left to sort it out. It's easier to glue together his madness the more pieces we see."

"Why doesn't someone just politically take out Stavros?" It was beyond frustrating. Here was a man in power who shouldn't be.

"He's entrenched. An institution. What would it mean to people in the Second Layer to know that we've let such a person in power? People don't want to know. They want to continue their idyllic lives. The Second Layer has it good. Why would anyone want to change that?"

More than one person on the line winced. "It's true," Mike said grimly. "Think of Layer Politics,

Ren. It's a golden age. No one wants to live like those in the Third."

"And Stavros and his policies provide us with an abundance of plenty. Keeps us thinking that way," Olivia said, before I could argue about making the Third Layer awesome with a little work.

"He hosts dozens of science and tech competitions. Puts loads of money into the STEM fields. The Department is very positive to engineers," Will said. "Figuring out who to recruit or keep an eye on, I'm sure, but he's considered a visionary because of his works."

"The only blip on Stavros' record before you came online, Ren, was the Dare uprising," Olivia said. "And he managed to weather that loss by placing responsibility on the countries that directly engaged Itlantes."

I frowned. "He would have had more of Kinsky's magic then, than he does now." It seemed strange.

"Maybe he feared what Sera McEllian Dare would do. There are deep, hidden rumors that no one speaks of, of what a Bridge Mage did with

Origin Magic before a dark age in the past," she said grimly.

Now there was no need for "rumors" of what a Bridge Mage could do with an Origin Mage's power. I looked at Axer, who looked steadily back.

I shrugged. "Okay, but if Stavros is keeping the Second Layer as a land of plenty with all the good things, why is a culling necessary?"

"I don't know," Olivia said grimly. "The Vanators go big, but many people believe small resets are a good thing. Recycling resets, for instance. Maybe his plan is smaller."

"We aren't talking about recycling, though."

"No."

"Why didn't you tell me?" I asked Olivia softly.

She didn't answer for a long moment.

"At the beginning, it was simply a bargaining chip. A piece of information on the chessboard. Like I did with Phillip, I would have used it for other things." Her voice shook. "But the problem with knowledge when crossed with emotion, is in how that emotion shapes and warps decisions. Once you were firmly ensconced within my heart, I could bear no longer to possess the knowledge that would send you right to him, into the pit of the beast."

Constantine jerked, and I looked to see reluctant understanding forming in his gaze.

I remembered how easily Olivia had given in to Marsgrove's deal of extending the deadline on revealing the secret. Quickly ceding any desire to give detail.

"I didn't want it to be you he wanted," she whispered as the last wards dropped right on Dagfinn's schedule.

I gave our connections a stroke as we came to a fork in the corridors. "So, we have to figure out if Stavros's ideals are the same as Helen's."

"Well," Loudon said. "I guess we are going with super sketchy Plan DoGA, then—Die on Glorious Adventure!"

"Loudon, I swear—"

"So, 01," Dagfinn said, firmly entrenched in codenames, even at the possible end of the world. "This is the part where you get to figure out which corridor to take. They both lead to the same place, but there's something weird about the space in the schematics. Usually a good bet that there are multiple pocket dimensions in play. Take heed."

I looked at the possibilities. They looked the same. I touched my cuff, and my fingers lingered on the clasp. I could use magic, or... I could use other means and give us a bit more time. I looked at the flaring thick gold thread connected to the shield around me and carefully twisted it.

A gasp, a laugh, and anticipation echoed. I knew you would survive. I knew you would find it. And I knew you would call. I've been waiting.

You helped us in Corpus Sun. What are your intentions?

I could feel him rifling through the data I let him access. Deliberately let him access.

You are getting so paranoid, Butterfly. And controlled. I approve. Go left.

I held firm. Amusement percolated down the connection from him.

Left, Butterfly.

I looked left, and excitement churned that was not my own.

Left, he sing-songed, but it was saner than normal.

Answers first.

Before you meet the devil? That seems fair.
I felt him rifling again. Your conversation was somewhat correct. Genesis Omega is Enton's attempt to play at God. I do support the part of the notion that... He trailed off, then started to laugh. Enforced truth. Lovely. You really outdid yourself. I must take more care in our mental space.

I learned from the best, I whispered in my mind, looking at the pulsing gold.

Flattery will get you the very heart of a mage. Truly fascinating, how you remade your connections. You left the one to me, but imbued it with honesty. I can tell you truth, or nothing at all. This is to both our benefits in this maze. I'm not leading you astray, Butterfly. You can <u>feel</u> the honesty in your creation.

I could feel his dark humor as I looked down at the gold thread and swallowed at the shine.

I still don't trust you.

You've always been the smart one. But I want you to reach your goal here as much as you want to. And I <u>know</u> this place.

I took the left corridor.

Constantine looked at me strangely.

Right, then left, then left again. Hurry now.

I followed the directions, picking up my pace.

"I'm mildly concerned at our sudden, deliberate path, while you feel conflicted," Constantine said casually.

"You should be," I murmured. "Watch me for possession."

He looked at me sharply, and his fingers wrapped tightly around my wrist.

The boy joins. Charming.

Constantine sucked in a breath, fingers constricting painfully before forcefully smoothing my pinched skin without letting go.

Axer's eyes narrowed on the two of us and he touched my other wrist.

Even less charming, Raphael said. Let's grab a better one.

"Ren," Olivia said stiffly. "Why am I hearing Verisetti?"

The lovely Miss Price, Raphael crooned. A much better addition.

"Ren," she said warningly.

I sent a mental summary packet.

Now, to work, Raphael said with relish. It is good for you to have your rabbits. They will ensure you survive to face Stavros.

I narrowed my eyes.

We aren't going to find Stavros here?

Assuredly, a sliver of him. But the Basement is a workplace, not his home.

Unsettled, I heard the dead silence across the feed.

This is the Basement, though? I asked calmly.

The loveliest of workspaces, designed with the brightest brains to lobotomize in mind.

Why didn't you destroy it?

I've tried. Failed. I've killed thousands in the attempts. The problem was always finding the entrance. Once inside, no problem. I _know_ this place. His mental voice became vicious. But the bigger problem with Enton Stavros is getting him where you want him to be. I had an opportunity...

His voice turned wistful and I felt all three of my friends twist at the connection.

"You would have killed Ren," Olivia said angrily.

Yes. But it's always been her path. She saved herself from the very beginning by making me flee her Awakening before I was ready. Enton would have had us both, had I stayed. Left, then another right, Butterfly, then...

Dark feelings mixed with triumph as we proceeded.

This is it. That door. This is what you want.

This was the Basement.

You have all the pieces for finding Enton. You just need to put them together.

I looked at the swirling patterns on the last door. The patterns were trying to hide their true nature, but I knew them. I sent Axer an image and held out my hand. Axer placed a completed puzzle box on top.

I opened the door and pressed myself against the adjoining wall as Axer quickly slipped inside. At his signal, Constantine and I hurriedly joined him behind a section of stacked crates inside a warehouse-styled room. The shadow cloaks wouldn't hide us for long, but long enough for this.

My heart lurched as we peered around the crates.

At first appearance, it seemed like a normal warehouse. Rows of storage units were piled along the walls with rows of shelves extending far beyond. Unlike a warehouse, the storage contents on the right were quite alive. Mages and beings of all ages and ethnicity stared back at me. The first row was stacked only two high, but the others behind it were ten high and at least twenty deep. Tubes and lines of magic whirled in curlicues of color into and out of the different grids.

And these weren't like the Awakening cells in Crelussa—where a mage would stay for a week or two. These cells were for long term captivity and held no privacy.

There was a different look and age to the gazes of the mages at the far back rows, from the ones at the front. The gazes of the ones to the back were deadened and older—as if all their emotion had been consumed over time, and they were simple husks. The ones I could see in the front rows appeared terrified, and the colors from their cages were sparking and flying. The ages of the mages from back to front descended like a macabre timeline of Stavros' experimentation.

A gruesome vision of pain and death painted the space to the left and the ceiling above.

Creatures and magical beings were attached to magic siphoning tubes and electric fields. Some were stretched out in the air as if they were a moment from being drawn and quartered, others were manacled to the ground. One specific dragon-looking creature was netted upside down on the ceiling. None of them were awake or alert—maybe the only positive in the entirely horrifying scene.

Vats—different ones from those at Crelussa—were stacked to the ceiling in the back of the room, connected outward to both the creatures, beings, and mages in long, clear tubes.

Five "work" tables were arrayed on the left, in front of the rows of storage shelves containing jars, containers, and tools. The storage shelf in the front pushed down through the floor and was replaced by another—this one with a solid front and a far more sinister purpose. Tools glittered on hooks and beakers of steaming liquids shone malevolently in the light.

A cell in a middle row on the right suddenly moved, its top swinging along a tube in the ceiling. It contained a giant fire-spitting lizard.

Five technicians with blank gazes worked around the space. None of them raised a gaze to us.

Hollowed out by Stavros long ago, do nothing to raise them yet, Raphael warned.

One punched in a code. The lizard suddenly froze in its cell and its body was pressed back against the glass. The cell tipped back to rest on one of the work tables, then melted downward, pressing the creature against the table, immobile. A small kit of tools raised into place at its right and I could see the spells that would exchange one tool for another with a flick—probably for one on the newly placed shelf behind.

I shivered. It was a far too elegant solution for containing something living and transporting it immobilized to work upon—tools already in place. I imagined that when they were done experimenting, the reverse would occur, neatly containing the creature in its cell and returning it to its spot in the grid.

I could imagine Raphael upon that table.

Months, I spent upon Table One, Butterfly. Be a love and destroy it for me, will you?

I was shaking. Constantine looked at me sharply, lips firmed, and stroked a hand over my hair. I smiled in reassurance, and he and Axer mentally debated next steps.

I felt Raphael disengage from the others so that it was only the two of us again. *Promise me.* Raphael's voice turned commanding. *Promise* me, Butterfly, that you will destroy it before you leave. <u>Without emotion</u>. Destroy it. Promise me you will do it <u>without emotion</u>.

I wanted to destroy everything I saw, but even with the truth imbuing our connection now I couldn't trust—

If you feel any emotion for the task, do nothing, he said seriously. But if you can do it <u>without</u> emotion, you <u>must promise</u>.

That seems unlikely, I said. Emotion was overwhelming me right now.

An unlikely task then.

Very well.

I could feel his triumph as he sealed the vow, then abruptly disappeared from my mind, like he had done all he needed to do.

Unease swept me. I looked at the empty faces of the workers in trepidation, wondering, while Axer and Constantine plotted out trajectories and strategies—Constantine pulling items from his cloak and slipping them into his roommate's cloak with activation spells and ownership.

This was not a place where normal people worked. The regular mages in the Department who sought security to ensure happiness in the Second Layer worked elsewhere. This was a slave driven hive of an operation. The empty faces spoke to those without emotion or soul.

And so, it was, when a man without a blank gaze strode into the room—a man with a face I had just seen in a painted memory, I felled him immediately with a blast of container magic pulled from Constantine's belt. And when I lifted the man's body, it was to Table One that I secured him with straps. Three dozen straps.

At the first hit of my magic, Axer had vaulted over the crates and immediately taken care of every blank gazed grunt in the room in coordination with the boys' quickly laid plans.

The automaton-like mages didn't put up a fight, which was even creepier. They were as still and empty in repose as their gazes had been in simulated life.

As Axer worked as quickly as he always did to secure a space, Constantine looked at Table One, then at me, eyebrows raised.

"We might need all of those straps," I said.

"Riiight."

Axer's container magic swept the man strapped to the table. He looked up at us with a glittering gaze. "Oler Mussolgranz. Not so dead after all."

I closed my eyes, but could feel the excitement moving through them.

"Get his magic," Constantine said, moving swiftly toward the table, pulling two containers from his cloak.

A cell moved from a holding area, its motions on autopilot, and was raised into place in the newest and shortest row, next to another familiar face.

Rosaria pounded on the glass, screaming, her voice and motions completely silent in the eerie stillness of the Basement.

Samuel and the girl with stars in her eyes pressed their fingers against their glass, watching her, and watching me. Magic zipped along the edges of their cells. Alive. And there were two dozen others of similar age around them. The Awakening mages since I'd come online.

Alive.

The relief was almost crippling. We'd made a gamble—let them take Rosaria, pinned with spells, to follow them to where we'd hopefully find the rest. All the rest. To the Basement. And Rosaria, our baited sacrifice, was still alive.

I was in front of her cell, hand raised, barely remembering having moved.

Rosaria pounded silently on the glass between us, her lips forming two words. "My brother?"

I pressed a hand against the glass of the mage I had failed last. "Alive. Safe."

I had put a thousand remote wards around that hospital, and Marsgrove had moved him to a secure location that even I didn't know.

"You saved him," she said, a silent sob forming around the words.

"No. You saved him," I said quietly.

She pressed her forehead against the glass, but I could still see her mouth. "I killed him. For a moment, I—"

I pressed my palm more firmly against the glass. "You killed no one. A lit bomb was placed in your hands. You aren't responsible." I closed my eyes, then looked over at Samuel. "And you will learn how to make that bomb into something else."

Samuel stepped sideways and touched the wall separating him from Rosaria, his other hand reaching to the girl with stars in her eyes, and suddenly I could hear them. "We are all connected, do you not feel it? We will help each other." Magic zipped along the cells.

"Makali Hōkūlani," the girl with stars introduced herself softly. "And I feel it."

"The man with death in his chest said he will destroy such connections," Samuel said, gaze pinned on me.

I immediately turned to find a release valve.

Constantine's hand gripped mine, pulling me into his chest. "Wait."

"What? I can't—"

"Ren," Constantine hissed. "You can't just release them. Any of them."

"He's right," Axer said grimly, still studying Mussolgranz.

I struggled. "I'm not leaving them like this." Asking me to leave the Awakening mages was asking me to cut off body parts, and I certainly wasn't going to let the tortured beings and creatures stay. "We aren't leaving them here. In the Basement."

Constantine turned me, so I was facing the last of the cage aisles. "Those in the front are still Awakening, and their magic needs stabilizing still—but worse, look at the brain scans of the ones in the back."

My gaze went to the monitor of one cell on the far left of the feral grid, far from the new mages. Symbols and magic swirled in patterns I didn't know. I called up one of the translation spells that allowed for alternate fields of study to be interpreted by laypeople. There was one for medicine related fields, gifted to me by Greyskull, and included in the "emergency pack" that Axer, Constantine, and Olivia had put together before I'd been expelled.

Symbols started translating in my mind as the spell took hold. And I could see what the boys were grimly pointing to.

"There is nothing registering in that cell, or the one next to it," Axer said. "And that's not to say what will happen when the creatures above us are released from hell?"

My gaze darted up at the myriad of creatures pinned to the ceiling. I licked my dry lips—short, quick open breaths drying them faster than I could moisten them. My hand shook. What would I do if I'd been sensory and magic deprived for weeks, months, however long they'd been here? Lash out, die of shock, overload...

"We can't leave them," I said.

Constantine released me. "No." He looked at Axer, gaze intense. "But we have other options. One, in particular, that it's time to take. No more hiding."

I hesitated, hand shaking uncontrollably, then nodded my consent.

"Okay," he said with a strange cocktail or relief and resignation, as if he thought I'd argue. "Don't touch anything while I do this."

I stared at the pinned bodies above, the caged mages in their cells, and my hand twitched toward the console. I shoved both hands into my cloak.

"Are you sure?" Axer asked him, stepping around the table.

"Yes." Constantine put on his ultra-game face—which let me know exactly who he was calling—and turned his head.

Axer immediately started opening wards using Mussolgranz's magic.

Cognizant of the many stares—some surreptitious, others not—from the hundreds of trapped gazes, I turned and walked to the tool aisles. Guard Rock jumped to the ground and padded alongside me. If I returned to the Awakening cells, I was going to release all of them, and damn the consequences. I looked over the assembled horrors. Jars, devices, incubators, conduits, and tools were lined up on shelves. I wandered through the first aisle of shelves numbly.

Dark shadows danced along glass containers and terrarium domes in the second aisle. Shadows like Kaine's. I peered closer.
Each vessel contained something slightly different—experiments at different stages of completion.

I wondered if this was how Kaine had been created. Had he been one of these small shadows? Had they fused a shadow onto a child's body? Had he been created from nothing? Had he grown from a shadowy wisp into the monster that he now was? Or had a Shadow Mage been taken as a child and experimented on?

My hands trembled in my pockets at what Stavros and Mussolgranz were capable of. Of what they had bred or destroyed to make Kaine. At what they would be doing next.

I closed my eyes and let the emotions come. Let them happen. When I opened my eyes, one of the jars on the lowest shelf had clattered closer, as if it had felt my emotions and was reacting to them.

A small shadow was inside. Thin, almost ephemeral. But there was something about it...

I crouched to peer closer. It pressed its tendrils against the glass with small, thin arms. The appeal in the gesture was apparent. It was a bad idea to reach out, but natural curiosity and empathy pulled me closer.

Guard Rock gave the glass a tap with his pencil.

The shadow pressed harder against the glass, pleadingly.

I looked at the other shadows growing and shifting in jars above and around it—malevolently or seductively pressing against their containers. Spiky, empty. Maybe replacements for Kaine. Maybe new beings to add to his army.

I looked back at the one that had captured my attention, and realized I was looking at my palms, and the container had somehow found its way into them. My fingers cradled the glass. Small, trembling tendrils pressed against the glass, reaching toward the heat of my palms and entreatingly toward my face.

I looked at Guard Rock, who shrugged and nodded.

"Ren?"

"Yes?" I called over my shoulder. The tendrils of shadow picked up speed, pressing, reaching for me, begging.

"They've arrived."

I stared at the jar, at the pleading tendrils. I tucked it into my cloak as I rose. "Coming."

Axer stared at me as I rounded the shelves, an expression on his face like he knew that I had touched and taken something. I swallowed and looked to Constantine, expecting him to start yelling, but he was focused on the entrance.

Stuart Leandred stood in the doorway. Grim-faced, he walked inside the space, ten mages wearing hazard gear trailing behind him.

Bellacia and Roald Bailey entered next. Bellacia's eyes were half-lidded and triumphant as she locked gazes with me. "Ren, my dear, dear, overpowered magelet."

Her fingers ran along my arm as she passed, spells flying to absorb every detail. "This, well, I will be processing this debt to you for years."

Her gaze paused on Constantine, then moved on. "You have your vow on that front and then some, as well," she said to me, without a second look his way, already working through fifteen different stories as she walked.

Roald Bailey studied me with dark, intelligent, dissecting eyes, and I felt a sense of unease.

"Now, Daddy, what did I say?" Bellacia called, without looking back.

"I'm still uncertain this is the way to go, Bella."

"Trust me," she said, gaze taking in everything. "Trust me."

He gave me one last look and followed her, powerful recording magic flinging from him in a burst of light.

Marsgrove came through next. Several officials followed in his wake, and immediately scrambled for defensive spells when they saw me, then scrambled even harder when their gazes landed on Axer. Marsgrove absorbed their spells in one raised protection spell and sighed. "Why are you still here, Crown?"

His voice implied that we should have disappeared the moment we opened the doors.

My eyes strayed to the Awakening mages. "I...I can't... We are going to stop whatever Stavros is doing, but I need...I need the Awakening mages safe." I needed to be able to think of other things, knowing they were safe.

"We will gather them," Marsgrove said, voice far quieter than I had heard it.

"But Stavros—"

"Stuart," Marsgrove called over his shoulder, looking steadily at me.

Stuart Leandred turned from where he was engaged in a tense conversation with Constantine. "Phillip."

"Permission to move the Awakening mages to Itlantes. They have facilities freshly prepared by some strange accident of fate."

Stuart's gaze went to Axer, who looked back with a calmness that was entirely false.

Stuart's eyes grew distant for a moment, "Permission granted by a 5-2 edict from the Council, though the two dissenting members are scrambling to repeal the decree, citing that we have been bamboozled by a Conquering Mage."

Marsgrove turned unimpressed eyes on Axer. "You've been upgraded. Congratulations."

Axer looked at him steadily, then turned to watching the proceedings. I noticed that he had removed his cuff.

Marsgrove flicked his fingers at an assistant, who was now punching codes in the console. The cells around the Awakening mages flickered and started to move.

I raised my hand, and Rosaria, Samuel, and Makali raised theirs. The cells turned, lined up end-to-end and shot through a tube.

There were a few tense moments, then, "Arrival complete," Stuart reported.

"They made it," Axer affirmed, gaze connected to mine.

Tension uncoiled in my gut and I gave a high-pitched laugh. "All of them?"

"Every single one."

Saved. I wrapped my hand around the edge of a shelf and let my chin drop to my chest, closing my eyes and letting the dark spots creeping over my vision blend into full black.

"Ren?"

"It's okay. Do your thing." I opened my eyes once the blood rushed back and focused on the floor. I could feel Axer casually step closer anyway.

They'd be fine. They'd be fine. Everything was going to be okay. The ferals were saved. Saved. And Stavros and his Basement unmasked.

"Crown. You did... You did well." Marsgrove touched my shoulder, then slipped away to supervise.

"Ren?" Olivia demanded.

I slid to the floor as all the Bandits' voices cut back in—Marsgrove's people raising communications to the outside world—and overriding the "mute button" that I hadn't realized I'd engaged.

"They are safe. Saved. Alive."

"We know," Olivia said softly. "You did it."

"We. We did it."

The Bandits commenced celebrating loudly over the comms as the authorities began systematically processing, recording, moving elements, and shooting us incomprehensible looks.

I saw Julian Dare enter, his eyes glittering with, I didn't know what, as he looked around. He looked at Axer and tilted his head. Axer tilted his head back, then nodded to an area of the Basement that Julian immediately headed for. I wondered why he wasn't going with his uncle, but then saw the conversation he was eavesdropping on.

Stuart and Constantine were having a low, tense argument in one corner while Axer remained near—alert to everything that was happening with the Leandreds and with me. Guard Rock jogged over to stand on Axer's boot, obviously deeming it the best guard spot.

Axer flicked a finger at me and suddenly I could feel the boys' connection and hear the conversation between Constantine and his father as if they were standing next to us.

"This will go a long way to rehabilitating your name, Constantine. But Stavros will blame this facility on Mussolgranz—magic knows how he survived and has stayed hidden—working in secret."

"Stavros won't be able to hold that argument for long."

"He doesn't need long. He has the Crelussa containers. He is hiding them legally, and it will take days—maybe weeks—to retrieve them," Stuart said grimly.

"Then you have plenty to work on. As do I," Constantine said. "I'm not coming with you."

"At the very minimum then, it shouldn't be hard for you to leave Alexand... You forgave him," Stuart said in a nearly disbelieving tone, looking at something on Constantine, some tie or magic that was visible to him.

"That is none of your business," Constantine said coldly.

I could see the anguish in Stuart Leandred's eyes. The desperation to be forgiven as well. To have his son back. But how did you forgive the unforgivable? What was involved in mending a relationship that was irreparably broken?

The despair on Stuart's face made me look away, unwilling to witness it.

"You… If you stay with them, you'll be dragged down with them," Stuart said. "You will be destroyed."

"Then there will be a lot more goodwill for you to do around the layer," Constantine said, unfazed. "Sad and tragically. All will benefit from your benevolence and sorrow once more."

I remembered what Constantine had told me about his parents. That Sashia had made Stuart want to be a better person—that he had changed from a greedy industrialist into a philanthropist. That change of heart had tripled again in the wake of her death, his psychotic break, and the destruction of his son. Like fixing the world might give him the clemency that he sought—trying to gain through the world what his son would never allow.

"You know that is not what I want," Stuart said tightly. "I did all I could for you. After... After I destroyed the son I had." He closed his eyes. "I will never be able to take back my actions or grief, and I deserve all the hate you give. But I will to protect you now as I have tried to in the past six years, as I should have always protected you."

"You loved mother more than you loved me." Constantine said it distantly. "I always knew that."

Stuart looked down at his hands. "I've only ever been capable of loving one thing. Power, greed, your mother, then you. All consuming. And the emotion consumes me before the next target takes hold. It was only after—" He broke off; looked at the ground. "After my grievous actions that I took the steps to become other."

"You are saying that there's hope for me. That I might love more than one thing?"

"You already do," Stuart said with an edge of wistfulness as he looked at the connections streaming around Constantine. "You already broke the first part of the cycle. You are in charge of your choices. As I am—now after so much work." He shifted. "Leandreds are masters of all minds but their own, until they choose, or are forced to a choice. You have shifted naturally. It took me the aid of mind healers to do so."

I stared at him and a lot of loose pieces abruptly made sense. How Stuart Leandred had gone from what was essentially a crime boss, or the nearest thing to it twenty years ago, to a powerful benevolent statesman who the people loved. Like Olivia had said, Constantine wasn't a sudden, rare mage. He had inherited Mind Magic abilities from his father—who could craft himself into whatever he wanted people to see.

If Stuart's focus had shifted completely to Constantine's mother and all her causes—she had been extremely beloved in high society, philanthropic circles—then he would have crafted himself into all that she desired.

And when she died... When someone died and they were all that you placed your emotional stability on...

Christian's death was still devastating, when I allowed myself to dwell on it. But though I'd put most of my energy into my brother's basket growing up, I'd always made it a point to know myself. To be in tune with inner Ren. And I'd had my parents, even though I'd felt isolated right after Christian's death—we were a tight knit family who just needed time.

"I remember well your abrupt switch from torturer to loving caregiver," Constantine bit out. "I would have rather you stayed consistent."

"Would you?"

"I do not forgive you."

"No." Stuart leaned tiredly on a decorative cane. "I seek no forgiveness from you. Only the chance to improve your lot."

"Buying favors, losing negative transcripts, and keeping me from expulsion. Yes."

"It was the only thing I could do. Now, I can do more."

"For a time, I had hoped I might find the end of your wire. Then it became more of a chore," Constantine said jadedly.

"Would that you had been less aware, perhaps." His eyes shifted to me. "Or maybe, it is just a good thing that events fell as they did."

Constantine smiled sharply. "So glad an Origin Mage fell from the sky?"

"No." He looked at me. "Just that she did."

The charged silence that followed made me itch at the elbow.

Constantine's lips firmed and a Molotov cocktail of emotions swirled within him.

"I've hated you for so long..."

Axer stepped toward him, but Constantine held out a hand to him without looking.

"Anger is what I lived on," Constantine said. "Anger and bitterness. It's in my blood, I suppose." His mouth crooked unpleasantly. "But so is intelligence. Why haven't you already gotten rid of Stavros?"

Stuart looked away, lips tight. "You think people haven't had concerns about him? Even without the damning evidence around us right now to prove it? You think I didn't know what he really was under that gentlemanly demeanor? Even with his mind locked far away where I can't reach it, I've always known. Everyone who encounters him for more than a minute, knows, somewhere deep inside. Even without our powers."

"The old Stuart got rid of those who opposed him. He was good at it. Like the reels show so well. No one stayed in business when you wished it otherwise. Entire operations went up in smoke the next day."

"Yes, I was once exactly like him, but for the scale and human horror," Stuart said, looking around the space. "But you know it isn't that simple. The more important question is how has he stayed in power? How did I? Why does the public turn a blind eye?"

Constantine grit his teeth. "By giving them what they want, so they conveniently ignore anything else."

"By being useful. By giving so much on one hand that people ignore what he is taking in the other. By keeping the monsters from fully breaching the gate—monsters who are always at the gate. So close to the gate, that they don't care that the occasional villager disappears. It usually isn't a villager anyone knows. Ferals are blips in a sea of comfortable ignorance. He doesn't take the known ones though, such as you and Alexander.

He would have taken you both long ago, if he could have."

"I'm surprised he didn't."

"All of those parties and social events that Maximillian, Sera, your mother, and I sent you to so early, some far too decadent for ones so young, but they got you both noticed. You can never be anonymous. Society's heirs all know each other by sight and magic. You can't go missing, if you are known. Disappearance costs the government far more."

"Society is a game. I never noticed."

"Don't be boring, Constantine," Stuart said, more harshly than I'd ever heard him. He was usually very conciliatory to his estranged son. "You know exactly why I did it. And you know why Stavros is in power."

"He protects our interests. And as long as little Apollo is fine, and everyone's companies are faring well, everyone is free to turn a blind eye. No one cares about feral mages who aren't even of this layer."

"No matter what kind of dirt you get on Stavros—pinning this horrible place to him—the only way his supporters will care is if he is seen killing an untouchable person in their eyes. And he's too careful for that. People are willing to let a lot of people they don't know die. Numbers on a spreadsheet. However,"—he straightened his fashionable coat—"you save a place like Crelussa Sanitarium and thousands of magicist children with ties that Stavros could never count on defeating... You find plans for his destruction of Tus Onus... Or Gliar Peit. Or whatever culling he's going to do with all the Awakening magic and a Bridge and Origin Mage at his disposal, and, well, now we have some ink."

I felt Constantine's echoing shock to mine.

Stuart's mouth firmed grimly. "Selen Vanator was a very close friend before I met your mother. But while I can nail the Department with Crelussa, Stavros will blame it on Helen Price. It will take more to ruin the Prestige."

"We find this evidence, and you will what?"

"I will make them see."

Constantine looked at him for a long moment. "Very well."

Over the comms, Olivia was trying to corral the others into moving into Phase 2, while Patrick was advocating for a little "celebratory time."

"Stavros's culling isn't going to wait for our celebrations, Patrick," she said firmly.

"Just one small—"

"What do you make of this, sir?" a tech asked Marsgrove, frowning at the console. "There's powerful magic here, almost like another lab space. But where?"

Axer stepped closer to them, Guard Rock traveling with him.

Another tech was flipping shelves, cataloging the contents of the Basement, and a third was flipping the rows of occupied cells. It was between one of those flips and the next that the Kinsky appeared.

"Con, Axer." I inhaled sharply.

I could hear swearing, but I couldn't look away, couldn't move.

A Kinsky, previously hidden by rows of shelves, was in full view. A small symbol rippled in the lower corner of the portrait and a heavy beat drummed in its paint, vibrating its frame.

Between one breath and the next, I was suddenly in front of it—like I had been moved by a godly hand from one spot to another.

Priyasha waved me back with panicked motions, pointing frantically at my cloak with one hand while the other pressed against her painted veil. The symbol rippled in the lower corner of her canvas.

"Do you have something else for me?" I asked, already knowing that wasn't the right question.

She motioned again, aggravated strokes of paint even more frantic, her head tilting behind her as she grew increasingly panicked. I started to back away, feet moving nightmare-slow.

I saw Kaine slither behind her a split second before I was lifted from my feet and pulled into the painting. The room turned, flipping in on itself like a moving tessellation—separating me in a clean slide from those running toward me, like I was on a turning face of a Rubik's cube.

I could no longer hear the others. Not the boys, not the Bandits or Olivia. Not Neph.

And I couldn't feel my magic anymore.

Chapter Twenty-two

EMPATHY OF THE LOST

P RESSURE PUSHED down on me and my cuff disintegrated as soon as the paint touched it. The paint was seemingly attached to me everywhere—like an animal stuck in a tar pit—leeching my magic so I couldn't use it.

"Struggling will just pull the magic from you faster. A small gift from one Origin Mage to another, though your predecessor had no idea the Pull would be used for this."

I could barely feel my friends, and I could hear none of their words. The connections were still there, but growing hazier, and I grasped onto them as the pull grew stronger.

Kaine smiled and his shadows lashed through the air, searching for weaknesses in my cloak and shields, and tearing apart both.

"I will kill Verisetti for the time I spent as his prisoner," Kaine said pleasantly as he worked. "But do you know the unintended consequence of combining with him for those months?" Kaine smiled. "Your shield set. The keys to all that he has created are now mine."

And through the pull, I felt my shields stripped from me, taking with them all the protections that I had relied upon forever. All except for the last shield—the last one he flipped into an amplifier. An amplifier and detonator.

"Verisetti embedded them in your very marrow. They will regrow, but how long will it take? One day, two? Far too long, I think, for you. You can't even control yourself with them."

He let me go, as abruptly as he had caught me, and my magic, raw and scraped and empty, started to slowly fill, but it was pulling the magic around me inside instead of regenerating my own. Kaine's gaze was taunting, daring me to use it.

I carefully touched the shield that was doing the equivalent of a First Layer countdown, only there was no countdown number attached, just a trigger—me.

I looked at the paint in the air around me and it rippled, but didn't part. And even though I could see points where I might break through it, something in me said I shouldn't. Axer had trained me far better than to just lash out without thinking through the variables. And something that was a mixture of a male and female voice said, Not yet. Not without incomprehensible loss.

I had always had my shields and my own untainted magic to rely on, but something within me that I had yet to identify was slowly eating it away.

"Come on, Origin Mage. Let's see your great powers now. My bet is on you taking out at least two layers. Enton set the seals up to obliterate each town they are in when destroyed by a regular hand. By you? Well, let's see what you do."

I carefully looked around me while I stored his words, letting them percolate into a pattern in the back of my mind. It looked like I was still in the Basement, and yet I could see nothing of the boys, Marsgrove, Stuart, the Baileys, or the others.

"This is a painted layer all its own." I could see the world-building elements. Could see the care that had been taken at first, then hastily finished by a less gifted hand. "Do you live here?"

"An in between, courtesy of your predecessor. And I live everywhere," Kaine said, slithering to the side, watching me carefully.

The jar tucked in my cloak shuddered with fear. I swallowed and held still, taking in more data, trying to act unconcerned.

The Basement was replicated around us—only small changes modifying the view in any way. But Mussolgranz was the only person in view—hazily in view, attached to Table One. I didn't know what it meant that only he could still be seen.

Kaine followed my gaze. "Ah, my lovely master, caught in the crossfire. We can't have that." He flicked his fingers and Mussolgranz flipped, still attached to the table, into our reality.

Kaine could do simple Origin Magic. My hands curled into fists to keep them still.

Mussolgranz flexed his arms and magic and the straps fell away. He looked at me dispassionately—a sterile scientist without feeling—and then paint rose from the floor, slithering up his body and reforming Mussolgranz into a form I knew far better.

"Take care of our guests, Archelon," Stavros said, painfully clenching his teeth, furiously cold gaze fastening on me. "Release the beasts and destroy the facility, if necessary."

Kaine flicked his wrist and the side of the room morphed into a long hall. He strode down the hall, the wall reforming behind him.

But not before I saw the swirl of it. The paint. A manipulation I knew. There would be other corridors, too, corridors I could take. I touched the flipped ward on me.

No! Not yet, not yet, millions lost, the scared voices said.

I swallowed. "We meet again, and yet not, Prestige Stavros," I said, trying to keep my voice calm. It was absurd that in all of this, it was a good thing that this was a Stavros facsimile, for I wasn't ready. With a bomb attached to my chest, it would have been Raphael's perfect scenario. But I couldn't afford the fallout. I started looking at the edges of the painted world, the hidden divots and thin valleys, looking for an escape without using magic. "Once more, a puppeteer from afar. You said when next we met, it would be face-to-face, and yet, here you are once more."

He bared his teeth. "You've made a liar of me time and again. I don't much like it, Miss Crown. I am a man of my word. But that isn't to say I can't do you some damage for all that you've caused me."

His hand whipped through the air, catching paint like it was frozen rain and throwing it at me. I automatically lifted my cloak, but with none of the protections that usually kept me functional, the paint shot through it and my shirt, sizzling as it splashed against my skin. I stumbled with the pain, contorting to try and get away.

Paint came again, and this time my body automatically reacted to the threat and raised an external shield. Paint rippled around me and there was a crackling boom in the distance. I could hear people scream—I could see a flicker of the boys and some horror swooping down—then silence and emptiness. I dropped the shield and stumbled backward.

"Why are you stopping?" Stavros said derisively. He flung another hand along a line of putrid green, and I dropped to the ground, but half of the splatter caught me anyway, sending electric shocks through me.

A cadaver consuming a body from afar, but he was powerful, and he was turning Origin Magic against me.

"You don't think I stole Kinsky's life and soul from him without taking the keys to the empire of his mind at the same time?"

My body went rigid under the next blast, but the painted world shuddered, and for a moment, I could see figures fighting around me, in the world on the other side. Axer had used an orb of my magic. I felt the echo of the pulsation as it exploded.

Wait, wait, the voices said.

Yes, okay. I could deal with pain. It took a moment, but I pushed myself roughly to my knees.

"I'm not sure if I'm displeased or impressed that you are this resilient," Stavros said. "It has cost me, and that forfeiture will cost you. You are in my kingdom now, Miss Crown."

There was another blast. Another orb. Stavros bared his teeth, pacing angrily as he looked at the shimmer vibrating around us. "All that I've built, and you think...you have the gall..."

Pain lanced through me again.

"You stupid girl. It was almost a good plan, too. If I wasn't completely prepared for such an eventuality. Such a loss."

I wiped the blood from my mouth and felt grim satisfaction as another orb vibrated the world around us. I couldn't feel Axer, who was probably trying to bridge my powers and connect, nor Constantine, who was probably having a complete cow. But I knew the magic was mine. Could identify the vibrations of it.

I pushed myself to my knees. "Quite a collection you had going, too, Prestige Stavros."

He smiled tightly. "It isn't gone yet, despite the loss of your little ferals."

"You are why there hasn't been a feral at Excelsine in so long." My breath issued harshly from my nose as I rose. "You take the strongest ones as soon as they come online. There haven't been enough to populate."

He smiled. "Is this a banal attempt at distraction? Waiting for your friends to save you? Well, as it happens, I also require a few minutes, and I do love to see the rage and realization of the unfairness of the world as it appears, and it always does."

He tweaked something in the paint and I felt the motion like he had reached in and was pulling my veins apart. A steady tug, like I was being drawn and quartered from inside. "No, there have been no loose ferals strong enough for an institution like Excelsine, radical mage haven that it's become. And it was easy to spin and sate the public after dear Rafi used ferals for his own means in Salietrex. Which is why when I heard about a feral at Excelsine, I knew."

I swallowed. It wasn't anything I hadn't known. I'd been marked from the first. Even Will, who had accepted me immediately, had known there was something sketchy about why there were no other ferals at Excelsine, even if he hadn't been able to verbalize why.

"It used to be that we'd add a single mage to the menagerie every month or two—the menagerie your little band is trying to ruin. But with your arrival in our world and the magic you so liberally spread, that timetable could be increased tenfold. Ah, look at you," he mused. "Trying so desperately not to attack me in anger. Afraid that your merry little band would pay for it? You'd be right."

I laughed, trying to relieve my rage and fear. "How did you decide who to keep alive?"

Why wasn't Christian in one of those cells?

"The instructions were always to take a feral and leave a replacement in its place. However, if something happened..." He shrugged. "There are always more eggs. Worrying about a broken egg is senseless."

"My brother was one of those broken eggs."

"And now he is dead. Move on."

Words in response were all choking me, the fury collecting inside the expanding bottle of my chest. "What do you want, with all of this? What is Genesis Omega to you?"

He smiled. "Why, I want the same as you, Miss Crown. I want to set the Third Layer to rights. I want to get our society back on track. Wars, terrorism, pestilence—"

"Half of those ills are from you."

"Yes." There was a smile underneath the fury still visible on his face. "We all play our parts. Some of us are simply assigned the wrong character to play."

"You think yourself the hero?"

"Oh, no, I am decidedly the villain of this piece. But it doesn't matter what you or I think. It matters what the mages of the future think. History will remember me in a polarizing, yet magnificent way. What sort of hero will I be looked upon, that I had the strength to undertake this task? They will view my actions and see a person who was willing to make the decisions that others could or would not make. Like you. You can't even sacrifice your least pawn."

"And you seek to sacrifice everyone. A monster."

"Not all. Many. And a monster I will be. But time leaches emotion from decisions. Makes results far more black-and-white." He smiled. "The way that I already view it. I could always see what was wrong with society. It was easy to see. I wondered why others couldn't, then I realized that their minds were far too small and their abilities far too weak."

"Like the non-magicals? You want to cull them, too?"

He moved, and I moved again, keeping Table One between us, as if that would help me.

He smiled. "The non-magicals are weak and dying. They kill the planet around them. But they have enviable technological minds, constrained as they are by physics, and every so often they produce magical children. Magical children who often have great powers. Why? What is it about these late blooming mages? What does it mean for our society if we take them out of play? I'm a scientist, at heart. I needed the data."

"So, the ferals—you were taking them, testing on them to see if you could sacrifice the entire layer?" I felt another orb erupt. Time...

"The entire layer? Dear me, no. You, dear child, are both the means to the end and the stopper in all of this. You are the prime example of why we need their stock, the cattle of their herds, no matter what the other data says. The outliers. You, a child raised in the non-magical world by non-magical parents. Your powers exceed so many others. If I were to eliminate the non-magical world, I lose the ability to find more of you."

"Just have to cull some of them, then?" I sneered.

"The weak. Mages, non-magicals, and magical beings—all the weak must be removed. They sap our resources, our magic, our time and energy. Gone." He wiped a hand. "The ones who prey on society. The poor, the indigent, the anemic, the stupid. It should appeal to you, really. For one who values intelligence and initiative in others—a self-starter, I think you First Layer types say—your new lower intelligence class will be all those of the middle. The entire structure will be strengthened. Like the way you are remaking the Third Layer—an otherwise brilliant strategy. Removing the decaying, decrepit parts, then strengthening all that remains. All those people who will never accept you, I can make them go away. You can help decide who goes."

"I'm not causing mass genocide."

"Are you not? What of the creatures you will uproot?"

"I'm making provisions for them."

"Cages? Pens?"

I smiled tightly. "That's the gift of being an Origin Mage. I can remake worlds within worlds for them."

"Without magic."

"Or maybe just with a different kind."

He narrowed his eyes. I felt a curl of victory, but turned the conversation quickly. "Those you deem weak give strength to those you deem strong. In the emotions that you disdain. Compassion, aid, community. Part of the human mindset involves developing tools to help those who are sick or disabled."

"But that's to my point." He leaned forward as if we were in concordance, but he couldn't hide the coolness in his gaze. "You cull the lowest denominator, and the tools developed become those that help the middle—tools that are more exceptional and thrust society on an even faster path."

"You deem yourself a philanthropist then?" I asked coldly.

"I deem myself the monster that will do what is needed," he replied in kind. "And history will hate and secretly celebrate me for it."

"I will not celebrate you."

"We'll see. I have nearly everything I need for Phase One. I need just one more thing."

"Phase One—the loss of a million, just to see what happens?" I said bitterly.

He smiled and rotated a multi-colored sphere in his palm. "I know what will happen. A million to set the stage. To see the forces clamber. What million is chosen? Why, you could have a say in that. Come willingly, and I will let you choose the first set. Even spare your friends should they fall within."

He held up his hand and instead of the device I was expecting, there was a giant cloud of magic, swirling and roiling. It was an oddly chaotic element for a man so precise.

My mind connected the points of chaos. I could see it—the roiling magic, the genocide, the decay of humanity. I could see how Stavros could do it, if he put pressure on just the right points of the layer system, which always hovered in the air around me now, even without my regular magic streaming within.

"So, is this the end of your villain monologue? Showing me your magic, telling me whatnot of your grand plan before I destroy you?"

"Oh no, dear. This was me giving your brain an exact run down of what is going to happen so that you can understand and draw the mental schematics I require of it." The whisper of magic fell over me again.

I took a step back, but the magic followed, sponging around my mind. I threw the last piece of the puzzle away before it formed.

He smiled and took a leisurely step around the table toward me, hand outstretched as my body arced backward. "Now you are perceiving the way of things."

I gritted my teeth and backed up another step. He was like Raphael, who always said he wanted me to "learn" before he used me.

"No, not like my dear servant at all," Stavros said. "I could have forced the knowledge within you from the start. I would simply do this."

He twisted his hand. Knowledge appeared in front of me in a cloud of magic. And like a sign in English appearing in front of me, my brain automatically read what it saw. The cloud of magic changed from one block to another. Some of the outside information slipped by, but the bulk in the middle pulled together. That was how I was supposed to tie two ports together? I had thought—

And that was how rocks became rivers? That made sense.

My brain followed the path of the images and diagrams.

"Dear Sergei's mind was like yours. All Origin Mages think along similar deductive and inductive lines. It is their outside parameters—their emotions and experiences—that color their paths." He tilted

624

his head. "It's so hard to recreate the manipulations of Origin Mages. I've been quite starved since he managed to kill himself."

Stavros needed my support. He needed me to give him the key to how my mind worked. Constantine had needed it to use my magic. He had pulled it from me with the leech, true, but I'd had to form it, and I'd only formed it out of curiosity. I could control my curiosity.

In this situation of life and death, literal life and death for billions of people, I could extinguish my curiosity.

"So, it's to be parasitical?" I asked, preparing myself. I'd known since I'd become a commodity, that this would be the end of the road if I was captured by the Department. "You worming in and taking control?"

"Crude tools. Who needs a leech?" he said, smiling that infuriatingly small smile. He lifted his hands and the entire atmosphere changed. Then he pulled.

I bowed forward, and my mouth opened, as if the emotions pulling out of me were corporeal.

"No, Miss Crown. I can simply remove the parts of you that possess moral quandaries. Or...unnatural ties."

My connection threads started to dim. Horror overtook me, then that too started to dim.

He smiled. "I can remove the horror and fear. And the love. Remove all that is your natural empathy. I misunderstood the depth of Sergei's grief, then consumed him as he died. A mistake I didn't fully realize until later. For I inherited part of his mind, but not the span to do the magic. I can visualize what I want, but I cannot make it happen."

He swirled out a pattern and I could see the broken pieces immediately—all the areas that needed to be fixed for his plan to work. I said nothing, but he smiled anyway.

"I know you know how to fix it. And I won't make that same mistake with you. I loathe the emotions that come with the connection he left behind. I have no desire to feel your teenage love, devotion, and angst. I need all that is you, but in pieces that can be manipulated around the whole. A jar here, a jar there. A conduit throughout. I simply have to remove the more useless parts of you that threaten the whole."

"No."

He smiled and sucked out my fury, directing it into a box inside his cloud. "Anger serves me as well as any other emotion. I care not which I take in what order." He pulled with his hand and a large chunk of fear abruptly broke away from me—and along with it, some of my magic. The cocktail pulled forth and flew into the cloud, pulsing the entire mass and making the color darken.

He closed his eyes. "You are like five of the strongest of them."

"Go to hell," I said, holding on to what I had left—dulled emotions I wanted to keep, dirty feelings and all. The ones that made me me.

He circled his wrist and pulled again. I groaned, heaving forward onto my hands and knees on the floor, a cocktail of emotions pulled from me in one long wisp, dulling everything left behind.

"Everyone worries about Bridges," he said. "Rightly so, of course, especially after Alexander Dare's little demonstration at Crelussa—and I will be utilizing such abilities when he comes to rescue you. Two bridges together, why the amplification will be amazing. But it was the reason I couldn't afford to go after Itlantes like I wanted. Those initial terrified rumors about Bridges, why, I spread those myself." He smiled.

"You're a Bridge," I gasped before the last bit of fear was pulled from me.

His smile didn't change. "If you want to be pedantic, I'm a Bridge of a very specific type." He directed the cloud to his chest and the magic absorbed inside him. He inhaled, flexing the magic outward in a bubbled, painted wave. "The more accurate description would be to call me a Hollow."

I caught my breath enough to say, "What is a Hollow?" Not even my bracelet had information on them.

"Both Bridge and Empath."

I stared at the painted floor swirling around me, then up at him. "I don't believe you."

He smiled. "Yes, I erased such information long ago, but who would believe it anyway? That's the most interesting part of the ability. Cognitively, it doesn't mean I have to care, I must understand. And I always understand."

"So, what," I said, rolling lethargically out of reach of his next pull while accessing passive information from my bracelet—the bracelet that held both the spirit of Christian and the enduring friendship of Will. I clasped the fleeting feeling, burying it deep. "You understand why people do what they do—you can even facilitate a response from them—"

"With precision." He smiled.

"—but you don't have any of the side effects of caring?"

"It's called cognitive empathy. But without all the nasty affective part that causes great men to be average."

He swirled through the paint and I groaned as another bit of love fled from me, causing another connection to dim.

"It makes me a decidedly excellent leader."

"And yet, not necessarily a great human," I spit. He took half that anger, too.

"In just a few minutes, I'll have enough of your emotion for you to willingly walk out of here and right into the lovely place I have set up for you."

"Never." I tried to hide the connections I had left, the strongest of them, covering them. Stavros simply lifted the feelings beneath, and one by one they started to die.

"Better to just let it happen, my dear. Easier. You won't care about your comrades soon anyway. Their love will seem like a burden to you."

"I'll never leave them."

He smiled. "Oh, you will."

The connection to Neph went gray. Worse, I suddenly felt nothing as I looked at it. I knew that this wasn't right, but there was nothing to connect me to an emotion.

I looked at the threads to Olivia, which were struggling to hold.

"Did you do this to Helen Price too?"

"Ah, dear Helen needed little work. Some people are simply built to hold the burden of greater things."

I tried to keep hold as the threads to Olivia vibrated—a hair from breaking. "You won't get me to work like this," I said, my voice scratched, like I'd been screaming. "My emotions are part of my creativity."

"Oh, indeed, that's why I have them. I'll feed a little emotion back into you, when needed. It's how people work best. Small motivations to do what is needed, then I'll kill those and find new ones. A lovely cycle."

He pulled again, and I arched up, watching the rest—the last—of my feelings disappear into his hand.

"And now...you will follow me."

"You lie. I know this, objectively."

"Do I? Do I lie?"

I tilted my head. Had he? Or had I assumed as such because I had felt repulsed or angry or terrified? What did those words even mean? I think I had known.

"Open the door," he said.

I'd never make it out. It was a sterile thought. I'd never make it out as me.

Who was I?

"There will be so many interesting things to explore, Miss Crown. You might even find the key behind it."

I looked at the door. Patterns swirled, making no sense.

"How do I open it?"

He smiled.

An influx of something fell over me. Magic—my own returned to me, but different. I looked at my hands, at the grayed-out connections that were rapidly decaying. One broke and fell.

Without sense or color, I had no notion of who it had been connected to. My memories said I would have cared at one time. I shrugged. No matter. It was cleansed now.

Would the world objectively be better with a cleansing? With an infusion of people who were better able to take care of it?

"Open the door."

With the influx of magic to my mind, the pattern on the door revealed itself as something logical.

I walked toward it, disregarding Enton Stavros's smile. I had no use of it or his regard. I only felt compelled toward an answer—the answer I would find behind the door.

Physical pain stopped me before I reached it. A sharp, physical pain in my midsection that radiated through my limbs and froze my feet. I examined the cause—it was a reaction to an embedded magic that was not my own, but that was hooked into something that was sluggishly regenerating at my core.

I needed to be elsewhere, and it was stopping me from that goal. I examined it further.

A vow. A simple thing. I remembered that the person who held the vow both lied and told the truth. I remembered him without the emotion that dull memory said had once colored our interactions. I looked at the vow, trying to reason out how to move past it.

It was a simple thing. Even more so because all the parameters were easily met.

There was a table, a table I cared nothing for, and as long as that was the case, I was to destroy it. Magic had made it so.

So be it. I raised my hand.

"What are you—"

I paid no attention to the voice. I had a vow that demanded to be met.

Without fanfare, I let the magic fly. Watched as the paint around it swirled and exploded. I tilted my head as the table broke, then shattered, and suddenly there were people and creatures everywhere—mass chaos and a brutal battle—and I was amid it all, while the world cracked in pieces around me. A shot of magic broke my arm, a dragon's razor-sharp tail opened my midsection, a spell shattered my leg.

"Stupid, stupid girl," Enton Stavros said from one of the cracks.

"You've said that before," I said dully, sliding to the floor. My head hit the ground and a grayed connection flared the tiniest bit gold, attached to something that was growing faster now within me. There was a sense of bone-deep relief through the connection that I couldn't share.

Never again, never again, never again. Never there, Raphael said.

No.

An animal with jagged teeth fell in front of me.

Stavros still has other means. Do not underestimate him, Butterfly.

Yes. There was nothing else to the answer, though. No fear or determination.

Something that looked like a dragon mixed with a tiger started to charge, gaze on someone behind me. It was going to run me down in the process. Magic, rough and raw, was mine again, leaking into the air around me, but I just watched as the beast charged. I had no further goal. No desire.

Magic shot from someone behind me, then the dragon tiger surged and fell.

"Ren." Constantine hunched over me. Flashes of light illuminated the air around him. Blood ran down his face and there was a singed quality to the skin around his neck. He was warm. He had my cheeks in his hands and his hands were warm, thumbs rubbing circles into my skin.

"Ren." I felt my left foot twist under the force of another stray spell. He frantically pulled a shield around us and magic seared over the split skin of my midsection. "Where are your shields? Where did you go? Why can't I feel you?"

I put my hand over his. "You are warm." I touched my elbow in the arm that no longer worked. "This was you."

There was a look on his face that I tried to objectively parse through the haze of disconnected reality—shock, anguish, terror, rage. I watched a myriad of expressions pass over his features. The pain of them seemed worse than that of my broken bones. Why would someone seek feelings?

His forehead pressed against mine, as if he could no longer bare to see whatever was showing in my eyes.

I could feel him pushing at the connection that had once existed, battering against it, trying to reform it. But his feelings battered against the decay like a bulldozer against old concrete—there was nothing to build, only more to destroy.

"Roald, you wanted proof about Prestige Stavros's abilities."

People were moving, fighting, recording. I stared at the ceiling.

"What proof," Stavros said, and a crack of thunderous magic split the room. A sickly mixture of Kinsky's, Kaine's, and mine roiled through the room.

There was a scream and the battle sounds grew louder.

"Constantine, dammit, move," Stuart Leandred said harshly, grabbing his son's shoulder. "She's been hollowed. There's nothing you can do right now."

"Oh," Constantine said implacably, darkness coiling around him as his fingers slipped from my skin. "I think that's quite false."

He turned without looking at me again, cloak flaring out behind him, but Stuart grabbed his arm while still holding defensive spells in front of them both. "If he can do it to her, he'll flip you, too."

"She loves easily," he said, shaking him off. "I, do not."

Constantine held out a hand behind him as he strode forward, and I could feel magic pulling from me in great waves, bridged from a source that required the minimalist of connections to work. With Axer's magic illuminating the air beneath Constantine's palms, my damaged magic traveled up and along his knuckles and wrist like liquid fire.

I turned my head, gaze pulled along with my magic.

From inside his splitting reality, Stavros was moving like painted smoke, killing the soldiers that had appeared during the time I was gone. Marsgrove was trying to destroy him systematically. But it was a phantom effort, for the reality of the world Stavros was within was not within Marsgrove's grasp.

Axer was hunched next to Marsgrove—his peril obvious as Constantine channeled the bulk of his magic—barely holding back Kaine and a fleet of snapping monsters while keeping a shield in front of Marsgrove and two others. Kaine got a shot in, but Axer just took the hit and didn't pull his magic back to him.

Stavros turned to painted mist and a killing beam aimed by Marsgrove went right through him. He came back into view, his eyes solely focused on the magic trailing from Constantine. "Dear boy, you play with forces far beyond your abilities."

"You poisoned Verisetti," Constantine said, stalking forward like a wraith of vengeance. "I will always hold him responsible for Salietrex, but you are responsible for making him. You will take nothing else from me," he said, before unleashing the full force of the hell he was dragging behind him like a whip.

Stavros's mist cracked into physical shards that hung suspended in irreality.

"I will make you, and all you hold dear, pay for this, boy," Stavros spit. "You will find that you don't know the definition of pain."

Constantine pulled the whip around and flicked it at the next shard, then the one after.

Shard after shard burst as Stavros flipped from piece to piece and Constantine destroyed each one.

Axer's magic rode beneath Constantine's like a wave, turning the crest of it to shatter each piece in turn like a great serpent slithering and striking after a fleeing rat.

The symbol winked in one of the shards. I reached a finger toward it. "The paintings," I murmured. The pattern slotted easily into place.

"I already have what I need. And you, girl, what are you going to do when all who you love, die?" He said as the painted cracked and splintered, making four, then ten, then twenty pieces of him, swirling broken in shards. "When they are before you, being pulled apart? I will allow you to care again, during those last gasps of breath. And you will give me what I seek."

"No."

"So it begins."

Constantine hit the piece containing the symbol with the last shot.

Axer whipped out Constantine's newest ribbon—one that I had been working with him to make into a storage space—and like in Crelussa with the bomb and my storage paper, it wrapped around the shards at the last second, and a muffled boom burst the ribbon into a hundred bits of fluff.

There was silence for an extended moment. "That was my prototype," Constantine said, breathing harshly.

"It works," Axer said.

And then the battle was back in motion, but this time with a fervor that was all push, push, push from the boys' side as Axer grabbed magic from every person they downed and pooled the growing mass between them.

If it had seemed like the boys were good at fighting together before, they were nearly seamless now. The creatures went down, Department grunts crumpled, and even Kaine, flinging Origin Magic—both mine and Kinsky's—wasn't slowing them down as they backed him into a corner.

Constantine pulled a vial from his coat. I knew what was in it. He had been making a concoction to take down Kaine since our first visit to Corpus Sun. Doubling down after the infections on campus. And tripling it after Stavros overwhelmed me on campus.

But Axer grabbed his arm before he could throw it. I could see them struggle, even if I felt nothing over it.

Kaine slipped through a crack in the floor.

Constantine balled up his fist, collapsed the magic and vial into the pocket of his cloak, then blew up Table Two with a guttural scream.

"We can't convert on it yet. You will get a chance to use it," Axer murmured too low for anyone to hear. I didn't know why I could hear it, but the echo of it seemed to be coming through the gold connection.

"I will," Constantine said viciously.

"You let him go?" One of the officials that had come with Marsgrove yelled at Constantine in disbelief. "You are exactly what they say you—"

Axer shot him in the chest. The man dropped to the floor. The other officials stepped backward.

Constantine stared at the downed man, chest heaving. "That could have been therapeutic for me."

"Thinking about how you will make Kaine scream in unending terror will have to do. Come on."

Both looked like they'd been through a war, but they were already healing extraordinarily fast, sharing magic back and forth—the pool of stolen magic still trailing behind them. I felt the combination of it descend on me, too, fixing my broken bones and damaged internals.

But when it touched anything other than physical ailments in me, the magic hit a wall. Constantine lifted me, trying to grow connections where they no longer existed.

He closed his eyes, his forehead touching mine again. "I can't... We need somewhere we can fix this."

"Her shields are gone," Marsgrove said. "And I know them well. They will take days, weeks, to heal without connection or magic. And her magic is...muddied."

"Time," Axer said grimly.

"There is no time," Marsgrove said. "Look around us. The end has begun. Stavros won't wait for her to heal. He knows it will take days. He'll be moving in the next forty-eight hours."

"He knows he's going to win," I murmured, remembering.

Axer's perfect mouth formed a smile ripe with bloodlust.

"Where?" Constantine was touching my face again, but he was looking at Axer, ignoring everyone else arguing around us.

Stuart stepped forward. "We have facilities—"

"No," Axer cut him off, gaze still connected to Constantine's. "Even now, they come." The hunters—both Department and bounty. He looked down at me. "Ren, I need you to come back."

Someone snorted in the background. "Gone bloody loony. Lock the lot of them up, we should. Did you see—"

I heard a body crash against something and fall. Axer crouched down next to me and pressed a hand over my heart. He looked at something above my head, then back at me. "Ren, I need you to come back."

I tilted my head to look at him fully. "I haven't lef—"

Guard Rock flipped over my face and stabbed me in the jugular.

A thousand things happened at the same time—people started shouting, Marsgrove started clearing the area around us, and Constantine scrabbled to hold me down as I knifed forward in anguish with every emotion rushing back in a painful waterfall of clogged feeling—and painted blood.

Hands scrabbled for me, healing the mortal wound immediately, and I grabbed two of them. I could barely stand the crippling intensity of their emotions. "He took my knowledge. I solved it. Most of it. We don't have time for the plan."

"Shhh, I know, we'll figure it out, just—"

Guard Rock hopped over our clasped hands, jabbed his stick into a hole in my cloak, slid it through my spilt blood, then vaulted from my chest before anyone could grab him. He slid lightning fast in a painted circle around the three of us, pencil tip dragging a circumference in the paint.

"What the ever-loving f—?"

But Guard Rock's circle completed before Constantine's question, and Guard Rock hopped inside.

I saw Bellacia and Roald, Stuart and Marsgrove, Julian Dare, and all the mages they had brought with them, and all the ones still trapped inside their cages. And behind them, with my vision freed, I saw what Stavros would do to the facility. I held out a hand, turned, and flipped the entire Basement into the bright sunlight of Gliar Peit, erecting a figure eight dome to surround both sites, holding it in stasis, but the magic was slimy, muddy. Thirty minutes, Bella, Marsgrove, I sent, then pressed the storage paper containing Vincent Godfrey Jr. and his men into Marsgrove's hands, along with the activation spell. Godfrey has tales of who hired him. I'm certain you will be able to pry those out. Free them, free the others, and grab what you can.

Guard Rock stabbed the tip of his pencil into the circle and flipped us into another world.

Chapter Twenty-three

WHAT WAS LOST

W E LANDED in a tangle, and as if the jolt of landing broke the last of Stavros's carving, a second waterfall of emotion crashed, igniting the embers of dead connections and leaving me gasping like I had been drowned.

I grabbed Constantine and my fingers scrabbled for any bare skin I could find, pushing cloak and shirt aside for unhampered touch, face digging into a warm throat like I was going to nest there.

"He took it, he took it, tried to take all of it."

"Shhh." Constantine's arms wrapped around me, and a bare palm pressed against the back of my neck. Relief so strong that it felt like he would choke on it pushed against me. "I have them."

I shuddered and let the ghosts of the connections in his fingers settle over the top of all that was broken, lighting destroyed pathways everywhere on me—like a trunk that had survived a forest fire, but all its branches had burned.

The embers started to fuse back together, slowly at first, then lightning fast, leaving me gasping with the mass mess of feeling and connection.

I pushed away and my hands fell against a marble floor a moment before I threw up.

A vapor of distorted paint spewed from me in an ugly mist.

"He's not in there," Axer said from my right shoulder, his magic running through me, searching every crevice in my chest. "And you can't collapse, Ren. Not yet. I'm sorry."

The floor sucked the mist down. Magic zipped along the imperfect marble pattern like a freight train migraine that was incoming on a train with broken tracks. Flickers of magic touched against the points where my fingers touched marble. It was strange, but it felt like the magic in the marble was surging up and fixing broken points of magic inside me.

"I know." I let my emotions run wild for a moment, acknowledging all of them—especially the horror, terror, and crushing anxiety of losing everyone—then pushed them gently into the background. I could feel Constantine holding back the tide of the connections with difficulty, letting through just small bits of feeling from the others to not overwhelm me. I could feel the boys both trying to hide all that they felt as well—letting the other absorb any overpowering emotions. I let a little of my own overwhelming gratitude through to their circuit, then let that emotion rest in the back as well.

I needed to be back to full strength. Deal first, collapse later.

I held out my hand to look at it, trying to bring the world back to rights as my view started swimming with magic. It would make brutal sense that I'd get a magical migraine after what Stavros had done. I shut my eyes, trying to let the magic running through the marble floor—familiar, yet foreign—finish its task.

"Stavros doesn't want to use me as a vehicle,"
I said, eyes still shut. "He has plenty of those.
Even when he tried to take me from Excelsine,
he just shoved me into the background to drive
my body where he wanted it, to secure the
surroundings until he could successfully port us
away. Using a person's magic means he must
accept some of the person inside. He must be
part of them. It's why he doesn't usually use
anyone's powers when he's riding them. Stavros
hates emotions. He's an empath." I laughed
without humor. "He wants to hollow... Hollow
me out. Make me more useful long term."

And Raphael... Raphael would have been an
in-between experiment. To see if Stavros could
manipulate the emotions of someone with so
much love into something else.

"To remove my ability to feel." I tried looking at
the floor again. The zips of magic had grown
stronger, like I was waking from a blind sickness
and was starting to see again. "He already
has what he needs for his version of Genesis
Omega. I saw it, tweaked it, certified it—but for
one piece. He can get it from me easily the next
time he sees me, but he wants me for other
things. To tweak variables in later pieces of the

destruction, and for rebuilding after, in the way that he wants. We still have a chance. We just don't have enough time."

The magic was fixing more than just my external senses. I could now feel the tension and panic in all my connections—all of them scrabbling on the other side—subtle differences between them. I closed my eyes, and brought forth the warrior side Axer had spent so long training. Soon, soon, I could fall into my reformed connections, but not yet.

Axer, permission given, softly rippled through my memories and conversation with Stavros, Constantine looking in, their magic connected.

Axer disengaged gently, fingers tapping. "We need to move fast."

"To where?" Constantine sounded resigned. "Stavros has the containers and the trigger. It's just a matter of pulling it. Tonight, tomorrow. As soon as he heals whatever damage we did, and you know it wasn't enough."

Axer didn't answer.

"Itlantes won't survive what Stavros is planning," Constantine murmured.

"No," Axer said, his own raw emotional reaction held back in the same way that he held onto everything that wasn't useful in the middle of battle. "It will be one of the first places he attempts to destroy. Selectively. He'll want some of the minds. Same with Excelsine. He wants to cull specifically. That will save some, and not others."

I could feel it, even though he held himself so tightly in control—the devastation that he knew could happen. Some of his family would be destroyed, and he'd have no chance to physically say goodbye.

My heart ached for him and my thoughts strayed to my parents and our friends at Excelsine. Returned emotions threatened to overwhelm me and tears welled in my eyes.

"Can we go back to campus?" I asked desperately, gathering my connections close, wanting last moments, wanting to experience that last hug. "Now that he's been exposed?"

"No. We are still expelled, and Excelsine needs to keep it that way for its own protection. We must believe that we will win. Losing is not an option. The Baileys, Marsgrove, Julian, and everyone else who viewed the Basement will spread the view and evidence, and it will put a dent in Stavros's reputation and public role, but it won't be enough, not in the time we need. At least half the people already after us will still be after us. I can feel bounty hunters heading this way right now—they are tripping wards along five different tracks Julian set up. We don't have time to flip public perception or to get rid of the bounties or hunters after us before going after Stavros. And though when trying to rouse you I was hoping you'd take us to an Origin Circuit spot, we can't stay in this one."

I looked up sharply, finally taking in our surroundings fully.

Soaring columns of gold formed a crown around the atrium, but that wasn't what caught my attention. The ceiling of the atrium showed a moving view of the Milky Way galaxy and the galaxies beyond. Black holes and dark matter. Supernovas, nebulas, and stardust. The magic constantly shifted and rotated the view as if I was viewing it in four dimensions.

The more I looked, the more things strengthened and expanded into view.

I sat back on my heels and stared. "Wow."

"You are finally appreciating good design, darling, if not adequate construction," Constantine said casually, over all the intense emotions simmering inside.

"It's beautiful." I reached up, as if I could touch one of the celestial bodies. I thought of Makali reaching toward the cosmos, and pulled my finger slowly down. She was still alive, I thought fiercely.

"I suppose I can see how after the turret, a half-caved in gold ceiling might be breathtaking," Constantine replied.

I tilted my head, seeing nothing but wonder. "I see space. Comets and solar events. And matter forming the strangest patterns."

I started to rise and Axer grabbed my shoulder. "Don't move."

I noticed that Constantine was carefully staying in one place as well.

"There are traps everywhere. The Broken Palace," Axer said, gaze canvassing the space and the magic all around, blue magic fluttering across his eyes. "Flavel Valeris' home. This is not a place we want to remain."

My breath caught. I looked around with new eyes. "Golden turrets, Con."

"I stand corrected," he said with a bit of reluctant amusement, though his gaze was still dark.

"The more obvious the traps," Axer said. "The worse that will be hidden beneath."

"Ren already contributed magic." Constantine waved a hand at the floor that had eaten my mist, posture tense. "I don't think we are going to remain anonymous."

"We could use the portal pad we got from the O'Learys on the way to Crelussa," I offered, staring longingly upward. How had Valeris done the spellwork? Were those real astronomical events taking place lightyears away, or like the falsely enchanted ceiling I had tempted Olivia with in our room?

"Not here." Axer's voice was grim. "We can't trust what is here."

"Because Valeris built it?" I mean, granted, he had killed millions of people—

"No, because this site, while a well-guarded secret, isn't unknown. Unlike Kinsky's lair, which was never found, Valeris's palace was well known in its day. It constantly shifts actual location, even now in the broken world through which it ripples, but he never made it hard to track. Valeris was very open with his magic in a society that welcomed his gifts."

"A bubble," I murmured. "He made a bubble that floats between."

Something flitted at the edge of my vision, and I looked sharply to the right.

"Something has been watching us since we arrived," Axer said in response. "But I cannot see what it is."

"Nor I," Constantine said grimly.

"It doesn't feel...harmful," I said.

The watching just felt—watchful. Not the paranoid type born from being watched for months. No, this type of watching, it spoke of Neph and how we had first met—watching each other surreptitiously from afar. A type of watchfulness that preceded good intentions, not bad.

I let a sliver of searching magic escape...and saw a shape duck back from far up the wall. Far up.

"What's the Third Layer situation on flying beasts?" I asked.

"Mixed." Clear magic encircled Axer's arm like a watery gauntlet.

Another little poke had my shoulders sagging. A papered claw wrapped around the edge of the wall and the tip of its spine poked around.

"It's a book."

Neither of them lost their tension. "Where?"

"Right there." I motioned to the book. "Come on out."

It ducked back in. But then just as quickly peeked back out.

"Ren... I see nothing." Axer was looking at the exact spot I was motioning to, as was Constantine.

"You don't see it, really?"

"No."

"Right over—"

"Even drained and half-dead, I do not doubt that you can see something that we cannot, especially in a place such as this," he said, on full alert.

Guard Rock dropped from my hood and started padding across the floor in a strange shuffle, dancing around the traps and snares crisscrossing the floor.

"Ren!" Constantine hissed.

I shrugged helplessly. Guard Rock was his own man.

Guard Rock got to the edge of the seal in the center of the floor, stared down at it without stepping closer, then looked at the book. He waved his pencil toward us. The book tentatively hopped out, and oddly, its cover was completely blank. It flew over, also making a wide circle around the seal in the center of the floor.

"What's the rock doing now?" Constantine asked resignedly. "Going to take us to Felrut Tears where we will all be swallowed by the Bog of Despair? Or maybe—"

The book landed carefully next to Guard Rock and they proceeded to have an incomprehensible conversation.

Constantine sighed, only being able to see Guard Rock's side. "Do I even dare ask?"

"Maybe the book knows something," I said. Guard Rock had been the one to bring us here. "Give them a moment."

I looked back at the ceiling and its glorious cosmos. Something distant exploded with color and blackness and sent shockwaves around the other bodies.

I looked at the marble column closest to us and watched little stardusts flicker over it. "The gold and marble are a little much, but it is beautiful. I know so little of Valeris," I murmured. "The Second Layer only highlights his downfall and the Third Layer whispers about him like a fallen god."

Axer looked down at me briefly, keeping his gaze mostly focused on the moot between rock and the book he couldn't see. "Valeris was a showman. Tales say that he was just as serious-minded and caring as the rest of your breed, but he understood the value of perception. And he made a lot of friends in high places." He ran a finger along a buckle on his chest and I could see magic spark, ready. "Of course, they all died with him. Took the brightest minds of the Third Layer out in one fell swoop. But he was quite the hit at parties, they said."

I grimaced. Great.

"I can only imagine what it was like, though." He looked up at the ceiling, his gaze distant. "What they saw before they died. They wouldn't have even felt that death. Only the wonder."

I touched his arm and let my magic connect.

He inhaled a gasp. Gaze already glued to the ceiling as it changed to my view—watching as a galaxy was born, cosmic events swirling in endless lines and patterns around it. Endless possibilities and explorations. I reached out with my other hand and grabbed Constantine's.

He didn't inhale at all. I looked over and saw that he was staring at me instead, gaze indecipherable. Then he looked upward, and I saw his lips part. Magic fluttered over his eyes in a pattern almost too quick to see.

Both pulled away, and their fingers went to their eyes.

"What a rush." Axer's hand moved to his forehead. The magic fluttering over his gaze steadied into a slower pattern, then stopped. He touched his nose and the suddenly dripping blood there disappeared.

"Oh my god." I reached for him, but he waved me off.

"Worth the ride," he said.

Constantine's nose was bloody too, and I stared at them aghast. I started to step back, but Constantine caught me before I could complete the motion, hand clamping around my upper arm, waves of calm running through his fingers and into my skin.

"As Alexi said, worth the ride. Do not worry over being exceptional, darling."

"You're bleeding."

He waved a hand and his face was once more immaculate. "And now I'm not."

"I can see the book," Axer said, gaze affixed on it.

"As can I," Constantine said. "Hopped up on Ren's magic as we are. And her magic is back—nearly cleaned even. Interesting, don't you think?"

Axer's calculating gaze lifted to the ceiling. "Not many know the true aim of the experiments Valeris was running. The speculation was that he was trying to get humanity off Earth. To deal with the population crises that the Second, Third, and Fourth Layers had started to worry about back then. To explore the unknown far from where the magic as we know it in the layer system reaches."

I frowned. "You think that's what happened that day? An experiment to leave Earth gone wrong?"

We were all made of elements. I looked up. Of stars. All the same elements, but in different combinations and concentrations across the galaxy. Therefore, magic must exist beyond Earth. It would make sense that we'd somehow be able to travel using it.

"I don't know." He looked around with my magic filling his eyes. "Valeris is seen as a grandiose eccentric now more than anything. The pertinent piece to present day policy isn't what he was doing but that whatever it was, the experiment failed. Badly."

So badly it had killed millions of people and devastated an entire layer for 70 years.

Guard Rock padded back. I scooped him up on my shoulder.

Guard Rock motioned at the book again, his pencil making the gesture at the side of my view.

The book tentatively hopped a step closer. There was no writing anywhere on its cover. An untitled book was unusual. And there was something otherly about it. Like it held a concept too large to comprehend.

"You know this book," I murmured to him.

Guard Rock tapped an affirmative against my shoulder with the eraser end of his pencil.

The book hopped a step closer, looking nervously at the boys. I touched the undersides of their arms carefully with my fingers. "They won't hurt you," I said to it.

Constantine raised an eyebrow.

But the book was looking between where we were physically connecting, and it hopped another step—this one a little more eagerly.

"I can't see a title," Constantine said. "What do you see on its cover?"

I shook my head slowly. "It's blank. Or maybe not blank—there's something otherworldly about it—but without a visual concept that makes sense, the way something that is incomprehensible might appear."

Axer shifted, his attention sharpening in the way it did when danger was near. "Hunters are here," he said. "They have one of the Origin Elite. They just broke through an entrance in a courtyard below. We have five minutes."

Axer pulled the new portal pad from his cloak. We'd get ten more minutes somewhere else, and then another ten—a series of endless jumps until we could find a safe port. Maybe.

The book hopped forward frantically, then motioned at me, then at the seal. Then it reached forward with a tentative corner.

I let go of the boys and reached out slowly, and made contact.

An image of protection and hidden worlds bloomed, then one of my magic swirling down the hole in the floor. My breath caught. The book hopped the last foot closer, anxiously, its spine twisting a bit as if listening to something in the distance. It opened its covers and a staircase built itself upon the page, tunneling downward.

I extended my fingers toward it. They were suddenly gripped in a larger hand.

"No," Constantine said, staring at the book with both distrust and a sharp, darkly-edged interest.

Guard Rock leaped from my shoulder. Constantine reached out to grab him with his free hand, but like a cliff jumper entering crisp water, Guard Rock had already become part of the page. His small legs pumped down the papered staircase and out of sight.

"Stupid rock." Constantine frowned fiercely at the book, gripping me more tightly as if expecting me to jump in next.

"The book said it will help us. Protect us," I said.

"And we are going to beli—"

"We have no time." Axer touched a finger covered in magic to the book's edge and the book stiffened. "If we enter, can we leave at will?"

It stiffly dipped the top of its spine.

Axer handed the portal pad to Constantine. "If I don't return in ten seconds, go."

Constantine's hand let go of mine and planted itself on his roommate's chest, eyes dark with irritation, before Axer could step inside. He shoved the pad back into Axer's hand.

"Stupid heroes." Constantine withdrew the cat from his cloak and set her down. She looked at him and Constantine pressed a finger against her forehead. "Analyze. Quickly."

The purple and blue furry monstrosity snapped her hundred needled teeth together, then walked into the page. Little bursts of paint colored the page around her, seeping into the grains, as she stepped onto the staircase. The book shook with a pleasant shiver.

The cat tipped her head at Constantine, and a whirl of magic lifted, then she padded down the steps with her three spade tails waving through the air as if tasting the magic. She disappeared into the crack touching the book's spine.

"We will survive inside," Constantine reported grimly. "There is life sustaining magic. The cat recognizes its kin to yours."

I could feel the shadows growing closer.

"Valeris's magic, then. I will go first," I said. The blankness around the staircase was as unnerving as it was exciting—something new. Something Origin made. "Just like Will's sketch." But my adventure now.

"No." Axer shook his head, stepping forward. "We won't be able to retrieve you, if you get trapped. The reverse, however, we know is in your power." Eventually, went without being said.

Constantine pushed him back. "She can't survive the end game without you."

"Maybe I'll just be the weird paper creature swooping down to save the day," Axer said with an entirely inappropriate edge of amusement.

I looked at him, horrified, then clasped the emotion to me. I never wanted to be without the ability to feel again.

Constantine looked skyward, then down at the book. "Stupidity is truly transmittable," he muttered, then stepped foot inside, sinking into the page, faster than either of us could grab him. Little violet, turquoise, and ultramarine zips of colors stained the paper as he fully sank inside.

We crouched over the top, tense.

Constantine stood in 2D form on the staircase, and breathed in deeply as the page turned to creamed parchment once more. He reached out of the book in a violet ripple of emerging 3D, then pulled his hand back inside. He nodded sharply at Axer.

Axer went next in a burst of blue. He closed his eyes once inside, then quickly motioned to me. I stepped into the parchment world in a wash of color. Lanterns lit at the sides of the staircase, like a black-and-white drawing coming to life. I could see the real-world shimmering above—like a dome into another world. It was a little like looking at Valeris's ceiling.

With that unsettling thought, I extended my head, shoulder, and arm out of the book and gathered magic to me. Footsteps pounded toward the room as my magic pooled—identifying me as the caster.

The book's page fluttered around me, feeding me bits of knowledge in how it kept itself hidden. I included a little of magic from each of us and layered that magic into the package I was creating. At the last second, I let it all go and ducked back inside the page, just under the cover of the book's spells.

The packet of magic shot toward the seal and was sucked into the center, just as a man wearing my brother's face rounded the corner.

Magic spewed upward from me at the sight, and I reached forward. A hand pulled me against a hard chest, another fastened around my mouth, and magic clamped firmly over mine.

The fake paused for a moment, but then he and the others—a dozen men all wearing my brother's face—flew into the seal. The book closed its covers, and all went dark.

Chapter Twenty-four

WHAT WAS FOUND

THE MAGIC clamping mine released and gently pulled the paint from me. I shut my eyes, feeling empty. I knew what Stavros was doing—in case I had shaken off his hard work—but still, wow, did his methods get results.

I let the rumbles of conflicting emotions rush through me. Deep breaths, acceptance. Anger wasn't going to help me—only meaningful action.

Both Constantine and Axer released me physically, feeling me settle.

A flurry of sounds echoed around me, and I opened my eyes to see books flying on wings of parchment, fueled by calligraphic ink and magic.

Paint droplets hung in the air from where Axer had pulled them from me, like splatters on an invisible page, and the books swept around, opening their mouths and capturing each, like a feeding frenzy in a giant fish tank.

I blinked, and reality coalesced. A domed ceiling and a single room encompassed us. Upward, I could see a dizzying bird's-eye view of the inside of Valeris's palace as the book we were within flew in slow circles around the room we'd just escaped from—its pages flapping a shifting view of dozens of men wearing my brother's face hunting through the palace, their movements slowing strangely the longer I watched.

Inside, Axer's magic was a physical presence around us as the books, who had finished snapping up paint droplets, circled hungrily.

A slow smile worked its way along my mouth as I looked around at the perches and papered nests. "We...entered a library? Inside a book?"

I looked back up at the domed ceiling, just as quickly. "If they have an Origin Elite, will the hunters be able to enter as well?"

"Doubtful. Neither of us could see the book without you actively infusing us. Even after using your magic extensively at Crelussa and Verrange. No, I think this is an active Origin Mage infusion. I think we are safe in here—" Axer looked around. "Or as safe as we can hope."

Constantine was at attention on my other side, his posture indolent, but his emotions tight. Guard Rock and the cat were watching with interest at his feet.

Guard Rock tilted his rock at them, then padded over to me. He jabbed at my pitted and torn cloak until he found the pocket he desired, then he slit the pocket with his pencil tip.

"Hey! That one was actually remarkably intact." The remains of the Origin Book splayed out on the floor, and I immediately tried to gather them back together.

The books started swirling faster.

Guard Rock poked at my hands, then the papers. He moved one page with his pencil toward another. Pushing them together into a destroyed book pile. The books immediately started flying in an agitated, tight circle above us, and the lines of Axer's body shifted, magic swirling under his skin.

Guard Rock sat on his haunches and poked the pile with his pencil again.

Nothing.

He did it again.

"Your rock is losing it," Constantine said, tilting his head back, but keeping his gaze moving between all the possible dangers. "How long until the cat turns on us, too?"

The cat bristled, offended, and bit his shin.

Smoke rose on the third stab of his pencil and Guard Rock swirled the shreds. Mist rose into the air and formed a constellation of points.

The books above us began to fly tight patterns through the constellation.

"Great." Constantine sighed, closing his eyes while painfully detaching the cat from his leg, then stroking it. He looked at Axer from the side of his eyes. "This is where we usually go on a field trip. It will have monsters and insanity. You'll love it."

Guard Rock herded us closer together, then shook his pencil and stamped it on the ground. His pencil was gripped in staff-ready position.

Constantine watched the byplay, strangely relaxed. "Your rock thinks he needs to stand guard with us now, when he didn't at a man-eating house. I feel concern."

I eyed Guard Rock, whose gaze swept the room. "Let's stay optimistic," I said, reaching out for the map displayed in the air.

"No one thinks that's a good idea."

"I think it's a good idea."

"You are full of bad ideas. Your vote doesn't count," he said, still strangely, loosely relaxed, as if he recognized temporary safety and was ready to grab it with both hands. "Neither of your votes count."

I very carefully sifted through the constellation points.

"This one." I pulled the pieces into my palm and concentrated. Maps and worlds shifted through my mind, then settled. "The Broken Palace, created by Flavel Valeris, currently in Third Layer

Golina—no, now in Olterre, now Flet." I shook my head as the switches continued unabated. "And inside of it, The Library of Broken Books."

"A myth," Axer said, looking upward at the book tornado that was forming.

"Hidden," I murmured. I looked around. "The Origin Book highlighted it as a place of safety."

I pictured the book winging off while we were off on adventure. I looked down at Guard Rock, who looked solemnly back. Whatever the book had been doing, I had a feeling I would find out here. Paint swirled upward in my throat, but I grabbed the swirls of ultramarine and violet lingering in the air and swallowed it all back down—more easily this time than any other.

"That was almost controlled," Constantine said, touching the back of my neck, grounding me with the residuals of the magic we'd called in Crelussa.

"I feel…" I frowned. "Not as bad."

Both exhausted and wired, yes. And I had nearly lost everything. But now that I could explore it, it was like there was a buffer between my world ending capabilities and the world ending.

"Maybe it's being here?" I looked around. "The palace? The library?"

I watched five books collect Ori's remains. They huddled over it, then started slowly piecing pages together. Hope filled me.

Bloodthirsty Bonds and Chains landed, but stayed just out of reach, hawkish pages stiffly rippling.

A tattered, well-used copy of The Twelve Black Steps landed at its side. I stared at it. It rippled its pages—death, decay, and ancient promise in the gesture and proposition. A memory played across its cover—of Christian tossing footballs with me, then tackling me as I crossed an imaginary goal line. We were both splayed on the ground, limbs akimbo, laughing.

"Oh, that is not good," I murmured faintly.

Death Magic landed next to it, examining me like one might a social curiosity.

Robberies Involving Mental Torture landed next to Bloodshed: One Hundred and One Ways. A scream of anguish screeched from its pages.

I shuddered. "Why are most of them, you know...?"

"Mad?" Constantine asked, poking the book with his toe so it shut before it could issue a second scream. "Did you think 'Broken Books' meant physically?"

"Why are they all so specific?" I clarified.

"Books are specifically created," Axer said.

Bookspeller's Last Moments—subtitled Now with 10 Accounts!—landed next to Ori, and the others made room for it. I grimaced. I really hoped those accounts had been given freely.

"Do all books of similar title talk?" I asked Axer, looking at The Twelve Black Steps.

"They are all born of the same tome. But they imbue their own memories once they are in the wild. You can determine the edition number with a spell."

I remembered the shopkeeper's words. "You give up a piece of your own soul for the kind of magic The Twelve promotes. And it doesn't work out how you think it's going to."

I remembered the brittle cracking of his face, like someone breaking from within.

I remembered what the pristine version on the Fourth Floor looked like.

"Yeah... I think we've got a first edition here."

The Twelve Black Steps bent its covers and pages to form a grisly smile.

Axer frowned. "The first edition went missing three weeks ago from the Royal Library in Ansolme."

Comprehension took me all at once, making my breath catch. I looked at Guard Rock, still holding wary court, and I looked at the remains of Ori. I had to swallow the emotion that threatened to drown me.

"The book was freeing them," I said. Saving its people, just like me.

Constantine swore and let his head hit the wall behind us. "No. Absolutely not. I only have the energy for one revolution."

I looked at the way the books were trying to piece Ori together. I watched the strings of the book connecting to strings coming from the others.

I looked back at The Twelve. I looked at the hanging tethers that had kept some of the books in place in a library somewhere. The magic was chipped in spots, as if something had taken a bite out of them.

"Did Ori free you?" I asked softly.

The book straightened its spine imperiously.

I watched it for a moment, thinking through the monumental issues such a course of action would cause. At one time, I would have given anything to have access to this book. Given my soul.

Flipped pages in Bloodthirsty came to rest on a spread that showed death and destruction—dismemberment and pain.

I rubbed the back of my neck and looked at the Ori's remains. "Plucked daisies and trapped innocents would be a lot easier to defend on the world stage."

The Twelve Black Steps stomped its spine and leaned forward, pushing pages into my view.

"No, I get it," I said softly. "You are rich with information and resource—a library is better for having you in it. And it only matters what you are used for," I murmured. "Just like me. Dangerous in the wrong hands."

"Like all of us," Axer said.

I inclined my head. I'd always taken comfort in that assertion he'd made to me what felt like ages ago. "But if you are free, it's what you choose..."

It regarded me steadily.

I looked at Guard Rock, and gathered his little body in my hands. He tilted his rock at me, pencil poised in question.

"We make things of magic, give them life, then refuse to set them free," I murmured. "Even eighteen-year-olds are free from their parents where I'm from."

I set Guard Rock gently down. He tapped his pencil lightly against my hand, then assumed his guarding position again.

I nodded at the book. How could I go about trying to free my people and not let the books do the same?

It relaxed a measure of its posture and backed away, as if satisfied.

"Ren, we aren't going to go around freeing books," Constantine said.

"No." I tilted my head toward Ori and watched as more books gathered and each page sparked a little more as the books worked. A smile worked its way across my mouth with an emotion that had been ripped from me in the Basement. Hope. "He's going to free them. And we aren't going to stop him."

I watched the first page of the Origin Book grow brighter.

Hope filled me. I looked at my hands and the connections brimming along, reaffirmed. I did feel better.

"Maybe when broken, I am fixed by surrounding myself with loved ones, too," I murmured. "Maybe each time the reformation grows stronger..."

"Or maybe you are gaining what you need to control the world," Constantine said flippantly, though I could feel the knot of his emotions—still not soothed from the Basement incident—and that he never wanted to test any theory of broken connections again.

He leaned back against the wall Guard Rock had herded us against, and whipping his ribbon against his palm. Three energy bars rolled down the satin and into his hand. He tossed them to us. "We could use a few spell supplies, if so, future potentate."

As if that was a switch—or the use of magic had been one—the books still circling broke formation.

Guard Rock crouched low, ready to flip into the air as one dove at Constantine. Constantine, as tall as he was, snatched the book from the air before Guard Rock could stab it. The book squawked as Constantine turned it over. Its cover read How to Be a Successful Dictator's Assistant.

"Cute." Constantine flicked it upward, sending it back into flight.

But the books were in motion closer now, and he pulled in another immediately—grabbing it as it passed. Part of the spine was missing, making the book flap erratically.

Grossly Illegal Ways of Communication was scrawled across its cover.

Guard Rock stabbed Axer in the ankle, then padded over to start constructing a pedestal in the middle of the room, pulling it into existence with his bloody pencil tip.

"I'm not certain whether to be concerned about your rock's continuously growing abilities," Axer said, flicking the flurry of converging books away with practiced ease, as he watched the pedestal grow taller as Guard Rock incrementally climbed and continued to draw higher. "Or amused that he just told me without words to guard the two of you for him."

"They are going to have to put all of us away at the end of this." Constantine turned the damaged book over in his hands, then pulled a piece of ribbon from his coat. He stretched it along the spine, securing it in place, and the book shuddered, then launched itself into the air and gave a shake, testing its new binding.

It made a single circuit around the room, then dove back to Constantine and opened its pages. He made a motion as if considering it—though with our magic freed again, I could feel his satisfaction. He'd deliberately patched that book.

Constantine sighed—falsely—and held out a finger. The book clamped it, then suddenly voices filled my head and the room. And the books became whirling dervishes in the air, flying faster than my eyes could process.

I blinked at the whizzing books, trying to catch their titles—but it was like trying to identify a single blade in a highspeed fan.

"But where are they?" Olivia's voice was strident. "I want to know now, Dagfinn."

"They are somewhere in the Third Layer—but their location is changing so fast." Dagfinn sounded as harried as he ever did when something was out of his control. "I've never seen something like this before. Leandred hasn't patched us back—wait, what, hello?"

"Yes?" Constantine answered in a bored voice.

A general feeling of relief and overwrought emotion encircled us, even as the books danced faster.

"Where. Are. You." It was more a demand than a question. "What happened? It felt like you died."

I stumbled through a quick explanation of where we were, putting off the answer to the other question as long as I could.

Guard Rock, pedestal deemed complete at around five feet tall, was holding some sort of court in the middle of the room—a small subsection of the books frantically zipping around him. He had raised Ori's remains up as well, and some of the books were buzzing closer to brush against the pages. Guard Rock held his pencil stiffly and motioned at us with his free hand—though his body remained wary and on guard.

"Valeris's Palace? The Library of Broken Books? Sure," Dagfinn said hysterically. "Find the lost city of Fier next. Then we'll move on to—"

"You aren't doing anything else until we get there," Olivia demanded.

I let out a shaky laugh. "Sounds good."

"I'm not kidd—"

Their voices cut out as the book shook itself free from Constantine's finger and flew off drunkenly.

The whirling books suddenly slowed to normal sweeps and curls, in a strangely united motion.

My emotions, so frayed and newly rejuvenated, decided to freak out, especially with the suddenly lethargic feedback I was hearing from Excelsine.

Constantine frowned and put a hand on my shoulder, his gaze on the inebriated communications book. Axer's eyes narrowed in the way that said he was trying to piece clues together.

Guard Rock motioned at one of the books and pointed at me. The book reluctantly flew over and landed at my feet. I crouched down, willing to do anything to get my mind off the repeated feeling of loss, no matter how temporary. The book hopped forward and held out a corner to me with some distaste. Temporal Specifics glittered on its spine. I quickly held out a finger, looking for answers. Knowledge filled me as soon as I touched it.

My lips parted.

Duty done, the book lifted into the air.

"Well?" Constantine asked, already reaching in to get the answer from my mind.

"The book said that we can only talk to the outside world for five minutes each hour."

"That is oddly specific," Axer said, and I could see the smile forming on his face, something absolutely catlike about the satisfaction in it as he figured it out just from that.

"Forty-eight hours in here is an hour outside." I looked up at the galaxies swirling outside. "And the magic to communicate between the two disparate times is destructive to the world here when used in large amounts, so it cuts off before any damage is done."

I looked at Guard Rock, who looked steadily back. "The gift of time," I murmured.

Constantine's gaze intensified. "So, we could stay here indefinitely, time passing barely at all outside?"

I blinked. "No. Could you imagine, we'd grow old in here while everyone outside remained the same." The thought made me anxious. I set a spell to keep track of time. "And the book said that anything over a hundred cycles would cause dementia and death in humans."

I set another time tracking spell, to be on the safe side.

"Hidden," he murmured.

"For four days," I said, reality showing me the possibilities and I slumped against the wall. "Four days. One hundred—well, maybe ninety, to be safe—to plan. And only eight hours to pass in the real world. We can stop Stavros."

Axer's eyes closed with something like bone-deep relief, then opened above a dark smile. His back slid down the wall to sit against it, head tilted back, an overwhelming languidness to his posture, like he had given himself permission to just...rest for a moment after days, months, years on duty.

"We can only communicate with the outside world for five minutes each hour of our time?" Axer was looking up at the books circling with a glittering edge to his gaze. His compass was spinning madly.

"Yes," I confirmed.

Constantine snatched another book out of the air, read its cover, then flung it back into flight and snatched another. He did this a dozen times while we watched.

"Just give them something," Axer said to him, a frankly concerning amount of smirk on his face as he leaned against the wall in a half-sprawl. "I'll make sure they don't eat you."

Constantine's gaze focused strangely on him for a moment, and a secondary tie that had been broken snapped fully back between them.

I could feel how much force it took for Constantine to hold the overwhelming emotions from his face as his expression became indolent as he looked back into the air at the circling predators. "Fine. Who wants a taste?" He touched his temple and pulled out a thin thread of magic, snapping it into the air. Like chum suddenly scenting the water, four books dove at him. They froze in front of him and I wondered how he had done that until I saw

Axer's fingers twitch in the held position he had at his side.

Constantine looked through his choices, pointing at the second to the right. "One chapter. You provide real time readouts on whatever we want for forty-eight hours. Forty-eight hours in here."

It vigorously nodded. Constantine tilted his head toward his roommate. Axer flicked his fingers, sending the three waiting books winging off. Easy. Like they had done this before in another library. Sometime long ago.

The selected tome—Communicating Off Grid—flew up to clamp his head like a strange man-eating hat. Constantine tried to look bored while the book duplicated whatever knowledge it was after.

Finished, the book shivered, then flopped open on a table Constantine raised from the floor. Constantine touched the open pages. A minute later, written data started to remotely write across the left side, but at a glacial pace of a single letter for each second.

The first line read: "How did you do that?"

I could almost hear the demand in each letter's slant. Constantine smirked at Olivia's handwriting. He responded, then touched another page that he labeled "news."

"In other news, the intense stores of magic held in Crelussa have been moved to an undisclosed location. Helen Price stated that it was clearly the target of the Origin Mage and terrorists that she was working with and will be kept in locked secrecy for now. Some lawmakers have expressed unease with these secrecy conditions, though, further putting the Department in a pos—"

Constantine checked his time spell. "Ugh. Watching any more of that write itself out will give me dementia in one hundred seconds. Boring. Let's set that to record."

He hooked up a spell to duplicate newsfeeds to another book, then traded two more written quips—and a single heartfelt response of mine—to Olivia's short follow-up sentence, as we waited for her to verify the time.

One minute had passed for them. Twelve for us.

Time.

I let myself bonelessly flop on the ground, suddenly understanding exactly what Axer's sprawl meant. I could just...do nothing for five minutes. The world probably wouldn't end in twenty-five seconds, Stavros wouldn't find us, no one would die. I closed my eyes and fought the sudden urge to cry. "Boring sounds great," I said.

"Yes." Constantine smiled. He flipped to another page and scrawled a detailed note. Olivia's handwriting came through ten minutes later.

"Perfect."

Axer was still splayed against the wall, but he had roused himself enough to have some sort of staring contest with Stealth and Tactics. Its brother tome had hunted him relentlessly at Excelsine. The book inched forward. Sacrificial Plays inched in behind it.

"What are you doing?" I asked suspiciously.

He tapped his bicep. "Plotting again."

I scraped myself from the floor and Constantine and I experimented with the communication gaps for the next hour. Olivia got one hundred paragraphs of ours to every few of hers. But it made it so that I could write out, in less stuttering sentences, everything that happened with Stavros.

Constantine, on the other hand, took constant opportunities to input all sorts of offensive things Olivia couldn't respond to in time.

Axer gave Stealth and Tactics his finger, while Sacrificial Plays vibrated behind it and Ludicrously Dicey Plans landed to wait its turn.

At the hour mark, we hooked back up for our five minutes of conversation with Excelsine.

"This is going to get old fast," Olivia said sternly.

"But, Ren," her voice was anguished. "You—"

"I know, I know. It's okay. It's all fine." It wasn't fine.

"It's not fine. We had to put Nephthys in a medical coma. We're just bringing her out of it now."

I shut my eyes.

"And, Ren..." Olivia hesitated. "The Department... Ren, Patrick's younger brother...he was attacked a few minutes ago.

He's still alive, but the curse... Lifen's aunt suffered the same a few minutes before. The cure is only held by obtaining a piece of the caster. Delia's family just made it out alive and has gone dark. Will's family made it. But Mike's... "

I choked on the knowledge. Stavros had said... "I'm sorry. I'm so sorry," I whispered.

"No. Stavros will be," Olivia said, voice implacable. "Find a way for us to get to you in the next six hours of your time. That's 30 minutes for us. We're scrambling, but will be ready. Tell Leandred no more irritating notes."

Constantine waved his hand at me in a lighthearted 50/50 gesture of compliance, but his emotions were dark and swirling with vengeance.

The connection stuttered a warning. Five minutes went by surprisingly fast when you were trying to stuff so much debilitating information in.

"Ren, the Kinsky paintings, Stavros...be careful in Valeris's home."

She was right, of course. Before he'd destroyed himself, Valeris had lived to a far greater age than either Kinsky or I. His breadth of knowledge, by years alone, would have been greater.

Looking around me at what he had built and imbued was all the evidence I needed of that.

But I could only be grateful. We needed to find Stavros, more than ever. We needed to destroy his plans.

Olivia gave a last strong embrace along the connection, then once more, we were alone.

"Wait," I said, looking at the time. "We had thirty seconds left."

"Yes." Constantine was already connecting to another call.

"Constantine," Stuart Leandred's voice was sharp. "What—?"

"There's no time. I'm sending you a list of names. You need to protect the people on the list. I'll contact you again in an hour."

Stuart said nothing for a long moment. "I'll take care of it. You have my word. Wait—"

Stuart stopped Constantine before he could disconnect. "Be safe."

Constantine nodded sharply and disconnected.

My friends' families... I looked over at Axer, who was watching us both from where Sacrificial Plays was hungrily attached to him, sharing its secrets.

"Reprisal. Stavros is going to—"

"You can't think about the others in singular right now," Constantine murmured, offering comfort through touch. "Once you are back—"

"I can't go back." I unearthed Kinsky's journal. Books immediately dove and formed a hungry circle around me. I looked at the closed journal, and thought of the dead woman depicted over and over by the same hand.

"Ren," Constantine murmured.

"I keep trying to figure out how to go back." I moved uneasily and let out a breath. It came out a little cramped and hysterical. "I keep trying to recreate what I've lost." I thought of the Kinsky. At the same woman looking back from every portrait. "Holding too tightly."

To Excelsine, to home, to Christian, to my friends.

I thought of the Third Layer wise woman, and her words on not knowing what it was to be without. "I know what it is to be without." Without connection. Without magic. Without aim. Without restraint. Without all four of those working together.

"Ren—"

"Kinsky lacked any connection but the one—and he lost it. Valeris lacked restraint. I have lacked all at different points, and Stavros would like me to stay that way."

"But I need to go forward, and in going forward, I might find again what I've been searching for." Home. I fisted my fingers, watching the magic swirl. "Because I can't go back."

If I wanted to go home, I would have to make a new path there. I had to earn my own freedom. And that started with getting rid of Stavros. Because I, and all those I loved, would always be hunted by him. And he would always be a danger to the world.

He had to be destroyed. Severed of power.

And the secret was in the paintings. It was time to confirm the answer I already knew.

Priyasha, Kaine's words about seals, the symbol on the two paintings... Pages fluttered open and the surrounding books inched closer.

I held the journal and closed my eyes. Show me.

The sturdy pages flipped, fell open, and then symbols, script, and knowledge burst into the air.

I tilted my head at the images. A pentagram with circular seals pressed into the five extending tips and pyramid seals at the interior connecting points of the pentagon within.

The points shimmered when each was touched. I gave the magic a twist, setting the images rotating into motion, the points shifting around the center, keeping that which was being protected safe inside. It was like how I was hiding the installation in the Western Territories. Not in a pentagram form, but in the way that each edge was secured.

Domes were far harder to erect in wards, but they gave an increased defensive edge, as it was a lot harder to peel a part away.

But five was a sturdy, secure number.

And the symbol at the center...

Constantine cleared his throat and I jumped to see him sitting on my right with a pile of string nets, ten filled containers, a series of half-finished projects, and one wrist flat and bare against the surface. Books were all inching around, trying to creep closer to me, only held off by a quick boot.

I looked down in confusion at the chair I didn't recall sitting in. "When did we make a larger table?"

Axer was curling magic into a series of containers across the table, a pile of glistening blades and stars freshly sharpened in front of him as well as all three of our cloaks and a slew of removed devices. One bare wrist was also sliding across the surface of the table as his fingers worked to guide the magic or mend a protection. His gaze slid over me, then, satisfied, returned to repairing the next piece of our arsenal.

Guard Rock swung his legs over the edge of the table next to Axer, watching the creep of books on the ground and in the sky. One of Guard Rock's palms was flat on the table as well, pencil ready in the other hand. The cat had its tail in his lap and was seemingly out cold, though I saw one eyelid slide open to peer at me, then slide shut again.

At least fifty books were in a hunching perimeter around us and were avidly watching—pages whispering.

Who had removed my cloak? When had I sat down?

Constantine raised a brow. "We couldn't break you away from your trance, but you responded to simple commands, and were at baseline on all measures, including your response to our connections. Alexi and your rock thought we should leave you to it."

His fingers lifted, and I could see him pull the protections they had been holding on the table into his fingertips. I noticed the soothing cream and tan tones of Neph mixed in with Constantine's violet and bronze, and bright ultramarine magic setting them indelibly into place—so much more stable than before.

"You are pulling from each other so easily now?"

And Neph, Neph was okay. So many ways for everything to go wrong, and so little time for me to be able to worry individually about anyone. I pulled shaking fingers down my face. All I wanted was to be able to hold all my people close. To stack into a huge pile under a blanket fort and not come up for an entire weekend.

Constantine let the magic swirl into the air to form a loose cover around the five of us. "Let's talk about you taking years from my life."

"I can't believe you let me not answer your call inside a place that as far as we can tell might be digesting us for a thousand condensed years."

And after completely freaking out in Verrange.

"I was told to try this new thing called trust. I can't say it holds much appeal so far." But he didn't seem angry.

Axer rolled his eyes, sealed the containers he was working on, and tucked three into each cloak.

"Did I miss the check in?" I asked.

"No, there are still a few hours to go," Axer said.

Constantine snapped his fingers twice between us and motioned at the journal. "Now to that, and your irritating meditation. Before I take the standing offer from When You Simply Can't Take It Anymore..."

A bedraggled book in the circle perked up.

I spread my fingers over the pages of the journal. I took a moment to carefully inspect the magic this time, seeing the threads.

"I thought at first Priyasha gave the journal to me as a warning. It's like the yearbook I looked through in Greyskull's office, but even more personalized. A singular view captured with all the sensory intensity of each moment. Kinsky's record of his journey to resurrect Priyasha." I looked up. "But it's more than that. Kinsky must have had just enough agency at the end to make changes to it after his capture and the revelation of Stavros's duplicity."

"This symbol." I tapped on the pentagram. "It was in the Crelussa Kinsky. And the one at Verrange. Sergei Kinsky's last move was to embed this journal with a way to reveal how to find his duplicitous master."

Axer stared down at it for a moment, then looked at me with a raised brow.

"What?" I pulled the journal against my chest. "I know what I saw. I know what—"

He reached his fingers to me and formed a picture in my mind's eye of what he could see. A jumbled mass of incomprehensible squiggles dotted a parchment page.

"Oh." I let the journal fall from my chest and looked down at the detailed and beautiful drawings. I pulled a picture of the page into my mind and when Axer opened a gentle mental palm to catch it, I set it inside.

His gaze sharpened along with his magic as he immediately passed the image to Constantine. "You saw this symbol at Crelussa?"

"Yes. It's a powerful warding symbol."

"Hidden from normal sight," Axer murmured. "But made by Origin hands." His gaze drifted to Constantine, who was grimly looking back at him, emotions firm.

"There was a Kinsky in Salietrex," Constantine said, finally. "We viewed it about fifteen minutes before..."

Axer turned to me, gaze intense. "Tell me about Ganymede Circus. What happened before Verisetti destroyed it?"

"I went to a black magic store, trying to resurrect my brother." I pulled a hand over the back of my neck. "That didn't go as planned. There was a layer shift. I went into an art store—the owner sucked. There was a Kin...." My voice trailed off.

"There was a Kinsky there?"

"Yes. But without the symbol." I traced it with my finger. "The woman had a paper for me, though, same as the others."

"You hadn't unlocked your power. The symbol might have been there."

"Raphael destroyed Ganymede because of a favor. He said that before he did it." A favor for Godfrey Sr. or Leonach or someone high in a Third Layer terrorist organization.

"But that doesn't mean he wasn't there for the painting. Did he ask you about it?"

"Yes. He asked me what was inside," I murmured. "The Library of Alexandria had a Kinsky, too. We escaped in it, and the library expelled all who remained outside. They never figured out what the terrorists were after."

"But they figured out who did it."

"Yes," I whispered. Raphael Verisetti, using my dolls.

"A man whose only goal is to destroy Enton Stavros."

My lips parted. It had to be right, then. All clues led down the same path as my intuition said.

Axer looked at me. "A pentagram hide. A powerful tool to hide something." His eyes were fierce. "Or someone."

"All of those towns Raphael destroyed," I murmured.

"I bet we will find a Kinsky was in each of them. That's how Stavros does it. That's how he hides. Five specific Kinskys are the seals protecting the sixth—or whatever is in the middle. Kinsky was prolific under Mussolgranz. The works are everywhere. It's a perfect camouflage. Verisetti probably figured out that you needed an Origin Mage to see the symbol at some point. He connected a leash to you to gain your power, but after another few strikes yielded nothing, he might have realized he needed you specifically. Someone the paintings—all connected—recognize." Axer smiled. "She knows. Priyasha. In all the forms she takes. In the memories that Kinsky imbued in her—in all the paintings of her—connected together, they know. They know they are protecting someone untrustworthy. Someone who caused the death of their creator."

"That's why Kaine grabbed the painting in Crelussa," Constantine said, stabbing a knife into the leather he was cutting. "He was protecting his master. One seal of five."

"And why Stavros was so furious with the destruction of the Basement seal—he's lost another."

"There are hundreds of Kinsky portraits, all over the layer, as Alexi said."

"And Verisetti, even imbued with your magic couldn't distinguish them. He needed you, but you were taking too long. He swiftly started looking for other opportunities to destroy Stavros—opportunities still provided by you, since Stavros was hunting you." Axer sat back, eyes closed, mouth curled. "And this...this gives us the shroud for Plan A."

I looked at him and nodded slowly.

Axer smiled. "We are going to finish Verisetti's job. We are going to rip all of Stavros's protections away."

"We can't do it alone," Constantine said.

"No, we have to get the others involved. And campus still has hold of them. We have to back Marsgrove into a corner that only has one exit."

"Marsgrove might do it without threat," Constantine said, looking down suddenly. The books had gathered together, top of their spines bent inward. "And the books are having a moot. No concern there. Rock, what's going on?"

Guard Rock motioned to me like, "One of these days, I'm going to stab him where he can't heal it," then pointed to the side and crossed his arms.

I cocked my head at a book that was inching closer. Temporal Physics and Interdimensional Travel in the Physical Age was sliding its cover along the tabletop in one-inch scoots.

"Are you...do you know how we can do what we need?" I asked it.

With a crack of displacement, it suddenly appeared right in front of my face and latched eagerly around my head. I squawked and tried to peel it away, but it held tighter and rifled through my thoughts and memories until it had six laid out in a grid in my mind. It let go and hopped back to the desk.

Constantine grabbed it, a spell on his fingertips.

I held out my hand to him. "Wait." I looked at the book. "You will trade for the knowledge?"

It solemnly nodded, pages vibrating in anticipation.

"What does it want?" Constantine asked brusquely.

"It wants the blueprints for building the inter-layer portal pad."

"Absolutely not."

I didn't look away from the book. "In exchange, it has a way for everyone at Excelsine to come here via a book on the Fourth Floor." It nodded eagerly.

"Do it."

I blinked at Constantine. "That was quite a change of tune."

"When the tune is obvious, you change it."

"How many can come through?" Axer asked, relaxing back in his chair, as if the entire war had just been won.

The book made a gesture, flipping a specific number of its pages.

"Looks like fifty, if I'm interpreting that correctly," I said.

"How many copies do you have in other libraries?" Axer asked it. "And do you visit them?"

It flipped five pages and dipped its spine.

He tapped his fingers on the table. "The Department is going to get the technology anyway. If they get you, no restriction will matter. Do it."

We sent the instructions to Olivia, and before the six hours was even up, the book's pages began to glow.

Chapter Twenty-five
REUNIONS

UNSURPRISINGLY, Loudon fell through first. Olivia, Will, Neph, Asafa, Mike, Delia, and the others quickly followed. Patrick fell through last and the pages glowed then dimmed.

There was a mad scramble, then Olivia, Neph, and I were tumbling to the floor, arms and legs bent in awkward, wonderful angles as we dragged each other closer.

"What a rush," Will said, cheeks red and eyes bright as he swayed, trying to take it all in. "Like my brain was squeezed through a tube of memories and then blended in time and space. I feel absolutely terrible," he said cheerfully.

Then he passed out. Two thumps echoed beside him.

Olivia and Neph seemed to be pushing back against fainting on pure determination. I held tighter and felt moisture slipping from my eyes.

"Did you really think we weren't going to come?" Olivia whispered into my hair.

"I don't want you to get hurt, too."

"I know," she said softly, pulling away to look into my eyes. "And things are going to get worse. But there's a time for worry and there's a time for action, and we are choosing which we follow."

A hand descended on my shoulder. I squeezed my eyes together then looked up at Mike. For a moment, everything was still. Like the world had frozen, and only the unending movement of dust in the wind was visible. A space opened in my chest, like someone had shoved a balloon in there and kept blowing, blowing, blowing, until they hit my ribs, pushing everything outward until it felt I might explode with the nothingness that was blooming inside.

"Mike."

"We are going to find the cure," he said, expression showing pain, immediate and fresh. "We are going to find the caster. We are going to stop this madness. And we are going to get rid of Stavros."

Patrick stepped behind him, eyes darkly glittering.

"Yes." My eyes filled with liquid. "Yes."

~*~

After reviving everyone and catching up on many, many fierce hugs, I introduced them to the library.

The Bandits took to the library's denizens exactly as I figured they would—with enthusiasm.

Guard Rock had become the official in charge of maintaining order, and had stabbed more than one book—and more than one mage—trying to sneak information without proper exchange. Things settled into order quickly under his watch.

At the one-hour mark, Asafa, Delia, Lifen, and Kita left to check in at Excelsine, and see what had occurred in their five-minute absence. After a quick discussion, it had been decided to split shifts between abilities and roommates, trying to give each group a member of each ability and pair, just in case something went wrong on either end.

There were still things to be done in the real world in real time, too. At Excelsine, they had been working hard to gather and energize all the resources that we had been collecting—the eyes and ears of the young, intellectual community. And they had started sending branches out to the other universities around the Second Layer—something that Axer had helped facilitate with the combat connections he had forged during the competition.

Contacting and putting those connections into play was a game of delicate balance and timing that we hoped would pay off on the world stage.

Inside, we were plotting a different plan.

"Once she's caught in the fly trap, she won't be able to get out. Stavros will specifically look for and remove triggers that act like the Table One mind job Verisetti laid," Adrabi said. "Ren's the one who has to be with him to destroy him, but she's useless once she's in his lair. Circular problem."

"He won't bring Ren to him whole," Will said, rubbing his finger in agitation along the table. How to Plan Your Heist hopped over each finger swipe like it was an invisible jump rope. "He can't afford it."

"Unless he thinks he's won," I murmured. Death Plans peeked hopefully over the side.

"He gets you, he has," Mike said baldly.

I looked at Axer, then Constantine.

"I don't like the people we might have to trust in this," Constantine said, throwing his string onto the table.

"Ditto," Olivia said tightly.

I looked at Olivia and Constantine in sympathy. "I know."

After a few rounds between Excelsine and the library, the connection was deemed stable. The combat mages came through for a few hours—holding intense conversations with Axer in the corner. The tension between Constantine and the combat mages was not zero.

Lox and Constantine were never going to be friends—they were too alike and different in all the wrong ways. Camille looked like Constantine could drop dead at any moment, and she wouldn't shed a tear. Greene and Constantine, on the other hand, had a tense conversation that seemed to end in mutual accord.

And Ramirez...well, Ramirez watched Constantine with the stare of someone who was plotting multiple endpoints—ways to make his best friend happy and bring Constantine into the fold, and ways to ensure that Constantine's body would never be found.

The Bandits and combat mages started rotating on a per-project basis. It was an elegant solution to visiting and securing the premises at Excelsine, though due to the time scale on the other side, they had to clump around the library's Fourth Floor, and clumping together was always a danger with the Junior Department still active.

"Stavros is going to know," I said. "About Valeris. That we could find something like this. He'll be able to put the clues together at the first report to reach his ears."

A ball appeared in Axer's hand. "That's where the art of the con comes in. That's why we make him think we are after one thing"—His hand flipped, and the ball was gone—"when really we are pulling another con."

Patrick's eyes glittered. "Pull the double bluff. The triple. There's always a way to make someone think you are on their side when you are not."

Constantine was watching Patrick sharply. Patrick smirked, a veil of mischief gathering back over eyes that continued to cast dark shadows.

Surrounded by dangerous books, dangerous mages, and the dangerous knowledge that we could all put together, we were ready to enact a risky plan.

"It's not going to be easy even in Plan A," Olivia said grimly, when we all gathered together for an hour inside to discuss the full parameters. "Evidence supports your pentagram theory." She turned a book so that I could see the page she was tapping. "Though without an Origin Mage's sight, it has always just been one theory in an endless sea of them about Stavros. In a pentagram hide, you must uncover each of the external points to find what is hidden in the middle—and where it is hidden. And in this case, who."

"Stavros."

Asafa tapped the page. "The intersections are the doorways to the center. Which means there are corridors between the seal endpoints and the doors." His fingers slid along the paths. "These are the routes that have to be taken, if part of the pentagram still stands."

"We finish Verisetti's work," Mike said. "Destroy the points. Expose him."

"Exposure will not be easy, even with all points destroyed. There will be a flipside, somewhere, even in the end," Axer said. "Just like in the Basement—a replication of the interior seal."

"But if we destroy the others and get him in the last one, he can be exposed. Maybe harmed."

Axer nodded. "It's an easier plan to predict. But it's far harder to destroy something from the outside. Time is against an attack from without. A siege is not in our favor. As soon as we start destroying the pentagram, Stavros will know. He'll know when the first seal is attacked, no less the last destroyed. He'll have every precaution and shield he's been working on for thirty plus years in place."

Axer tossed magic into the center. "No matter what, we're going to have to split up. That's the only way any of this works."

"Absolutely not," Olivia said, steel under her words.

"You know the end game, Price," Constantine said wearily. "Alexi is right. And we're going to need people at the sites simultaneously anyway."

"When did the two of you become friendly again?" she asked aggressively. I could feel in our bond that she had expected him to agree with her.

Constantine lifted a brow. "You expected me to be reasonable and consistent?"

She growled.

"We all have our specialties, Olivia, though usually no one cares about a specialty for hail," Mike said, twirling a thread of wind around his finger, lips tight. "We need to cover all parts of this plan near simultaneously. Sacrifice is inevitable, but the end game can be ours if we commit. I know you are committed. I know you will play your part. The rest of us are committed, too, let us play ours," he ended softly.

I looked away.

Olivia's lips pulled tight. "I don't like this plan."

"I don't either," I whispered. "But if we want to beat him, we have to do it before he knows we switched the game."

"It's a bad game."

"The board was set before we were ever on it. We were never playing a good one, but we can make it ours." I looked around the table and saw the determined faces staring back. Even Olivia's.

I looked at the magic displayed in the center of the table, with our circular plans swirling around it—with the sacrifices that we might have to make. So many parts with so much risk.

"Verrange is gone," I said. "But Kaine could have put the Crelussa painting into play again already, elsewhere. It was likely Salietrex was a seal. Maybe Jauvine, too. Which means Stavros has a way to patch the seals or move them.

But once you start loosening a pentagram hide, it is never quite as strong as the original. Like patching tape on a broken toy." I looked at Olivia. "We have to hit simultaneously. But even if that plan fails, he'll still want an Origin Mage to remake the entire construct completely. From scratch. Better this time. He'll want me."

"I don't like this." And it was interesting, here at the end, that Olivia, that Constantine, had been the two at different points in time—Constantine earlier, and Olivia still now—to be the ones to hold out so fiercely. "We almost lost you."

"I know," I said painfully. "But not this time. That's what we are doing—we are going to make certain every one of us is standing at the end." I had to believe that. "Together."

Grim resignation and a veil of determination descended, and she nodded sharply. "Yes."

Asafa cleared his throat, the others exchanging short nods. "So, locating the remaining seals... Dagfinn? What do you have for us?"

Dagfinn didn't hesitate. "Five sites. Two extremely likely candidates, the other three good options as second tier hits."

"Pull them up," Axer said.

Dagfinn enlarged the hologram.

It was interesting how the Bandits—a bunch of independent and rebellious troublemakers—had automatically deigned to listen whenever Axer spoke.

"Darpin Sloughs. Fels Hollow. Picquant Moors. Shayvale Castle. Spartine Prison."

The oxygen in my lungs felt like it had been lit on fire. "Why the prison?"

Dagfinn blinked. "Why...not the prison?"

Someone elbowed him, and I heard "brother" harshly whispered.

"Oh. Ohhhhh, right. Well." Dagfinn coughed. "Er, that's one of the two... I mean—"

"It's okay, Dagfinn," I said gently. "Spartine Prison has a Kinsky?"

"It...has a Kinsky with the date and hit parameters you provided. Now, no one can see the symbols like you can, but Verisetti tried to hit the prison three separate times. The motive was attributed to prisoner liberation by the media each time, but—"

"But he was probably trying to destroy a seal." I pulled my finger across the hologram, rotating it. I forced myself not to look at the prisoner section.

"Also, the location pinged as a hit on our earlier Basement list. A few people we were tracking went into the prison—Department folks—then disappeared, only to reappear elsewhere later."

"There are ports inside the prison," Axer said.

"Yes. But our flagged villains didn't go into those rooms." He pulled up a subset of schematics. "Government specs are supposed to show all port entrances and exits, even restricted ones. It's a violation of building codes, otherwise someone might add in magic somewhere, not knowing that there's already a space, and next thing you know—" He made an explosion with his hands.

"You cross-referenced, and the unmarked porting room has a Kinsky," Olivia said, getting back on topic. When Olivia decided she was in a plan, she was in.

"The unmarked porting room has a Kinsky," Dagfinn confirmed.

Axer nodded, unsurprised.

"I know some people who can scout the sites." Dagfinn looked a little furtive. "No names, but they hate the Dep—"

"Julian can help." Axer sketched a communication rune and tossed it across the table. "He knows the security measures and can give a rough sketch of them. He is...taking a leave of absence from his duties, as well as being off island. He can help you gather information. He'd be pleased to do it."

Will and Dagfinn exchanged uneasy glances, then looked at me. I shrugged. I didn't trust Julian Dare much either, but if he could aid us...

"Show me what you have on Darpin Sloughs," Axer said.

Dagfinn brought that one up, and they started dissecting it as well.

I tuned out. I had little doubt we'd have the correct hit list by the end of the day. Axer could pull on all my knowledge, at this point, by just curling his magic with Constantine's and tapping into the right thought. I happily left him to it with full permission.

I tapped on Constantine's confidence games device instead. Patrick went suddenly silent next to me. I looked up to see him staring down at it.

Crime Families and Punishment immediately landed next to him. Disloyalty, Dishonor, and Death followed.

"You can't trust an O'Leary," Patrick said, eyes on his family's device.

I nodded and tapped the con above Five Man Act on our list, scrolling through the parameters. "So, I've heard."

His eyes glittered as he looked at me with a faint smile. "You heard me talking to my father last term." He waved a distracted hand. "He has his plans. And his desires. The Department stole our generational ward stones some ten years past under cover of continued 'evidence' lockup. Motivation and revenge are easy lures for my family," he said darkly.

"Along with family ties. Loyalty."

Patrick's eyes went blank as he stared off into the distance. "We'll have to see, won't we?"

"We'll save your brother."

"We'll have to see on that, too," he murmured. I stroked our connection thread, which hadn't fully recovered, but was still there, still attached. The connections had to be upheld by both sides. All of Patrick's were dimmer than before, though, and it made me want to cry. Sacrifice. "Get to have my fun first, though, don't I?" His expression turned jovial like his continually flipping emotional switch had locked into place again.

"Only if you want," I murmured. "I'm serious, we can—"

"Yes, Crown." He sounded so tired suddenly, letting me see his strain. He gave me a smile. "I know. With you there is always a choice. It's a novelty. Don't be concerned. O'Learys always come out on top."

He leaned back and shut his eyes.

"All Department prisoners go to Keating Glen first," Dagfinn was saying, as I tuned back in to the other conversation. "It's procedure. They get wiped of tracking spells and anything else before being run through the system."

"Then some stay there, while others go to a stage further down," Saf said, running his fingers along the path.

"Where would they take one of us?" I asked.

"Depends on who they get." Axer tapped one of the buildings in the hologram. "You or me, we'd get processed quickly. Fifteen minutes, maybe. Stripping spells and unbreakable null cuffs and tailored spells. Stavros will already have subroutines set to subdue our magic, and he'd want us quickly. Kaine is the only one who'd be allowed to transport us, though, so we'd have just that small bit of time before he arrived, if he wasn't already on the premises. Price and Constantine would get nearly the same treatment we would, though they'd be held until Stavros needed them. Maybe underestimated and allowed a bit of magic even. Bau and Tasky probably too. One of the others gets caught, they go to maybe stage two or three. It depends on how they'd rate their status and what surgeon they'd be sent to."

"Most of you would probably stay in Keating Glen," Greene said. "It's where they keep most of the prisoners."

"If we incapacitate Keating Glen..."

"Then they'll have to use the holding cells of the next best alternative."

"Spartine."

Axer nodded. "Spartine."

"And the protection levels?"

"Different levels of protections are used for different kinds of prisoners."

"So, Patrick—"

"Would rank as high volatility. A trickster. They wouldn't trust him."

"And Will?"

"Tasky would still get held in the highest security because of his ties to you. But would they expect trickiness from him? They'd be less likely to. A distinct advantage." He tapped the page. "We need a high level of security, but a low level of deception risk."

"The space where Stavros is?" Greene said. "It can't be large. And it can't be filled with workers. No one ever says, 'I work in the Department's secret torture lab' and though people claim to have seen Stavros personally as a point of pride, the truth is always unsubstantiated."

"Politicians lie," Constantine said languidly, twisting a stringed net.

"There are many secret torture labs," Ramirez said. "He can visit any of them by hopping a ride."

"Who would be allowed to travel where he is, though?" Greene asked. "Kaine, probably."

"Cuffed, tortured victims?" Will contributed.

"Raphael was tortured by Helen Price. Extensively," I offered. "They both have said so. Now, maybe the torture took place in the Basement alone, but Raphael was worked on by Stavros personally. Does your mother know where Stavros is?"

"She doesn't need to know where he is, if she has a connection to him," Olivia said briskly. "He can just open the door for her. That is, in fact, how

I'm sure they do things. Stavros has to open his side."

Uneasy silence met that statement.

"Price's mother," Green allowed. "Mussolgranz. That irritating praetorian from campus."

Darkness roiled through Constantine, Axer, and Olivia at the reminder of Tarei.

"Likely more of the empty vessels you saw in the Basement," Camille said tightly. "Nothing to trust or not trust there."

Axer nodded. "We get to him on our own, outside of all the spells, those are the people we have to fight."

"Lovely," Constantine said, stretching back. "One for each of us."

"We all need to go over Crown's memories," Greene said. "Sorry, Crown."

They pulled the entire set from the Basement and put it in a viewing ball. It was too hard to experience again, so I chose to sketch and use the time for the dozen enhanced storage papers I needed to construct.

"Ugh. I need to vomit somewhere," Lifen said, giving my shoulder a squeeze, when they were done.

"We already knew what had to be done after Crelussa," Mike said tightly. "Four thousand attempted murders of kids. But this...millions..." Mike looked up, and there was no second-guessing in his gaze. "I will see this stopped no matter what. No matter what, Ren."

I had to look away, close my eyes. That I would lose one of them in this was too probable.

"An Empath. A Bridge. A Hollow. Wow, listening to that was worse than the summary I already knew!" Loudon said.

"This is all just fantastic," Delia said, stabbing a knitting needle into a glowing scarf, held in the chompers of a book titled Deadly Creations at her side. "Nothingness. Loss of self and others. I'd rather have death and dismemberment."

Neph, who I'd thought would be the most upset—and indeed, her emotions were all quite clear on that front as she viewed the memories—was surprisingly the one straining for every horrifying detail.

"Affective Empathy. High intelligence. Hubris," she said softly. "His model for humanity is already set. He assumes motivation according to the basest of emotions. And while that likely bears true in an overall sense, such views can lead to overestimation in the micro. Enton Stavros under and overestimates emotions. Anger, love, vengeance... He has manipulated each for six or seven decades. There are no surprises for a man like that."

Axer flipped the sphere in his hand. "Give him what he thinks he'll see..."

She nodded, and looked up at him, resolute resignation in her gaze. "And he'll see nothing else."

Loudon clapped his hands against the table. "Well, we're all going to die. I'll let Adrabi know," he said cheerfully, standing.

Delia, Lifen, Kita, and Camille rose as well. The hour to get caught up was over—Adrabi and Lox were the only ones keeping tabs over the book at Excelsine—and it was time to shift members.

As the others exited, the remaining Bandits and combat mages put their heads together, tablets out, and started flipping through books and texts. Fully formed books popped up for some, while others were using specialty search spells that projected pages, text, and diagrams into the air.

Temporal Physics and Interdimensional Travel in the Physical Age flashed, indicating incoming mages.

Adrabi and Lox tumbled through...

...along with someone no one had planned to see. My breath caught.

"She whammied us, but passed the vow. I feel terrible," Lox said, and both staggered, then fell. I didn't watch to see who helped them stand.

Stevens, who had landed on her feet, strode over and gazed down at me, something fierce in her usually cold expression.

I looked around and saw everyone watching, magic ready on many fingertips. But Stevens had none on hers. And she had passed the vow we had put into place on the other side—a self-preservation vow that had been demanded by the books. Stevens couldn't mean anyone or anything harm inside.

"How did you find us?" I asked.

"Your little squad, though brilliant, is conspicuous. And they can't escape administrative magic, no matter how much they try."

"You tracked them."

"Grey, Phillip, and I have been keeping track since you left. The world is in tumult. Each hour is critical. Mwamba sends his regards." She threw five of our shield field prototypes and I caught them against my chest.

I swallowed around the lump in my throat. "Thank you. Tell Professor Mbozi thank you," I whispered.

"He demands a recollection of the box's use at Crelussa, when you are back on campus."

I swallowed and nodded slowly, achingly, looking down at the fields we had created together. "I can't wait to use up seven hours of his time."

"You exceed," she murmured. "You've exceeded."

I wiped at my eyes. It was like someone else telling me I had done an outstanding job. "I've made a bit of a mess."

"And yet, you exceed."

I looked up at her. "We will."

She looked me over for another long moment. "Show me where to set up. Time constructs are terrible for the skin."

I looked at her, hope filling me. "I thought you said you were the person most dangerous to me."

"Yes." She smiled—and for a moment, she was Stavros's daughter through and through. "I'm also plenty dangerous to him. Timing, Ren. All information was locked within me long ago with no way of telling anyone what I knew. Locked down by him. And when I'd finally found happiness, he took it away."

And I could see it, suddenly, within the memories of the yearbook. A cold girl who had never experienced warmth, suddenly befriended and brought into a tight fold by a laughing, golden boy, alongside his dark tattooed friend, a powerful mage who was also trying to escape being born to the dark, and an offbeat mage who liked explosions and made me think of Loudon. A cold girl who had become enlivened, enriched, and...happy. I looked at Olivia, who was clenching her fists.

"I've had ten years to plan." Stevens regarded me for a moment. "You were a surprise. But I had years to plan for something. An event or hope that I could cling to. A person that could end what I knew father might someday start. And with you, I know who the targets will be. And I bet you have a plan for that. I have an alternative offering."

Axer shifted around her, like a predator examining prey. She watched him from the corners of her eyes without turning.

He looked to me, to Constantine, to Ramirez, then back to her as he finally stood in front of her. "We do have a role for you, Professor, if we can trust you."

She looked at him and held forth her bare right wrist—an action that caused more than one person to inhale sharply. Though some mages freely showed their personal markings, most wore some sort of cover, or expediently kept their control cuff over top. Stevens was not the sort to bare hers. Ever.

A broken set of five rings was tattooed so deeply in her wrist, that it looked as if they had been carved there. One of the rings was mangled and pitted, another was so sharply thinned that it looked like it would break with any physical movement, two were worn and scarred but still trying to clasp together with all the others, and the fifth was also still clasped, but dim.

"He took everything from me, long ago," she said, securing her cuff back over top. "Give me whatever vow sealant you want. I will see justice finally served. I will see him gone."

Axer looked at me, then nodded.

Vow taken, and our plans revealed to her, Stevens returned to Excelsine to retrieve her things and to bring another inside.

Greyskull was eagerly mobbed by the Bandits and pulled into construction tasks. No one needed a vow to know where he stood on Enton Stavros's downfall. Greyskull and Will put their heads together immediately, going over permissions, tattoos, and vows.

After a quick intro to the library, Stevens began unpacking supplies and calling on books. An eager one helped set up a working lab.

Five hours later, with occasional aid from Greyskull, Constantine, Will, Greene, Adrabi, and Neph, we had batches of things far beyond our initial planning.

"Thank you for helping," I said to Stevens, who was quietly stirring.

She didn't say anything for a long moment. "You are one of my brightest students. I expect you to excel next year."

I swallowed down the clog in my throat, the one that said we both knew that wasn't likely to be possible, and nodded. "I will."

Constantine had been helping frequently, but he had gone off with Neph to execute one of the most important steps. He returned as we finished up another potion, connections shining from him. Stevens looked at the connections, then sharply at the vials in Constantine's hand. "You will indeed surpass me one day."

"I will."

For a second there was a ghost of a smile curling her lips, then it was gone. She withdrew the pair of silver earrings and cufflinks that we had imbued with modified versions of our shield field, as well as a slew of other spells. We fiddled with the magic and encapsulation effects of the connections for another two hours. Then finally, finally it was done.

I looked at the earrings and took a deep breath. It felt like safety. Like a heat resistant glove for fighting a dragon—what we were making was slim, but at least there was a chance.

Stevens held up a tiny vial of the brightest green with a sliver of a sickly ochre weaving through it, as if seeking escape. "I've been holding onto this for many years. To be used two steps before the end."

Constantine's gaze greedily devoured the vial. I could see his hands itching to grab it. "We could have used that at Crelussa."

"And yet, you survived without wasting a priceless artifact," she said.

"We should reverse engineer it first," Constantine said, gaze fixed on the tiny vial.

"I've tried," Stevens said briskly, breaking the seal. "And failed. Be glad I didn't try more. There's just enough for this."

I looked between them. "That will hide the wearer?"

She smiled grimly and poured the mixture carefully on the earrings and cufflinks, then let it set. Thirty minutes later, I felt nothing from the jewelry. No magic of any kind. Each piece was neutered. And when Constantine lifted one, I could no longer feel him.

I quickly made him put it back down, getting a taste of what he'd felt when Stavros had severed me.

"You are certain the spells still exist underneath?" I asked, rubbing at my elbow.

Stevens lifted an earring and turned it between her fingers, the feel of her going blank, as if her magic no longer existed. "Without price, this potion, and only three vials in existence—the formula lost to the world in the mind of a scientist who fell with The Golden City. Apropos that we use it for this."

To stop the end of a world.

Her gaze lifted to mine. "Two steps before the end, Ren. We are counting on you. Hold your emotions tight."

She tucked the earrings and cufflinks carefully into her cloak pocket and left without further fanfare or farewell. Constantine gazed at the pocket where she had stored the jewelry with something close to desire as she disappeared.

I poked him in the side. "What say you we figure out how to make that potion, after?"

Hooded eyes shifted to me. "Marry me."

"I thought we were already engaged?" I asked, yawning.

"Don't say such lovely things, darling. I'll hold you to them."

I patted him on the shoulder. "I'd probably be fine in a harem, actually. More people to do science with."

"I don't think you understand what a harem is." He looked amused, though, which had been my point.

With Stevens' departure, we were far past a thirty-hour cycle inside, and fatigue was catching up.

I yawned again. "Oh, I almost forgot. I figured out what we needed while working with Stevens. Vampire containers."

He raised a brow. "Vampire containers?"

"Evil ones. You know, you stick one against someone and"—I sucked in my cheeks—"drained. My magic to create the container, yours to make the person pass out, and Axer's to leech it all in. We can probably get some of Neph in there, too, to make the person have good dreams. Don't have to be totally evil about it, though the people we are going to use them against totally deserve it."

He bent down and looked me in one eye, then the other.

"I haven't been possessed."

"Right." He straightened back up. "You want to make containers that drain a mage's powers? You want to give me an army of zombie magic? I accept."

"No, that's not what I—"

He smiled.

I pointed. "You'll be working with Axer on it."

His smile grew. He leaned in. "Cute, that you think Alexi won't put in worse."

My fingers triangled over my brows and pushed out above my closed eyes. "Con."

"We'll get it done. No worries."

"Now I'm really worried."

"You should have thought of that before trusting either of us, and especially both of us together."

"Ugh." But I couldn't stifle a third yawn.

"Come on." He shifted me toward the sleeping nest that Neph had constructed at some point while I wasn't looking.

I looked at her suspiciously, then up at Constantine, then to Neph again. "Did you make me tired?"

She looked back with a raised brow. "After you've been working nonstop in a draining temporal environment for thirty hours on end? Would I have to?"

I looked between her and Constantine, then face planted in the pillows and turned to burrow deeper. "You can't fool me. I'm on to you both."

Like me cashing it in was a signal to everyone else, the others abandoned their half-finished projects and flocked over to talk, tease, and relax.

Our connections gleamed, and I touched them all and smiled.

Sleeping arrangements turned hilarious, though, as everyone hunkered down to get a few hours rest. Neph was uninterested in any sleeping position that wasn't plastered against my side. Olivia quickly claimed the other side, glaring at both boys, who seemed more amused than anything.

I let sleep take me, and followed the gold threads to where I knew they would lead.

Chapter Twenty-six

SHADOWED PLOTS

R APHAEL WAS sitting on the sand, staring out at a vast ocean in the twilight. Stars whirled in the heavens of the dreamscape.

"I loved the sea once," he said, his only acknowledgment of me sitting beside him. "Until all those Kinsky's with their salt spray. I specifically started targeting the ones with ocean backgrounds after a while."

"Which ones were successful?"

"Jauvine, Cadmiat. It was easier to narrow options once I had your magic. I nearly had the first, as well, lucky number one, but Stavros moved the painting in Salietrex just in time. But too much time has passed, he's remade one of the two I did get, at the very least."

Neither Constantine or Axer would call the location lucky.

"We are going to destroy the remaining seals," I said quietly.

He lifted a handful of sand and let it slip through his fingers. "And by the hand of victory, you shall be delivered into the arms of old," he murmured.

"You don't think we can do it?"

"I do not doubt you will try. I grow weary, Butterfly. Infected by figments of the past." I could see a shimmering golden tattoo twine along his skin. "What will be wrought from it, I cannot say."

"I need your knowledge, but without riddle as we draw near the end. And I need to know how to craft one of your spells."

He smiled. "You solved my riddles just fine, Butterfly. And it was a game that made me experience an emotion I had thought forever lost. One for which I thank you. No, don't look at me like that." He looked away. "I can experience no regret, not if you want me of sound mind to help here upon the shore of nevermore."

I looked at the stars, willing my dream eyes to dry. "You've seen Stavros. Physically. Face-to-face."

"Yes. He's worse in person, if you can conceive such a thing. The embodiment of all that is soulless." He looked at me. "Though perhaps you can believe such—he was almost present, inside of you."

I shuddered, but pressed on. "Did he visit you physically in the Basement?"

"No." Raphael reached out and swirled the air around me dipping into shared memories. "He didn't even visit in his own form in the painting you entered. You have to go deeper."

I nodded. "He can embed himself in others remotely—that's how he got me. But the drones, the truly hollowed, and you—initially must be delivered to him in some way."

Raphael held up his palm and the sky swirled with an unpleasant memory, showing me an image. "There was a spot in the Basement that opened."

"The painting."

He smiled. "It never looked like a painting. It was always disguised as a door. Tricks and guises. You'd enter the door and stand in a long, decrepit corridor to hell. A between. Where you are neither here nor there. Where you waited for judgment—to house the devil or be smote forever." Raphael looked at me. "To enter Hell or be returned from purgatory. That is where he wants us both. For once you enter that passageway, you fall under his dominion until he releases you. Forevermore."

"How did you escape?"

"Oler wanted to do extended tests, and Enton doesn't like others in his space for long. So I went back to Table One. For months, I awaited an opportunity, sanity dwindling with only a single image to hang onto—a picture from Excelsine that I had managed to tuck away—and a single emotion—revenge—that Enton himself strengthened. He was going to take and turn my revenge against enemies he wanted gone. Make me think they were the ones I needed vengeance upon. Turn me into a weapon with continually fluid targets. He was going to move me back to his domain and rekindle a lost emotion—devotion—but to make himself the

748

focus. Never." There was a bit of the old insanity in his eyes for a moment, before he got it under control.

He ran his fingers through the sand. "I found an opportunity. Oler would bring outsiders, specialists, in to see his experiments sometimes. I grabbed one of the ones Oler loved best—used the last of my will, flipped the protections on him and slaughtered everything I could in my escape." He looked to the side. "I never found the Basement again. Stavros was too smart for that. I have long wished I had taken my time to destroy it or mark it, but I was desperate to be gone from that place, and what was left of my mind fractured almost completely in my exit. It is easier to see now."

There was so much and so little to say.

"I'm sorry," I murmured.

"Yes."

We let the waves provide the only sound for a half rotation of the sky. But I could feel dawn emerging and the others waking, and time was not on our side.

"Can Mussolgranz physically travel to Stavros, if he calls him?"

Raphael tilted his head. "Yes. And you have deduced correctly. Helen. Kaine. And a few of the praetorians, before Kaine consumed them. I saw no one else there, though there could be more. Oler's assistants maybe. Enton doesn't share space with others well. Ironic, really."

"I just need to find the passageway to Stavros then."

Raphael looked at me and smiled. "I've always loved that about you, Butterfly. But, no, your confidence, though earned, will not help you once you are there. Your magic will not aid you. Stavros has complete control over that entryway. He can tailor the spells for each mage's abilities—and nullify all extra magic he finds. You will never unlock the magic of it, not in time. Sergei Kinsky set it up before he understood he was sealing his own doom, and the seals have been repeatedly refined since."

Kinsky had done it because he thought he was fighting for something more important than his own freedom—his lost love.

"So, one can only enter under Stavros's complete control?"

"That is why I chose the alternative after my escape—to bury him so deeply that he could never escape."

But I could see that Raphael felt this a poor alternative, too. It didn't solve the problem of Genesis Omega if Stavros had a remote switch. If he had options, which he almost assuredly had.

Stavros was an ultra-planner. His alternative plans would not be weak. But his overconfidence in his own planning was our in. That and his reliance on only himself.

Raphael seemed to follow my thoughts and his gaze grew distant. "A man who stands alone is a man consumed by the river, Butterfly."

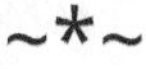

With timers set to remind us of when and where we were, the "new day" inside our hideout provided a full slate of machinations and grim planning.

Like testing the spell from Raphael, which was eagerly and darkly embraced by the more mischief-bent of our number.

Mike, Patrick, and Lifen worked the curse angle with Constantine, Neph, and me, our heads bent together, all morning. With tainted and untainted magic samples from each of their loved ones—pulled through family magic spells—we came up with a test that would identify the caster's magic. Family magic was quite special when used for good purposes, and I could reluctantly see why people argued for life hooks—though I had too many bad examples to be swayed to that side.

Stevens and Greyskull had tasks in real time to take care of, so they had given us the parameters for a draught that combined with Origin Magic, might extend the stasis of the victims to four days. Enough time to find the cure in the real world once we had what we needed.

It had to be.

When we finally emerged from our last grueling session, we had a concoction that only required an appropriate container that could stay near the victim.

"Washcloth. Headband. Hair tie," Lifen agreed. "Something innocuous and soft to rest against them without someone taking note. Price, where's Peoples?"

I looked around the library. We were missing five.

Olivia waved her hand from a table where she was neck deep in books. "Delia, Kita, Greene, Ramirez, and Straught left for testing. Said they'd be gone for the afternoon. Should be back in"—she checked her timer—"an hour."

She flipped a page. "Trying to trick their way into other rooms on campus using the enhanced phys-changing spells and the magic of the rooms." Crelussa had been good, but was not enough for what we needed. There was too much that could be undone.

I looked back at her. "Delia's not terrorizing Anastasia Kaparov again, is she?"

"If her enchantment can get her in Kaparov's room after all the pranks she's pulled on that girl, it can get her in anywhere," Olivia said with a grimace. "And if she can get into one magicist's room…"

She could get into more.

"Everyone was inspired by Professor Stevens's potion, Verisetti's mastery, and your blobs. Loudon, Asafa, and William are certain they can place the resulting spells into an implant with Greene and whatever duplicitous witchcraft Ramirez is capable of, so they are over there practicing." She pointed in their direction without looking and they gave a cheerful wave. "If they get past the magicists, we are greenlit."

Even Bellacia—who was still off campus with her father, writing articles against the Department as if she were the one with an extended timespace—with her eyes and ears everywhere, had lost contact with the increasingly paranoid. And recent articles had put her at increasing odds with some of the most fanatical of magicists. There were even vows that had to be taken to enter certain dorm rooms now.

"How is Delia getting around the vows?" Lifen asked. "If she's using administrative magic, it won't help outside Excelsine."

"Patrick gave her something to skirt most vows. Don't ask what," Olivia said grimly. "We all need some plausible deniability in case any part of this insane plan gets uncovered."

That led to a spirited discussion (argument) on the insanity involved.

No one wanted to outright say, though, that if at least one of us didn't go to prison for life after this, then all of us were dead.

I wandered over to where Axer was stretched out at a table in the corner, his hooded gaze staring at the tendrils of Kaine's captured shadows—the ones Kaine had been trying to infect Axer with every time they fought. The shadows swarmed in malevolent swirls inside the nullifying jar.

There was a book stalking around the table in a brooding, irritated way. It was just far enough away that I couldn't read its title.

I sat across from Axer and he gave me a brief smile before his focus was back on the shadows, as if they would do what he wanted from will alone.

"You can't really think planting those back on you is a good idea?" I asked, grimacing. "There's got to be a better alternative."

"There's an alternative. I just don't know that we want to take it." He looked at me.

I winced. "Raphael seems better, but what would those even do to his mind? His trustworthiness is still questionable."

"Quite."

I frowned at the malevolent shadows and shuddered. Who would want to touch them? It wasn't like they were... I blinked, looked at Axer, and bit my lip.

"I can't wait to see what you are about to reveal." He leaned back with hooded eyes and a smile, like an entertainment was set to unfold.

I sighed and called my cloak over. Looking furtively around, I saw everyone's heads deep in books, projects, and plans. Fishing out the container I'd put there, I brought it into the light. The shadow winced, then when it noticed its surroundings, the edges of the tendrils did what I could only describe as a jump for joy, swirling happily around the glass.

"It's okay," I whispered. "I didn't leave you there."

The shadow pressed its tendrils against the glass, like small webbed fingers searching for contact. I touched the glass, and it pressed a smudged tendril against the same part.

"So that's what you took."

"Hmmm?" I asked, watching the pure joy in the little shadows' movements.

"In the Basement. That's what you took," Axer said.

I looked over at him and winced again. "Yeah. Sorry."

"You know, Ren, I long ago decided to trust your instincts." He uncrossed his legs and removed them from the table, then motioned for the jar. I put it in his hand. The shadow shifted anxiously to the back of the glass as soon as it was placed in his hand, but then slowly crept forward and pressed a tentative shadow toward him. He tapped a finger gently against the glass. The shadow stared at his tapping finger, then did a little backflip swirl and started tapping back eagerly.

He played with it for another minute, then set it down.

Placing the jar next to Kaine's shadows caused an interesting reaction. The shadows in Kaine's jar frantically started leaping at the little shadow like they were compelled to get to it, and the little shadow fled to the other side of its jar in terror.

I snatched the jar with the little shadow and tucked it in my elbow.

"They weren't doing that in the Basement." I sent Axer the memory. I had excised it from the memory dump to the Bandits...for reasons.

"Maybe those weren't Kaine's."

A book started creeping down the table. Not unusual in our present circumstances, so I ignored it.

I bit my lip and looked at the jar. "How old are you? What do you eat?" I hesitated. "Not people, right?"

It flew around, forming various shapes.

"What are you two doing?"

I jumped and pulled the jar straight into my midsection, hunching over the top. "What? What do you mean?"

Olivia was standing behind me, hands on her hips. "You were talking to something that you were holding." Olivia's gaze was flat, not even attempting to play at misdirection. "Are we doing this?"

I sighed and untucked the jar, reluctantly scooting it into view.

Olivia stared silently at it for a full ten seconds, before looking at me flatly. "That's why you didn't include that in your debriefing. What else did you touch in the Basement?"

"Nothing! Just this. It...it ended up in my hands?"

She looked at me, eyes judgmental. "It ended up in your hands?"

I waved them at her, then waved them at the jar.

"Is that supposed to be some magical jar call?" she asked.

I slumped. "I felt bad for it. It didn't belong. I couldn't leave it there." And I had known I'd be in trouble for taking it.

"It looks like a shadow. Part of what makes Kaine."

"But it's not Kaine. It's innocent."

She stared hard at the jar. "How do you know?"

I waved my hands again, pantomiming that I just did.

She sighed. "Pick up a jar in a basement of horrors. What could go wrong?"

The book that had been stalking the table, then creeping toward us, was suddenly next to us, and I finally got a good look at the title of the book as it bent down to peer into the jar, finally willing to be part of things.

Shadow Magic.

"No, no, absolutely not." Olivia started swearing as the little shadow cocked its shadowed head and pressed a tendril against the glass to the book. "We aren't releasing that thing in here! Ren."

And Axer... Axer leaned back, crossed his hands behind his head, and smiled.

~*~

Shadow Magic firmly and malevolently waited for another turn, while Axer was discussing something with Tactics and Trickery in a Slippery Age and Patrick was trying to use trickery to gain access to Planning Your Heist for Maximum Bloodshed.

An actual drop of blood was dripping down its cover.

Waiting for my glass film to set, I meandered over to where Constantine and Olivia had been working together for five hours. Or, working alongside each other. Guard Rock was sitting on the edge of their table, legs slowly rocking back and forth as he watched the room.

A book perked up and fluttered its pages as I drew closer—Universal Motes on its cover.

I blinked at it. "You know everything?"

It flipped its pages and I could see building blocks of stars and planets and comets. Molecular components and compounds. "I...I want to read you. A lot. But I'm not certain you are in the four-day plan. We aren't going to space."

"We're already in space, darling." Constantine hefted Guard Rock, who began stabbing his palm immediately. "Every rock is a space rock."

I smiled, and Guard Rock flipped to the table and scooted over to make room for me.

"Out of your four-day plan, but any and all explanatory, high-level pieces about Corpus Sun and the Western Territories' atrium need to be added to my work folder," Olivia said, furiously writing something that looked like a section of a speech, 'If I choose to end this world, I can. and you won't be able to st—'

Constantine leaned back. "Life on Io. Might be better than here. You could build a new world somewhere else."

I frowned. "I think my instincts only know how to work with the life-giving compounds it knows. All life I know runs on current Earth parameters. I wouldn't have the first clue how to make a moon of Jupiter capable of sustaining life when the working components of life there would be completely upside down from Earth."

"You could learn."

"We can always learn," I agreed.

And after having all my people in one spot, I could see the allure of it. The hoarding aspect. I could understand Constantine's previous desire to hide away.

He raised a brow at me, reading the thought. "I'm always right. I thought you knew that."

I patted his arm. "I do."

"Despite the allure, you wouldn't survive that type of life." He flipped a page, far more languidly than Olivia's precise economy. "You are too vibrant to hide."

"Surrounded by friends?" I said wistfully.

"Closeted away without the scientific possibilities you can learn from others. Where's the next Mbozi? Stevens? Where are the Third Layer engineers that you've been trading information with?"

"But for safety's sake—"

"You won't truly be safe until Stavros is gone." He looked away. "I recognized that. I just didn't want to confront it." He pulled a string through his fingers. "I had thought we could be happy, just the two of us hidden away. But you'd wither.

Your connections to the others... And I...well, maybe I can see my way to having others near."

I squeezed his arm.

A huge tome was opened in front of him, but instead of the way Olivia was hunched in battle mode in the middle of her eagerly chattering books, Constantine was lazily flicking search and copy spells to a paper stack that was growing larger at Olivia's right hand. I read the spine of the book in front of Constantine—Be First and Master the Dialogue.

I frowned. "What are you doing?"

"Price has all of us working on the side on a resolution to your reintroduction to campus, society, and the political landscape," he said drolly.

I blinked. "What?"

"We aren't going to get much of a window," Olivia said from her pit of jostling books. "After we win, we have to move quickly. Whoever gets there first and controls the political landscape will win the Origin Mage war. We don't want the dialogue controlled by others."

"Win?" I echoed.

"After we depose Stavros, then get you back on campus," she said impatiently. "Keep up, Ren. You aren't usually this slow."

"Right." I cleared my throat. "So...we are working on contingency plans?"

"Actual plans. You don't think we are going to fail, do you?" She looked down her nose at me, glasses sliding down to unshield her eyes. "We aren't." We won't.

"Er, of course. What do you want me to do?"

"You? Finish the Kinsky glasses." She shooed me away.

"Don't you want me to resear—"

"No. Your innocence works best in our favor. We will handle this." She pointed between Constantine, her, and six of the books. "It will be brilliant and decisive, and you will speak it and believe it without having crafted it with deception in mind. You keep to your 'Aw shucks, anything to help the world' attitude, and we'll take care of the rest."

I opened my mouth, then shut it abruptly. I thumbed to the workspace I had claimed as mine. "I'll be over there."

"Excellent."

I paused and looked back at Constantine, then Olivia. "Are you making plans for Constantine and Axer, too? And all of you?"

"Senator Leandred has this one covered." Olivia pointed at Constantine. "Not including Dare, the rest of us will be combined under the 'saved the world, free pass' clause I'm drafting. The combat mages are working Dare's angle, which is just as tricky as yours, and needs to include might and bite. He already has an overwhelming plethora of goodwill in the combat community, where those qualities—might and bite—render respect. The victory tour across layers, combined with not seeking anyone's aid in this whole debacle, has shown him not only as resilient and self-sufficient, but strong as a partner. That he doesn't need aid, even when hunted by all, but still offers his own aid when needed, gives him a very strong bargaining position. Military power. If Dare survives intact, he will slide out on top on that wave. Might makes right, and if the young military leaders side with him, the rest will follow. They are just waiting to see if he survives."

She shook her head, grimly. "In twenty years, the Dares are going to rule this layer and more."

"Well, thankfully they are on the side of good."

Olivia looked down her nose at me again. "I love you. Get out."

"Right. Leaving." I slowly backed away.

I worked for a few more hours on the glasses and dolls we needed for the first part of the plan. I leaned back to stretch all the knots and kinks out and noticed the combat mages were walking through the room, observing everything—shifting battlescapes and planning boards—in the air as they walked.

"We can use the Crelussa mages," Ramirez said to Axer. The pieces in the air moved with his question.

I rubbed at my chest. "Will it put them in jeopardy?"

They looked over at me.

"They didn't ask to be involved," I said.

The Awakening mages had given their power and connections to us—they'd been part of their own rescue. And though the Department tech who I'd left their safety in the hands of had turned over the site ward keys to the countries themselves, there was always a chance the Department would talk their way into having the countries turn over the charge of the mages to them before the end.

Camille shook her head. "There were too many magicist children involved—they can't just make them disappear. They made a large gamble with that play—well, not such a large gamble if they are going to start killing people on a mass scale, but they still need public sentiment to be in their favor for as long as possible. They needed for you to take the blame. They may try and distort the children's memories to make you three the villains—it will feed nicely into the conspiracists' theories, but the children will stay physically safe. Not like what would have happened if you hadn't intervened. Or what still might."

She looked at me, and any lingering trace of animosity was gone. "It's in your connections that you will win."

I rubbed my arms. "Stavros can take them away."

"And you will get them back," she said, secured in her own opinion as she always was.

We've got this, Axer said gently, mentally. Finish your glasses and get some sleep.

I nodded and checked the time. It was closing in on the time we had set up for our second night time.

I worked on the glass film and dolls until my eyes started to cross and Neph was leading me to the "nest."

We passed Will and Mike, who were engaged in an intense conversation inside a constructed hologram of their room. Will was sharing memories en masse. "I know you are worried. Whenever you need a good memory, take one of mine," he said. "Full access. If I know it, you know it."

"Your family—"

"I don't know where they went." Will smiled sadly. And I heard what he didn't say—It's better that I don't know.

Mike closed his eyes and inhaled deeply. "We'll get them all back."

"I don't want—"

"Stop."

Will looked down and nodded, swallowing roughly. He deliberately didn't look up as Neph and I passed—deliberately staying walled in the facsimile of their room. When he looked back up at Mike, he was determined.

"Take the memories. Look, I have this one from Ren's birthday party. Olivia karate chopped my arm and Neph, Ren, and I all ended up in a pile in the hall. Oh, and Ren's mom hit me over the head with a broom the time before that. And Ren carried me around in a paper where—"

I could see the memory of it as he displayed it to Mike—with Will's papered view of dropping from the window, going on adventure, and heading back, all while he was strapped to my chest. I could see the street signs and house numbers as we jogged past. 257 Maple Avenue was even in the right spot—not as I had last seen it, flying through a tornado.

I looked over to see Patrick watching it all through narrowed eyes—a book on broken bonds hovering nearby. Saf, who was working memories into a pair of his own augmented reality glasses, clasped his hand on his roommate's shoulder. Patrick allowed it for a moment, then shrugged it off and stalked over to the other side of the room, the book following in his wake.

"You want to know if he's okay?" Saf asked me, as Neph and I drew nearer. Saf's eyes remained on his task. Eight completed game controllers sat on the table next to him.

"No. I know he's not okay." I knew what it was like to have a brother attacked. "Can we do anything, though?"

"I don't know," Saf murmured.

"I don't like this."

Saf looked up and his gaze gentled. He gave me a sympathetic glance. "That's why we are willing participants—above and beyond it being the right thing to do. Thought you knew that, Crown."

I looked at the memories he was weaving together, along with the echoes of our bonds, just as Neph and Constantine had done for me. "I don't like sacrifice," I whispered.

He didn't say anything for a moment. "We are all called to moments when we have to choose." He twisted one memory around another. "When we have to decide between easy and hard. And sacrifice should never be easy, Crown. But sometimes it has to be made."

~*~

By the next afternoon, Neph and Ramirez were finished with their project and ready to set everything in place with Camille and Delia to one side, Green and Lifen to the other, and Lox and Adrabi helping secure the ends. Suggestion, duplication, illusion, hidden, metal device, righteous belief...

Constantine was finishing the null cuffs and control devices with Will, Asafa, Patrick, Loudon, Dagfinn, and Mike.

Axer had been working with them, but when I was shooed away to paint, he detached himself and came with me.

I removed a canvas. Axer pulled a club chair into existence.

"You got stuck on apocalypse duty? Makes the most sense of anyone."

"Stuck? Hardly." He let himself slouch down, his head on the back of the chair, looking up at the domed ceiling. I didn't look up. I knew what I'd see. More imposters wearing Christian's face, trying to find us. "Watching you paint is a rare treat."

I twirled the brush in my fingers. "You are going to like the monsters I make."

"Of course. You'll have made them."

My cheeks warmed. He was still looking at the ceiling, but I saw him smirk.

I sighed and opened my paints.

I looked at my paints, at my brush, at the canvas, waiting for the overwhelming urge to overtake me.

I'd been shooed over here, but I felt no need to paint. I wanted to paint. But I hadn't needed to paint since...

"It's all of you," I said softly, looking around. "Of course..."

Axer looked up.

The desperate urges had gotten better with Constantine. Better again with Axer joining us. Better when we'd hooked into everyone, then when Constantine had regenerated every connection, and settling fully when everyone was together.

I shook my head and looked back at the canvas. And let it come.

Let it flow from my brush—the hopes, the dreams, the fears, the plans, the connections, the crippling terror of Stavros. Victory. Defeat.

It swirled in a mass from my brush onto the canvas in glittering silvers and golds, exploding everywhere on the surface until I was gasping with the effort.

And then Axer was next to me, pulling his finger through a line of silver that signified him.

"What, I, how did you—?"

He gently turned my chin, forcing my eyes to follow the direction of my head. The contents of the entire room were swirling in a funnel around us. Guard Rock's limbs were splayed out as he swooped around and around. Books were fiercely flying through the currents like big wave surfers who had finally caught the swell they'd been waiting for.

Every single mage inside was staring, mouth agape, eyes lit by the flashing gold and silver lights. Except Constantine, who was smiling and Axer, who looked triumphant.

"So connected you didn't even realize," Axer's voice was strangely soft, as opposed to the harsh tornadic wind forming the background beat of the room. "Look at this. Effortless."

The magic streamed from me in patterns that all hooked together. Everything made sense in the swirl, and the beauty of it vied with what it had taken to create it. What had been needed to bring me to this point. The swirl caught more speed with my emotion. "Did you see what I painted? Did you see what I might do?"

"Yes. And I can see you right now—lit up from the inside, creating world-ending magic like it was an easy broom sweeping enchantment."

I thought of my earlier paintings, of the death and despair. The swirl turned darker. I thought of Kinsky's painting. Of the longing and loneliness.

"What the hell is going on?" Olivia demanded, picking herself up from where she'd just been ejected by Temporal Physics and Interdimensional Travel in the Physical Age. She'd been discussing last minute "things" with Marsgrove.

I jolted. Axer didn't move. But then, the number of times I had seen him surprised could be counted on one hand with fingers to spare.

"Ren is painting."

"Ren is painting? What, the air?" She plucked Guard Rock from the tornado, tossing him safely onto the table. He landed on his feet and took two steps across the papers strewn on top, as if he was going to dive back in, but Olivia shot him a stern glare and he slumped his rock and sat. "What is going on?"

I called a marble to my left hand and abruptly pulled the tornado into my palm, collapsing the magic inside the glass and forcing everything floating in the room to land softly.

Axer eyed the marble as I tried to calm my racing heart. "Not even winded this time," he mused. He looked at me. "You are getting better."

"Yes," I said, and for the first time, I meant it. I felt better. Even after Stavros tried to rip out all the parts that made me, I had been stitched back together. I looked around me. I could always be stitched together if I had them.

I looked at the canvas.

A world was forming, blooming into different worlds of possibility, both creation and destruction—but for the first time, I controlled what the product would be.

"Stavros will know. All of our plan. He'll be able to read my mind. Our expressions. We need to get rid of his powers."

"How?" Olivia demanded.

Axer dipped the same painted finger in the line that was Constantine on the canvas. He lifted it and watched as the paint glittered, changing the properties of the magic always around him—properties he'd have to change back—but for now he just watched the changes. Like Constantine, he, too, had been touched by Origin Magic. Died repeatedly from it and worked up a resistance.

He looked at me in question. I shook my head. "It didn't help me last time," I said. "Stavros has to have an immunity."

Constantine prowled closer, as if called. "Not to everything."

"Not to something temporary," Axer agreed.

Constantine looked at the paint on Axer's finger, then turned his head to look at his roommate. "Tears of the Fallen?"

Axer nodded. "Tears of the Fallen."

"I love that one."

"I know." He smiled and wiped the paint on the back of Constantine's hand.

Constantine immediately turned and strode to his makeshift lab.

"Wow. Great. So happy I left for fifteen minutes." Olivia tossed the test glasses onto the table, hands going to her hips. "Phillip said the sight lasts five minutes, then the magic ends. He wished us good luck."

Satisfaction swelled, as did hope, and I began duplicating the finishing touches in the other pairs of glasses and on the storage papers with the paint. "Five minutes is all we need."

Chapter Twenty-seven
UNSEALING THE DEVIL

B Y THE THIRD morning of our library stay, the news reports outside had started to shift.

"What happened at Crelussa? This is a question burning every feed this morning. The Department has firmly denied all evidence and witness accounts in favor of the Origin Mage, and against the Department, claiming the Origin Mage responsible for all negative events. But there have been enough conflicting reports now to render questions that even the staunchest Department acolyte can't ignore."

I could see Bellacia's delicate touch and devious mind in many of the different news reports. Seeding in bits and pieces about people being unnerved. Not dripping in the evidence, dripping the emotional components attached to them.

I flipped to watch the recording of the news conference that Bellacia had sent. Shelle Fanning looked tired. Morven Jance was visibly riled.

"We aren't returning the magic to Crelussa," Jance said. "Absurd. Not while the Origin Mage is still active and ensuring that we, the safety and security of this layer, can not enter. It is for the safety and security of the entirety of the Second Layer that we capture her before returning the magic to its former place. I entreat each of you to do your part. Furthermore, fifteen thousand troops from a cross-section of patriotic countries have formed a barrier of magic around the sanitarium. Nothing is getting inside."

"And nothing gets out. Neat and tidy," Baxter Roberts, Bellacia's favorite reporter said.

"I dislike your tone, Mr. Roberts."

"But what about the strengthening rumors that the Origin Mage is the one who saved the site. That the Department triggered the destabilization. That the Department set the terrorists upon the site in order to take charge of the containers."

"Absurd."

"There is, in fact, some evidence that this is not entirely conspiracist in nature. There were recordings—"

"Manufactured by a mage capable of such dangerous things."

"Vincent Godfrey Junior—"

"Is a terrorist."

"This administration has a record of—"

"Keeping this layer safe? Agreed."

"You can't keep the magic away," a man in the crowd said. He was wearing medals and seals of state. "Our country stands with the others in wanting the Origin Mage leashed, but we do not accept the Department's hiding of five tons of Awakening magic."

"It is not hidden, it is secured."

"You have provided no coordinates for the individual security councils to ascertain—"

"Why would we do that? Why not just give them to the Origin Mage?"

"With all due respect, Secretary Jance, we—"

"This is a matter of layer security and you will respect that."

A reporter touched their throat. "Secretary Jance, Secretary Jance, we've just received news that Priority Five has been halted. Senator Leandred—"

"No more questions."

Olivia muted the hologram.

"The media is turning," she said. "Public opinion will be next. And Priority Five has been halted indefinitely. Senator Leandred is a force, make no mistake."

"Bellacia has a full interview with Godfrey Jr. where he says that agents of Enton Stavros gave them the information on Crelussa and the go ahead. That the terrorists were set up. The Baileys are pushing for a full audit of the Department. And people are coming on board." There was something in Olivia's eyes that had been missing for weeks too—that same insidious emotion, hope. "We might get a political solution."

Patrick muttered something in the corner.

She whirled on him. "We need a political solution. At least partially."

Patrick closed his eyes. "I know. But you aren't going to get everyone on board."

"We don't need everyone."

A few of the more vocal supporters of Stavros had been working the media feeds, too.

"It isn't a surprise to find Bremia, Tu, and Koghslov working with Stavros," Olivia said. "The heads of those countries have always had their own plans. And whatever Stavros is planning to do—working with him as a head of state ensures that your country stays as limited in the cull as you want. Get rid of your enemies inside, but keep the rest of your people safe? A huge win for leaders who don't mind making 'hard' choices when it comes to lives."

It's what Stavros had offered me—a choice dripping with blood.

"Such choices only work when people who agree with them are in power, though," Mike said. "No one making these types of choices is thinking of how they would feel if it were their enemy's finger on the button."

"Let's go destroy the button."

Four hours in the real world since we'd hidden ourselves, we let loose a series of eight dolls wearing my face and magic in the middle of the Great Forest in the Second Layer.

Showing up in the Second Layer set off every buzzer, tracker, charm, and ward that had been set against us. Kaine showed up, as expected, as well as just about every enforcer in the Second Layer—all converging on "my" position.

Having no objective other than to keep them busy, Asafa, Patrick, Loudon, Kita, Will, Neph, Lifen, and I did just that—remotely, like Raphael had done posing as Emrys. To no one's real surprise, the dolls driven by the gamers did a ton of damage, even with each successive doll being made to look and act weaker as it ported to the place where the next, weaker doll was waiting and turned into flower seed as the new doll took over.

Though Patrick slipped when Kaine, wearing Stavros's face said, "Come to me now, and I'll give your friends the cure that will rid their loved ones of their ailments. Do not, and I will ensure they all die."

There had been a lot of...mayhem after that.

The last doll was taken by Kaine in blood, shadow, and decay. I hoped that Mussolgranz liked his present.

In coordinated strikes under the cover of our fanfare, Axer and Constantine took out Darpin Sloughs, Marsgrove and Julian Dare crippled Keating Glen, Camille and Ramirez infiltrated Fels Hollow, Lox and Greene hit Picquant Moors, and three other combat mages that included plucky Johnson—who it had never occurred to me was the son of the Provost—confirmed and took out Shayvale Castle's stamped Kinsky with a piece of Axer's magic and a storage paper.

Wearing a pair of my glasses to verify the stamp, three were confirmed seals. Those three were now confetti.

Fels Hollow, unfortunately, had not been a seal. But Camille and Ramirez found the Awakening containers hidden deep in the catacombs. Within minutes of the discovery, Stuart Leandred had the containers tagged, moved and under a magical decree that needed five days of negotiations to unseal.

He was also on the feeds as if he'd planted himself magically within. "We know it's been a public concern, and we thank the Department for agreeing to put the containers under the Council's watch. They responded quickly to the request for release. We still have questions about the move in the first place, however. And we will work with every country to determine our next plan of action."

The celebration after that was fierce.

Axer and Constantine's signatures had stayed successfully hidden during Darpin Sloughs. We were close. So close.

One seal was left.

Stuart Leandred was a force of nature, and he was determined. Political things that we could have never accomplished, even with all our power, were being set into motion.

"Your dad is pretty awesome," someone said, clapping Constantine on the shoulder as we watched Stuart leave Council Hall. "I'm glad he's on our side."

Constantine said nothing, just raised a brow, but I could feel his conflicting emotions. I could feel the way they were starting to settle just the slightest bit when reference was made to his father.

Stuart Leandred never made it home.

Chapter Twenty-eight

REPRISAL

THE OTHER members of the Council who had started to array themselves against Stavros were missing as well. The public uproar was immediate, fierce, and terrified. But the Department worked above all the countries in the Second Layer. And while the countries were scrambling, emergency appointments to the Council were made—all by the Prestige—and went into immediate effect.

"How can he do this?"

"Can he do this?"

"How have we never realized that was a power the Prestige could wield?" the media pundits said.

Within minutes of their appointments, the new Council was already sending people to find and move the Awakening containers.

We had no time left.

The first domino was flicked.

Stevens and Greyskull fell to coordinated strikes that left all within the blast range in a comatose state. The duplicitous spells took down fifteen teachers, twelve staff, and ninety students. Ramirez was one of the students, Lifen and Asafa, two of the others. Most of the victims were connected to us in some way.

Their bodies were moved to Medical and quarantined. Junior Department members slipped inside and recorded all the bodies, and gleefully spread the news and recordings. I had never seen Camille look grimmer as she watched people she had been friends with celebrate the attack.

Ramirez was laid out next to Stevens and Greyskull. They looked perfectly preserved in their inert states.

Listening to frequencies, Dagfinn reported that multiple students were claiming to the

Department that they had been in on the plan. Loudon carefully took down their names. But it was Inessa Norrissing who'd been the one to spring the trap. She had secretly confessed to one of her conspirators over a "secured" frequency that she'd been given the spell by an unnamed source.

We all knew who the source was.

"Inessa always was a bit of dullard," Olivia said scathingly.

We were all on edge.

Chancellor Barrie closed Medical to all but those with medical needs. No visitors, no guests. And the ward with our friends was put under quarantine.

"So, it begins," Olivia said, putting a last piece into play.

Marsgrove disappeared from campus a scant ten minutes before the enforcers arrived to carry out the arrest warrant issued by the new Council.

The Council couldn't do anything about Medical—hospital regulations were tied into the fabric of society like Justice Magic. The Medical ward would stay closed until quarantine was lifted.

But they could force Chancellor Barrie to open the school's borders. Anyone could now leave.

It was a victory for all those in league with the Department.

They didn't know it would be their doom.

"Everything is moving fast," Dagfinn said, fingers and magic flying. "No dithering, no more set up, they won't draw things out and neither can we. Both good and bad for us. We have reached go time."

"We still need to find Mussolgranz. We were expecting him at Darpin Sloughs. And he hasn't touched the doll."

"Do we need him?"

"He's an outli—"

"He has the cure," Patrick argued, coiled and irritable. Alone now, it was apparent how much Patrick relied on Asafa. I had never seen them apart before. Patrick was gripping his pocket where I had seen him put the glasses Asafa had been making.

"We don't know—"

Patrick leaned forward. "If this all goes tits up, I want that cure. Stavros offered it to Crown. He offered it attached with a vow. We are getting that cure."

Mike watched from the side, also white knuckled.

Olivia looked at Patrick, expression grim. "Yes. But it's secondary. You know that." It took effort for her to say it.

Patrick's face darkened for a moment, then smoothed out. "Got it, Your Majesty."

Olivia looked down, and for a moment I thought Patrick was going to drop the facade and comfort her, but he held firm, role chosen.

"What if Mussolgranz is already with Stavros?"

"In those who care little for others, power shares only while it remains convenient."

I nodded. "Raphael said Stavros prefers to remain alone, kept company only by those he's working on."

"So Mussolgranz is hiding somewhere separately."

"With his scalpel and dubious grasp on morality."

"In a place where he can use them."

We exchanged looks. "Spartine."

I closed my eyes.

"Part of Spartine is a research facility that conducts tests on the prisoners who are never leaving. You must have a specific clearance to enter the labs. And that clearance is controlled by the Prestige of the Department."

We exchanged glances.

"Good place for Mussolgranz to be now that the Basement is gone," I admitted, shoulders slumping.

"Good place for Mussolgranz to be," he concurred.

"Someone needs to tag the waterfront there."

Everyone looked around with the same ill feeling descending. The combat mages were currently making certain Medical was locked down.

"O'Leary and Givens, that one's yours," Axer said, almost distractedly, gaze firmly on the prison schematics.

Everyone looked at the pair. My heart rate skyrocketed.

They need this, Axer sent me mentally, soothing some of my panic. O'Leary's been on the edge of madness for days.

Patrick's eyes had gone dark as soon as the news about Medical had come through and Mike was tight-lipped. Will was barely keeping it together whenever he looked at his roommate.

But—

You have to let everyone do their part. Axer sent another soothing stroke to soften the words.

"Mike—" Will was fretting again.

Patrick smirked. There was a lot of darkness in it. "Don't worry, Tasky. Givens and I got this."

Will looked uneasy. "Why don't you let me—"

"Nah. You'd try saving the puppies, too. Ain't got time for puppies, Tasky. Only marks." His language had increasingly included a lot of odd quirks over the past few hours—shedding one skin to put on another.

"But—"

Patrick stepped over to him, eyes steely. "You get caught, it's game over. The weapon only you and Crown can carry? Going to need that." Patrick's eyes went empty. "Besides, I need to be a hero too, right? Givens and I will do it. Say your goodbyes, Givens."

A flash of cold swept through me.

Dark determination—of two different kinds—flashed across both of their faces. Mike grabbed the back of Will's neck. "It will be okay. I'm the master at hail. We'll be back in no time. I'll even let you skim the room when we are back on campus. Maybe we'll find my shorts."

Delia was looking at the ground, unwilling to watch. Neph tugged her into her arms.

Patrick looked back at me. "See you on the flipside, Crown. If we don't see you before...well then, you kill Stavros for us, you hear?"

~*~

And like Stuart Leandred, Mike and Patrick never returned.

"They aren't dead," Neph said, one arm around Will, one hand on my knee.

"O'Leary broke the vow," Constantine said, looking at the threads he held. "He broke his connections."

We all exchanged grim looks.

Inside the library during our last hour, we traded in our separate tables for one large one, our numbers more than halved. The mood was tense as we waited.

"Stuart Leandred and his entire inner circle were pronounced missing earlier today. Sources say that they went on a call to attempt to bring his son and the Origin Mage back in line, but that they never returned. Speculation is that they were obliterated by the Origin Mage at the Leandred scion's request. Sources who knew

Constantine Leandred at Excelsine say that his relationship with his father grew even worse over the last few months when he showed an interest in Ren Crown."

I stared at the Department feed, numb.

Constantine roughly shoved his papers to the side. "Stop listening to that. You didn't do it. I called him."

I looked up at him. I didn't say anything, just sent my emotions—sadness, horror, love—at him. He shuddered and dropped his elbows to the desk, roughly rubbing his fingers through his hair.

"I've hated him forever. Seven years out of nineteen is a long time to hate."

I didn't say anything, just continued to offer my support in a steady stream of emotion, leaning in to press my arm against his. What could I say? That his father loved him? That he wouldn't blame his son? That he had worked to try to be a better man, but that didn't mean Constantine had to forgive him for what he had done?

Constantine shuddered again and let his head drop on top of mine. "It doesn't matter."

It very obviously mattered. And dealing with death was an intimate part of my existence now. But in this, I had no words. Only comfort.

"As opposed to the lies being spread by the Department, Stuart Leandred had delivered a number of damaging and destructive reports mere seconds before his untimely disappearance. The Department immediately tried to hush them, but they were released to public frequencies and spread too quickly. Public fervor is starting to lean heavily toward Stuart Leandred's disappearance being a conspiracy led by the Prestige. Ironically, Department sources are trying to claim the Origin Mage's involvement. But every damning piece of evidence had to do with the Prestige and those close to him. The hunt for the Origin Mage's capture has accelerated. Some, however, are advocating a trial now, a stark contrast from—"

"The Department can't control it. The media is turning," Olivia said from across the table as we all determinedly finished our last pieces of work. "Wide public opinion will be next."

"Yes," Axer said. I could see his magic combining with mine to twirl around Constantine.

"Bellacia is unraveling the web. Stavros has been the one running the anti-feral sentiment. He is the one who seeded it into magicist circles most strongly. It boosted the magicist agenda, which has always been about protecting one's own people." Olivia flipped a page. "And they don't like to be hoodwinked. They will serve him up. He's not going to wait. This is it."

I scrolled through Constantine's illegal confidence game device—Five Man Act, Old Man and a Firebrand, Three Man Sneak, Treacherous Don, Center Fitting, Scope of Tears, Death in a Style...

Axer leaned over and his finger flipped the list to technical gambits. He tapped one highlighting "Drill Sandwich" and it popped up a complicated series of images and specs. "This one. We'll need your friend Dagfinn working with other darkcomm mages."

"The labs will be gone. He'll have to take you to where he is."

"But he'll have other measures in place there. Higher forms of control. He's a sociopathic empath. He'll know exactly what to use."

"And he'll rely on it."

"That's part of the problem with taking over the world," Olivia said. "In order to think you can do it, you have to believe you can. And it means you approach the tipping point where confidence becomes overconfidence."

I scanned the schematics for Spartine, running over the plan one more time.

"There are five possible paths," Axer said. "The two for low security are less relevant. We aren't going to be looking for footpads and embezzlers. The middle tier sends to an interesting web. But the two for high security lead to a set of paths that interconnect. Level 5 will be individual cells with complete nullification parameters. Level 4, however, is for prisoners being manipulated mentally and allows for low level spells. Because the mage is trapped by the mind, a regulation of magics and a few enchantments to make the mage more comfortable are allowed."

I looked away. "Like making the air cooler and the pillow softer? With enough food and water available?"

His piercing gaze pinned me until I looked back. "Yes," he said resolutely, but gently.

"Do you think this will work?" Will murmured.

"It has to," I said.

The library shuddered around us—slowly at first, then it started to pick up speed, shaking with magic. The books took flight like a thousand crows lifting from a field. Universal Motes solemnly landed in front of me.

I swallowed and closed my eyes. "He's begun."

The time for planning was over. Stavros was initiating the first cull.

I opened my eyes and looked at the tense, beloved faces around me. "As soon as we leave the library and temporal field, we'll have twenty minutes. I went over the pattern with the books—once started, it takes about twenty minutes to complete the magic he will use."

Twenty minutes for Stavros to wipe out twenty million people.

"I can't start my part until he completes the setting of the grid. Which will equate to five minutes' passage outside," I said, trusting in math instead of falling to terror.

"We have to be in position by then." Axer looked at Olivia.

Olivia lifted her chin. "I'm ready. I've been ready for this since the day of my emancipation."

"Ren?"

I felt the shuddering of the library. Inside we had minutes to spare that we would not have outside of it. "Valeris let his power get out of control," I murmured. "Kinsky let his power get under control. Valeris was too strong in his grip on the powers available to him, Kinsky too weak."

I touched the journal. "Kinsky wanted a quiet life. A life with his projects. A life with the girl."

I looked at Valeris's beautiful temporal library and the palace beyond. "Valeris wanted progress and prosperity for the world."

"Ren?"

What did I want?

If I had been asked what I wanted before, it would have been safety, security, and happiness, for those I loved. But to ignore the cost, or to ignore what happened to people outside of my family and friends was something I could no longer do. The world was greater than my circle.

Sacrifice.

My fingers drew along the edge of the journal. "It all comes back to that. For what happens to a Kinsky or Valeris or Crown without a tether? Without a center? And so... What does Ren Crown choose? Does she choose to keep her family and friends safe, or does she choose to save the world? For the saving of one is at the cost of the other. If I'm on my own, I lose my humanity, but if I'm surrounded by those I love, I thrust those I love into the center of the storm."

"Trust in your friends' choices," Axer said.

I tilted my head. "I do. Of course, I do. And yet, deep down, I lose my drive to do anything except protect all of you when circumstance strikes."

"Find a way."

I smiled. "Do better?"

He didn't say anything for a moment. "You always do. So, trust in us to do our part. That we are not pawns for you to protect."

"I've been told I'm terrible with pawns." I touched the threads at my elbow.

"You are too good with them. That is the problem."

"Each of us has a reason we are here, Ren. And you made certain that everyone connected to you would make their own choice. Even Verisetti, with the truth spell addition, can choose not to use the connection."

What does Ren Crown choose?

"Yes," I whispered. "I'm ready."

We gathered our supplies. The books arrayed in two long lines, watching us solemnly as we left.

Universal Motes blinked, and I gave it a small bow.

Then we all walked up the stairs and out into Valeris' palace.

Chapter Twenty-nine

ALL IS LOVE; ALL IS LOST

OUTSIDE of the library, the world was shaking violently. Stavros's lights zipped along, looking for their victims.

I had wondered if he'd just target all of us first. But the input parameters for the spell were too broad, and yet too restrictive—he'd already decided who he was using it for before I'd seen the spell, but hadn't shown me who.

Besides, he wanted more than one of us alive to be used—he'd want to make our ends personal and painful.

The seal in the center of the floor started swirling as soon as I looked at it. Universal Motes had been very helpful.

Butterflies jammed together in my chest. I didn't know how I was going to survive what needed to happen. Spartine, Stavros, the culling, A... I closed my eyes. Forward. Go forward.

I quickly formed an image of the destination and shot the coordinate packet toward the seal. It was sucked into the center, opening a vortex.

I let a half-smile curve my lips. "Look, Con, it's like..." My words trailed off. "What?"

He was staring moodily at the seal. He looked back at me with that same strange cocktail of emotions, but something was finally winning—resolve.

He stalked back toward me, eyes intent.

"What is it?" I asked, butterflies becoming eagles jamming in my chest. "Second thoughts? Something's wrong? What—"

His warm fingers slid along my cheek, then wrapped into my hair. He leaned down to rest his forehead against mine and closed his eyes. "The ribbon. I lied."

"What? We aren't engaged?" I asked, smiling shakily, curling my fingers into his shirt. "I have to show up to family dinners as your weird second cousin?"

He opened his eyes and looked into mine. "It doesn't mean family. Not like that. Not to me."

And his emotional connection opened cleanly, without the muddle he usually hid his true feelings within. And it was love, clear and without artifice, shining there.

I stared at him, breath caught in my chest. "You—"

His emotions were wrapping around me, free and clear and relieved. Like honey and copper—sweet, tangy, and charged—gentle, consuming, warm, passionate, and resolute. "No tricks. No games. No expectations. No lies—not to you, not ever again."

Stunned, I watched him pull away.

He looked at peace for the first time in weeks. Months. Then he looked down at our connection threads and I wondered what on earth he'd see.

He looked up, and a smile, brilliant and all-consuming split his face. He backed up slowly. "Interesting. See you soon, darling." He winked, turned, and flipped over the edge of the seal and through the vortex.

I stared, lips parted, cheeks warm.

"Did he just...?" I asked, my fingers carefully touching my cheek, needing to be certain.

"Tell you he loved you?" Olivia said, eyes on the ceiling, foot tapping the floor.

"But he, and all the girls, and..."

Axer smiled. I could feel their bond, solidly tight.

Axer reached forward and in a mirrored gesture put his forehead to mine. "Tell him he can court you as long as I get to chaperone. For the next ten years."

He pulled back and winked.

"That's...what?...no!"

But he, too, was gone, laughter trailing in his wake.

Olivia was looking at the shaking, domed ceiling like she wished for a murder stick to drop from it. A large one.

Will's jaw was somewhere near the floor. Neph just looked amused.

Delia sighed, then said, "That sigh was for Mike. He would want a sigh recorded here."

"In that case," Olivia said. "I would like to put forth—"

Delia elbowed her hard and Olivia let out a little oof of air.

"Are you going to chaperone, too?" I asked. I felt along my chest, my arms, at the connections there, and wow, okay. Wow.

Neph laughed outright. It was a reassuring sound as the world shook.

"No, while Delia, Nephthys, and William are waiting for those two morons to clear the hallways, I'm going to take the other vortex path you open." Olivia looked down her nose and pointed at the seal.

I quickly opened the second path.

But before she hopped inside, she grabbed me and pulled me to her. "Don't die," she said into my hair as we clung to each other.

"You neither."

"Be careful."

She wrapped her arms more tightly around me and laid her cheek against mine. "You, too." She tore herself away and dove inside the vortex. It closed behind her.

"And then there were four," Will said.

"Tasky, I'll kill you if you just jinxed us," Delia said. She was on edge, wanting to get to the prison. She had lobbied to go through with the boys. I heard the jar clinking in her coat as she shifted. "Also, Dagfinn said we are clear to move, and we are about to have company, Ren."

We all jammed together into a fierce group hug full of knocked heads and entangled limbs. "Good luck."

I tore away and threw out the first set of coordinates again. The three of them jumped inside, I shot a spell at the hunters rounding the corner of the palace, shot another set of coordinates inside the seal, then dove through the fourth vortex.

I slammed into the ground. Outside of the palace, the world was vibrating.

Guard Rock jumped down from my hood.

"It's you and me, buddy," I murmured. He poked my boot in support and solidarity and began his preparations. We would get five flips.

I whipped out the plethora of devices we'd need as Guard Rock drew his ritual circle.

"You ready, Crown?" Dagfinn asked over the communication network that Constantine and he had constructed. The network was tethered to Constantine and a large vat of my magic, instead of to any part of the layer system.

"Thirty seconds." I initiated all the spells, pulling up copies of Dagfinn's feeds. "You in Medical now?"

"Terrible case of the strumps. Contagious. Wildly contagious. Can't even arrest me until two days have past. Instant death to anyone who enters."

I grinned, then looked at the feed of Delia, Neph, and Will. My smile thinned. "I should be there with them."

"You can't be there, Ren. You know that. Hold tight. Hey! Found Givens! They are moving him through the prison," Dagfinn said to the comms at large. "Looks like Level 4."

In the deserted hallway at Spartine, Delia drooped in relief—it was the news we'd all been waiting to hear.

"They dumped him in the less restricted cell block. Look, he's got a pillow."

I stared at the cell through the surveillance feed Dagfinn had hijacked. Mike looked terrible. My hand started to shake. Guard Rock poked me hard. I swallowed and nodded.

I called up the magic of the layers and the puzzle pieces that Stavros had given me. I shifted them into position.

"What about Patrick?" Delia demanded.

"Negative."

In the multitude of feeds, different transportation spells activated around the prison, making one cell open into a lobby, another into a mess hall, another into a laboratory.

"Labs are on level one, four, five—" Dagfinn was listing what each person saw along with what the surveillance feeds showed.

The surveillance discs looked just like they did in the Second Layer Depot—blinking on the wall with a thousand eyes shifting in a thousand directions. But now, we were using those sinister-looking surveillance feeds for our own purpose.

In the feed showing Will, Neph, and Delia, two prison guards turned the corner and startled abruptly at seeing the three of them. Neph raised a hand, but before she could do anything, the guards' eyes went strangely blank.

"Something's not right," Axer said, turning the corner and walking past the guards, paying no attention to their inert forms as he quickly cataloged Delia, Neph, and Will—making sure they were who they appeared to be even though he had seen them five minutes before. Satisfied, he looked at the hall's wards.

I called up a second set of strings that held the world together and attached them to the seal I was building.

Constantine rounded the corner behind Axer, and motioned offhandedly at the guards. Both guards blinked, then blankly looked up at the ceiling. "Yes, this part doesn't involve enough stab, stab, spin, thrust for you."

"I'm going to get rusty," Axer said. He crouched and put his finger on a ward along the floor, then stood and, battle focused, motioned for the others to follow along the path. They passed another eight women and men peering strangely at the ceiling.

"Lies," Constantine said blandly, good mood threatening to overtake his usually excellent game face.

Axer smiled. He looked at the others and pointed in two directions. "The first of the Awakening canisters are to the left. And the main guard tower is to the right."

Quick, solid hugs were again exchanged, then Delia turned right, and Neph and Will went left.

"And then there were three," I murmured, slipping a ward underneath the one Stavros was laying.

"Darling, no," Constantine said.

"Love admit-and-runners don't get to have a say."

He smiled slowly. "I'll remember that."

My ward was yanked and burned. "Shoot." Stavros had finally figured out what I was doing, and I could feel him start to fight—feel him send out magic to pinpoint my position. "Here we go."

In the feeds, guards poured into hallways and through portals, and so did people I recognized. Fighting erupted, and it became hard to discern who was whom across the changing surveillance landscapes.

In one, a man I semi-recognized was fighting Axer.

"Alexander Dare. The warrior. The prodigy. The protector of the people. The fighter for justice." The person spit blood, smiling crazily. "Always keeping to the rules of the field. Stavros will remake you into a real warrior."

Before the man could lift his hand again, there was one wrapped around the back of his head, gripping it. The man froze, as if his entire body had stopped listening to commands from his brain.

"Here's the thing," Constantine whispered into his ear. "That most people don't know. Alexi and I are far more alike than anyone understands. You think he's the good guy." Constantine laughed lowly, almost seductively. "That was your first mistake."

The man dropped to the ground.

"The guards are tied into revivification wards in case of prison outbreaks," Dagfinn said across the comms. "They will be shocked awake in eight minutes. I'm trying to see if I can recode the magic to put them out again immediately, restarting the eight-minute clock."

I was forced to stop watching as the wards around me shrieked in alarm.

I held out my hand to Guard Rock, who nodded. The wards would hold for thirty seconds more. Now that we'd started, we needed every precious second.

Golems poured into the building, surrounding our warded circle and Kaine strode through.

Something about the golems made the hair rise on the back of my neck. "There's something wrong with the guards," I said to the others. I shook my head slowly, and sent an image of the first guard through the communications loop.

"Yes," Axer agreed. "Piecing enchantment. Watch for them to reform into something else—dragons, vampires."

Kaine began thrusting shadows against the ward circle.

"I told you they'd come back in some grisly fashion," Olivia said grimly. "Status check, I'm at my position."

"They are..." I stared at them. Bile rose in my throat. The ears. The nose. The hair. The eyes. My mind did exactly what Stavros wanted—piecing together the separate pieces and forming a whole across the lot. "They aren't dragons."

"Do you recognize the pieces?" Stavros's mouth appeared on another portion—Christian's eyes staring sightlessly at me over Stavros's moving mouth. He sneered at the circle. "I feel your magic. Interesting, that you have recovered so quickly. How so, I wonder? And what do you think you are going to do?"

"Stop you."

He laughed and reached toward the thinning ward. "How are you going to stop me and keep hold of those threads, my dear?"

"Now," I shouted at Guard Rock.

He stabbed his pencil down and flipped the circle.

I barely kept my grip.

It took Stavros only two minutes to find us at location number two.

I shuddered as I observed my brother's dripping features.

"It was time to overhaul the guards." Stavros smiled. "You gave me an excuse and liabilities aren't tolerated. You keep giving us pieces of you. We are piecing you together in the workshop now. A little Pinocchio girl. We will have your abilities, whether piecemeal or altogether in one package."

Kaine shot a shadow under the circle and as it sliced through my shield, I could feel elements of my own magic in it. Flying backward, I hit the ground and my head hard. The threads almost slipped free.

"Ren!" Multiple shouts came through.

I gritted my teeth. "M'fine."

"Do you need me?" Constantine asked tersely.

"No. I'm fine." I dragged myself up.

I could hear Constantine swearing over the background of the battle noise and saying he should have gone with me.

"I'm going to take all of your little friends," Stavros said. "And line them up one-by-one in front of you. I'm going to make you kill each and every one of them. Then I'll let you have your emotions back. Just for an instant."

Another shadow started to breech the circle.

"Now!"

Guard Rock flipped us again.

I didn't even try to rise from the ground this time. The magic was overwhelming. I could feel people dying. One, two, a thousand, a million. I had known, I had known this would happen. We had known there was no way to stop Stavros's first hit from happening, we just had to stop it after.

And that meant the cull would be successful, at least initially.

"Shivit, we just lost Delia, and at least a hundred students on campus. He targeted Second Layer mages with Third Layer ties."

Tears fell down my cheeks.

Even Bloody Tuesday with the unreality, the disconnect of watching people I knew drop around me, hadn't been this brutal. This overwhelming feeling of death.

"Do you like my choice?" Stavros said, appearing again with Kaine and the horrible misfit versions of my brother. "So messy, those with ties between layers. We need things to be orderly when we make our real changes. But you could have saved your friend. I would have spared her. She—"

"Shut up." And I was yanking the magic back, flipping it. Using the knowledge from Death Magic and The Twelve Black Steps—using the reverse of what the books were usually used for. I had ten minutes from the time the first person fell to revive them without consequences.

Somewhere in Spartine, Delia was heaving a breath.

"You fool!" Stavros yelled.

"Go!" I shouted.

Guard Rock flipped us.

We had one more flip.

"Can you take out Stavros?" Constantine asked me.

"No," I said grimly. "He's protected. But I can save twenty million. He gave me the key. I've got them. Thirty seconds." I gritted my teeth and pulled.

I felt his fingers sliding along my arm and, in the feed, saw him guarding Axer's back.

Axer was destroying the western wing of Spartine.

I saw Bialto, the Third Layer champion, and two others who looked too closely related to be anything other than family—along with an array of other Third Layer fighters behind them. They were wearing our cloaks. If they were caught, the Second Layer would blame the Third. Call them terrorists. Strip them of their legal rights to travel to the other layers. And still, Bialto had come here to fight.

Axer. He was fighting because Axer had asked—for a cause they had all agreed upon that week after the championship. A championship that Axer had influenced—a win for the Third Layer instead of a huge win solely for himself.

And now...it wasn't just a good political move that Bialto was fighting for. The fight had just become extremely personal. Bialto's expression was absolutely and utterly enraged. How many people did he know who'd been targeted?

I pulled harder. Another million gasped a breath, two, three.

In the feeds, there were combat mages I had never seen, and more streaming in from all corners of the four layers.

Magical beings, creatures, shifters, and the largest feline dragon hybrid I had ever seen, were fighting the praetorians and devouring everything in their path.

War healers were weaving in and out of the fighters, casting their own magic to revive, to protect, to repel.

"You will regret this," Stavros said coldly, his empty shell standing outside the last circle.

Guard Rock stood, ready.

And suddenly, I could see the change in the Spartine fight. New guards swarmed from portals wearing new faces and forms—their forms changing with each person who met their enchanted eyes—forming pieced together versions of someone the fighters on our side had loved and lost.

And I knew the moment that one of them turned into Sashia Mayr Leandred. I saw Constantine freeze, for just a second. Saw Axer grab and throw him from harm. Saw the hand with a null cuff fall and attach to Axer. Saw the transport doorway open.

And my hands were full of the dead, the remaining ten million I needed to save, and the world-breaking magic around it.

There was nothing I could do about Axer. Not if I didn't want to let ten million people die, not if I didn't want to end the world.

There was nothing I could do about it. By design.

Axer was nullified. The portal doorway was open. And it wasn't any grunt that was taking him. It was Mussolgranz reaching through with a pair of hot tongs.

Constantine looked up at one of the small surveillance devices on the wall Dagfinn had tapped into, directly into my eyes, and his fingers slid along the skin of his elbow, regret and determination in his gaze.

My eyes went wide. "No. No."

Constantine was in a defensible position. He could get out.

But he was already moving, tossing the cat safely from his cloak and diving in after Axer while throwing a spell at Mussolgranz.

"Fall back!" Lox yelled. The combat mages immediately initiated a series of complicated maneuvers to retreat to a designated location in the prison. The cat scampered after them, and Greene scooped it up.

Constantine and Axer's connections stuttered, then went dark.

My legs gave out and my pelvis hit the back of one splayed calf, trapping it limply against the ground. I stared at the empty space in the feed and held on with all my might to the lives in my hands.

"Dammit Leandred," Olivia said quietly, then all the voices in my head went dark.

Constantine had been the hub.

He'd been the hub for weeks, plastered against my side.

Stavros was laughing. I saw the praetorians. Saw Kaine. But if Kaine was here, he couldn't be carving into Axer and Constantine yet. My heart squeezed.

"Weakness. Who is your best ally now, Miss Crown? Soon you will have none. You should let go, my dear," he said soothingly. "What is a million more? I can give you your enemies. You will need to make some...choices."

And he flashed a recording along the wall.

I let the tears fall, holding firm, pulling another hundred thousand back, even while I watched the recording play.

Mike was setting charges along the waterfront, his attention elsewhere as the shadows lengthened.

Patrick was behind him, downing a potion. I saw the potion do its work, loosening and breaking all the ties that had formed through Excelsine.

"Time's up, Givens."

There was a certain amount of regret in the darkness underlying Patrick's voice that made Mike look up and step back automatically. "What do you—"

Five O'Leary thugs stood behind him. I recognized all of them from the supply drop. Five Department forms stepped from the shadows.

Mike stiffened. "So, you picked a side after all."

Patrick smiled darkly. "A side? Nah. A broadside, maybe. No shot across the bow." His fingers darted through the air and made a little explosion as if they had hit something with a force to sink it.

"That's the thing I love about O'Leary's." The man smiled cruelly, as he looked over the lack of non-family connections on the third son. "You can always be bought."

"You say it like we'd find it an insult." Jameson O'Leary, Patrick's father, stepped into view from where he'd been shielded behind the others. "Let's see it."

The man held out his hand. Three rose sapphires and an elixir rested in his palm.

O'Leary looked hungrily at the sapphires.

"From your old family treasures, yes?" The man idly rolled them around in his hand. "Still a bit of power in them. Let's hear your traitor tales."

Patrick's face tightened. "We test the elixir first, then we play."

"Feeling sentimental? I'm feeling generous." The man smiled and handed over the entire vial. An O'Leary scooped it up to test. "Unusual in a thief and villain. And I know the sapphires are what you really seek."

The tester nodded confirmation of the elixir and Patrick relaxed.

"Now, my information?" the Department thug said.

Jameson O'Leary grinned savagely, eyes on the sapphires, and pulled Mike forward. "Got something better than tales. This one knows a little of everything," he said roughly. "Especially whatever the Tasky kid knows. Always included, always listening, high memory retention. Has all the Tasky kid's memories. And those are worth gold if you want dirt on Crown."

The man's eyes narrowed in on Mike. "The Givens child?"

"Got his family, didn't you?" Patrick said roughly, an unmistakable directive in his tone.

The man slowly smiled. "Yes, I think we will have quite a use for him." He looked over at Patrick and his smile grew edged. "And you and yours, while we are at it."

"Naw. See that's where you aren't thinking." Jameson tapped his right temple. Fifteen more men bled from the shadows around him. "You gotta be quicker than that with an O'Leary.

Now hand over the sapphires and your travel passes."

The man eyed the new shapes. The odds were pretty even. He turned back to Patrick. "The passes weren't part of the deal."

"Maybe not the part you planned." Patrick smiled and the men behind him tapped weapons against their palms like the prelude to a knife fight.

"You won't last a week with those passes."

Patrick laughed. "Then you shouldn't be bent out of shape about giving them over."

The exchange was made, and Patrick shoved Mike forward. "No hard feelings, Givens. Maybe you'll save your family this way."

"Eat dirt, O'Leary."

Patrick's hand went to his chest. "Now that hurts." But his eyes were cold above his smile. "See you on the news. Probably in a body bag." Patrick tipped an imaginary hat and whistled as he gripped the passes in his hand.

"Everyone will know what it means to cross an O'Leary." He grinned savagely and disappeared.

The recording winked out.

"Go," I whispered to Guard Rock.

We flipped again, our last flip.

Eighteen million people revived, two million to go.

Stavros found us within twenty seconds.

"You are just so determined. How about this one, then?"

He flashed up a second recording.

Mike was staring blankly at a white ceiling. Two men were bending over him—Oler Mussolgranz and a dead-eyed minion.

"His resistance to the mind pills is quite extraordinary. There is no evidence to such skill on his reports."

Mussolgranz hummed. "Excelsine is well known for hiding rare abilities among a diverse and extraordinary population. Even better to receive such a subject. I do so love experimenting."

Mike groggily moved his head.

Mussolgranz smiled. "First things first, though. Information before experimentation. Tedious, but research requires munits, and munits are delivered by others. Let's make this quick, shall we? You give me your memories of everything, boy, and I will be quick to reorder your brain into something new. You'll barely feel it. You'll just be...free."

Mussolgranz pulled magic upward and the images going through Mike's mind were visible in the air.

"Go to hell."

Mussolgranz smiled again. "You don't have the capability to avoid my serum. So, it was really a question of courtesy."

The drip of the serum hit the memory like oil spilled in water, immediately breaking into separate drops, like a thin spatter of toxic clouds over Mike's mind.

"Really quite amazing what one finds in the minds of the university. One of your own professors developed this serum. Our Prestige's daughter. To force the truth from another. Causes a catatonic state in a non-magical human, of course. But in a concentrated dose, a mage can be kept under thrall of the questioner for quite some time."

Mike shouted one last time as the magic formed into one cloud.

"Tell us where Ren Crown's family lives."

"No." But it was weaker this time, and the toxicity grew. The picture of an address from a memory came to mind, but he blocked it just in time.

"Tell us."

The memory grew clearer.

"No."

"Tell us."

"No."

"Dear boy, you will tell us."

The film wiped away all thought to disobey. Mike started screaming and the knowledge flashed in the air.

I closed my eyes at the same time that I felt the wards on my parent's house break.

The ties to them ripped away.

"And now, what do you choose, Ren Crown?"

I yelled and yanked the entire net around the culling, putting the world back into order.

Stavros smiled. "Temporary fixes. Like the state of your parents' lives. You have fifteen minutes."

I grabbed Guard Rock and our supplies and threw us through the portal pad.

I slammed into the hard floor of the Western Territories' atrium.

The low-tech communications network Constantine had embedded in the compound stuttered to half-life.

"He has them," I said, breathing heavily.

"We saw it." Dagfinn's voice was tight and grave, all grim seriousness. "Bailey made your feed live. Crown—"

"It's all over the feeds," Olivia said. She sounded winded. "And twenty million people are witness to Stavros trying to murder them. And to Ren saving them."

"Even his supporters, even if they want the whole Third Layer destroyed, can't advocate for mass genocide and survive the forming mob crowds. They are shutting up and slinking away," Loudon said. "The hunt is on, we could—"

"He has them," I repeated.

The comms went silent.

"Do you—"

"No," Olivia said forcefully through our communications, interrupting Loudon. "We stick to the plan."

"But the plan—"

"I know," she said grimly.

"Losing Leandred... What does that mean?" Loudon said. I could hear him chewing his fingernails.

"They are still alive, just nullified," Olivia said. "We know Stavros wants Dare. But Leandred..."

No one knew what would happen if Stavros or Mussolgranz got hold of Constantine. Stavros hardly needed a mage with Mind Magic capabilities, however rare. Though...

"He'll want to gloat." I hit my palm against the floor. "He won't kill them—either of them. Not if he can use them. He'll want to gloat."

"But—"

"And he can use Constantine against Axer," I said, ruthlessly overriding. "He knows they're bonded. It won't be hard to test the strength of the bond. He'll use Constantine if for nothing else than to kill him specifically in some game or test for Axer down the line. Constantine's not a disposable pawn for an opening gambit." I touched my elbow with its still vibrant threads.

But if that was a miscalculation...if he did kill him... I raked my fingers through my hair. "They are both still alive. We can't do anything about it now. We have to hurry. We have to go forward with the notion that Constantine still has a part to play."

That he would remain alive.

"Ren, if he's kil—"

"No. No alternatives. This will happen the way I say it will." I ground my finger into stone. I took a deep breath. "I did not end the world. I will not end the world. I will do what is needed to save it. I will reach the end. I will remove Stavros. And then, and only then, will I deal with everything that fails on the way."

I repeated the litany in my head. I clenched my eyes shut. I couldn't end the world if one of them died.

"We need our backup plan. Just in case," Will said. I could feel his agony. He would have seen what happened to Mike through my feed.

"Yes," I agreed. Constantine wasn't here to kill me for the decision. I tightened my lips. No, I couldn't think of what might be happening.

"No," Olivia said.

"We need him."

"I don't trust him."

"We need him." I pushed away from the floor and pulled the portal pad.

"I can be there," Neph murmured. "Do you—"

"No." I closed my eyes. "I need you there. Find Mussolgranz. Delia, the secondary diversion?"

I didn't directly ask if she was still capable. She wouldn't appreciate it.

"I'm on it," she said with a level of darkness that we would need to heal afterward. "I know where our combat mages are holed up. Camille shared their battle frequency yesterday."

I nodded. "I have ten minutes, then I'm going in."

"As Stavros expects you to," Olivia said grimly. "Hell, if you weren't going to leave a bunch of nameless ferals, you aren't going to leave those two idiots. And you definitely aren't leaving your parents at his mercy. He knows you will come."

I looked at the magic pooling in my palm. "Let's not keep him waiting."

~*~

I gripped the address Greyskull had given me the last time I had seen him. Before... No. I had to trust that everything was going to be fine. I couldn't think of any of the others.

"What does Ren Crown choose," I whispered.

I took a deep breath and wrapped the portal pad around me. I emerged on the doorstep and looked at the door plate. 257 Maple. Funny Fate, so funny. I slipped the paper into my pocket and wrapped the knocker against the door.

A man opened the door—a man I had only seen before in memory.

Lachlan Lassiter.

And behind him—

"Hello, Butterfly."

Chapter Thirty

ANOTHER PERSPECTIVE

M ike

Explosions rocked the prison.

"About time," Mike muttered. It had been hours. He had started to wonder...

There was little magic in the cell, by design, but the mind spells necessitated the barest magic be available.

Precise, beautiful hail tore from his finger and sliced the ward. He sneered at the console techs, who were freaking out about the attack happening somewhere in the prison, broke the lock, and let hail fly. Their bodies flopped to the floor.

Amazing what kind of cell they'd leave you in when they thought you broken. When they thought you were one of the easy ones.

Not Alexander Dare. Not Constantine Leandred. Not even Patrick O'Leary. They would never have put Patrick in one of these lower security cells.

And yet, no one under Level 4, and none of the combat mages—man, he hoped those were the combat mages—wreaking havoc below could get to Level 5.

Mike ripped the canisters and security cards from the fallen techs and broke the capsule wedged in the back of his mouth while putting his hand on the face of the unluckiest one. The tattoo swiveled under his skin and he felt the change overcome his features.

No, the likes of Alexander Dare would be in the maximum-security cells.

Under the assumed face, Mike limped down corridors streaming with guards. Bloody hand prints painted the walls where he couldn't keep his body upright. No one gave him a second look. There were others with wounds much worse. He looked at the skin on the underside of his arm. The arrow tattoo grew ever larger as he drew closer, pointing each direction that he needed to travel.

Everything hurt.

He got to the correct bank of cells, the arrow growing thick and dark. But then suddenly, the arrow split, a tiny slice pointing left, while the larger piece pointed right. He shook his head. That couldn't be correct. He looked right first, seeing exactly who he had expected to see, then looked left.

"Dammit, Leandred," he muttered.

Leandred and Dare were in cells on opposite sides of the maximum-security corridor, staring at one another in silent communication. Leandred was in rough shape—beaten within an inch of his life at some point in the past ten minutes. Dare was scuffed as well, but he seemed strangely unharmed. Perhaps Stavros wanted to keep him healthy. Who knew with that guy.

The intensity of their connected gazes was freaky, though. Mike sighed. Damn Ren for having the worst taste in men.

Leandred looked at him and smiled, as if he'd heard that thought.

"Probably did," Mike muttered. His brain was laced in the asshole's magic. It was the only way he'd survived that hack surgeon.

"Here to stab us in the back, Givens?"

"Hardy har har, Leandred. You like your cell?" Mike worked on the magic locking the cells down. "You weren't even supposed to be here." His bloody fingers slipped, and he swore. Will and Ren were far better at this. Even Olivia had tried her hand at lockpicking with Ren for a roommate.

"Performance issues?"

"I'll leave you in there, Leandred."

Mike glanced quickly at the opposite cell before giving in to the inevitable—it was the reason Ren had given it to him in the first place—and shot a sliver of wind into the locking mechanism while using the leech Ren had tailored specifically for him to undo the locks. Dare looked bored, splayed against the wall, but his muscles tightened, waiting for the lock to spring. He'd always made Mike nervous. Even as the one he always bet on, his sports hero on the field, Dare had been an unbeatable force, not a person. It had been a real nut kicker to find him on the periphery of their group, slowly tunneling inward.

"Should I leave you two alone after this?" Leandred asked languidly. He still had access to some magic. They had locked down Dare totally, but left Leandred with a bit of magic, just like they had with Mike. Underestimation.

"While you sit in your cell and we leave?" Mike asked. "I'm still deciding."

Constantine's grin was lazy, but edged. His only real emotions were ever displayed around Ren, and she wasn't here. It made him dangerous and unpredictable in any circumstance that didn't include her.

"You are right to beware."

"You know, a little more shutting up and a little less loosity lips would do you a world of good," Mike warned.

Leandred opened his mouth.

"Constantine."

His lips shut with a snap at the calm utterance of his name from the man in his opposite cell.

Mike worked more quickly. "You weren't even supposed to be here, Leandred. You were the backup," Mike said.

"As I still am."

"In there?" He said it sarcastically, but Mike wondered if Leandred had deliberately chosen to be taken, knowing he might not be locked down as tightly, just to keep an eye on Dare and make sure he got free.

"Plans sometimes go awry." Leandred carefully waved a broken hand, the other one clasped to his chest. Not enough magic to heal, then. "No harm done."

Dare looked sharply at him. It was obvious that harm had been done to Leandred.

"You exercised loose lips in there, too, didn't you?" Mike said.

Leandred didn't say anything, but surprisingly, Dare tightly offered up, "He forced Mussolgranz into a ten-minute coma and got in the way when the assistant tried to take my eyes."

Mike felt the bile rise in the back of his throat. "Right." The locks clicked open and they both were quick to exit.

Two more explosions rocked the building.

"They didn't take them, is the point," Leandred said, limping with difficulty into the hall. "And we needed them. They take too long to regrow properly. Amateurs."

Mike disengaged their nullifying cuffs. Dare's magic burst free—the power bending the walls with the wave of it.

"They are coming back with collars as soon as Mussolgranz wakes. Two minutes, give or take one," Dare said, already reaching out and healing Leandred like it was just that easy—fixing all those wounds. "We need to either wait and take them out or get to the rendezvous point."

"How is everyone else doi—"

Dare interrupted him, tipping Mike's head back.

"Uh, buddy?"

Leandred came to look at him over Dare's shoulder, two sets of eyes boring into him.

"Doing five things at once with no one to watch her back," Leandred muttered.

Dare put his hand over Mike's face—who was now fully freaking out and positive he was going to die—and pulled. The little leech clung to him a moment more, then detached.

Dare cradled it in his hand, looking at it sternly. It squiggled guiltily in his palm. Then he handed it to Leandred who smirked at it and let it burrow into his fixed wrist.

Mike felt only relief.

Dare released him, watching him with those unsettling eyes that scrutinized a field before demolishing any and all participants.

"It was part of the plan," Mike said quickly.

"Of course, it was." Dare dismissed him completely, and Mike felt even more relief to be free of that gaze.

"Someone scared of their hero?" Leandred taunted him. He seemed in a strangely good mood.

Freaky.

"I will put you back in there." Mike pointed. The identity spell he'd stolen released and he shook it free.

They rounded the corner, stopping only when they saw the line of Department soldiers blocking the hall, wards shimmering around them to block their physical and magical signatures from appearing.

Kaine slinked down the hall. "Did you really think anyone trusted you, boy?"

Mike looked steadily at Kaine, though his heart was beating triple time. "No."

"Then why would you think this paltry escape plan would work?"

"Escape?" Mike smiled grimly. "Thinking that was your first mistake."

If he was going to die, this was a worthy cause. And this stand would do.

Mike happily threw the first shot.

Chapter Thirty-one
ENSNARING AND ENSNARED

I COULD HEAR the fighting elsewhere in the prison, could feel the ground shake. Could feel Axer and Constantine come back online. I closed my eyes and took a deep breath.

Stavros was waiting. And he had my parents.

I stepped up to the last stamped painting.

"The fewer who are between you and Stavros, the better. Variables. Better to go straight there," Axer had said, moving chess pieces in the library.

Straight to Stavros's lair.

I carefully tucked all such thoughts beneath the layer of paint in my mind, letting it erase them, allowing only the fear and determination to remain.

Priyasha looked out sadly from her frame. Stavros watched me, coldly furious, from inside a small portrait on the wall behind her. "Do invite her in," he said to Priyasha, then disappeared.

Priyasha reached out, almost unwillingly, and enveloped me inside. I could feel my magic as it was bound. The few devices I had brought with me to get to this point disintegrated. God, if I had tried to bring anyone with me in a storage paper, or hidden Guard Rock... I shuddered involuntarily. All my connections went dark.

But she held me within her painted arms before flipping me behind, and I could hear the whisper of her paint against my cheek.

I do not regret the years I had with Sergei. Not even the wisps of me in these enduring memories do I regret. I feel your turmoil, and the pain of your loved ones' loss, and I give you one last gift. I felt her painted fingers coat me. I can do nothing against he who holds my strings, but the destruction of the others makes those of us left stronger. And I can give you the protections I have, as love is not an emotion Stavros guards against. Take heed, though, the protections will only last so long. Good luck.

Her smudged fingers slipped from my cheek.

I caught the paint before it fled. Kinsky loved you, I said.

She smiled. I know. And I, him.

A corridor whooshed past me, and Stavros was before me. The last net of spells tightened around me. I had no magic to call. It was the entry price I had paid.

I looked around me, at the inner sanctum of Stavros, at the towering walls of paintings surrounding him. Priyasha was looking back from each one.

"That's why Kinsky's lair was never found."

"I had hoped that the idea of the Origin Circuit would prompt you to try to navigate it. You would have been mine the instant you set finger to this spot."

I thought of the mirror in Okai. "I have seen things that temper curiosity. And the Origin Book was always cautious of this spot."

"Unfortunate."

I stepped carefully into the atrium and felt the paint wrap around me. I needed to time things so very carefully. And to find the way that Stavros planned to cull. The button that he would push. "How many did he create?"

"Thousands. Each day, ten more. Trying so hard to find the right likeness, the one that would bring her back."

I looked at my feet and thought of my hundreds of trials with Christian. "You used him. Told him you could help."

"He was wasted on his own pursuits. Look at this. What do you see?"

I looked at the towering pictures. "I see someone who loved wholly."

"I see someone who couldn't let go. But you let go, didn't you? Shoved your brother into the dirt, found new replacements."

I choked down the fury and the other debilitating, unhelpful emotions suddenly clogging me, and concentrated on the ones I could count on. I counted on my Olivia ones. My

Axer, Constantine's, and Neph's. "I know what you are doing."

He smiled. "Knowing doesn't really matter. It's how you are feeling that does."

He circled around me. "Look at you, with your miserly emotional protections, thinking that any of them matter when it comes to the end. I have all the time in the world to work on you. No one can get to you. No one can find you."

"But you don't have all the time, do you?" I asked ruthlessly. "Because your house of cards is falling. You don't have the public's blind support anymore. You've failed here at the end."

He gripped my chin, then let go and smiled. "You bring out the emotion in me. I will hurt you even more for it." He stepped back. "You are just coming into your powers. Given a few years, you would have been able to find me without subterfuge, without using the paintings at all. Luckily, you possess little skill in the art."

"Luckily," I said, letting bitterness show, and allowing the paint in my mind to hide any other thoughts. I looked around at the dizzying array of Kinsky portraits. "An endless supply of seals. Convenient."

"When needed." He straightened his shirt sleeve. "They allow me to be anywhere, should I need it. And they protect me." He smiled and looked derisively at Priyasha, who looked steadily back. "She protects me. Even when she knows that I'm the cause of his death. But she can do nothing—I drank too deeply of his magic, enough to trigger all the protections she doesn't want to give."

"You've enslaved her memory."

"You speak as if she's real."

"The memory of her is real," I murmured. "The love that went into her creation was real."

"And yet she sits there, day after day. Barely moving. Useless."

I thought of the journal, thought of all the Priyashas who had tried to help me. "You underestimate love."

"No, it is you who overestimate its value."

"Are you connected to all of them?" I looked around me.

His brief hesitation caused my anxiety to calm. "Of course I am. Come now, we have important things to do."

"Small problem with those containers disappearing once more?"

A wave of emotion was abruptly pulled from me, leaving me staggering against my bonds.

His hands fisted, then loosened. "I'm being hasty, when I want you to suffer. The containers are easily found. Your little Third Layer girl hid them, and she will tell us where before you kill her."

I gritted my teeth. Painted shadow curled around my throat as he squeezed.

"I do wonder how you got your connections back so strongly, and your mind. Making me have to work to take it again." He prowled around me. "It was hours ago that I ripped them from you. No one heals that fast."

"Maybe I'm just that durable."

I felt my wrist break. Tears sprang to my eyes.

"So many different types of torture to choose from. I, of course, prefer the kind that you can never heal from." He swung around. "Wake up, Miss Crown."

Something shifted abruptly in my brain and I started to fall before I knew what was happening. A shift so severe; a fall in a nightmare.

I plunged into dark, churning waters then woke, gasping for breath.

"Ren, stay down. I think you broke your wrist. It's okay. The police will be here and an ambulance."

"What, who—" I looked up and my breath stuttered so hard that I started coughing, pain spasming in uneven spikes in my chest. "Christian."

"Yeah?" He looked at me even more worriedly. "I think you hit your head. I'll never convince you to go to the dance with a concussion—I have a friend who promised upright behavior on pain of death—"

"No." I grabbed him, my fingers unable to grip his shirt and sliding uselessly to the side. "Christian."

"Holy...! Ren, fine, no Homecoming manipulations! What part of broken wrist did you not understand?"

"Any part. You're alive."

He looked disturbed, then his gaze softened. "Of course I am. Two guys saved us. And we're magic. Look." He held up his hand and I could see a ball of blue flame, so like Axer's.

"Axer," I choked out.

"Yeah, he's right over there." Christian pointed.

"No." I shook my head refusing to look in the direction he was pointing.

"He's right there, look. He and his uncle said we can go to a magic school. Learn all sorts of neat things. There is even a sport like football that I—"

"No." I grabbed his shirt desperately.

"What?" He looked surprised, then grinned—and oh, it was the bright, mischievous smile just like I remembered. "Are you embarrassed because you took a hit?"

"No. I'm devastated." I closed my eyes, then opened them to get a last view. "Because I wouldn't know Axer's name. Not if this were real."

"Ah, a flaw," said a different voice, and I woke, gasping on the tiles, paintings of Priyasha surrounding me. "Strong minds are the most challenging, but even they can be quieted, if the lie is tempting enough. Isn't the lie tempting, Miss Crown?"

I didn't respond. It wouldn't be truth to say no, it would only be bluster. But Christian wasn't alive, and, "I don't want to live in a world you create about my brother."

Something lit in his eyes. "But that is the beauty of it. You create the world with a simple nudge to bring it into existence. I only interfere when things are going too well. The mind needs balance, after all."

"Inject a little nightmare?" I asked spitefully.

"All for the best. The mind wouldn't accept it otherwise, at least not at first. I've been quite thorough in my experimentation."

He moved.

"It was a little project I did with Sergei. Sergei was such a sensitive soul. And he created the most complicated story worlds. Though they were always so fraught with sadness and melancholy. He was far happier when I put him under."

I licked my lips. "With your implanted emotions."

He shrugged. "He accepted them for a while. Long enough to nearly complete phase one, but not long enough for the real cull." He gave an exaggerated sigh. "He figured it out. Killed himself. People are always rushing to complete their life's work. And I am no exception. It is a flaw I have not overcome."

"You sicken me."

He smiled. "You think yourself above such acts? Let's go for a little stroll."

He flipped us and suddenly I was looking through the left eye of a Spartine guard, with Stavros's presence riding next to mine and looking through the right. The guard moved with purpose down hallways and corridors to the cells made to hold murderers.

"No," I said, trying to back away from the guard, but Stavros just pressed me harder against the man's mind.

The hunters who had killed my brother looked up from their cells and jumped to their feet. I wondered what they saw. My face and Stavros's linked together and overlaying the guard's?

Nausea rose.

"How do you feel, Miss Crown? Right now? Knowing the men who murdered your brother, under no orders of mine, stand before you?"

The one whose face I knew best scrambled, pressing himself against the back wall of his cell. "Prestige, Prestige, please."

I could feel my emotions targeted. I could feel Stavros's fingers sifting through my head. "Kill him, Miss Crown. Go ahead. Have your revenge. I have no need of hunters who don't know what they have in their hands."

"Prestige, please."

"Go ahead, Miss Crown. Lift your hand."

Instinctively, I let a finger rise, and watched as the guard did the same. I balled the fingers into a fist. "No."

I stepped away from them, making the guard move back. One foot. Two. Then ten. "No," I said to the guard. "You will rot. Somewhere I never have to think of you again."

The expression on the man's face was one of abject relief.

"Pity." Stavros waved a hand and the man started to choke. I reached out to stop it, but the hand no longer responded to me.

And then Kaine was next to us, watching with a dark smile. "I have them, Prestige."

"One more moment while I torture the girl. Then you will present yourself at the portrait."

Through the guard's left eye, I desperately searched behind Kaine, looking for the others, but there was no one there.

Kaine chuckled darkly, watching me. "I killed the one, and the other two will be my puppets soon."

Stavros pulled us away and I dropped to the floor. This was my only chance. I had no magic to call, no devices, but I wasn't without. I wiped my hand against my tearstained cheek, then swiped it along the painted ground. The paint wasn't ultramarine. It wasn't violet. It wasn't green. It was silver-specked gold. I let my eyes shut and laughed. Of course it was.

The ground and world shook around us with the potion I had ingested.

Stavros grabbed me by the back of my neck. "Stupid girl."

"Everyone keeps saying that," I said, not struggling as he bound the paint within me and the painted wall in my mind fell. Don't look, don't look...

Stavros bound my wrists behind me, then looked at a painting where Kaine was prowling in a window behind Priyasha.

"Bring them!" Stavros bellowed.

He looked back at me, fingers curling around my neck. "You used up your only move to, what, dampen me? Your magic can't override Sergei's in the world that HE built. That I built. You think I can't fully regenerate in a matter of minutes?"

"I'm sure you can. But now you know I resist." I bared my teeth.

Fury banked beneath a bland expression. He stepped backward. "You try me. I haven't been so tried in a long time." Even with dampened senses, he still had full use of the world around him. An upright table formed from the floor. He started strapping me to it. "I will be the king. And you will be my sword."

"No."

"You want to rid yourself of your destructiveness, just like Sergei after he learned of Valeris, after he felt that he had somehow poisoned Priyasha, but it is part of you. Creation can't exist without it. You must destroy something else in order to create. You must tear down worlds in order to build new ones. You must have dark ages, in order to have enlightenment."

"No," I swallowed, struggling. "I don't believe that. Some of the most magnificent pieces have been formed by building on top of something else. By leveraging a structure already in place."

"In so doing, you suffer all the original's faults."

"Or gain its solid mass."

He laughed. "We can quibble on words all day. You can even leverage some of your favorite things—I had planned for a number of things to survive, but the core of this world needs to be torn down and reconstructed. We need better stability and security."

"You will lose."

He shook his hand and looked at his hands. "It's been a long time since someone has touched me with magic. Sergei tried to dampen me, once."

"I know."

He narrowed his eyes on me. "Do you?"

"You think you have everything planned out, but that was a surprise, wasn't it?"

His eyes narrowed further, and he tugged a painted cord. "Bring the machine," he said to another portrait. A window appeared in the background of the portrait and Mussolgranz looked up from whatever he was working on in his temporary Spartine lab.

I looked warily at the cord.

Stavros smiled. "Oler perfected the way to both prevent a future Origin Mage from killing himself or from hurting his master." He leaned down. "I will be taking all of your emotion from you in fifteen minutes, Miss Crown. But first...well, first, I think you need to have an example made."

He opened two portrait portals with a swirl of his fingers.

Mussolgranz strode through, eyes cold and eerily triumphant. Two assistants wearing half-melted portions of my brother's face marched gruesomely behind—one carrying a sword, one a device.

Kaine entered through the other portal, pulling Axer and Constantine behind, trussed and nullified. I inhaled sharply.

They all looked terrible. But nullified, I couldn't feel the extent of their injuries.

Kaine jerked them to a halt and his shadows tightened even more fiercely around them.

Axer and Constantine's expressions looked about as pleased with this outcome as Kaine looked smirkingly triumphant. Constantine's expression promised ultimate bloodshed as his eyes tracked the Shadow Mage, and turned even darker when he caught sight of Mussolgranz.

"Where's the other one?" Stavros asked indifferently. Even dampened, he checked that the appropriate measures he had predefined were in place on each of the boys. Axer would require different precautions from Constantine, and vice versa.

"He didn't make it," Kaine said, a smirk pulling over his teeth.

I looked at the boys. Axer slowly shook his head to both sides. I looked down, unwilling to let Stavros see.

"Oh, dear. One of your friends didn't make it? Well, I did warn you about the casualties." He touched my chin and tilted it. I put every loathing emotion into the look I shot back.

He smiled and let my chin fall. "A few minutes more, and I'm going to pull those thoughts and emotions."

"Come see the carnage." Kaine tapped his temple and let his eyes slide shut, shadows swirling in glee around his face.

"In a few minutes. The idiot girl thought she could win by hitting me with a dampener."

"That's going to cost her," Kaine said, opening his eyes and staring fiercely at me.

"Indeed. And those who undoubtedly provided it," Stavros said, and flicked a device. Constantine fell to his knees, knocked forward by an internal blow. "I'm going to take my time with you, boy."

"Thought he could end me with some concoction." Kaine shoved a shadowed claw under Constantine's jaw. "Got a shot in."

"Ah, that's why the entry magic indicated you are the slightest bit off." Stavros waved it off and Constantine bent forward again, spitting blood onto the floor.

"He failed." Kaine grinned nastily at Constantine's bent head. "So much failure for you, boy." Constantine set his jaw.

"Oler, get the... I didn't ask you to bring a sword," Stavros looked at the sword held by the assistant on Mussolgranz's left. "Get rid of it."

The assistant threw it to the side without looking, eyes blank. The sword clattered to the ground. Stavros turned to Mussolgranz with a sneer.

Mussolgranz sneered back. "Last minute creations. They killed my best one."

Stavros pulled his own sword from a portrait, then walked over to Axer and placed the blade against his neck. Axer tilted his head back, lips firmed.

Stavros let the flat side of the blade slide against the skin of his throat. "Not even burned by it. Been practicing with Origin Magic, have you? I should simply slit your throat. End your life right now. Put you in stasis. Or maybe leave you to rot."

"Do it," Mussolgranz said eagerly, entire face lit with the possibility of it. Unease took me.

Axer stared back without expression, but I could see the edges of copper and turquoise bleed around him.

"You still need him," I said desperately, pulling at my binds, pulling Stavros's eyes back to me.

"Poor Oler needs someone to die to cover for his failures," Kaine said tauntingly.

"You wish," Mussolgranz sneered.

But Mussolgranz's responses seemed to have the opposite effect on Stavros and he pulled the blade from Axer's throat and let it fall. It melted into the floor. "Now, now, Oler, you overextend your emotion, patience is rewarded."

Mussolgranz's eyes flashed for a moment before he got himself under control, but Stavros was already opening the next portrait's portal.

Helen Price walked through. My heart picked up speed. I pulled my lips between my teeth, unable to hold in the emotions.

A familiar, hostile gaze narrowed in on me. She shook her head, disgust plain.

Kaine smiled from his corner.

I looked at Helen Price with steely eyes, keeping my emotions locked down, as she looked around the space, taking everything in with her sharp gaze.

"I have them," she said to Stavros. "None of these mages should be here, though, especially not the Origin Mage. I can set up a new Base—"

"The girl can do nothing without my say so," Stavros said coldly. "And I tire of games. I would have thought you had tired too, Helen. It is time. Bring them."

I struggled vainly. "What did you do with Olivia?"

Helen looked at me, gaze cold, and held up a finger that dropped, as if showing the movement of a body with its strings cut. "I got rid of her."

Hold it together. Hold it together...

"I hope you have life insurance," I said woodenly.

She smiled coldly. "The best." She reached through the open portal and pulled two more people through. The portal closed behind them.

I swallowed as my parents were pushed into view. Dressed in work clothes, my mother was still wearing her jewelry, and that was always the first thing she shed. They had been taken as soon as they'd entered the house from work, or maybe even before. My eyes darted between them, unable to help myself from drinking in their features, regardless of the circumstances.

"Ren, honey, it's okay." My mother's eyes were so blue. Like sapphires.

"Poor non-magicals," Stavros said. "Look at them, with so little life inside. But it's curious. They still stand. Did you do something to build resistance to the magical world within them, Miss Crown? Or is there something hidden within them—something dormant, that produced you? Perhaps we will run a few experiments."

My heart stopped for a moment. I looked at Helen, whose eyes briefly narrowed.

"They went into cardiac arrest twice in the Depot," Helen said. "Non-magicals are frail, though these two are slightly hardier than some I've tested." She sliced my father's cheek with her fingernail.

I pulled against my restraints, bringing Stavros's eyes back to me. He smiled. "We could still make a deal, my dear. You must realize you have lost. Badly. Things can be easy."

"I thought you didn't need my consent."

"Naught but for purposes of time. So much wasted already."

I stared at my parents. They stared eerily back for a long moment before my mother reached toward me. "Ren."

"Don't worry. I'll get you out of this," I said.

Stavros laughed benevolently. "Out of their magic-null meat sacks? Undoubtedly." He looked them over with disdain. "Non-magicals. Their null stench is nauseating. How can anything be so...dull?"

"Don't you dare hurt them."

Stavros smiled. "I'm not going to," he said. "You are." He shoved my mother at me.

Chapter Thirty-two

GOLDEN CIRCLES

I KEPT contact with my mother's eyes, with my father's gaze, switching between, last looks.

My mother's fingers smoothed down the hair at the side of my face, her fingers pulling around my ear, leaving a piece of her behind. I felt the touch and closed my eyes at the feeling of home and magic seeping within my earlobe. I held tightly, not letting it go.

Stavros clapped his hands together. "A fine victory. A fine gathering. All of you nullified and trussed like First Layer turkeys about to be baked."

Kaine tapped his fingers against his chest. I watched the way they tapped. "They shouldn't all be here in one place," he said, sneering.

"Agreed," Helen said briskly.

"Now, now, it's a day for celebrating," Stavros said benevolently. "And none of them can do an ounce of magic." He motioned, and indeed, we were pretty dead in the water. We had known this is what would happen if we were ever trapped here.

He walked toward Constantine. "I think we'll start with you."

"Thank you," I said abruptly.

Stavros's eyes narrowed, though his mouth was still amused. "Young love already withering? For what, dear girl?"

"No. Thank you for bringing us together." I let the feeling of home seep down to my core.

"Bringing you together? You give me credit for the formation of your group?"

"Not a chance." I took a breath and let it loose, forcing myself to smile. "Thank you for bringing us all here."

A hard smile on my face, I let the magic release. My cuffs burst apart. I watched realization wash across Stavros's features. But I already had his world in my hand.

"Kill her parents," he said to Helen Price, scrambling backward. "Oler, use the device."

Oler Mussolgranz swiped a cufflink from my father. "Better, I think, for you to die first," he said as he picked up the dropped sword and shoved it through Stavros's chest.

Stavros stared down at the steel, then stumbled.

Mussolgranz fell to his knees, the magic around him starting to swirl. He laughed, high-pitched and hysterical, his eyes on Stavros and the blade, his hands shaking. "Felled by an Awakened object. Felled by my hand. Felled by that which I never anticipated when I set her upon her path."

Stavros choked, blood sputtering from his mouth. A painted hand reached from a portrait and pulled him inside in a last bid at protection. I could see him try to get to another painting. He was trying to heal himself, but the sword wasn't letting him. The paint in the portrait started to sear around the edges.

"An interesting object," my mother said, walking forward and removing her remaining earring. My father removed his second cufflink. "An

Awakening object, made to fight monsters. An apt goal."

My mother's features abruptly sharpened from their normal soft curves. And my father grew an additional two inches, tattoos blooming everywhere along his exposed skin. Magic burst from both, like a constricting net suddenly cut free.

Ganix Greyskull gently took the first cufflink from Mussolgranz—along with a tattoo—and put it into the hand of the assistant who had dropped the sword. The tattoo slithered back onto the assistant's wrist. "Thank you, William. The permission magic worked exactly as expected, though I must say that I thought I would be doing the stabbing."

He crouched down and pressed his forehead to the side of Mussolgranz's head.

Stavros jolted—the first truly surprised expression I had ever seen from the man. He looked back at my mother, who was no longer a brunette, but a cold, familiar blonde. "Trickery. Family tragedy. How banal," he said.

Lucille Stevens, formerly Lucille Stavros, watched the portrait calmly. "Funny, isn't it, how hubris can unmake a man?"

"I felt you dying. I can still feel it."

"Such lovely talents at Excelsine these days. One wonders if Alexander Dare is ever truly on campus with a friend who can feign it for him like the one who is lying next to my half-dead corpse. And you'll have gotten your reports, of course, from mages who were fed it by little birds wielding big pens instead of swords. All led by two of my most troublesome and brilliant charges."

"What have you done?"

She smiled. "Taught my students well." She stabbed the stem of the earring she hadn't put into my earlobe into the canvas and Stavros gritted his teeth in pain. Stevens left it sticking out of the canvas, nullifying the magic within. "You took him. Them. From me," she said, just as absurdly calm.

"You never did learn to curb your feelings. Broken."

Lucille Stevens, one of the most composed people I had ever met, tilted her head. "You overestimate your own liberation."

"I overestimate my enemies'." A bolt of magic shot toward her from another portrait, cutting and deadly. But with his abilities neutered and my hold on the painted world, it was without the force it would have once held.

Greyskull reached up and palmed the spell.

"Ah, the doctor," Stavros spit. "With his vow. I'm surprised you didn't bring dear Rafi."

"I didn't need to," Greyskull said, tattoos flashing.

Mussolgranz lifted his head. "Enton, dear boy, patience is rewarded." Gold light twinkled around Mussolgranz's frame, and his features bled and turned dark and gold. Raphael's eyes closed in deep relief—like a profound wound had started to clot.

"Kaine!" Stavros's voice went a pitch higher.

Kaine's eyes bled ultramarine blue. Shadows flew from him, up, around, dancing happily in the air, then settled in his reformed hand. Axer's hand.

"Helen!"

Helen Price ignored Stavros, watching Axer with a pinched expression. "That's great. Just great. Nice, Ren. Just give the Dares the world. Ugh. I don't want it anyway." She shook her head, freeing herself of her guise. Olivia finally looked at Stavros with her own eyes and bit out, "Mother is unavailable."

Marsgrove's pinstriped form rose from where "Constantine" had been kneeling. And Constantine shook free of the features of his roommate. Even knowing, even having seen their signs, staggering relief nearly felled me. Constantine was supposed to have been Mussolgranz. As Axer, he'd transferred to the most perilous role—the protections against them limited by their assumed forms, just in case.

"A bit of an overdone affair, Crown," Marsgrove said, shaking out his suit front and wiping the blood from his mouth. "I approve."

I wanted to say, "When Alexander Dare pulls a con, it is thorough," but there was something I needed to know more.

"Mike?" I asked desperately, as Constantine strode forward with the other assistant—Neph, shedding her guise—and together they reconnected me fully, everything blooming intense silver and gold. "Is Mike—?"

"Fine," Constantine said gruffly, fingers checking my wrists. "A bit roughed up. Said you owe him at least one blizzard practice space. He and Peoples are gathering the others from around the prison right now. O'Leary's bringing Bailey."

Stavros let out a growl.

It turned my attention back to him. "Surprised?"

He bared his teeth at me.

I prowled toward him. "You had to think you had won. You had to think it was because of you that you won, too. Patrick? An O'Leary? You believed he would turn, and therefore you accepted that turning." I let the Treacherous Don confidence game rotate above my palm. "You accepted Mike's information about my parents because you thought it was given under duress—instead of plotted with deceiving you in mind and carefully cultivated by Mike and Will pretending to exchange information and memories—most notably my parents' address, a closely guarded secret. You believed you were gaining it through trickery. And therefore, you believed you had my parents. Who you never had. Hidden beneath a magic so heavy, you couldn't sense that one of them was your own daughter. Brought to you by a trusted servant. Confident of your victory, you never doubted."

The Treacherous Don morphed to the Five Man Act with all of us located around our target. All roles other than Stavros's and mine had multiple people filling the parts—Olivia, Greyskull, and Stevens, Kaine and Axer (which had turned into Kaine/Axer/Constantine), Mussolgranz and guards.

"Destroying the seals to find you...that was a good gambit," I said. "And if we'd located you at the end of it, we'd have run with it, but it was never the main plan." I let the cons extinguish. "It wasn't the one where you'd let your guard down. Where you'd think that you had won."

"You think you've won?" he spit.

"I think you are scared."

"I have all of the codes pre-programmed. And I'm not without you." He threw out the last of his magic, trying to hollow me.

I batted it away with the freshly surging connections Neph and Constantine were sharing in abundance.

Rage flew through me, nearly unchecked at what Stavros was trying to do again.

Nearly unchecked.

I took a deep breath, hand holding him firmly in the painting. Priyasha stood above him, a silent sentinel who had been forced to protect his sanctum and life, but nothing else. I could see her magic seeking to keep him alive, but she stared at me, her face relaxing into a sort of hungry peacefulness.

I took another deep breath.

The thing Stavros lacked in his ultra-empathy, was the ability to attach to the emotions himself. He understood it in others, used it, but didn't share it. Understood it, but didn't feel it.

I wanted to feel it, though. Even the sadness. Even the tragedy.

I allowed the rage to flow through me. Acknowledged it. Then let it flow away, down the stream. Steady.

Anger, sadness, happiness, they made me stronger, but they also made me weaker. It was the balance, the understanding, that I needed. To feel the emotions, but not to make decisions within the emotions. Decisions made at the height of anger, or even happiness, were decisions influenced by things outside of reason. But being entirely of reason, without influence, like Stavros, wasn't ideal either.

I looked at the boys—who were standing shoulder-to-shoulder now, where weeks ago, there would be stab wounds in their backs. Felt all the Bandits, who had banded together—a bunch of miscreants who had found a purpose—including Patrick, with his newly reconnected connections and vows courtesy of a completely fit Asafa sitting completely unharmed in Medical.

I looked at Neph, Will, and Olivia, who had been with me on my first adventures. At

Greyskull and Stevens, whose fingers were encircling Raphael's wrists, as if he might disappear—Marsgrove at their side. At Priyasha, leaning forward in her frame.

I looked down at the spot which the rage was trying to erode, but couldn't touch. At the spot where my brother's memory would always hold firm, where my parents still firmly resided, even if their house was no longer the place I called home.

Love.

And I let go—let the spot release its stone hold and spread to overtake all else.

"No," Stavros said.

And for once, the smile was on my face, not his. "Absolute power corrupts. So does absolute love, but from the opposite view."

He struggled to stand in the frame.

"You were right." I looked up at him through a section of escaped, wild hair—with heavy-lidded, certainty in my gaze. "I rely far too much on my friends."

He backed away.

"Here's the thing," I said, almost gently, pulling the silver-gold from me in a long banner of satin magic. "You were expecting me. Corrupted by power and rage. And that me, you knew how to conquer. But you didn't get that me. You got the me that is part of a bigger whole. You got us. And us doesn't just include Origin Mage powers. It includes Muses, and Bridges, and Mind Mages, it includes Sirens, and Scholars, and physical geniuses. It includes people who can manipulate frequencies, back door magics, and weaponry. And more importantly," I leaned forward. "People who can put all of those things together into a very disruptive unit."

The net reached farther, wider—Excelsine, Crelussa, The Western Territories—spreading, spreading, spreading until it reached all corners of the earth in all five layers.

"You didn't just get me. You got us. And we? We defeat you." And I cast the magic at him.

Chapter Thirty-three

HOW IT ENDS

THE MAGIC of the last seal faded and broke like a bubble popping, pulling the whole room fully into the Second Layer.

Bellacia smiled as she recorded it all. "And thus, the veils come down," she murmured. "And a new empire will be born."

I watched the last of the magic fall, carefully pulling it into the storage system that we had set up just for this—the ten of us at points around the sword that Will had set up in the middle. "Can't we just, I don't know, have a republic? With like, benevolent leaders interested in the common welfare of all people?"

Her tinkling laughter was her only response.

I sighed.

"Ren, you have an opportunity." Her eyes glittered. "An opportunity for greatness."

"How come no one promotes an opportunity for fun and happiness?"

"Because it's boring and unambitious."

"Sounds anything but," I said wistfully.

"What are you two discussing?" Olivia demanded.

"Door B," I said, looking at the media and authorities who were porting and pouring in around us.

"Door B?"

"Where I'm the weapon of mass destruction in case of emergency, but a fun-loving nerd from day to day."

Olivia stared at me. "Did you read my notes?" she demanded.

"Yes. Republic?" I asked hopefully.

"Watch Alexander Dare and don't go off script."

I sighed.

It only took three spells before everyone in the crowd stopped trying to capture Axer. The combat mages who were pouring in behind him just made the crowd stand that much more at silent attention. Ramirez was a silent shadow at his side.

The magic used to defeat Prestige Stavros, as well as what he had been trying to do, had been covered extensively already. Connecting the majority of the free worlds together in spirit, in order to defeat one man, had made few of the details secret. We were all a part. And yet, fear was still dominating many expressions.

Axer looked out over the crowd of journalists without emotion.

"Yes. We could rule the layer and there is little you could do about it," he said. The fear already on their faces turned closer to terror. "But that's not what is going to happen. What's going to happen is that we are going to work with you and with the other layers. And in exchange, you will allow us to live freely. No restrictions, no binds—other than an Oath to Serve which is being drawn up."

"Oaths are breakable," a reporter said.

"Immediate notification to the Council will happen if it's broken, as well as dire consequences. But as long as the oath isn't broken, you will leave all of us alone."

And I could see the might of it. Standing there, issuing an ultimatum. Demanding a concession right then from the lawmakers.

"The council will be given the drafts. Senator Leandred and all council members and staff have been located and are currently being treated for their injuries. Senator Leandred will recuse himself due to his conflict of interest, but we expect the council to decide on these matters quickly so that we, as part of our greater society, can continue living freely, as we just assured for all."

It was a nice touch. Very Olivia with its reminder and threat.

"Where's Raphael Verisetti?" someone asked.

"Vaporized," Marsgrove said, voice clipped.

My gaze slid to Greyskull automatically, who did not look at all devastated by such news.

A phoenix with a broken wing slid across his neck and disappeared beneath his circular collar.

"Miss Crown, can you confirm?" someone said.

I looked at Greyskull's neck and nodded slowly. "Vaporized."

"What about Oler Mussolgranz?" another reporter demanded.

I winced. Sending in Raphael to take Mussolgranz's place had had consequences. Mussolgranz had been able to hide from Raphael in the Basement. Raphael hadn't wasted his opportunity at having the man before him.

Marsgrove firmed his lips. "He is in a comatose state."

Greyskull had said it didn't matter if he came out of it, either. The man was gone.

"Archelon Kaine? Helen Price?"

"They are within custody. They will be questioned extensively."

"What about you, what about questioning you, Dean Marsgrove?"

Marsgrove looked down his nose. "I will also be available for questioning."

"And Ren Crown? What about her?"

I lifted my chin. "I will help, I will be an Origin Mage, I will serve society. But it will be all societies, not just those in the Second Layer. Create a commission that answers to the people of all layers, with transparent communications and discussions. And from that commission, I will take assignments."

"How can we trust you?"

I nodded in understanding. "It is unnerving to know that someone has the power to change the fabric of the world. But it is a truth of the magic worlds that the existence relies upon the system that was put into place. I, too, will be under oath. There will always be people who have power and people who do not. I will not be forced into grievous servitude or hiding because I have power. I have responsibility to my power, and to my communities, but also to myself."

I looked around the crowd. "Do not mistake my desire to help with a desire for chains. Do not forget what I am. I will not allow myself to be chained because some government desires control. I will not allow you to chain me at all. Do not try." I said it calmly, but let a little of my power flow into spirals in the air. "Form a commission. Work in a way that brings equality to all, and I will gladly work with you. I want nothing more than to live my life as one of you."

Olivia stepped up, and I stepped back. "I will be taking questions on Miss Crown's behalf from here." She pointed to a reporter. "You, go."

The crowd erupted with questions.

Julian Dare stepped to her side, as did a mussed Stuart Leandred and the members of the Council who'd been recovered.

The rest of us eased back from around the podium.

"Well, Phillip, you can clean this up with your cousin," Stevens said curtly as Olivia pinned the crowd firmly under her thumb with help from Bellacia's planted questions. "I have places to be."

Stevens turned on her heel.

"Yup." Greyskull stepped backward more slowly, still watching Marsgrove intently. Stevens paused, waiting for him—for Greyskull and his tattoos—to catch up.

Marsgrove's fingers curled into his palms, and for a long moment, I wasn't sure how the moment would play. "Go," he finally said, gruffly.

They didn't wait for a further response, disappearing together.

I looked up at Constantine at my side. His arms stayed crossed for another moment, then loosened. He touched the back of my neck, seeking comfort. "Forgiveness suits me ill."

"It's hard for us all," I whispered, leaning in. "But I think...I think it gets easier, the quicker it comes."

Constantine looked over at Axer, who had gone to stand with Julian, pointing out Stavros's detailed notes to the crowd and the triggers Stavros had been planning to use.

Constantine's face softened. "Perhaps." He touched my cheek and wiped the silver-gold tear there.

Mindful of the crowd, I pulled fingers through my tangled hair and checked our spells for something to do that didn't include responding to that touch. I could feel Constantine smiling.

Neph leaned into me on the other side. She felt amused again. And relieved. So relieved. I squeezed her hand. Will was windswept and elated on her other side. Guard Rock, hidden from prying eyes, prodded me from inside my cloak. I'd recovered him from the vent I'd stashed him within before going to meet Stavros.

I looked back to the podium. To where Julian Dare's gaze was plotting, even as he said all the right things. The vacuum left by Stavros wouldn't go unfilled for even a day. But it was enough that people would be more wary, would watch all those jockeying for position—might see them with eyes that were predisposed to find ulterior motives.

Julian would not be exempt from scrutiny. Even from us. Maybe especially from us.

Being for the "good" was all well and great, but power is might still rang true. And we'd be watching.

Make new friends, stand up for yourself, be the best Ren you could be. Christian would be pleased.

I touched the bracelet around my wrist. I love you, always. Thank you.

Chapter Thirty-four

HOME

MY REAL parents were back home, wards reengaged—and strengthened. Safe and sound after their adventure in the safehouse Marsgrove had tucked them into. They had asked if I wanted to stay. Stay home with them.

Home.

I looked at all the threads flowing in and out of me. The red ones of my family were as strong as ever. And even with the wish for Christian to be intertwined there, we were healing, each day. All of us.

I had promised I'd be back for the weekend. Maybe with some additions who could use a good home visit too.

Home. I looked up. I had more than one home.

"Give me your finger," Marsgrove said.

I held it out, the butterflies in my stomach fluttering in anticipation, and looked up.

The atrium was wide and open, and a long ramp spiraled upward along the rectangular edges of the walls. Doorways dotted the sides of the wall to my right.

Hanging in the middle of the atrium was a giant compass surrounded by five concentric silver rings, each rotating in various directions around the ones inside it. The edges of the rings were rippling in an asynchronous, nonuniform pattern as well. The inmost ring lay mostly flat, with just a bit of a slow ripple. The outermost one was wildly changing, even in its thickness.

A smile spread my lips at the thoughts. The past. The present. My future.

On the floor, directly beneath the enchanted gyroscope, was a large stone with Rosetta-styled carved markings. The view through the windows showed the building edged a large circular grassy space. Thousands of students stood on the grass. Endless sky appeared through spaces between the buildings across the grass circle.

"Well, go on Crown, hug the Shinar Stone, we haven't all day. I need to write over a dozen acceptance letters for your new feral friends."

I looked up at Marsgrove and couldn't contain my smile. "Yeah, okay."

I wrapped my arms around the stone, bloody finger pressing into its surface, and closed my eyes. The campus magic immediately wrapped around me, like it was welcoming back a lost beloved child. A silver and gold tear escaped, dropping onto the stone, and as I let go, the writing on the stone grew brighter, shimmering, and a nearly invisible layer of something pulled away with my movement, then snapped from the rock and settled on me.

There was a rumbling, then a golden light whooshed and sprung into place.

Marsgrove sighed. I grinned.

"Go on then." He motioned tiredly, though he couldn't hide a small smile. "I need a drink."

Not being able to stand it any longer, I ran to the glass door and threw it open. Top Circle spread out before me, overflowing with mages.

I couldn't see the Magiaduct, but I knew what I'd see when I walked there—a golden net spreading across the entire complex. The Bandits, the Combat Squad, the Justice Squad, Bess, Sari, Isaiah, and all those who had ties to me—even Bellacia and Peters, individually—had volunteered to be linked in through ties that bridged the entire superstructure.

On the steps in front of the Administration Building, Constantine was leaning back against the nearest column, brow raised, the end of a purple and blue tail sticking out of his pocket. Axer was leaning on the column at his side. The combat mages were in a combined group behind him.

Olivia was standing a step away with her hands on her hips—telling me in no uncertain terms that I was taking too long. Neph was standing calmly next to her, Guard Friend waiting patiently on her foot. Guard Rock jumped from my pocket and sprinted over, pencil waving in the air with all the news he had to tell as he ran into an eager embrace. I could feel Neph's anticipation to sweep me up the moment I stepped past the threshold. Will bounced on his feet next to her, Justice Toad in his hands.

Delia, Mike, Patrick, Asafa, Dagfinn, Loudon, Kita, Lifen, Adrabi, Sari, Bess, Peters, Isaiah, and all the others stood arrayed around them. Bellacia smirked on the other side of the steps, recording it all.

The professors—Stevens, Mbozi, Greyskull, Harrow, Wellingham, and all the rest—stood to the right.

I looked behind all of them and saw the faces of the student body—most anticipatory, most open and welcome. Welcoming a student back—one they wanted on campus.

I looked up to the dragon-filled sky. Ori, patched and free, winged through the air currents. Magical creatures surrounded him, along with five other flying tomes and the dragons and phoenixes I'd made for Axer.

I put my hand on the side of the doorframe. Magic lit and spread down the steps, along the grass, shooting tendrils out in every direction. The mountain lit up from the inside, hastening the spread.

Shouts combined with cheers, and I could feel the community magic accepting this new golden rush, could feel it seeping into me beneath the relit administration magic. I looked at the threads of color and love connecting us.

Constantine winked at me and surreptitiously twirled some bit of golden residue that would undoubtedly be used questionably at some point in the future. Axer sighed. Olivia glared.

I grinned and stepped outside.

Author Note

Thank you for joining Ren on her journey. It's been an exciting, illuminating, and extremely special six years writing this series and I can't wait to explore what comes next.

For deleted scenes, goodies, and what is in the works: http://www.annezoelle.com

And you can reach me directly at: anne.zoelle@gmail.com.